ACKNOWLEDGEMENTS

First, thanks to all my technical advisors on this project: Pete Groseclose for keeping me up on the inner workings of guns, Reno Brown for his poker expertise, Charles Cox for his encyclopedic knowledge of trucking, Kelly McDermott for all her help with helicopters, and, of course, my Vegas connection, Tom Shear.

None of my books would have been possible without the continued support of my family. As always, thanks so much for the ideas, editing, constructive criticism, and tolerance.

Finally, thanks to Simon Lipskar and Kelley Ragland for all their suggestions and enthusiasm.

And there went out another horse that was red: and power was given to him that sat thereon to take peace from the earth, and that they should kill one another: and there was given unto him a great sword.

—Revelation 6:4

Chapter One

"Five-card draw, gentlemen. Now let's start paying attention, okay?"

Brandon Vale shot the cards out of the deck, skimming them across the table to the five nervous-looking men surrounding it. After a quick glance at his hand, he slapped it down next to his teetering mountain of loot and scanned the faces of his opponents. All were staring at their cards as though they contained the meaning of life and, based on his experience, they would continue to do so for a lot longer than necessary.

The tinny sound of machine-gun fire started on the far side of the room and he turned in his chair, squinting at the television bolted to the wall while he waited. The lenses in his glasses were only two weeks old, but had never been quite right. Prisons tended not to attract the top people in their fields and the fact that the optometrist who had given him his exam was half blind himself didn't speak highly of his qualifications.

They were good enough, though, for him to see the unmistakable outlines of tanks and running men accompanied by the increasingly familiar sounds of war. Sudan, Israel, Iraq, Afghanistan—one of those sandy countries full of people who liked to fight over crap that happened a thousand years ago or all that "my God's better than your God" nonsense. He knew the type, of course. You couldn't swing a dead cat in his chosen profession without smacking the hopelessly self-destructive, truly violent, or utterly sociopathic. If you were really careful and lucky, though, you could avoid them. Not so easy if you lived in Baghdad, he supposed.

The men sitting in the chairs bolted down in front of the TV were separated into knots of similar skin color: black, brown, and a few white guys who were basically sturdier, meaner, more impressively tattooed versions of himself. All perked up a bit at the violence.

The story quickly faded into something about the Federal Reserve, though, and its audience sagged in disappointment. The truth was that they were only there in hopes of catching a glimpse of Ann Coulter or some other talking-head hottie.

Brandon Vale squared himself to the table again and examined the man responsible for the prison's rather somber viewing habits. He probably weighed about the same as an Italian sports car and was roughly as fast and powerful. His skin was preternaturally dark, making the whites of his eyes seem to glow and partially obscuring a tattoo of a hooded KKK guy dangling from a graphically broken neck.

As one of the prison's many converts to Islam, Kassem was always interested in following "the struggle" while hanging out in the rec room. And after what happened to that neo-Nazi power lifter, there weren't many people willing to argue.

After a quick round of timid betting, Kassem slid his discards across the table. "Three."

Brandon had barely dealt the first one when the man suddenly jumped to his feet, causing the floor to shake perceptibly.

"You're dealing from the fucking bottom of the deck, you bitch!"

Brandon shook his head calmly. "I wasn't, actually."

"Oh," Kassem said, obviously disappointed. He sat back down to a cautious round of polite laughter.

Brandon had landed in prison for a fairly sizable diamond heist in which the jewels had never been recovered. That, in addition to the fact that he'd refused to rat out a single person he'd ever worked with, had given him some basic credibility and maybe even a touch of mystique. The bottom line, though, was that he was still a skinny, thirty-three-year-old guy who hadn't been in a fight since grade school. And that girl had kicked his ass.

He'd been there only a few days when Kassem had "asked" him to join the informal prison poker club. Being a guy who was always interested in a profitable enterprise, Brandon had been quietly watching the games from a safe distance and had noticed a few unusual complexities. It seemed that the people involved played hard and recklessly until about fifteen minutes before lockdown. At that point, they started tossing away good cards like they were dipped in

anthrax and let Kassem win everything on the table—
generally cigarettes and IOUs for unknown services
to be performed at some future date.

Since Brandon didn't smoke and wasn't anxious to
perform any mysterious prison services, he'd decided
to remain at that safe distance. There was no refusing
Kassem's invitation, though, and he found himself in
the awkward position of having to tell the truth: That
he was an on-again, off-again professional gambler
and brilliant card cheat.

Miraculously, Kassem had been bored with
winning—though still completely unwilling to lose—and
saw Brandon as just the diversion he needed. In the
end, they'd negotiated a deal that worked for everyone.
The other players would donate a few "chips" to
Brandon at the beginning of the game and he would
sit in, helping them with their technique and teaching
them to spot cheats. Then, at the end of the game, his
winnings would be distributed based on an arcane calcu-
lation that had less to do with how people played than
it did with who was the most physically dangerous. A
good facsimile of life, actually, and one from which he
was now happily exempt. His relationship with Kassem
had made him instantly untouchable, giving him an
opportunity to get to know virtually everyone incarcer-
ated there and become almost universally popular. An
achievement previously thought impossible.

"I think this is the last hand," Brandon said, giving
fair warning to everyone that it was time to discard
anything promising and lose everything they had.
Betting turned from cautious to manic.

"To you, Kassem," Brandon said.

"Two pair. Deuces and threes."

Those at the table who hadn't yet laid down their hands groaned subserviently and dropped their cards. All except Brandon.

"Well?" Kassem said.

"You really want to see what I got?"

"I want to see."

"Think you can handle my game?"

"Put your fucking cards down before I bust your pencil neck," Kassem said, laughing.

Brandon slapped his cards down. "Five aces. All spades."

This time the groans were a little more heartfelt.

"I swear, I don't know what I'm gonna do with you guys," Brandon said, as the guard signaled for the room to be cleared. Kassem offered his hand, and when Brandon pulled away he had a thick, hand-rolled joint in his palm.

"Get some sleep tonight."

"Hey, thanks, Kas."

These generous little gifts went immediately to Brandon's psychotic cellmate, calming him enough for Brandon to actually relax in his bunk and read. These fatties had been instrumental in his quest to get through the classics, though he had to admit to counting the comic book adaptations of *Moby-Dick* and *Tess of the D'Urbervilles*.

He took his place in line and began shuffling silently out the door, squashed uncomfortably between two profusely sweating mountains of murderous flesh. It didn't matter, though. His mood was currently immune to such minor irritations. In an hour his cellmate would be lying in his cot, stoned out of his mind, while Brandon lost himself in the inner workings of samurai society. It wasn't most people's definition of a stellar evening, but it was the best evening allowed by his current situation. And what more could you hope for but the best?

"Vale!"

He leaned out, crinkling his nose when it got too close to the armpit behind him, and squinted at the guard pointing to him with a nightstick.

"Front and center!"

Brandon leapt out of line and jogged back the way he'd come, stopping a few feet in front of the man.

"Yes, Sergeant Daly?"

As the guards went, it was generally agreed that Angus Daly was second most sadistic, third most corrupt, and a runaway winner at taking himself the most seriously. His uniform was always starched into something resembling cardboard and his hair was cropped into a flattop that came to an impressively sharp point in the middle of his forehead.

The oddest thing about Daly, though, is that he was one of the few people Brandon had ever met who hated him. He saw Brandon as some kind of int-*I*-lectual who looked down on workingmen like himself and who, after serving his time, would collect his hidden diamonds, move to the Costa del Sol, and live out the rest of his life dating supermodels. So Daly had taken it upon himself to make sure Brandon's time at that particular facility was as unpleasant as was practically possible.

Not that he'd been physically abusive in any significant way. What fun would that be? No, to his credit, Daly was more imaginative than that. Clogged toilet? Brandon was his man. And the tools and gloves necessary always seemed to have been conveniently misplaced. Warden's car stuck in the mud? Brandon was always the guy on the back bumper.

"Sir? Can I help you?"

Daly continued to stand there silently, waiting for the last of the long line of men to disappear around the corner. Then, simply, "Follow."

Brandon did as he was told, walking a few respectful paces behind the guard. He shoved his hands in his pockets, suddenly feeling a bit cold, but knowing it was just his imagination. Despite all evidence to the contrary, the fewer people that were around, the less safe he felt. It was something about the gray rock the place was built from. The crumbling mortar. The heavy, artistic archways that evoked craftsmen long dead. He wasn't generally superstitious, but he was sure the place was full of ghosts. And Daly's weird fifties persona didn't help. Sometimes Brandon thought he might be the head ghost. That one day, when they were alone, the old guard would spin around and there would be a rotting skull where his face should be.

Daly finally stopped and unlocked a heavy steel door that Brandon had never seen open. It was painted roughly the same gray as the walls, as though it had been purposely camouflaged. Probably an effective strategy for most of the inmates, but it had the opposite effect on Brandon. He'd always wanted to know what was on the other side. Until now.

"Mr. Daly?" he said hesitantly. "Where are we going?"

Daly shoved Brandon through the door and followed, locking it behind them.

The corridor they found themselves in was barely lit and ended after only ten feet at a similar door. Something about it felt really wrong. "Excuse me, sir, but—"

"Shut the fuck up!"

Daly pushed a rusty button on the wall and a moment later a loud buzz erupted from the door at the other end of the corridor. He pointed and Brandon started for it, listening to the dull echo of their footsteps swirling around him. He had to use his shoulder to get the door to move, but when it finally did, a wave of cold, wet air gusted in. A quiet, commanding grunt suggested that he should continue.

He'd never seen the tiny courtyard before—it was one of the many sections of the prison that had been cheaper to close off than to renovate. The ground had turned to thick mud beneath the monotonous drizzle that had been hanging over the area for the past few days and Brandon was forced to curl his toes to keep from losing his shoes as he walked.

"This way," Daly said, starting purposefully across the yard. The lights from the guard towers caused the razor wire atop the stone walls to flash dangerously, but didn't penetrate to their level. Everything around them was dark, cold, and wet.

Brandon continued to follow along obediently, trying to figure out what it was going to be tonight. Probably a glitch in the septic system needed checking out and Daly'd wanted to wait until there was some good deep mud to make it even more unpleasant.

Of course, Brandon had thought about breaking out. A lot, actually. Particularly the day he'd spent cleaning roach carcasses out of the kitchen after the exterminators had gone. It wouldn't have been all that tough. The problem was less how to get past the walls, though, than how to negotiate the miles of wilderness and rural countryside that surrounded them. But even that was surmountable. The real issue was that those diamonds everyone thought he had didn't exist, and his sentence wasn't quite long enough to trade in for a life on the run. The best—only—course that made any sense was to keep out of trouble, talk loudly about Jesus whenever the warden was within earshot, and keep his fingers crossed for early parole.

He shaded his eyes and looked up at the closest guard tower. It was empty. He slowed a bit, searching unsuccessfully for human silhouettes in the other visible tower and then trying to make some sense of their absence. Typical for him, he was concentrating so hard that he didn't see Daly's nightstick until it hit him in the stomach. Not hard enough to drop him to his knees, but easily hard enough to double him over and make him gasp for breath.

"Move!" Daly said in an unusually quiet voice.

When Brandon just stood there bent at the waist and slowly sinking into the mud, the guard moved behind him and used the nightstick on the back of his legs. He felt a flair of pain, but again not enough to send him to the ground. Just enough to prompt him forward.

Brandon allowed himself to be herded toward a narrow metal gate that had, at some time in the distant past, probably been used for deliveries. When they reached it, he turned toward Daly, who was now only an outline, backlit by the glow of the spotlights behind him. The shadow of his arm moved and Brandon flinched, but the guard was just holding something out.

"What . . . ," Brandon gasped, still under the effect of the blow to his stomach. "Is that—"

"Take it," Daly said, shoving it into Brandon's hands. It turned out to be an elaborate cell phone. The large screen was dark, but when he pushed a button, it came glowing to life. What was going on? Daly had never outright beat him before—no one had. And the phone . . .

He spun around when he heard the rattle and creak of a key turning in an old lock and watched Daly open the gate and then step aside.

"Sir? What are—"

"Out."

"What?"

"Step through the gate, Brandon."

"I don't think that's . . . Sir, if I've done something to—"

"Get the fuck out!" Again, not a shout. More of an enraged hiss. As though he didn't want to be heard.

Brandon didn't move. Had Daly gotten bored with his petty humiliations and decided on something a little more drastic? Was he going to force him outside the walls and then sound the alarm?

"Sir, I don't think—"

Daly's hand shot out and closed around Brandon's throat hard enough to cut off the breathing he'd just managed to get back under control.

"What don't you think, boy?"

Brandon grabbed the man's wrist, but it just felt like wet stone.

"That's right! You *don't* think. You're just another piece of shit crook who was too stupid not to get caught."

Daly moved forward and Brandon found himself being pushed back. He released the man's wrist and put a hand out, just missing the gate and instead getting a handful of the wet, crumbling wall. A final shove and he fell, landing on his back in the soft mud. He jumped immediately to his feet and lunged toward the gate, only to lose his footing and fall again as Daly slammed it shut. A moment later he was on his knees with his hands wrapped around the bars, watching the guard back away.

"Mr. Daly," he shouted through the sound of heavy raindrops falling to earth around him. "Open the gate! Let me back in!"

The guard continued to back away, his teeth flashing when he passed through a narrow beam of light. It was the first time Brandon had ever seen him smile.

Finally he stopped and, still staring directly at Brandon, swung his nightstick right into that well-tended widow's peak. He staggered to the right, then a bit to the left, and crumpled to the ground.

Brandon just knelt there, his wet hands going numb around the cold bars. This wasn't good. Not good at all. He was soaked through with rain and mud, two feet on the wrong side of a prison gate, with a mind devoid of intelligent thoughts. He craned his neck and looked behind him through the water cascading over his glasses. The dim light bordering the wall quickly faded to black as the prison's lights got lost in the rain and distance, but he knew that somewhere out there the forest started. How large and how dense it was he could only guess. He'd never bothered to find out. What would have been the point? He'd made his decision to serve out his term a long time ago.

Finally, he pulled himself to his feet, giving the gate a hard tug to confirm that it was indeed locked and taking one last look at the dazed guard. A few deep, calming breaths did absolutely nothing to help him grasp what had happened. The only thing that he knew was that he was cold and scared. And that everyone would think he'd attacked Daly and escaped . . .

The phone!

He spun and dropped to his knees, crawling around until he found it partially submerged but still glowing green. He wiped it off and began scrolling through the menu, trying to find a number. Nothing. Why would Daly give this to him? If he were caught with it, there would be questions. He hit redial. Nothing.

"Shit!"

The rain was coming down even harder now and he could hear thunder that with his luck would bring lightning.

The bottom line was that he was screwed. Fully and completely screwed. Making a run for it would end with him being easily caught and then screwed some more. Giving up would start his screwing a few hours sooner. Maybe getting hit by lightning wouldn't be so bad after all.

"Shit! Shit! Shit!"

His mom had once told him there were always options, it was just a matter of whether or not you were smart enough to figure them out. He'd be willing to bet that piece of philosophy came from having never been on the wrong side of a prison wall in a Noah-and-the-ark level storm.

He struggled to his feet again and began backing slowly away from the gate, watching the towers as they came into view. Somehow he wasn't surprised to see that they were manned again.

"Hey!" he shouted, holding his hands in the air. Another step back put him into the beam of one of the spotlights and he shielded his eyes with the phone he was still holding. "Hey! I give up! I'm not trying to escape! This is all a mis—"

The crack of a rifle shot and the screech of a round

going past his ear made him duck, but he managed to keep his hands up.

"Goddammit!" he shouted, trying to be heard over the rain. "Stop shooting! It's me! Brandon! I'm—"

The second round went by his other ear and he heard it hit the mud behind him with a sickening splat.

He just turned and ran.

Chapter Two

"It's a little late to turn back now. For everything."

Edwin Hamdi was visibly nervous. Agitated even. His suit and tie exuded quiet dignity and European tailoring but couldn't hide the subtly fidgeting hands and the way his dark skin stretched over his cheekbones. Richard Scanlon poured two scotches and handed one to Hamdi before crossing the expansive office to a grouping of leather chairs and sofas in the corner.

Outside the closed door, the rest of the building was dark. Scanlon had set security at a very high level—not wanting to repeat the errors of other government contractors and agencies that made the papers for misplacing critical hard drives, documents, and God knows what else. The entire complex was meticulously evacuated and locked down at seven every evening. No one but he and the people working directly with him at that moment had the authority to stay.

"How's he doing?" Hamdi asked.

Scanlon looked at his watch. "It's just started. I'm sure everything's fine."

"You're sure? You're not getting updates?"

Scanlon shook his head calmly. "I'm not an operational person, Edwin. I signed off on the plan and now I've handed it over to people with experience in this kind of thing." He pointed to the phone on his desk. "They'll call me if there's a problem or if they need to make a change."

Hamdi took a sip of his drink, his lips tightening either in reaction to the liquor or extreme disapproval. Probably the latter.

"This is a mistake, Richard. There's no way to control him. Even before all this, the situation was turning unpredictable. I'm beginning to question the likelihood of our succeeding in this."

Scanlon nodded thoughtfully and stared into the crystal glass in his hand. Hamdi was a man of almost unfathomable contradictions. Abstractly brilliant, yet focused to the point of single-mindedness. Outwardly dignified, but deeply passionate.

Hamdi's Egyptian father had run a company that exported cotton to the United States and it was through that business that he'd met the American woman he married. Young Edwin had spent most of his childhood on the move, suspended—perhaps trapped—between the two cultures before landing in a New England boarding school. After he'd graduated, he'd gone on to Harvard and then to Oxford, where he'd earned a doctorate in Middle Eastern studies.

Despite his American heritage and the fact that he had no apparent religious convictions, there was something fundamentally different about him.

Something hard to come to grips with. A subversive undercurrent that occasionally surfaced, but then was almost immediately gone. It made Scanlon question whether the people of the West and East would ever be able to truly understand and trust each other when he himself couldn't fully trust this man he'd known for so many years. But then, faith wasn't something that had ever come easily to him.

"I'll be honest with you, Richard. I'm beginning to regret having approved this. You've been incredibly effective at bringing in some of the best and the brightest to work on this . . . project. How is he going to mix with the men you already have in place?"

Hamdi had an uncanny ability to see the gray in any given situation, but was blind to the gray in any given individual. To him competence was measured in the weight of one's degrees, the cut of one's hair, the amount of starch in one's stark white shirt. Anyone who didn't display these symbols of conventional success was somehow defective in his mind.

Of course, in this case he was right. Brandon Vale was defective.

"You're right, Edwin. They probably won't be able to keep up."

Hamdi leaned forward, his voice rising for a moment before he became aware of it. "Even with impossible responsibilities resting on our shoulders, facing a mission that simply cannot be allowed to fail, you enjoy antagonizing me, don't you, Richard?"

Scanlon smiled and took a sip of his scotch. The problem with doctors of Middle Eastern studies was that they tended to get a bit lost when faced with situations that had no historical precedent. It was hard to be too critical, though. Hamdi had the imagination and the courage to embark on this fool's errand, and there was no question that he could make things happen that Scanlon himself couldn't.

"If you have another suggestion, Edwin, I'm listening."

Hamdi didn't respond, instead turning and staring at a blank section of wall, reminded of the fact that it was one of his rare failures that had left them in the dangerous situation they were now in.

He had promised that Scanlon's company would win a two hundred million dollar contract from Homeland Security, but that was before the terrorist attack on the Mall of America brought security funding to a grinding halt. There was nothing like pictures of little American girls separated from their limbs to send politicians scrambling. Currently—and for the foreseeable future—virtually all Homeland Security contracts were on hold until the completion of yet another lengthy government inquiry that would ultimately recommend even more bureaucratic layering and complexity.

So now his and Hamdi's backs were against the wall, and Brandon was the best thing—the only thing—they'd been able to come up with.

"You've never been one to dwell on decisions that have already been made, Edwin. Why don't you tell me what's on your mind?"

Hamdi turned back toward Scanlon, but didn't

seem to be able to fully focus. "I think you know what's on my mind, Richard."

"Do I?"

"I want to be certain that we have the same understanding of Brandon Vale's usefulness to us."

"Yes?"

"He's a tool. That's all. No. That's not entirely correct. He's a syringe. Precise, effective, and safe—as long as you remember to discard it after use."

Hamdi didn't have an identifiable accent, but his speech had an odd cadence and lyrical quality that had come from a life straddling Egypt, the States, and England, and that gave everything he said additional weight. Combined with his natural charisma and intensity, it was difficult at times not to be mesmerized by him.

But not impossible.

"Is this really something that we need to talk about right now, Edwin?"

"Better now than when things turn desperate. And they will. We both know that eventually they will."

"I'm not necessarily arguing with you on this point, but let's give Brandon a chance. Let's see what he can do before we start planning his disappearance. All right?"

The silence between them extended for almost a minute before Hamdi finally put his drink down and stood. "I'm going to give you some rope on this, Richard. But I'll tell you now that we're not finished with the subject of Brandon Vale."

Scanlon nodded. "I know."

Chapter Three

The fact that the intermittent crack and hiss of gunfire had been replaced by the dull wail of an alarm was probably a positive development, but at this point "positive" was a fairly relative term. Brandon had escaped the illumination surrounding the prison and was now wading through the mud in what seemed like a sea of ink. He kept moving away from the light, not allowing himself to look back, partly because of the effect it would have on his night vision, but mostly out of fear of what he might see.

He tripped for what seemed like the hundredth time and again landed face-first in the gritty muck. The rain was coming even heavier now and he was breathing hard enough to choke on the droplets. He almost vomited but managed to hold down the corned beef and frozen peas he'd had for dinner.

He started again, shaky and increasingly cold, heading for the tree line he knew was there but still couldn't see.

There was no sign yet of anyone following, but that didn't mean much since the rain was deafening him and he still refused to look back. Maybe they were right behind him. Maybe they were waiting for Daly—

the injured party—to regain his equilibrium enough to properly line up crosshair and skull. Maybe he was just about to pull the trigger.

Brandon ducked involuntarily and ran in an uncomfortable crouch, slowing his progress but hopefully presenting less of a target to that mean-spirited, fat, James Dean wannabe psycho. Okay, maybe he wasn't actually fat. But he was a mean-spirited psycho and Brandon refused to get his head shot off by him. Not that the alternative of getting shot in the ass and dying of old age sitting on a rubber donut in his cell was all that attractive. It wasn't fair. He hadn't done anything. Not to Daly. Not to anyone at that prison.

He finally made the trees, entering them without slowing and taking a few painful branches to the face before raising an arm as a shield. After about fifteen graceless feet, he stopped and slammed his back against the broad trunk of a tree. It turned out to be about thirty seconds too late, though, and this time his convulsions left peas and corned beef splattered down his pant leg.

He always talked about taking advantage of the exercise equipment in the yard instead of sitting on his butt playing cards. But what had been the hurry? How could he have anticipated that Daly had this kind of initiative? He'd seemed so happy forcing Brandon to empty rat and grease traps. What would he do for entertainment now? Oh, yeah. Shoot him in the ass, catch him, and ensure that his plaything would be at his disposal for the rest of his natural life.

Brandon's breathing evened out enough to spit a

few times and the stitch that had knitted itself in his side began to ease. He started to lean out around the tree but then caught himself. What was there to look at? He already knew that they were coming after him. What he saw wouldn't affect his decision about what to do, so it was just mental clutter. Not what he needed right now.

Options?

Few.

He could circle around toward the prison and take a stab at sneaking into the courtyard in the confusion—making him the only guy in history to ever break himself *into* prison. Chances of success? Ten percent. Chances of survival? Maybe twice that if he was lucky.

Brandon wrapped his arms around himself and tried to ignore the cold rain that had soaked his clothing. If he just stood there, he'd probably freeze to death. How long would that take? How the hell should he know? What was he? A forest ranger?

What if he just stayed put and concentrated on keeping warm? The darkness and confusion might give him time to explain himself and emphatically give up before anyone could get a bead on him. On the other hand, the darkness and confusion could be just the excuse Daly needed to shoot first and ask questions later. Who would doubt a viciously attacked, God-fearing prison guard if he said he thought he saw a weapon?

Finally, he could keep running. But what chance did he have? He'd probably either break a leg or poke an eye out in the next hundred yards, and even if he didn't, he had no plan, no idea how to get to the road, no clue where that road led if he found it, and no allies on the outside. Even worse, he was the master of the thirty-minute mile and wearing a prison uniform.

The rain wasn't hitting him directly anymore, instead rolling off the tree behind him and down his back like some half-assed Himalayan waterfall. The thunder was an almost constant drone now, blending with the prison alarm in a way that made it hard to discern where one started and the other left off. Not exactly good for the concentration.

After a few more moments of thought, he decided that heading back to the prison was his only hope. No one would be looking for him pressed against the wall waiting to get back in. And once he was inside, it would be a lot harder for anyone to shoot him under false pretenses. Too many witnesses. The big draw-back here was that if he survived, he would not only have his sentence extended until doomsday, but he'd get his place in history as one of the stupidest criminals of all time. With just a little more bad luck, he'd be immortalized in the J. Edgar Hoover Building tour alongside the guy who wrote a bank holdup note on the back of his personal check. Now there was something to be proud of.

Brandon wiped at his glasses with a muddy sleeve and came out from behind his tree, cautiously pushing his way back through the dense foliage toward the clear-cut surrounding the prison. He'd made it about ten feet when he came to a sudden stop. The phone in his pocket had begun to vibrate.

He'd completely forgotten about it. Could Daly be tracking him with it? Some of them had built-in GPSes now. Was he calling to say he was only ten feet away?

Brandon grabbed the phone in a muddy fist and was about to throw it, but then stopped. None of this made any sense. The escape, the phone, Daly. So far, his overdeveloped sense of curiosity had been nothing but helpful to him in life, but it was hard not to remember his father's warning that it would get him in trouble one day.

He looked down at the phone, noticing for the first time a wireless earpiece taped to the back.

What the hell? It wasn't like things could get all that much worse.

He stuck the little speaker in his ear, securing it with the tape, and pushed the answer button.

"Hello?"

"Get going, Brandon. Move away from the clearing and start bearing left."

"Who is this? Daly? Why are you doing this to me? I—"

"Shut up! There are twelve men with dogs and guns coming across that clearing right now. They're not coming to catch you. They're coming to kill you. Is the earpiece secure? Did you use the tape?"

The voice came from someone smart and decisive—definitely not Daly or anyone who would hang around with him. Brandon opened his mouth to give whoever it was a piece of his mind but then realized he didn't really have anything to say. Instead, he touched the earpiece and confirmed that it was stuck on.

"It's in there."

"Then get moving."

He didn't. "How do I know you're not just trying to get me to keep going so it looks like I escaped—"

"As opposed to how it looks now, Brandon? Listen to me very carefully. You're a smart guy—we both know that. But right now you're cold, tired, and confused. So you can do what I tell you and let me get you out of this, or you can stand around asking stupid questions until somebody shoots you."

Brandon hesitated. "I can barely see to walk in here and those guys will have lights—"

"Quit whining and start moving, goddammit!"

The truth was that the upside to the best plan he'd come up with on his own was spending the next twenty-five years inside. And while prison hadn't been as bad to him as it had to some, he didn't see himself growing old there. Better to get shot, maybe.

A moment later, he was on the move, getting tangled, slapped, and jabbed by branches and sliding uncontrollably down steep banks all at the behest of the disembodied voice in his ear.

"Bear left a little more—about eleven o'clock."

Brandon smashed a shin into a jagged rock and stopped, bending at the waist again but managing not to vomit. There was nothing left in his stomach.

"Why are you stopped? Get moving!"

"I'm stopped because I'm tired, soaking wet, freezing my ass off, and probably being led into a fucking ambush . . ." He thought he heard the excited barking of a dog rise above the storm, and he spun around, staring into the darkness.

"Fine. Good luck to you," the voice said with a tone of indifference that sounded pretty convincing over the static-ridden connection.

"Wait!" Brandon shouted, cringing at the sound of his own voice. "I'm going, okay? I'm going."

He started forward again, bearing left and cursing himself for his pathetic flash of pointless defiance. Even Kassem would have seen through that bluff.

"Okay, you're doing good, Brandon. Keep your pace up. You've only got about another minute."

"To what?"

The question was ignored. "Can you see a light in front of you?"

"No."

"Keep going."

He did as he was told, stumbling forward and looking for a hint of anything unusual. Another thirty seconds and he caught sight of something. It was too dim to make out if he looked directly at it, but his peripheral vision could just pick it up.

"I think I see something. It's kind of greenish—"

"Go toward it! Double time!"

"Okay, I'm—"

The phone went dead.

Brandon stopped short. "Hello? Hello!"

He hadn't trusted the guy on the other end of that

line, but at least it had been a human voice. Now, in addition to being frozen, lost, and hunted, he was alone. His teeth began to chatter as he pulled the phone from his pocket and confirmed that the line was dead.

"Shit!"

He looked over his shoulder, but could only see blackness. They couldn't be far behind though. The forest was thick enough that he probably wouldn't see their lights until they were just about on top of him.

Turning back toward the glow, he pushed forward, feeling his heart rate rise still more as he came to the edge of a small clearing. He half expected to find Daly standing there with a .44 Magnum, grinning ear to ear.

Wrong again.

The light was coming from a single glow stick hanging in a tree. But that wasn't all. Dangling next to it was a thick vinyl duffle. Brandon took it down and began digging through it. A pair of boots, a towel, a set of thin farmer-John underwear, and a light, water-proof black jumpsuit.

He stepped close to the trunk of the tree, getting out of the rain as much as possible and stripped. After drying himself off as best he could, he put on the clothes, finding they fit perfectly, and reveled for a moment in the sensation of spreading warmth.

There was also a small backpack in the duffle containing a water bladder with a hose to allow him to drink on the run, a few energy bars, and night vision goggles that he was familiar with from a job he'd done a few years back.

He slung the pack on and stood, noticing for the first time a Polaroid photograph hanging next to the glow stick in the tree. It was a shot of the equipment he'd just put on, neatly laid out on the ground, but with one addition: a rather serious-looking hunting rifle.

He powered up the goggles and looked around, but couldn't find the rifle. Most likely because it wasn't there. Whoever had set this up wasn't stupid. The men from the prison would track him here and be drawn to the photo by the glow stick. Nothing slowed down a thirty-grand-a-year prison guard like the thought that the guy he was chasing might be sighting him in from a hundred yards away. No real point in actually providing the rifle, though. If this thing came down to shooting, it was over.

The phone began vibrating again and he reached down and picked it up.

"Are you ready?"

A few seconds ticked by before Brandon answered. "Yeah."

Chapter Four

"You wanted to see me, Richard?"

Catherine Juarez stood in the middle of the office, hands clasped behind her back and foot tapping casually on the carpet. When she was a child he'd paid more attention: to the way she'd grown, to the dramatic changes in appearance that inevitably accompanied changes in fashion, and to what people more knowledgeable than him called phases. Now that she was a woman, though, it occurred to him that he didn't ever really look at her anymore.

Her brow furrowed and the tapping of her foot became a bit more energetic as Richard Scanlon silently caught up on the much more subtle changes that had taken place over recent years.

Her hair was dark, almost black, falling thick around her shoulders and partway down her back—not the businesslike cut preferred by the other women in the office. Tan skin spoke partially to her father's genetic influence and partially to her lifestyle, as did her athletic build. Or maybe it was just that the older he got, the more fit these thirty-somethings looked.

He'd hired her for a variety of reasons: her unusual combination of extraordinary intelligence and humanity, her creativity and courage, the deep loyalty born from their long history together. Interestingly, though, her appearance hadn't entered into his decision at all. Ironic that it was about to become so useful.

"Richard? Are you all right? What did you need?"

Scanlon leaned back in his chair and continued to examine her from across his desk. "What do you do after work?"

"Do you have a new project? I can stay late if you—"

He shook his head. "I mean, in the general sense. Are you dating anyone?"

"Excuse me?"

"A beautiful girl like yourself, I assume you have a fair number of suitors."

"Nobody says 'suitors' anymore, Richard. Are you feeling all right?"

"What about that musician? What was his name? Adrien? Allen?"

Her expression melted into one of confusion. But with just a hint of suspicion. "Adam. That was in college, Richard. Ten years ago. I can't believe you remember him."

Catherine was the closest thing he'd ever have to a daughter, and while he certainly had never tried to insinuate himself into her personal life, he paid more attention than she would have guessed. The young men had always been around, but never seemed to stay around. He wasn't sure why.

"What about that professional skier? You seemed to really like him."

Her expression remained so constant it had to have been a conscious effort. She'd definitely felt something for that one. It had been obvious even to him.

"I'm guessing that there's a point here somewhere," she said, avoiding the question. "But I'm not sure I want to know what it is."

He pointed to the door and she walked over to close it.

"I've had a thought," he said, motioning to the chair in front of him.

"About my love life?"

"My understanding is that there is none."

"That's funny. Thanks."

"I've been thinking that since you seem to have some free time, maybe you should take charge of Brandon Vale."

She blinked a few times. "What?"

"Brandon Vale. I think you should be his contact."

"I don't understand."

"Am I not being clear?"

"Richard, I came here from the NSA. You know what I did over there—you got me the job. I'm an analyst, not an operative. Certainly not a handler. I don't know the first thing about it. Particularly handling a career criminal."

He waved his hand dismissively and then began drumming his fingers on the arm of his chair. "Of the eighty people I have working for me, only seven know anything about this operation—and frankly that's too many. I don't have a lot of people to choose from for this assignment, Catherine. You know that."

"Yeah, but every one of them has more operational experience than me. A *lot* more."

He nodded slowly. "You hated your job at the NSA."

"That's not true! I—"

"Come on, Catherine. I pushed you into that job. The CIA had gone to shit and the FBI wasn't much better. But I think I was wrong. To put you in a cubicle like that . . ."

"Richard, I appreciate what you did for me. The NSA was a great opportunity and a really good job."

"And yet when I asked you to come here and work for me, you couldn't get out of there fast enough."

"I like you," she said. "And you offered me more money."

He smiled. "You ride a motorcycle to work every day."

"Good gas mileage and it's easy to park."

"And the judo lessons?"

Her speech became a bit clipped as she got increasingly annoyed. "I can't stand aerobics."

"And the hunting?"

The uncertainty was completely gone from her face now and she'd moved fully into pissed-off territory. "Venison is less fatty than beef."

He nodded and tilted his chair back in a submissive gesture that suggested he wasn't looking for a fight. "I'm serious, Catherine. I've given this a lot of thought. I don't need someone who can kill him with a piece of dental floss. I need someone who can think fast and improvise. Look, Brandon isn't an evil or violent man. He just has an unusual take on morality."

She didn't respond immediately, and it seemed like she was using the time to beat down the intrigue subtly registering in her eyes.

"From what I've read, he has no take on morality at all."

"Don't start feeling too superior, Catherine. At this point, we aren't exactly what I'd call law-abiding citizens."

"That's different, and you know it."

He shrugged. "Obviously, I could send one of our former military or CIA people, but Brandon isn't going to respond to that. Trust me when I tell you he has a problem with authority."

"I'm not sure how my involvement helps."

"Oh, come on, Catherine. You know exactly how it helps. You're about his age, you're wound a hell of a lot looser than a former special ops guy or spy. And, as much as I hate to admit it, a little sex appeal is going to go a long way here. I mean he did just get out of prison . . ."

"What are you suggesting?"

"Oh, don't be such a prude. I'm not suggesting anything. Other than the fact that we're going to go with a soft sell here."

"A soft sell," she said, shooting for skepticism but missing the mark a bit.

"A soft sell," he repeated.

They sat there in silence for a few moments and

then she started shaking her head. Once she got going, it seemed like she couldn't stop.

"No way, Richard. Okay, maybe I have, somewhere in the back of my mind, thought about moving a little bit into the operational side. But there's too much at stake to just throw me out cold—"

"So you don't think you can do it? Maybe you're right. Brandon might be more—"

"Don't try reverse psychology on me, Richard. I'm not twelve anymore."

"Too obvious?"

"Yeah."

"The jet's waiting for you. You're going to be late."

She shot him an angry look but didn't say no. He knew exactly what she was thinking. She resented being railroaded into this but was absolutely dying to do it. Which side would win out?

The question was answered when she rose and started for the door.

"If you have any problems with him, call me on my secure line. Don't come in through the switchboard."

Of course, it was unlikely that Hamdi was listening in on the phones there—the security at the office was state of the art. But if their roles were reversed, Scanlon would be doing everything possible to keep a close eye on things. If there was a problem, he wanted a chance to deal with it before Hamdi found out. Brandon was a more critical piece of manpower than any of them wanted to admit, and it would be best if everything gave the appearance of going smoothly. Though it almost certainly wouldn't.

"Your secure line," Catherine said, tilting her head slightly to one side.

She was smart enough to know that there was more power behind this than just him, but she was also smart enough not to ask questions.

"Oh, and one more thing." He pointed to the tan jacket and matching knee-length skirt she was wearing. "Maybe we could sex that up a bit?"

Chapter Five

Brandon Vale released the car's accelerator and looked at the GPS in the dashboard. Then he floored it again. The sensation of his back being pressed into the leather seat was liberating at first, but he knew it was just an illusion.

The road he was speeding down was lined with broad trees and thick foliage, all beginning their transition from deep green to the more vibrant and varied colors of fall. It was really beautiful, and under normal circumstances he might have pulled over and gone for a stroll. These weren't normal circumstances, though.

He released the accelerator again and this time drifted to a stop on the gravel shoulder. The combination of running desperately through the woods, driving all night, and looking for cops around every corner had left him way too tired. The few coherent thoughts he'd entertained since getting in the car and starting out on its preprogrammed route had long since deteriorated into a mess of paranoia, fear, and fantasy. He'd never been particularly strong or fast or tough. His only edge was the ability to think straight, and now even that had failed him.

Yesterday he'd been a little more than a year from finishing out the sentence he'd been handed for that stupid diamond heist. Now he'd assaulted a guard and escaped from prison. Oh, and left behind a picture of a rifle. Couldn't forget that. No doubt he'd be nailed with threatening the life of a federal agent or something and get another five thousand years tacked on.

He was thirty-three now and no matter how his fatigue-addled mind spun it, he wouldn't see the light of day until he was a hundred and six if he let himself get caught.

Maybe he should just go back and explain himself. He tried it out loud in the empty car: "So the guard just threw me out, I swear! I assumed it was an over-crowding issue and I wanted to do my part to improve the prison experience for everyone, so I took off. Oh, and I was just kidding with the picture of the gun. Wasn't even loaded. Seriously."

He rested his head on the steering wheel and tried to control the dizziness and nausea that had been coming in waves for the past few hours. It was even worse than when they'd read the guilty verdict that had sent him to prison. At least then he'd had some anger and indignation to hold on to. It was bad enough to get sentenced to prison for something you hadn't done, but to get blamed for a sloppily executed and not particularly lucrative diamond job just added insult to injury. Why couldn't he have gotten nailed for something he *had* done? Maybe that elegant little caper in Atlanta. Now that thing had been sweet . . .

He lifted his head from the steering wheel and

shook it violently. "Pull it together, Brandon! And think! Time to get yourself out of this."

He made his third search of the interior of the car, more to get his blood circulating than in an expectation of finding anything. When he'd gotten in, there had been a change of clothes, a few bottles of water, and a couple of sandwiches wrapped in foil.

Otherwise it had been—and still was—empty. Not so much as an errant potato chip stuck between the seats.

He threw the car in gear again and made a screeching U-turn, driving up the wrong side of the road and skidding to a stop in front of a mailbox with the number 186 stenciled on it.

This was it, the address that had been programmed into the dashboard GPS. What was at the end of that long, narrow drive? Death? Doubtful. Too much effort had been expended to get him there. He'd made a lot of friends in prison, but it wasn't like most of them wouldn't have shivved him for a carton of smokes. The best he could have hoped for was that they'd be briefly conflicted about it.

"In or out?" he said aloud, wondering if someone was listening. Probably. Listening and watching.

He turned up the winding driveway, coaxing the car forward. Within a few seconds, the road behind him disappeared and a haphazardly maintained single-story house began to reveal itself. He wasn't sure what he'd expected—maybe some modern concrete and glass monstrosity with gun turrets. This was kind of a larger version of his grandmother's old cottage. She used to stand on—

Focus, dumb-ass!

He eased to a stop only a few feet from the house's faded porch and stepped out, leaving the car door open and the keys in the ignition.

A quick check of the front door suggested it wasn't locked. No point in knocking. It seemed that he was expected.

There were no gunmen or muscle-bound guys with flattened noses standing in the entry to meet him— just a bunch of doily-covered furniture that looked and smelled old.

"Honey, I'm home!" he shouted, not sure what else to do. His voice echoed through the house and a moment later a woman with a thick head of long, dark hair appeared at the end of the hall. She was actually wearing an apron.

"Good timing. Dinner's almost ready."

Then she disappeared again.

He stood frozen for a few seconds and then started forward. After everything he'd gone through, the least he deserved was a decent meal.

Chapter Six

The sun had set and now the sky's fading glow competed with illuminated storefronts and the headlights of cars inching along the clogged Jerusalem street.

Jamal Yusef lifted the cup in front of him and took a sip of the thick coffee it contained, the caffeine mingling with the adrenaline already coursing through him. He twisted around and held up three fingers to the waitress working the tables lined up along the sidewalk. She gave him a hard, suspicious glare and then an aggravated nod.

Despite the fact that the temperature had dropped ten degrees with the sun, he couldn't stop sweating. Grabbing an already damp napkin, he dabbed at his forehead, catching a thick drop before it started down his long, straight nose. It was the fifth time he'd done it and he cursed himself silently. The Jews at the adjoining tables would be watching for anything that could be construed as out of the ordinary.

He smiled easily, as though in reaction to the carefully crafted small talk coming from the man across the table, but he was actually focused on the movie theater across the street.

The line had begun to move about five minutes ago, and he watched the animated conversations of the people slowly disappearing through a set of heavy double doors. Their expectation was that they would be treated to the latest Hollywood blockbuster— apparently the story of a professional wrestler's family travails. And that expectation would have been fulfilled, except that the cousin of the man sitting opposite Yusef was attending the film as well. A very devout and passionate Muslim, he had entered with a significant amount of plastic explosive wrapped around his left leg. It was now inevitable that within a half hour, hundreds would be either dead or horribly wounded. And what was Yusef going to do about that? Sit there and let his coffee eat away at the ulcers he was convinced were growing in his stomach.

It wasn't exactly the life he'd imagined for himself.

His parents, both still alive and living near Chicago, were immigrants from Lebanon—people proud of their heritage and observant of their religion, but also anxious to provide opportunity for the son growing in his mother's womb.

He wondered what they would think of the path he'd chosen? How they would feel about the fact that he'd allowed the CIA to lure him into their ranks with the irresistible promise that he'd be the first of a new generation of operatives—a generation that understood its opponents and could move silently among them. The first step in a completely revamped intelligence machine that would promote peace, freedom, and equality around the globe.

But now here he was, trying to reconcile his dreams with what he'd become. And what exactly was that? One of the men who trained him had suggested that Yusef refer to himself as Bond. Ayatollah Bond. Rendered with an exaggerated combination of Arab and British accents, he'd taken it as a good-natured gibe. But now he wasn't so sure. On the verge of exercising his de facto license to kill, the joke came back to haunt him.

When he'd finally completed his training, Yusef's assignment—his only assignment—had been to penetrate as deeply into the al-Qaeda network as he could. What he had to do to accomplish that mission was unimportant. In fact, his involvement in the planning of this attack on Jewish civilians had been officially, if quietly, condoned by his superiors. That didn't make it any easier to live with, though. More and more, he lay awake at night, trying to force himself to consider the bigger picture—what these few casualties would eventually allow him to accomplish. It didn't help him sleep, though. Nothing did anymore.

Pathetically, his great achievement in all this—the only thing he'd done in a long time that didn't stink of evil—was convincing the men carrying out the attack to target a theater playing an R-rated film in order to reduce the toll on children. And that, in this part of the world, was what passed for a benevolent deed.

The man sitting at the table with him looked at his watch for the ninth time in the last thirty minutes and Yusef reached over to grip his wrist in what would appear to be a simple gesture of friendship. He spoke just loud enough to be heard. "Don't do that again."

Muhammad's teeth flashed dangerously before he caught himself and gave a nearly imperceptible nod. He was almost six-foot-five, with a thick black beard and eyes so filled with God and hate that they had lost sight of everything else. While discipline and obedience were hardly his strengths, he knew he was responsible for most of the attention they were getting and didn't want to do anything to jeopardize what he had convinced himself was God's will.

The men who were physically carrying out this attack weren't part of the cell that Yusef now led. Beyond consulting on the details of the plan, he'd managed to keep his people out of it—insisting that they had a greater purpose and that they couldn't risk the possibility of exposure. Of course, Muhammad had been violently opposed to sitting this one out, but the promise of a future opportunity to kill millions of Jews in one glorious action had calmed him. For now.

The waitress appeared with the coffees and Yusef thanked her, attempting a few pleasantries that she didn't return. Not that it mattered—his primary concern was that she depart without looking at Muhammad, who was staring at her like a lion choosing its prey.

And why not? Muhammad was an animal—an arrogant and ignorant man to whom God was just an excuse to vent his rage. If used carefully, though, he could be an effective tool.

The young woman moved away and Yusef slid one

of the fresh cups of coffee toward him, using the motion as an opportunity to glance across the street. The line leading through the theater's doors had dwindled to a few stragglers standing at the ticket window.

In some ways, he supposed that hope was beginning to glimmer. Edwin Hamdi was having a minor success in convincing the U.S. government of the painfully obvious: The root of the problem was not Osama bin Laden, or Saddam Hussein, or the Iranians. The root of the problem was ever growing hatred of America. Whether that hatred was justified or not was utterly irrelevant. In the world of politics, perception was reality.

If Americans could be convinced to concentrate on changing their image as brutal Crusaders, the terrorists would be marginalized. While it would be a slow and unsatisfying process, fraught with compromise and sacrifice, it was the only clear path to peace. Well, not entirely clear. There was still one insurmountable stumbling block: Israel.

In the early 1900s, this land had been Palestine, the home to fifty thousand Jews and over half a million Arabs. Certainly, it was understandable that the Arabs would have been alarmed at the growing immigration of foreign Jews to the land that had been their home for thirteen centuries. And it was equally understandable that these Jews would want to flee the persecution they'd suffered in Europe and return to the land of their god.

The fighting had begun quickly and continued to the present day. Only now mankind had entered a technological age where a single zealot could gain the power to kill millions in pursuit of political justice, or God's favor, or revenge.

The roughly three thousand people who died on 9/11 had prompted Afghanistan, Iraq, the Patriot Act. What if New York and its millions of inhabitants disintegrated in a tidal wave of nuclear fire? Or Washington? Or Los Angeles? In the face of that kind of destruction, would the Americans willingly give up their freedom and equality for the promise of safety? Would they let out a uniform, bloodthirsty cheer as millions of innocent Arabs died in their retaliation?

He wasn't even sure what terrorism was anymore. Was it defined by the type of weapon used? The target? The involvement of governments? Intent? In some ways he envied Muhammad's unwavering faith. More and more, he wished he could close his eyes and wrap himself in that same moral certainty.

But he couldn't. The truth was that the argument over Israel wasn't a question of right and wrong, but of right and right. And, as such, it was a dispute that could never be resolved by conventional means.

Yusef used a subtly shaking hand to bring his coffee cup to his lips. It was completely cold. He glanced at the waitress who returned his gaze with a barely perceptible smile on her lips. Even she was a terrorist—using the only weapon she had available to express her racist displeasure at the Arabs fouling her café.

A familiar sense of hopelessness washed over him— the same one he had conveyed to the CIA's deputy

director for operations a little more than a year ago.
Ayatollah Bond or not, his infiltration of al-Qaeda
wasn't going to change the situation in Israel.

Instead of accepting his resignation, the DDO had
quietly introduced him to Edwin Hamdi, whose plans
for neutralizing the Muslim terrorist threat went well
beyond the peaceful measures he publicly endorsed.
Hamdi didn't have ideas as much as he had solutions.
And solutions were what Yusef had been looking for.
Or at least that's what he'd thought at the time.

Though he'd known it was coming, the explosion
across the street actually surprised him. He threw
himself to the ground as the horrible sound of it
attacked his ears and the heat blasted his skin. Before
he could even cover his head, he felt a powerful hand
grab him by the collar and drag him beneath the table
that was already clanging loudly with the impacts of
falling debris.

Yusef blinked hard, trying to clear his eyes of the
dust billowing over him. The reverberation of the
explosion faded to an eerie silence that was quickly
broken by the shouts of bystanders and the screams
of the wounded.

Muhammad released his collar and once again
bared his teeth through the narrow slit in his beard.
This time, though, it wasn't an expression of anger
or indignation, but one of joy. He motioned with his
head and Yusef looked in the direction he indicated.

Propped precariously against a concrete planter,
only a few feet away, was a human leg still enveloped
in a dark blue pant leg. Yusef stared at the leather

loafer dangling from the lifeless foot, fighting back the bile rising in his throat. He wanted to look away, but to what? The charred bodies of both the dead and the living? The panicked people who a moment ago had been drinking coffee and peacefully talking about the trivialities of life?

How had he ended up so far from home?

Chapter Seven

"There's beer in the fridge," the woman said, opening the stove and examining something inside. "I understand you're not a wine drinker."

Brandon couldn't bring himself to fully commit and paused in the doorway, taking in every detail of the small kitchen. It, too, had that generic grandma's-house feel, though the dusty smell was covered up with something else. Cooking onions maybe. He crouched, confirming that there were no thugs hiding beneath the dining table and then went for the fridge. It was empty, except for a six-pack of beer on the top shelf. His favorite brand. Why wasn't he surprised?

The woman turned toward him and smiled with what he assumed was practiced unease. Impressive. Very disarming.

"I'm not the greatest cook, so we're grilling. Steak, potato casserole, and salad. My mom says it never fails."

"The bar isn't that high. I've been in prison. Name?"

"My mom's?" she said, seemingly startled by the question.

"Yours."

"Oh. Right. Sorry. Catherine. Rare, right? The steak?"

He nodded. She was even prettier from the front than the back—and that was saying something. Straight, elegant features with just enough softness to keep her from looking icy, flowing dark hair, and a slim, athletic figure packaged in a pair of low-rise jeans and a shirt that she was constantly tugging down in an unsuccessful effort to obscure the brown skin of her belly. She seemed to be about his age, though the complete lack of wrinkles around her eyes and mouth made the estimate difficult. Either Botox or very good genes.

"How long?" he asked.

"What?"

"Till dinner?"

She shrugged. "The grill's heating up. I haven't put the steaks on yet."

He turned and started back down the hall.

"Where are you going?"

"To meet your friends."

"There's no one else here."

"Yeah. Right."

There was no basement, so he started in the far corner of the ground floor, following a careful pattern that included the backs of closets, beneath furniture, and behind curtains. Then up the stairs for a similarly regimented search of the bedrooms, ending with the master. Nothing. No well-armed assassins, no obvious bugs or cameras. Just a whole lot of faux antiques, doilies, and carefully framed needlepoint pieces with uplifting sentiments. In order for this to get any weirder, space aliens would have to be involved.

There was an open suitcase on the bed and he pawed through it, finding clothes suitable for every occasion, from manual labor to formal wedding. The matching shoes were lined up neatly along the wall. In the bathroom he found a shaving kit, a set of electric clippers, and a pair of stylish wire-rimmed glasses. He took off his own glasses but hesitated before putting on the new ones, not sure he wanted to know what they might tell him. Finally he slid them on his face and, as he'd feared, they weren't the screwed-up prescription the prison optometrist had given him. They were dead on.

He looked into the mirror with his newly cleared vision and let out a long breath. "What have you gotten yourself into now, Dumb-ass?"

He hadn't cut his hair since his trial, and it now hung in his face, weighted down by dried mud he'd picked up the night before. Turning on the faucet, he splashed some cold water over his pale face and then felt around for the towel next to him. He hadn't spent much time in the sun over the past few years—content to sit in the shade and read during exercise time.

Brandon plugged in the clippers and five minutes later, his hair was a uniform half inch. With the new glasses, it created a disguise that would fool all the blind people and about half of the mentally challenged, unless they were really paying attention. His only hope was that the media would let out a collective yawn at the inelegant escape of an obscure, nonviolent diamond thief.

"Looks good," Catherine said when he walked back into the kitchen. "Everything fit okay?"

After a gloriously lonely shower, he'd chosen a pair of jeans, a white silk shirt, and a reasonably fast-looking pair of tennis shoes that might prove useful. The stink of nervous sweat was gone and he was almost ready to accept that his time in prison was just a bad dream and he was actually a married insurance salesman living in the burbs.

"It must feel good to be out of prison," she blurted when he didn't answer her question about the clothes.

"Yeah. Nothing like a hot shower and a steak to make you forget that every cop in the country is looking for you with the idea of either shooting you or putting you away for the rest of your natural life. I'm just having an outstanding day."

Her expression took on a brief deer-in-the-head-lights quality and then she beat a hasty retreat to the back deck. "I'll go put the steaks on."

When she returned, she seemed a little better composed. "I have a proposition for you."

His eyebrows rose unbidden.

She held a hand up. "Bad choice of words."

"Right."

"Look, we need the help of someone with your . . . skills. Actually, we need a miracle worker. And that's your reputation."

He didn't answer, instead standing there mesmerized

by her performance. This woman had undoubtedly been trained to snap his neck like a twig at the slightest provocation, yet she played the nervous innocent with such depth and conviction that even he was almost fooled. He'd worked with some talented people in the past, but no one like this. How was it that their paths hadn't crossed before?

"In return, we'll give you a new identity, enough money to live on for the rest of your life, and a little vineyard in South Africa. Paid for, of course." She pulled a photo of the vineyard off the fridge and held it out toward him as though it was proof of her complete sincerity.

He didn't look at it, instead pointing to a small jar on the counter. "And if I don't? Is there cyanide in there?"

"It's garlic salt."

"You say."

She shrugged—an oddly appealing gesture that made her shoulders disappear briefly into her hair. "Nothing so sinister. If you say no, I just walk away and wish you luck. You can either try to get out of the country or turn yourself in and take your chances with the courts."

"That seems kind of unlikely to me."

She put on an oven mitt and used it to retrieve her casserole from the oven. "It's a pretty nice day. I figured we'd have dinner outside."

They ate in silence on a wooden deck surrounded by thick hedges and flowers. The sun was still high and its heat overpowered the fall air. Even the weather seemed to have been set up to put him at ease, to rock him gently into a sense of well-being and trust. No harm in giving in just for a little while. He was out of prison, having a pretty good dinner with a beautiful woman, and there was nothing he could currently do about it. If there was one thing his mother had pounded into him, it was that if the moment was good, for God's sake live in it.

Catherine finished her steak, eating with the careless velocity of the terminally uncomfortable, and tapped her gorgeous lips with her napkin.

"So? Are you interested?"

He almost wanted to say no just to watch that perfectly nonthreatening demeanor suddenly turn black. To see if she still seemed so disarming when she was pointing a gun at his face.

The sad thing was that it wouldn't have been all that radical a change from his past relationships with women. When you lived like he did, generally the best you could hope for was a cute sociopath. Despite the fact that Catherine was undoubtedly on the verge of killing him at any moment, she was clearly a step up from most of the women he'd dined with. No relationship was perfect, after all.

"You're staring," he said. "What?"

She seemed embarrassed. "Nothing."

"If you've got something to say, say it."

She remained silent for a few seconds apparently gathering her courage. "Okay. I was wondering why you became a criminal."

"Oh, so now we're getting personal? You're going to try to get in my head?"

"It's not like that. I—"

"Psych degree?"

She shook her head. "Political science. I'm not trying to pry or anything, but you've got to admit, you're kind of . . . interesting."

"Am I?"

She nodded. "You got a near perfect score on the math portion of your SAT and then just left the English portion blank."

"You know, that's confidential information. You could get in big trouble for looking at those records."

She smiled. Just barely, and she looked away first.

"I like math problems," he said. "The English stuff was boring."

"And yet you never did better than a D in a high school math class."

"Politics. The teachers had it in for me."

He finished the last bite of steak, reveling in the fact he could chew without worrying about breaking a tooth on a piece of bone. "My father was a con man and a gambler," he started. "Not a bad guy, though. Not really. He always wanted me to go to college and even saved the money to pay for it. I did a few classes, but it didn't suit. Dad was pretty upset. I think he just wanted a lawyer in the family so he could get a deal on fees."

"Really?" She seemed to be hanging on his every word.

"Well, maybe. He's one of the few people I could

never read. Honestly, I think, deep down, maybe he felt responsible for having exposed me to it."

"Crime, you mean?"

"Yeah. It's all I knew from as early as I can remember. I was always surrounded by crooks. Scams. Whatever. I didn't see it as good or bad. It was just the world I was born into."

"That's so fascinating," Catherine said, putting her elbows on the table and resting her chin in her hands. The intensity of her gaze amplified to the point that he felt like he was a rock star and she was an adoring groupie.

"Fascinating? You really think so?"

"Definitely. I mean, not the story itself, but the way you tell it so convincingly. None of it's true, right?"

Brandon grinned broadly. "No. I guess not."

"I'd love to hear the real story."

"You don't already know it?"

"Just the bare facts. Your father is still alive—a retired accountant with barely a parking ticket his whole life. You traveled all over the world when you were young, apparently with your mother—"

"Do you know what happened to her?"

"No."

"Oh," he said, trying not to sound disappointed. "So?"

"What? My story? My real story? It's complicated."

"That's okay," Catherine said. "If I'm good at anything, it's complicated."

When he looked up again, she seemed to have leaned even farther over the table. He knew he should just keep his mouth shut, but there was something about her that made him want to talk. Prison must have scrambled his brain.

"My mother's hard to describe. She was beautiful and brilliant, but mostly she had a light inside her that was so powerful that you had to experience it to understand it. Everyone who ever met her loved her." He paused for a moment. "I know that sounds like an obituary cliché, but in her case I mean it. Actually, maybe it would be more accurate to say that everyone who ever met her was *in* love with her. Men, women, old people, kids. If you walked down the street with her, men would give her flowers and ask her to dinner right out of the blue."

"So that's where you get it."

"Get what?"

"Your job tends to revolve around getting people to trust you."

"Oh, I suppose that's true. But I'm just a bad copy of her. There's really no comparison."

"So how did a woman like that end up married to an accountant from Sacramento?"

"I have no idea how they met, actually. He was just in the right place at the right time, I guess. Mom had . . . Well, she had lots of relationships."

"But she married your father. And as far as we can tell, they never divorced."

"The difference with that relationship was that she got pregnant. She was young. Nineteen at the time," he said, continuing to push his food around his plate. "From what Dad said, she mostly stuck around for a couple years, but then started doing some trips. And they got longer as time went on. She wasn't the type for a house and a family and a dog, you know?"

"So your father raised you."

"Mostly, yeah. Mom'd show up a couple times a year for a few weeks. Then, one summer when I was . . . I don't know. Eight? She asked me to go to Europe with her. I couldn't believe it."

"I'm surprised your father would allow it."

He smiled and shook his head. "See? You still don't understand. No one could say no to her about anything. She'd left, but Dad still loved her. I don't know which of us was more excited when she showed up on our doorstep—him or me. That's why he never divorced her. Never got remarried."

"We have records of her traveling and you traveling with her, but there's no real record of her having a job. And no record of your father ever giving her a significant amount of money."

"No."

"So she was some kind of criminal. A con artist."

Brandon took a deep breath and let it out. There was a time when those would have been fighting words, but he was older and had mellowed on the subject.

"Not really. I mean, she sort of transcended that label. People *wanted* to be near her. And they gave her things. Money, places to live, plane tickets, food, clothes. Whatever. But they benefited just as much. And when she left—like she eventually always did— they were really sad. Sometimes even devastated. But

I don't think they would have given up that time or wanted the things they'd given her back."

"Strange life, though. For a kid your age, I mean."

Brandon shrugged. "I saw the world and had experiences that were pretty unique. And in the end, I wasn't any different than anyone else. I wanted to be with her. As much as it hurt when she was finally gone, I wouldn't give up the time I spent with her."

"But you don't know what happened to her."

"No. Dad hired a guy who traced her as far as Russia, but the trail went cold there."

"Did you ever try to find her?"

He shook his head.

"Why not? I would think you'd have contacts that would be pretty useful."

"She's dead. What is it they say about the bulb burning the brightest burning the shortest? She wasn't meant to get old."

"But—"

"Can we change the subject?"

"Sure. Sorry. Why don't we go back to the original question? Why did you become a criminal? If it wasn't really your mother's influence, and it certainly wasn't your father's . . ."

The sun had gone down and he couldn't help looking over the back fence as the trees lost their color. He could jump over it and run. But then what?

"Who says I'm a criminal? I'll have you know I was wrongfully—"

She held up her hands, silencing him. "Hypothetically."

He started tapping his fork on the table, listening to the dull clack of it fill the air. Was this a setup? Were they trying to get him to admit something? What would be the point? He'd never done anything all that bad, and they'd already put him in prison.

"Funny story," he said, finally. "When I was in school, I actually considered going to work for the FBI. Hard to picture, isn't it? Me as an FBI agent?"

"Oh, I don't know," Catherine said. "Why didn't you?"

"Police work isn't like what you see on TV. Ninety-nine percent of it is complete boredom and you never really accomplish anything. Bust one drug dealer or terrorist and there are five to take his place. Then you have the bureaucracy to deal with. Imagine your life being ruled by some fat bureaucrat lifer who spends all his time pissing in corners." He shuddered dramatically. "Crime, though . . . Now that's a good time. Seventy percent fascinating intellectual exercise and thirty percent full-on rush. Leaving zero percent for dealing with some asshole in a toupee who's planning on giving you a shitty annual review because you made him look bad in a meeting."

Catherine nodded with what he'd swear was real understanding.

"Deep down, everybody wants to be a criminal, Catherine. You know that. It's why everyone's seen *The Godfather* ten times. Hey, did I hear you say something about dessert?"

★   ★   ★

The refrigerator was visible from the deck through the glass door, so Catherine retreated to the pantry and stepped inside. She wanted nothing more than to close the door and stand there in the dark, but wouldn't let herself do it. Not that it mattered. Brandon Vale was probably already over the fence and headed for Mexico by now. In fact, she hoped he was. Almost.

A few deep breaths and she felt slightly calmer. It was hard for her to imagine what Brandon's mother must have been like—that anyone could have burned any more brightly than he did. Actually, he looked just like the passport photo of her that Catherine had spent an inexplicable amount of time staring at. Even long dead, Aisha Vale still glowed.

Of course, Brandon wasn't as startlingly gorgeous as his mother—on a scale of one to ten, probably an eight compared to her twelve. But he had the same wide-eyed, almost childlike expression, the same open smile that made you feel like you were the only person to ever see it. And beneath it all, the same subversive undercurrent that made you completely uncertain as to what he was going to do next. What the hell had she gotten herself into?

She tugged up on the low waistband of her jeans and down on her shirt, cursing herself for letting Richard talk her into wearing them and then walked smoothly from the pantry to retrieve a carton of ice cream from the freezer. Out of the corner of her eye, she could see her guest balancing his chair on its two back legs and examining a blooming rosebush intertwined with the fence. A surge of adrenaline went through her at the realization that he was still there, but she wasn't sure why. Excitement? Fear?

He was a professional criminal, she reminded herself. While the stress of all this was killing her slowly, it was probably just another day at the office for him.

There were only a few bites left in the carton when Brandon leaned back in his chair and ran a hand over his distended stomach. Catherine had given up fifteen minutes before, content to just watch.

"So why did you, Catherine?"

"Why did I what?"

"Become a criminal."

She felt what little calm she'd put together in the pantry abandon her and he leaned forward to study what was obviously an unexpected reaction to his question. She managed to regain her composure quickly enough that most people would have never even noticed the lapse. Unfortunately, he wasn't most people.

"I don't know. I guess I felt like there wasn't any other choice."

Chapter Eight

Edwin Hamdi sat motionless in front of the empty desk—once used by John Kennedy—and waited. He'd spent a fair amount of time in that particular chair, staring through the increasingly thick glass at Washington and trying to find a comfortable position. As near as he could tell, there was none.

When he'd published his first book on Middle Eastern politics and culture, he'd expected it to sell a couple of thousand copies that would clutter the shelves of university libraries all across the country, dusty and unread. It was a bit of a shock when the word of mouth started. While it would be an exaggeration to say the books flew off the shelves, they definitely began to move. Not in numbers that would impress a romance novelist or celebrity biographer, but not bad for a young college professor.

This, of course, had led to a few tentative invitations to various news programs, though it seemed that most producers were less concerned with expertise than the danger of professorial lecturing turning off their audience. Their fears turned out to be unfounded. Hamdi's unusual ability to explain the Arab mind to Americans, combined with the passion and logic he brought to disassembling the conventional wisdom, had left more than one television opponent shouting for him to "just shut up!" Suddenly, he was a talk show favorite.

His popularity and the near unfailing accuracy of his predictions had eventually made him known beyond the circles of producers looking to keep their viewers from channel surfing when they were occasionally forced to watch something more complicated than the latest celebrity divorce. Politicians had started to call, asking opinions and advice, and eventually that had led to a minor position as a national security consultant to the prior administration.

Unfortunately, that post turned out to be more of a publicity stunt than anything else. The president had been set on continuing the destructive eye-for-an-eye strategy that had become so popular with his constituents. In his mind, the tangible act of catching and punishing a terrorist was easier to explain in a sound bite than the admittedly complex business of preventing the genesis of that terrorist in the first place.

Hamdi had been quickly and quietly fired for speaking inconvenient truths—a fact that had been picked up in a small way by the media when a number of his more grim predictions had, inevitably, come true. And that would have been the end of his career in government if it hadn't been an election year.

He'd been toying with the idea of another book in his new office at the University of Virginia when the call had come. Not from an advisor or a consultant, but from the challenger personally. A few days later, Hamdi was working as a well-publicized national security advisor to the man soon to become the leader of the free world.

"What now, Edwin?" President James Morris said, entering and slamming the door behind him.

"A full theater was destroyed in Jerusalem."

Morris fell into his chair. "How many dead?"

"We're not sure at this point. Over a hundred, I would guess. More than that injured."

Morris jerked forward in his seat and slapped a hand down on his desk. The entire world works its ass off to get things moving in the Palestinians's direction, the Israelis finally give back Gaza, and what happens? The whole thing collapses into a goddamn civil war. And terrorism? It increases! Those people in Gaza are worse off now than when the Israelis were in control."

Hamdi remained silent, aware that any questions arising from the president's occasional outbursts were entirely rhetorical. These mini tantrums, while endlessly terrifying to most staffers, never really came to much. In fact, Hamdi saw them as evidence that, while certainly a skillful politician with the requisite survival instincts, James Morris actually cared. An unusual trait in Washington.

The president jerked his chair around and stared out the window for a few seconds, then spun back to face Hamdi. "Go ahead, Edwin. Say it."

"Sir?"

"Say I told you so."

"I don't see how—"

"I'm serious. You know you want to. Say it."

Hamdi folded his hands uncomfortably in his lap but managed not to start wringing them. "I told you so, sir. But I'm not sure what you could have done with the information. Were you going to say that you opposed self-rule by the Palestinians because they couldn't be trusted to run their own affairs? That you believed the Israelis would do whatever they could behind the scenes to sabotage Gaza's future? You'd have made enemies of everyone involved."

Morris's expression hovered between a smile and a smirk. "Very nice, Edwin. Very smooth. I'll make a politician out of you yet."

Hamdi didn't respond. When he'd gone to work for this administration, he'd quickly learned to quash the measurably correct, but overly forceful outbursts that had made him so successful on television. This was not the time to make a mistake that could cause him to lose the power and access his position afforded him. Not when he and Richard Scanlon were on the brink of solving a problem that the world believed irresolvable.

"There's more, isn't there?" Morris said.

"Yes, sir."

"What?"

"We have it on good authority that Israel is going to reoccupy Gaza."

"How good?"

"Consider it a fait accompli. We're already seeing troop movements."

"I swear to God, if there's ever a World War III, these assholes are going to start it."

"I can't argue with that analysis, sir."

"Nothing we can do to stop them?"

Hamdi shook his head. "It was their plan all along. Show the world that giving in to any Palestinian demand would just increase misery on both sides, then move back in."

"In your opinion."

"Excuse me, sir?"

"Do you have proof of that? That it was their plan all along?"

"No, sir," Hamdi admitted. "But—"

"Then it's just your opinion. And one I don't want to ever hear repeated."

Hamdi admonished himself silently for making the statement—no matter how accurate he felt it was. While it was well known that Israel was one of the foundations of Middle East instability and aggression toward the West, he had to be very careful in the way he presented those arguments. The Jews and their American lobby already hated him and missed no opportunity to undermine him. Any verbal misstep would be lauded as final proof of his anti-Semitism—a label that they had turned into an unfailingly deadly weapon.

"Yes, sir. I understand."

"So, how do we react?"

Hamdi remained silent.

"Come on, Professor. I'm asking you to lecture me on the Middle East. It's your favorite thing to do in the world."

"After the mall explosion, it seems politically impossible to come down on the side of the Arabs," Hamdi said.

"You let me worry about the politics, Edwin."

Hamdi crossed his legs and leaned farther back in the chair, mentally reviewing what he was about to say and making sure that his voice remained quietly respectful.

"Did you know that apartheid was originally a good idea, sir?"

"Excuse me?"

"It's entirely true. The original concept was that South Africa would be split evenly and equitably amongst the tribes. The thinking was that they had never been able to get along and never would be able to get along. An astute observation, in some ways. Perhaps not so astute in others."

"But separation isn't working, or Gaza wouldn't be in the situation it's in today."

Hamdi nodded. "*Partial* separation isn't working. As with many half solutions, this one is causing more problems than it's solving. Israel is still heavily involved and their security caveats are so onerous that Gaza can't be considered truly sovereign."

"So you're saying split the country in half with a tall, thick wall and put the Arabs on one side and the Jews on the other."

"It would be a step in the right direction. Though, honestly, it wouldn't result in peace. Both groups want *all* of the land. I think you'll find that in the long term neither group will give up its rights to a single square foot of land that they believe was given to them by God."

"It sounds like you're telling me it's hopeless," Morris said. "Is that what you're telling me?"

"I didn't—"

Morris stood, supporting himself with fists pressed into Kennedy's blotter. "I've listened to you, Edwin. I've listened to every word you've said. If I show any more goddamn respect for Islam, I'm going to have to grow a beard. I've started the process of normalizing our relationship with Iran. We've spent tens of millions of perfectly good dollars hiring Arab PR firms to polish up our image across the Middle East. I've criticized the Israelis for reckless attacks against civilians. Not just remained silent, mind you. Actively criticized them. And worst of all, I put a political gun to my head and told the American people that if we're going to reduce our reliance on Middle Eastern oil, they're going to have to sacrifice. Do you know how much the American people like to sacrifice? Not a whole hell of a lot."

Hamdi opened his mouth to speak, but Morris cut him off again. "You know where all this is getting me? Nowhere!"

"You haven't created new terrorists, sir. And that's a vast improvement over the policies of the last admin—"

"You know what? I can't show a voter a terrorist I didn't create. But the Republicans can damn well show them what's left of the Mall of America."

"I know, sir. And I wish I had something more

constructive to tell you. The truth is, you'll never eradicate terrorism. There will always be someone out there with a radical ideal and the knowledge of how to build a bomb. But you can do a great deal to minimize *organized* terrorism. We've seen it happen in the IRA, in Corsica, in the Basque country. People's lives improved and these terrorist groups simply lost their relevance. They became a solution to a problem that no longer exists."

"The Middle East isn't Europe."

"No, but I'm convinced that the same general principles apply. You only have to look at Israel to see where draconian enforcement measures take you. What has their brutality and racism gotten them? A country that's slowly sliding into chaos. We don't want to follow the Israelis into failure. We want to follow the Europeans into success. Unfortunately, though, those kinds of changes don't happen overnight."

"Pushing for economic and political reform in the Middle East isn't going to do anything about the question of Israel," Morris said. "We're talking about a group of people who just want one crappy piece of land that most Americans wouldn't pay two cents for. And the goddamn Arabs can run the rest of it right into the oil-soaked ground."

"Unfortunately, whether they're right or wrong, the Palestinians consider it *their* crappy piece of land, sir." Hamdi said. "The sad reality is that we're trapped. We can make every effort to be evenhanded in disputes between the Jews and Arabs, but we can't go so far as to make enemies of the Israelis. They're far more dangerous than the Arabs will ever be. In the past, they've proven their willingness to spy on and attack us if they feel it's in their best interest. They are, very simply, much more effective terrorists than the Arabs. If we ever began to support Arab causes to a degree that worried them—if we ever tried to force their hand—I can personally guarantee you that they would attack America in the most brutal way possible and leave a trail back to the Palestinians."

"You're full of strong opinions today, aren't you, Edwin."

Hamdi knew he should remain silent on this particular point, but he couldn't. "That's not an opinion, sir. It's a very dangerous fact."

Chapter Nine

Brandon rolled down the window and adjusted the car's side-view mirror, burning his fingers on the sun-heated metal in the process. The white Chevy tailing them was unimaginative to the point of looking government issue. The major difference between it and the one he was riding in was that instead of being driven by the lovely yet undoubtedly deadly Catherine, it was piloted by a square-built man who looked like he'd spent his childhood pulling the wings off flies. The guy riding shotgun looked marginally less Gestapo, but that was probably just the reflection off the windshield talking.

"Could you move that back, please?"

"What?"

Catherine slammed the accelerator to the floor and changed lanes, squeezing into a gap in traffic about six inches longer than the car. He could see the surprise on the face of the chase car's driver, despite the fact that this was about the tenth such pointless maneuver Catherine had performed. They seemed to be the equivalent of a nervous tic for her.

"The mirror," she said, ignoring the chorus of

honks coming through the open window. "Move the mirror back. I can't see."

Once he'd readjusted it, she raised his window and cranked up the air-conditioning, trying to dry the sweat beginning to stain the back of her blouse. Though all evidence seemed to be to the contrary, she continued to exude more apprehension than threat. Not that she really needed to be all that intimidating—the guys behind them were doing a good job handling that angle. They'd been waiting on the tarmac when the private jet that had delivered him and Catherine arrived. And that was yet another thing to worry about. He'd looked into private jets once— stealing, not owning—and knew that the one they'd arrived on was worth at least twenty million, confirming again that whoever was behind this thing wasn't your average criminal loser.

Catherine slammed on the brakes and they were briefly surrounded by a group of Japanese tourists crossing the street. The chase car hadn't managed to fully catch up yet and was hanging three cars back, but the guy in the passenger seat had popped his door open slightly and was staring straight at Brandon. Making a run for it seemed like a good idea on so many levels, but suffered from a few logistical issues. First, he couldn't seem to figure out how to unlock his door, and second, he wasn't such a fast runner.

"So . . . ," Catherine started hesitantly. "Can I ask you a personal question?"

"Why not?"

"In Chicago. How did you get away with the money?"

He turned in his seat to look at her. "That's it? That's your personal question?"

"I'm just curious. From what I read, you'd have had to make it from one side of the city to the other in less than five minutes. It's not physically possible."

"I don't have any idea what you're talking about or where you're getting your information about me. I'm a law-abiding citizen falsely accused and erroneously convicted."

"Come on. What would it hurt to tell me? What if you just give me a hi—"

"Maybe you're just a cute cop and all this is a setup. Maybe you're just trying to close the files on a few unsolved cases."

"You think I'm a cop?" She was vaguely pleased.

"Not really, no."

The bright sun coming through the window created a halo around her hair, taking her face slightly out of focus. He concentrated on that for a moment, then down her torso and to the legs protruding from her cotton skirt. "Honestly, I'm not sure what you are."

She looked over at him and, as if by clairvoyance, stepped on the gas just before the light changed to green. One of the pedestrians had to break into a jog to avoid getting clipped.

"Did you just imply a question? Is that curiosity I'm hearing?"

She was, of course, referring to the fact that he

changed the subject every time she began rolling around to what she wanted from him.

He shook his head. "I know everything I need to and almost everything I want to."

"Oh, really? What is it you think you know?"

"Well, you're a very classy and well-funded outfit, despite your taste in cars. You want something stolen and you can't figure out how to get your grubby little hands on it. So you give a guard some money to throw me out of prison and set it up so I can't really go back. Then you have me chased through the woods by a bunch of guys with guns to see if I still have what it takes to help you. Now you're feeling good about the fact that I'm between a rock and a hard place and you're going to spring what's probably an impossible job on me while you butter me up with images of a vineyard in South Africa." He took a breath. "Pretty close?"

She didn't react at all, instead concentrating on weaving through the traffic in a way that seemed more like meditation than impatience. Brandon pushed his seat back and turned toward the window, gazing at the graceful lines of the Stratosphere as they passed by. If there was one positive thing that had happened to him in the last forty-eight hours, it was ending up in Vegas. The city was, more than anywhere, his home. He knew every casino, every strip joint, every cheap diner. Hell, he'd worked in about half of them at one time or another—covering the full spectrum from front-office suit to dish-washer.

"So if that's everything you need to know," Catherine said finally, "what is it you *want* to know?"

He rolled down the window again and subtly felt around for the latch on his seat belt. His stop was coming up.

"Where they found you."

"Me? Why?"

"Because I've been around a lot of criminals over the years and they all have a certain . . . I don't know. A certain je ne sais quoi. You don't have it. Which means either you don't belong here or you're the most amazing liar I've ever met."

"If I don't belong here, then where do I belong?"

"Advertising. You look like an advertising person to me."

"Do you know a lot of advertising people?"

"Not a single one, actually."

They rode in silence until Brandon saw an almost imperceptible shaking of her head in his peripheral vision.

"What?"

"Nothing," she said.

"Come on. What?"

"Nothing . . . It's just that . . . Well, it's funny. I actually thought about going into advertising when I was in college."

"Why didn't you?"

"I wish I had."

The Treasure Island hotel and casino became visible ahead and Brandon leaned a little farther toward the open window. The entire front of the building was dominated by a man-made lagoon with life-size floating pirate ships. They were props in what had been "The Battle of Buccaneer Bay," an over-the-top exhibition of sword-wielding pirates and dangerous-looking stunts that an old girlfriend of his used to perform in. A few years before he'd been sent away, she'd given him a tour and explained how it all worked.

He'd heard that show had been replaced with a more sexed-up version now, but the set looked pretty much the same. Or at least he hoped it was.

"I'm not feeling good about that," Catherine said suddenly, disrupting his concentration.

"Huh?"

"You said I was feeling good about you being between a rock and a hard place. I'm not. It's just that you don't understand how important this is. We—"

"Do you gamble?" he asked, trying to change the subject while he searched the rearview mirror for the chase car.

"Do I what?"

"Gamble. Do you gamble. We're in Vegas."

He finally spotted the vehicle tailing them. Catherine's opportunistic driving had left it four cars back in traffic too thick to move through. They were traveling at about ten miles an hour at this point, though it looked like the cars ahead were starting to slow. Treasure Island was only about twenty yards away.

"Slots sometimes," she said. "That's about it."

"Slots are for suckers, you know."

"You sa—"

Brandon pressed the button on his seat belt and pulled himself through the open window all in one semigraceful motion. He had his butt on the sill and was trying to slip the rest of the way out when Catherine's hand clamped around his ankle and threw off what he'd hoped would be a balletlike maneuver. Instead, he fell backward, ramming his head into the asphalt with his legs still inside the car. The driver of the truck coming up alongside them slammed on the brakes and narrowly missed running over his face.

"Brandon!" Catherine shouted. "Get back in the—"

He managed to get his free foot out of the window and used it to push against the door, holding his pants up with both hands. A moment later, she lost her grip and he was free.

Traffic around him had completely stopped, and a few people had gotten out of their cars to watch. A little more scrutiny than a guy in his position really needed, but his audience was unintentionally doing its part to slow the guy who was bearing down on him from a few cars back.

Brandon struggled to his feet and slid across the hood of the truck that had almost run him over, landing on a sidewalk full of staring tourists.

"Look out!" he shouted, shoving his way through them. The man chasing him was already halfway across the same hood Brandon had come over.

The crowd on the sidewalk thinned a bit as he ran, stumbling gracelessly every time he looked over his shoulder. The guy was only ten feet back now and closing fast. Brandon faced full forward and ran hard, skirting along the railing that bordered Treasure Island's huge lagoon for a few seconds and then throwing himself over it.

He was five feet into what was about a ten-foot fall when it occurred to him that the performers never came to this part of the lagoon. For all he knew, it was six inches deep.

He heard the splash when his feet hit, and tensed for an impact, but instead felt the water slide over his body and cover his head. He opened his eyes and looked up at the railing, seeing the wavy form of the man who had been chasing him, along with countless other people pointing and shouting soundlessly.

He kicked his feet and started swimming underwater toward one of the large ships, surfacing only when the burning in his lungs became too much for him to stand. A glance back confirmed that the man pursuing him was moving along the railing toward the hotel, but not diving in after him.

Brandon went under again, making it to the back wall and skirting along it, starting to feel dizzy from lack of air. Despite his increasing disorientation, though, he found what he was looking for: an underwater passage that was used by the stunt people to get back into the hotel. He ducked through it and broke the surface, feeling his head clear as he gulped in air and looked around him at the locker-lined room stacked with dry towels.

Chapter Ten

"Slow down and tell me exactly what happened," Scanlon said, closing the door to his office and giving it an extra shove to make sure it was fully latched.

"I lost him, that's what happened! I was stupid. I thought . . . I let you convince me that I could han—"

Scanlon held his hands up, but she ignored him for one of the first times in her life. "I let him roll down the window and jump right out of the car. How could I have been such an idiot? I didn't think he'd run."

"Catherine . . ."

"You've never met him, Richard! You can read reports about him all day long, but when you're actually sitting there with him . . . Even with everything I knew about him, even knowing he was playing me . . . I let my guard down."

"But you got along?"

"What?"

"You liked him. And he liked you, yes?"

"What the hell are you talking about? He isn't capable of liking anybody—of anything resembling a normal relationship. He just uses people." The words came out a little angrier than she intended.

"I'm not sure that's entirely true, Catherine."

"With all due respect, Richard. Trust me. It's true."

She finally fell silent, moving behind a chair, as though she could hide there, unable to meet Scanlon's eye.

"You weren't there as an enforcer, Catherine. I'm sure you did more than anyone else could have to win him over. I'm not holding you responsible for this."

She stared down at her hands. Whether he held her responsible or not, she *was* responsible. She'd been put in charge. He'd been in her car. And now he was gone. There was too much at stake for these kinds of stupid mistakes.

"What happened to the chase car?"

"It wasn't their fault. There was a lot of traffic and I wasn't careful enough to make sure they were behind us. Daniel's feet hit the ground probably before Brandon's did. But he was too far back."

"Does Brandon still have the phone we gave him?"

"He had it when he ran."

"Is it working?"

"In theory it's water and impact proof."

"It has a built-in GPS, yes? One that transmits even when the phone's turned off?"

She nodded submissively. "No signal. Either it's not as tough as the specs say or he pulled the battery out."

Scanlon walked behind his desk and dropped into his chair. "Clever boy."

"Richard?"

He looked up at her.

"I . . . I'm so sorry. I know that—"

He waved a hand dismissively. "Relax, Catherine. And sit down. There was no sure way to play this. If

I'd assigned an entire SEAL team to watch him and he wanted to walk away, he would have figured something out. That's why we want him, right?"

"But I should have—"

Another wave of the hand. "Maybe we can make this work for us. Use it as a chance to prove a point. Or maybe not. I don't know. The bottom line is that this was never going to be an easy courtship."

He turned his chair to fully face her as she finally sat down. "I assume he knows basically nothing. That he changed the subject every time you tried to tell him why we broke him out of jail."

"How did you know? Did you bug the—"

He shook his head. "The less he knows, the less motivated he thinks we'll be to find him. How much money does he have?"

"None. I mean, we didn't give him any."

"IDs?"

She shook her head. "He didn't give us time to make any."

"Do we have a photo of him with the short hair and new glasses?"

"No, but we can Photoshop the one we've got."

Scanlon drummed his fingers on his desk. "I assume his prison escape hasn't gotten much press in Nevada."

"None at all, really. It's more of a local story up north."

"Okay. We're going to have to risk it. Quietly fax a photo of him to our friends in casino security. Tell them he's a suspected cheat and to contact me if they see him."

"What about his accounts?"

Scanlon leaned a little farther back in his chair and let out a long, slow breath. They'd done a great deal of research into Brandon Vale and found a number of his bank accounts spread out across the country under various aliases. The problem was that there was no way to know if they'd found them all. Worse, they'd never turned up any documents relating to those aliases, making it likely that he had IDs stashed in places they couldn't track. Probably just buried in the woods along with a stack of hundreds. Someone like Brandon could be counted on to be well diversified in that area.

"Drain them," he said finally. "Let's not make this easy for him."

Edwin Hamdi watched the flashing light indicating that he had a call on the secure private line he'd had installed. It had been a precaution, really. Nothing more. Nothing he'd expected to ever use.

"Hello, Richard," he said, when he finally picked up. Scanlon was the only person with the number and had been given instructions to use it only in the event of a dire emergency.

"He's gone, Edwin. He jumped out of a moving car on the Strip."

Hamdi's breath caught in his chest for a moment and he glanced up to confirm that his door was shut, despite already knowing that it was. "How could this happen? He's one man, wanted by the police! How could he get away from your people?"

"It was quite a production, actually. You'd have been impressed."

Hamdi's jaw clenched at the lack of gravity in Scanlon's tone.

In the beginning, the only significant weakness in his plan was the overreliance and irreplaceability of Jamal Yusef in the Middle East—a situation that couldn't be remedied and therefore had to be endured. Then Congress had suspended all new Homeland Security funding, leaving them without the resources to go forward. And now this.

"What does he know?"

"Nothing."

"Don't you—," Hamdi shouted, but then caught himself and lowered his voice. "That seems very unlikely to me."

"Relax, Edwin. I handpicked everyone involved in this and none of them know anything about you—no one but me does. And Brandon's completely in the dark. All he knows is that someone broke him out of prison, and the only face he has is Catherine's."

"But he was told what we wanted from him. He can use that—"

"She never got the chance. He kept changing the subject. Figured we wouldn't put as much effort into finding him if he didn't have any information."

Hamdi tightened his grip on the handset but didn't speak, just breathing into the phone. It was becoming harder and harder not to look back fondly on the cold war. In retrospect, it had been nothing but a game. Two opponents, playing for insignificant pieces, neither daring to make a meaningful advance. Errors—even serious ones—rarely cost more than brief embarrassment or the loss of secrets with no long-term significance. But now the world had changed. The U.S. government, still accustomed to the glacially paced, low-stakes competition with the Soviet Union, was struggling to adapt to a completely new enemy. An enemy that could appear from nowhere and kill thousands—perhaps millions—for no rational reason at all. It was a difficult transition and one that wasn't moving fast enough to avert disaster.

"Are you going to be able to find him?"

"I think so. I hope so."

"You hope so?" Hamdi said. *"You hope so?"*

"I'm not going to make promises about something I can't control, Edwin."

Hamdi didn't immediately respond. He was becoming increasingly concerned about Scanlon's attitude toward this little thief. He didn't seem to be treating him as the necessary—and ultimately temporary—evil he was.

"And if you do find him?"

"I don't understand the question, Edwin."

"I think you understand it quite well."

"What do you want me to say? That I'll take him out back and shoot him? Unless you've come up with an alternative you haven't told me about, we're stuck with him."

Hamdi nodded silently. "Then perhaps it's time for you to be a little more forceful in the way you convince him what is and isn't in his best interest."

Chapter Eleven

The maid shook her head disapprovingly as Brandon stood there in a towel, dripping all over the carpet and telling his sad story about going to the pool and forgetting his key. Or maybe she was shaking her head at his atrocious Spanish. It was hard to be sure. After a little begging and a few of his best embarrassed grins, she finally used her passkey to let him into a room he'd chosen based solely on the fact that no one had answered his knock.

"Gracias!" he said, ducking into the room and pushing the door closed before the maid could peek inside.

He latched the chain and pressed his back against the wall after confirming that no one was in the bathroom or asleep in the unmade bed. Maybe his luck was changing.

He powered up the laptop sitting on the desk and then began rifling through the open suitcase next to it, hoping the room wasn't occupied by a couple of five-foot-tall, middle-aged women.

It turned out it was a somewhat taller middle-aged man. Brandon slipped on a very roomy pair of plaid shorts and a golf shirt that would be perfectly complemented by the collection of black socks and brown dress shoes that were his only choices. On the bright side, the loafers were actually the right size.

He heard someone talking outside and froze, but they just passed by. If there was one thing in life that drove him nuts, it was relying on luck instead of planning. But how the hell could he plan for getting thrown out of prison by Betty Crocker's much hotter sister? Sometimes you just had no choice but to improvise.

The overall effect of the clothes wasn't as bad as he expected. Except the socks. He took them off and slid the loafers back on. With a little luck, people would think he was going for a baggy, neo-preppy thing. Luck. There it was again.

After another nervous glance at the door, he sat down in front of the laptop. There was no password and he made a quick inventory of its contents. All business stuff—no credit card numbers or anything else he could use. But it was connected through the hotel's WiFi, so he pulled up Explorer and started tapping in addresses.

"Shit," he muttered after a few minutes of effort. Mostly he was pissed off, but he also had to admit to being a little bit impressed. He'd checked four bank accounts and all four had come up closed. That was almost a hundred grand of emergency funds up in smoke. No wonder Catherine had gone for the filet. He'd paid for it.

Another ten minutes confirmed that these assholes were really irritatingly efficient. His net worth had sunk to sixteen thousand dollars—Canadian, no less—in an account in Banff. What was even more annoying was that he didn't have any way of accessing that money personally. He could use his still-operational Internet bill-paying service to send him a check, but he had no ID to cash it, and Vegas was a notoriously suspicious town. He could, however, send checks to other people. Real people with identities and lives and houses and families.

Ironically, he hadn't stashed a single ID or bag of cash in Vegas. The idea was that it was the first place anyone would look for him, so he'd have every reason to avoid it. Yet another mistake in what was becoming a long list of mistakes. His closest stash was in Salt Lake City. And, of course, there was no guarantee that instead of fake driver's licenses and cash, he wouldn't find a herd of well-armed goons or a booby trap. But what choice did he have?

Brandon removed his glasses and squinted against the bright sun. He could see well enough not to bump into anyone and skipping the glasses would make him slightly less recognizable. Of course, crossing the road was going to be fairly death defying. What was it the bumper sticker said? Live on the edge: There's a better view.

After only a few minutes of walking along the Strip, the heat had plastered his new shirt to his back and his hand was sweating profusely around the sixty dollars in his pocket. He'd found it in a pair of slacks hanging in the closet of his unknown benefactor and was reluctant to release it since it was all he had to live on for the foreseeable future.

His best—only—option was to make it to Salt Lake and take his chances getting his IDs. Then buy a reliable old truck and head to Central America for a few years. If he could track down some local talent, he might even be able to pull a small job or two and live a fairly comfortable little lifestyle. A quiet hut by the beach had never really been his vision of paradise, but it beat the hell out of a prison cell or a coffin.

But first, a little information. This Catherine woman knowing everything about him while he knew nothing about her and her playmates had to go. It was time to balance the scales a bit.

He wandered over to a pay phone and thumbed through the yellow pages until he found the section for private investigators. He found a national outfit that he'd never used and dialed the number. Admittedly kind of dull, but the truth was that PIs were a great way to gather information without introducing the often unpredictable criminal element.

"Hi. I'd like to hire an investigator, please."

"You've got one," came the pleasantly motivated voice on the other end of the line. She sounded cute, too . . .

He punched himself in the forehead. "Focus!"

"Excuse me?"

"Nothing. Sorry."

"What can I do for you?"

"I need information on a private plane and a house."

"What kind of information?"

"I dunno. Whatever you can get."

"Yo! Could I get some more peanuts over here?"

The bartender frowned and dipped the bowl behind the counter, returning it filled with what was to be Brandon Vale's dinner.

He'd managed to get a room at a dive hotel about six blocks away by wiring double the price of the room into the front desk guy's personal bank account.

Thank God for dishonesty. Without it, the world would just plain cease to function. It could be a bit of a two-edged sword, though. The clerk had drawn the line at kicking Brandon back any cash. He obviously was only confident enough to play if it was the hotel and not him that was at risk.

Brandon crammed a handful of peanuts in his mouth and washed them down with a small sip of Pepsi, careful not to accidentally swallow the maraschino cherry floating in it. That was dessert.

While he chewed, he pulled out the phone Daly had given him and turned it over in his hand. It was a heavy model, built for durability more than sleekness, but beyond the dents and scratches it had gotten in their short time together, it had no identifying marks at all.

Who were these guys? The more he thought about it, the more he was sure that Catherine was no career crook. More like a combination between June Cleaver, Salma Hayek, and that nervous old dentist he used to go to. Crook or not, though, she had someone big backing her. The mob? Probably not. He had a pretty good relationship with those guys. If they'd needed something, they'd just ask. A foreign outfit? Maybe. Probably. Between the Asians, the South Americans, and those damn Eastern Europeans, you could hardly breathe anymore without catching the eye of some overseas psycho killer.

"South Americans," he mumbled before jamming another fistful of nuts in his mouth. Catherine did have a kind of south-of-the-border look. And those guys loved buying private jets with all that drug cash. But what could they possibly need him for? Next to selling coke, all other enterprises were almost comically unprofitable.

He looked down at the phone again, memorizing the location of each button and testing his dexterity by punching a few. Satisfied, he slapped the battery back in and began quickly scrolling through the navigation screens. Within a few minutes, he had confirmed that the address book was empty, that the calls he'd received during his escape were from a blocked number, that there was no history of calls going out, and, most interestingly, that there was one voice message. He put the phone to his ear and played it.

"Brandon. Come on. Where are you going to go? What are you going to do? Let's talk. That can't hurt, can it? Call me."

So earnest, he thought, yanking the battery back out of the phone. He just wanted to run into her arms every time he heard her voice. But then, who wouldn't?

He finished his Pepsi in a single swallow, catching the cherry between his teeth and dumping the rest of the peanuts in his pocket. The bartender had his back turned, chatting seductively with an older woman who had the look of a Mary Kay rep. Their eyes were firmly locked together and Brandon took the opportunity to skip out on his bill.

Chapter Twelve

One of the unfortunate by-products of his father's unfailing honesty and his mother's lack of hard and fast criminal skills was that Brandon never learned any of the more practical survival-type crimes. Things that you could use to get by if you really had your back against the wall. What he wouldn't give to be a decent pickpocket right about now.

On the bright side, though, his mother *had* been cursed with an obsession for poker and Brandon had inherited her aptitude, if not her style. He was a little rusty from spending the past few years playing with Kassem and his entourage, but in the end poker was like riding a bike.

He held his cards close to his chest, peeking at them for a moment and then sliding a few chips onto the table under the watchful eye of the dealer. The other people around the table weren't as bad as he'd become accustomed to—rating between a two and a four and a half on a scale of one to ten. Based on his current financial situation, he'd walk if he calculated the table's average skill level above a three. He didn't need a challenge—he needed cash.

A guy who looked like he'd mugged an Elvis

impersonator for his shades called and aimed his shiny lenses at Brandon. He was the four and a half—a man whose body language suggested he regretted that poker wasn't a contact sport.

"Nines over deuces," Brandon said laying his cards on the table to a chorus of frowns from the other players. Not Elvis, though. He just smiled.

"Three sevens."

Brandon looked around at the carefully created chaos in the casino while the dealer gathered the cards. Above him, people were floating by in fake hot-air balloons and model ships, tossing stuff to the crowd. Music blared, vividly costumed performers danced, tourists smoked and fed coins to the slots. As far as he was concerned, the Rio was the best of the bigger casinos to get lost in.

A quick glance at his new hand revealed that it was crap, and he laid it back down on the table, trying to decide what to do. Elvis's eyebrows came up slightly, and the chunky lady next to him let her cigarette quiver perceptibly between her gloss-smeared lips. Brandon had been playing for nearly two days straight and had thirteen hundred dollars in his pocket—more than enough for a fake mustache, a cowboy hat, and a rusted-out truck that could make it to Salt Lake.

"I'm out," he said, sliding a couple of chips to the dealer and taking the rest for himself. "Hey. Do you have a business center?"

"Susan Fallow, please," Brandon said into the phone as he sat down in a small booth neatly arranged with office supplies. There was an audible click and then the cheerful voice of his private dick.

"This is Susan."

"Hey, it's Brandon. Do you have anything for me?"

"Yup. You got a fax?"

He gave her the number and a moment later the printer next to him began spitting out pages.

"The house you wanted to know about is owned by an elderly couple who've retired to Arizona," she said. "They rented it about a month ago and got all the money up front—in cash, apparently. I talked to the wife. Nice lady. Chatty. The lease was signed by a Ray Bradburn. I've checked the name, but come up with zip so far. Do you want me to—"

"Nah, it's fake."

"Seems likely based on the cash thing."

"What about the plane?"

"I managed to narrow it down to three possibilities based on your description and the general flight plan. The first is owned by a private individual named Robert Palmer—like the singer. He's a retired real estate developer. I forwarded you some newspaper clippings on him."

Brandon retrieved the pages from the printer and shuffled through them, finding a carefully posed photo of Palmer smiling out from beneath a hard hat.

"Ring any bells?"

"Nope," Brandon said. "Never seen him before in my life."

"I don't know exactly what you're looking for, but this guy seems pretty much on the up-and-up. Well known in the community, gives a lot of money to charities, lives in a modest house . . ."

"Next," Brandon prompted.

"The second is owned by a New York law firm."

Brandon perked up a bit. Interesting in a John Grisham kind of way.

"There are about a hundred attorneys working there. The link to their Web site is on one of the pages I sent you. Do you see it?"

"Uh-huh," Brandon said, typing the address into the computer on the desk. A stuffy home page with limited information appeared.

"You can get into individual profiles on all their people through that site. It also talks a bit about some of their bigger clients. They do mostly corporate work."

He clicked through a few profiles, examining the serious, smartly coiffed headshots. It would be interesting to see if he could find Catherine's beautiful face in there anywhere. Advertising had been his first-blush reaction, but he could see lawyer, too.

"Is any of this exciting you?" Susan said.

"I'm not getting sweaty or anything, but I kinda like this one."

Maybe someone he knew had told his lawyer about the job Brandon had been planning before he got busted. Then that lawyer got to thinking about it and figured it sounded pretty profitable.

"The third is owned by a corporation: American Security Holdings, Inc. It's some kind of government contractor, but I can't figure out exactly what they do. They're privately held, so the information isn't just floating around in the public record."

"Uh-huh."

"I did get you a filing that lists the officers and some other basic information. I could dig deeper, but it would cost you more."

Brandon found the document she was talking about and began flipping through it disinterestedly. The law firm was clearly the front-runner. Shady bunch, lawyers. He got to the last page and ran a finger down a list of the ASHI's board members.

"This is good stuff, Suze. I need a chance to go through it and then I'll ca—"

"Brandon? I didn't catch that. Could you say it again?"

He didn't respond, instead staring down at the words printed above his index finger.

Richard Scanlon, CEO.

"Brandon?"

He slammed the phone back into its cradle and shoved the fax pages down the back of his shorts.

The corridor seemed impossibly long as he walked briskly up it, keeping his nose pointed at the floor. It eventually led back to the casino, but not before going beneath God knows how many little black bowls in the ceiling that hid the casino's surveillance cameras. He was going to be okay, he told himself. He'd been basically living in the casinos for two days and nothing had happened. The gods would really have to hate him to—

"Excuse me, sir?"

He kept walking, acting as though he hadn't heard. A moment later a thick hand slipped around his left biceps. Then another clamped on to his right.

"Hey, guys, I realize you're just doing your job, but somebody's lying to you. I haven't done anything."

Well, other than breaking out of prison and the whole life-of-crime thing before that. But why nitpick?

"If you want me out of here," he continued, "I'm gone. Seriously. There's no need for any rough stuff, right?"

They ignored him and continued half pushing, half dragging him forward in a well-coordinated effort that suggested they'd done this a few times before.

When they turned right, away from the Rio's exit, Brandon tried to dig his heels in, but it did nothing other than cause him to lose one of his loafers.

And on they went—through a set of metal doors, down a bare concrete hallway, and finally to another metal door that they opened by slamming his head into it.

At precisely the right moment, one of the guards stuck a foot out and Brandon tripped, bouncing off a Dumpster and landing hard on the hot asphalt. The hotel guards weren't the only ones experienced at this kind of thing, though, and Brandon immediately rolled into a ball, covering his head to mitigate the damage from the inevitable kicks he was about to absorb. He tensed, but nothing happened. A trick. They were waiting for him to look up so they could get a shot at his face. Unfortunately for them, he was nowhere near that stupid.

A moment later their footsteps started to recede and he heard the screech of the metal door closing. He still didn't move, though.

"Brandon?"

When he opened his eyes, he found himself looking at a set of subtle but artistically painted toenails.

"Come on, Brandon. We both know you're not hurt. Get up."

Instead, he just lay there, soaking in this latest humiliation. Finally he moved his arm from in front of his face and squinted up as Catherine's expression of irritation faded into one of mild disgust. "When's the last time you took a shower?"

Chapter Thirteen

This time they were taking no chances.

The comforting blandness of the Chevy Impala Brandon jumped from two days ago had been replaced by a much more intimidating black Suburban with deeply tinted windows that didn't roll down. He was sitting in the back, belted to the seat and hand-cuffed to the man who had chased him down the side-walk in front of Treasure Island.

Brandon examined him out of the corner of his eye, trying not to be too obvious. He wasn't super heavily muscled like the guys in prison, but was certainly broad-shouldered and narrow at the waist. His hair was a little shaggier than seemed natural and framed features that could be described as chiseled, but by a vaguely careless sculptor. Overall impression: extremely dangerous. His old prison protector Kassem probably outweighed this guy by a hundred pounds, but if they got into it, Brandon wouldn't put money on Kassem with less than nine-to-one odds.

"So where are we going?" Brandon said. The silence in the car was starting to get to him.

Catherine glared at him in the rearview mirror but didn't answer.

"Are you gonna kill me? You are, aren't you?"

Catherine mumbled something that he couldn't quite make out. Best guess: "I wish."

"Are you mad? Go ahead and say it. You're mad at me."

She twisted around in the seat with enough force to make him jerk back. The guy he was cuffed to seemed a little startled, too.

"You know, I break you out of prison, I cook you dinner, I make you a really attractive offer, and—"

Brandon jabbed a finger toward the windshield and she turned her head just long enough to avoid a slow-moving minivan.

"—you don't even have the courtesy to just say no. Instead you jump out of the car on a crowded street, risk getting us all caught, and, in the process, make Daniel and me look like complete jackasses in front of our boss."

Brandon glanced over at Daniel, who nodded in agreement as Catherine turned back around and flung the SUV onto an off ramp.

He tried to just sit there disinterestedly, but the silence started eating at him again. It was nuts. They were probably taking him to a pre-dug grave out in the desert and he was sitting there worried about her being pissed. He didn't ask to be broken out of prison. Just who the hell did she think she was?

He drummed his fingers loudly on the edge of the window for a few minutes and then began tapping out a similar rhythm on his knees. Finally, "Okay, okay. I'm sorry. I'm sorry if I made you guys look stupid."

She glared at him in the rearview mirror again, but this time it seemed a little forced. Even the psycho next to him seemed to relax a bit.

Another few miles and they were gliding through an area with a distinct industrial feel. Not old and broken-down or anything, but packed with boxy buildings that always housed things like plumbing suppliers and propane companies. Catherine slowed and turned onto a short street that dead-ended in an enormous windowless bunker of a building surrounded by a razor-wire-topped chain-link fence. The gate began to open as they approached and then immediately started to close behind them as they coasted into the empty parking lot.

Brandon was vaguely aware of the handcuff being removed from his wrist, but focused mainly on the building filling the windshield. The sun had hit the horizon, throwing everything into shadow except the razor wire. That glowed like fire. Just like it had in prison.

Catherine jumped out, a little nervously he thought, and pulled open the back door. Brandon swung a foot to the ground but then stopped when Daniel grabbed his sleeve, waiting for the inevitable threat. If he was a betting man—and he was—he'd put his money on "If you run, I'll kill you," though the more simple and to the point "Run and you're dead" was a distinct possibility, too.

"Nice jump at TI. Not too many people get away from me."

★   ★   ★

In light of the heavy metallic clunk the door made when it closed behind them, the interior was a bit of a surprise. Instead of medieval torture devices, the building was full of plants, cubicles, and private offices tucked behind thick birch doors. There was even a fireplace. Clearly no expense had been spared to disguise the fact that it wasn't much less of a prison than his home of the past few years. For whose benefit, though, he wasn't sure. The place was empty. Dead silent.

"I'm taking you to meet my boss," Catherine said. She grabbed him by his collar and pulled him to within six inches of her face. "Are you listening to me?"

He'd actually been examining the desks that were within view, trying to find some shred of information he could use. There wasn't anything, though. Not so much as a sticky note or grocery list.

"I heard you. Something about your boss."

"I'm taking you to meet him!" she said, a little fast to sound natural. "It wasn't the original idea, but it's kind of hard to make plans with you around. I wish we could have gotten you some clothes."

He followed her to what looked like a reception area and rolled his eyes when she started trying to straighten the wrinkles she'd made in the collar of his stolen golf shirt. On the bright side, though, it gave him a chance to really look at her without making her nervous. Her eyes weren't actually the dark brown he'd expected. More of an interesting color of green.

"Now, it wouldn't hurt to show him a little bit of

respect, okay? Say hello, and then try to limit yourself to answering ques—"

"Yes, massa."

"See," she said, finishing with his collar. "That would be an example of the kind of attitude I don't need right now."

He followed her through the door, frowning deeply as a man with a thick head of gray hair stood and came around his desk.

"Hello, Brandon," he said, offering his hand.

The wrinkles creasing his face suggested character and wisdom more than age, and there wasn't even a hint of a paunch to strain the expensive leather belt holding up his slacks. What an incredible disappointment.

Instead of shaking hands, Brandon swung wildly at the man's head.

He missed by nearly a foot, causing him to lose his balance and pitch forward until his momentum was abruptly halted by the older man's fist connecting with his stomach. Brandon sank slowly to his knees, listening to Catherine's unintelligible shouting and trying to hold down all those free peanuts.

The man crouched down, bringing their faces almost level. "As much as I hate to admit it, it's good to see you again. Really."

"Fuck . . . you," Brandon managed to get out. Maybe he *should* throw up. The carpet looked really expensive.

"Wait a minute," Catherine said, the anger gone from her voice now. "You two know each other?"

Richard Scanlon rose to his full height again and leaned back against his desk. "I'm afraid so. Brandon used to work for me."

"I . . . I don't understand."

"Would you like to explain," Scanlon asked. "Or should I?"

Brandon managed to rise unsteadily to his feet and ease himself into a chair, but wasn't ready yet to speak.

Scanlon nodded his understanding and pointed to the remaining empty chair in front of his desk. Catherine sat, glancing over at Brandon with a hint of genuine concern that she couldn't entirely hide.

"By the time I got completely sick of the FBI and quit, I was the assistant director in charge of counterintelligence. But if you remember right, years before that, I'd run the FBI's office in Vegas."

"I remember," Catherine said.

"I still had friends in the area and that's how I ended up being offered a job as the head of security for a corporation that owned a number of casinos here. I resisted for a while, but you probably also remember how bored I was. There's only so much golf you can play."

He walked over to a low table pushed against the wall and made himself a drink. "About a year after I took the position, Brandon here used a false identity and work history to get a job in my office. I have to admit, though—fictitious résumé or not, he had a real ability to get things done. And even better, he'd forgotten more about gambling than many of my 'experts' would ever know. So, as you can imagine, he moved up quickly and eventually began reporting directly to me. In fact, I'd go so far as to say that I thought we'd become pretty close. Hell, if you hadn't been working in D.C. at the time, I imagine I would have introduced you two."

"Looks like you finally figured out a way," Brandon said, at last able to suck in enough air to get a few words out.

"Excuse me. I believe I was telling a story? Anyway, eventually I wanted to move Brandon up—essentially into the position you hold now. But, obviously, I don't have a very trusting nature, and so I hired an old friend to do some checking into his background. It didn't take him long to find out that I had one of the slickest and most accomplished criminals in the world working for me."

Brandon remained focused on Scanlon in what, at this point, was a rather pathetic effort to stare him down.

"Why?" Catherine said, turning toward him. "What were you doing?"

He didn't answer, so Scanlon answered for him. "He was casing the place. Right Brandon?"

"Whatever."

"Obviously, I wanted him gone," Scanlon continued. "But it turned out that beyond firing him for lying on his application, there wasn't much I could do. He'd never actually been convicted of a crime. He was too clever for that. Weren't you?"

Brandon held a hand up and raised his middle finger.

"You can imagine how embarrassing this was for me—the head of security for a multinational corporation getting duped by some thief. And it would've been even worse if he managed to pull off whatever he was planning . . ." Scanlon's voice trailed off.

"Go on," Brandon said. "You're just getting to the good part."

"I'm sure you tell it much better."

Brandon scooted his chair around so he could face Catherine directly. She looked understandably confused.

"So Richard's pissed off because I made him look bad in front of all those fat, rich, white guys he hung around with. Suddenly, he comes up with a brilliant idea to make himself look better and get rid of me. He calls the cops and together they frame me for a local diamond heist."

Catherine's head swiveled toward her boss and he nodded. "We think it was a group of Nigerians, actually. But they were long gone and the police were looking for a collar. It worked out for everyone."

"Not me."

"I suppose not. It was a shame, really. A smart kid like you could have done well working for me. I'd have paid you more money than you needed and you wouldn't have had to spend your life running around the edges of society like a cockroach."

"You can just go ahead and stow that cockroach crap. The way I see it, you framed me for a crime I didn't commit, then broke me out of jail, and unless I miss my guess, now you want me to . . . let's see . . .

steal something? Probably something huge. Shit, I'm not crooked enough to work for you, asshole."

Scanlon walked back to the small bar at the edge of his office and refilled his drink. "You may be right."

Brandon sank down in the chair and fixed his stare on a blank section of wall. He was really screwed now that he knew about Scanlon's involvement in all this. It was something the old man wasn't going to just forget. He had way too much to lose.

"Okay, fine," Brandon said, more to play for time than anything else. "So what's the job?"

"Does that mean you're interested?" Catherine said.

"It means I'm not really in a position to not hear all my options."

"Options?" Scanlon said, stifling a laugh. "What options? I'm offering you a wealthy retirement in South Africa. What would you prefer? Twenty more years throwing prison poker games?"

"I'd prefer to get you."

Scanlon shook his head, a barely perceptible smile on his lips. "I doubt the opportunity will present itself. Let's be realistic here, son. You'd be an escaped convict accusing a former FBI assistant director of breaking him out of jail. What is it you used to say? That doesn't even pass the laugh test."

"So what if I do what you want? What guarantee do I have that you won't just get Catherine here to lure me into her boudoir—"

"Please . . . ," she moaned.

"—and stick a knife in me. Even I think I'd be a

loose end at that point, and I remember how you feel about those."

"One of the reasons I thought of you on this," Scanlon said, "is that you never rolled over on any of your old comrades. I know they were trying to offer you a deal—"

"You're not an old comrade."

"Brandon," Catherine cautioned.

"I probably should have just leveled with you in the first place," Scanlon said, talking more to himself than anyone else. "It would have saved everyone a lot of trouble."

Brandon shrugged and kicked his feet up on Scanlon's desk. "Yeah, whatever. What's the job?"

"Oh, nothing that should cause someone like you any problems. I want you to help me steal twelve tactical nuclear warheads from a Ukrainian organized-crime group."

Brandon let his feet drop and leaned forward in his chair. "What?"

"You heard me."

"I'd think you were kidding, but I don't remember you having a sense of humor."

"I'm completely serious."

Brandon grinned and put his feet back up on the desk. "Somebody's selling you a bill of goods, Richard."

"How do you mean?"

"I'm surprised at you. Why would an organized crime outfit take on the risk of smuggling those things into the U.S.? They'd sell them where they are and let the buyer take on the shipping risk."

"I never said they were in the U.S. They're in Ukraine."

"So call the Ukrainian cops then."

"There's still a lot of corruption there. If we talk to the local police, word of it would be on the street in an hour."

"Then call the army, or the CIA, or whoever it is that does this kind of thing."

Scanlon leaned against his desk again, a defeated expression crossing his face. "My friends in the government are split on whether it's good information or a hoax. They've come down on the side that it's not a hard-enough piece of intelligence to assign the kind of resources necessary to resolve it."

"Bullshit."

"I know it's hard to believe," Catherine interjected. "But these kinds of decisions are made all the time. Thousands of threats come in every year and they can't all be acted on. Plus, the government, in its infinite wisdom, has decided to concentrate our resources on wars and a missile defense system that doesn't work. Loose nukes haven't become a political hot potato yet, so they're not being prioritized."

"But *you* think it's a valid threat."

"I think there's a damn good chance," Scanlon said. "Sure as hell good enough for someone to look into it."

Brandon didn't answer immediately, instead mulling over what he'd heard. "I don't get it. What's this to you? You're not even in the government anymore. What makes you think you're so much smarter than they are? Other than your generally high opinion of yourself, I mean."

"Long story. Have Catherine tell it to you sometime." He pulled a piece of paper off his desk and held it out. Brandon reluctantly took it.

The marginal spelling and grammar couldn't hide the e-mail's hysterical tone. It was clear that the "mercandise" was being bid out to a number of "intrested partys," and would be immediately handed over to the first group who made a reasonable offer that they could back up.

"So are you interested?" Catherine said.

Brandon chewed his lower lip and continued to stare down at the e-mail. He desperately didn't want to be. But the truth was, he loved to steal stuff. And not just for the money. A really difficult heist was the ultimate rush. A horrible, self-destructive addiction that was virtually impossible to break.

But this was a whole other level. He tried to imagine a nuclear bomb going off inside the United States, but honestly couldn't get his mind fully around it. How many would be killed? Thousands? Tens of thousands? More?

"Tell me about the nukes," he said. "Just to satisfy my curiosity, though. Not because I'm agreeing to do anything."

"What do you want to know?"

"Stuff I'd need to steal them."

"Okay. They're hundred-kiloton weapons—"

"What's that mean?"

"Think five times as powerful as the ones we dropped on Japan."

"Now, see, I don't need to know that. That just makes me nervous."

"Sorry. I'd hate for you to feel nervous. How's this? There are twelve of them—all the same. Each is about five feet tall, cone-shaped, and maybe three feet in diameter at the widest point."

"Weight?"

"Four, maybe five hundred pounds."

Brandon frowned. That kind of ruled out shoving them down his pants and making a run for it.

"We believe they're being stored in a cave in the Carpathian Mountains."

"The what?"

Scanlon ignored him. "Maybe a hundred men guarding them, mostly former military. Fairly sophisticated weapons, but probably no sophisticated alarm systems or anything like that."

Brandon blinked a few times. "Let me get this straight. You want me to walk into a Ukrainian military camp in the middle of the—What were they? The Carpathian Mountains? And steal five thousand pounds of nuclear bombs. Is that right?"

"Well—"

"And just how would you suggest I do that? Pretend I'm the UPS guy? No, wait. Maybe I could cut the phone lines and jimmy their window? It's a military base in a cave, for Christ's sake!"

"But everyone says you're a genius," Catherine said.

He let out an exasperated breath. "See, that's a common misconception. I'm a reasonably creative guy who has a screw loose and, instead of getting a real job like everyone else, decided to be a crook."

"But—"

"You know what makes it easy to steal stuff in the U.S.? First, people rely on technology they don't understand as good as me. Second, they're all insured, so they really don't give a shit. And three, because they hire drowsy, overweight, six-dollar-an-hour security guards who are about as effective as my grandma. And my grandma's dead."

"I think you're underestimating yourself," Scanlon said. "You've stolen things that people very much cared about, protected by alarm systems they understood perfectly, and that were guarded by good men."

"Don't blow smoke, Richard. Yeah, I'm good. In fact, I like to think of myself as the best. But this is a military operation, not a criminal one."

Scanlon went back to the bar, this time returning with a second glass, which he handed Brandon. "Hard to imagine, isn't it? What would happen if one of those went off in an American city?"

"It'd kill a gazillion people. I get it, okay?"

"Believe me, that would barely even be the start of it."

"Hey, you can't put all this off on me, man. It's you government psychos that caused this."

Scanlon smiled ironically. "Yeah, the world would be a wonderful place if there were only thieves—"

"Kiss my ass. You know how many people I've hurt? I mean physically hurt? None. And what about all the people I help? Think about what goes into alarms alone: engineers, computer programmers, sales people, manufacturing. Think of how many people work for insurance companies." He pointed at Scanlon. "And what about cops? What would you have done without people like me, Richard? You'd have had to get a real job."

Scanlon sat down and sipped his drink for a few moments. "I'm not going to defend my life to you, Brandon. And I'm not going to ask you to defend yours to me. We're who we are and we've done what we've done. Now what about the nukes?"

Brandon sniffed at the drink in his hand, checking for the odor of poison. Not that he'd really know what it smelled like. He saw a movie once where Jodie Foster said it smelled like almonds.

"I can't steal them, Richard. No one can."

He didn't look particularly surprised. "On to plan B, then."

"Does that involve my body being picked over by coyotes?"

"That's plan C," Catherine said, giving his arm a strangely reassuring squeeze.

Scanlon's laugh lacked even the slightest sinister edge. "So, Brandon. Tell me. What do you know about Ukrainian organized criminals?"

"Complete psychopaths," he replied. "I stay as far away from those eastern bloc wackos as I can."

"A pretty mercenary bunch, then?"

"Slit their own mothers' throats for fifty—" Brandon fell silent for a moment and then took a satisfying swallow of the scotch in his hand. "You'll have to excuse me. Prison's made me a little slow. How much are they asking?"

"No set price yet. But two hundred million ought to take them off the table."

Chapter Fourteen

Richard Scanlon's hand hovered over the phone for a few seconds before he finally picked it up. "Hello, Edwin."

"I'm hearing disturbing things."

Scanlon nodded silently. If there was one positive in all this, it confirmed that Hamdi did indeed have ears inside his organization. Not that he blamed the man. Their relationship was built more on a sturdy foundation of mutual respect than trust per se. Sometimes Scanlon felt as though they were two battle-weary fighters circling each other in the ring.

"What things?"

"That Brandon Vale is aware of your involvement in his escape. Do you deny that?"

"No."

The only response from Hamdi was a slightly elevated rate of breathing.

"In fact, he and Catherine are in my break room right now."

"And you were going to tell me this when?" His voice had transformed now, increasing in pitch and volume to the point that it sounded . . . dangerous.

"I wanted to talk to him first. To see where he stood."

"And just where is that, Richard? Where does this little thief stand?"

"Honestly, I think it's better this way, Edwin. He isn't a good puppet. We'd have to deal with him constantly trying to cut the strings. We've already seen the prob—"

"Don't rationalize, Richard! It doesn't become you. This was a serious error. Catherine was an unknown to him. Now he knows about you and that means everyone—*everything*—is jeopardized."

"I disagree. The more information he has, the better he can help us—if he decides to. And this has no effect at all on your level of risk. As you're well aware, no one but me knows anything about your involvement."

"That's not entirely true, is it? I've been a strong supporter of your company in Washington. If you go down, I could be dragged down with you."

"I don't see—"

"We need to get rid of him, Richard. And we need to do it now."

Hamdi was an extraordinarily intelligent and practical man, but one prone to occasional bursts of slightly self-conscious emotionalism. A cultural propensity toward martyrdom, Scanlon had once thought, and then admonished himself for it.

"That would certainly be clean, but it would leave us back at square one, wouldn't it? We can't afford that, Edwin. You know we can't. The Ukrainians are no more than a few weeks from selling the first of those warheads and we don't have a backup plan."

Again the only answer was the hiss of breathing.

"Is there any chance Congress will loosen up and release the funds for my new contract?"

"How many times do we have to go through this?" Hamdi snapped. "They're completely frozen until the commission report on the Mall of America attack comes out. And that won't be for at least two months."

"Kind of ironic, isn't it?" Scanlon said, trying to move off the subject and inject a bit of calm into the conversation. "That a study on a terrorist act could potentially facilitate the most devastating terrorist attack in history? Maybe the most devastating attack of any kind in history. It seems like an easy decision to me, Edwin. We go with Brandon. Not because it's a good option, because it's the only option."

Of course, Hamdi knew all this. His protests were motivated half by frustration and half to soften Scanlon up for the inevitable second part of this conversation.

"I think we both understand now that this isn't a long-term accommodation, Richard. We get what we can out of him and then we get rid of him. There's too much at stake here to risk—"

"I think you're being a little narrow-minded. Give him a chance to prove himself."

"I did. He escaped and tracked you down over the course of forty-eight hours. What if he escapes again tomorrow? You think he won't use what he knows to make a deal? He doesn't owe you anything, Richard. Quite the opposite. Are you willing to risk the lives of millions of people on Brandon Vale's reliability?"

Of course, what Hamdi was really talking about was his own life. More specifically, the possibility that the eminently unpredictable Brandon Vale might find a way to exercise power over it.

Scanlon pulled out a low drawer in his desk and propped his feet on it. "Brandon may not have a degree from Harvard, but there's no denying he's brilliant at what he does. And as for reliability—how many of your fair-haired government people would have kept their mouths shut and gone off to jail like Brandon did? Ivy Leaguers tend not to deal well with maximum-security prisons. They're also a little squeamish about breaking the law. They have lines they don't easily cross. Brandon has those lines, too, I suppose, but they're a little hazier."

"Do you have a point?"

"Yeah, actually, I do. Unorthodox problems sometimes require unorthodox solutions. Hell, even if we didn't need something stolen, Brandon makes my short list of potential employees."

"In for a penny, in for a pound. Is that it, Richard?"

"I was thinking more that the pot shouldn't call the kettle black."

"Look," Hamdi started, enunciating carefully, "I know you were undecided on what to do with Vale when we were finished with him, and at the time I understood that. But I think it's a clear decision now. We have to be realistic. Whether he can help us or not, when we're finished with him, he has to go away. Agreed?"

"Let's say I'll keep an open mind on the subject."

"Fine," Hamdi said, though his tone suggested it wasn't. A moment later the line went dead.

Scanlon replaced the phone's handset and took in a deep breath, holding it for a moment, and then letting it out slowly. One thing he had to say about Brandon Vale. He sure as hell was a lot of trouble.

Chapter Fifteen

Brandon dug a pizza box out of the refrigerator and tossed it like a Frisbee onto the table.

"What are you doing?" Catherine said.

"Dinner. What do you think I'm doing?"

"Put the pizza back."

"What are you talking about? It's pepperoni and sausage." He fished a six-pack of Coke from the back with one hand while lifting the foil on a piece of pie with the other. Apple. Wouldn't you know it? He was allergic to apples.

Catherine picked up the box and pointed to the name JIM scrawled across it in Magic Marker. "It doesn't belong to you."

He frowned and stared at her for a moment, watching the comprehension slowly flush into her face.

Satisfied that she was once again clear about his shaky moral underpinnings, he checked the freezer. They were Ben and Jerry's people. Nice.

"Finding everything all right?" Scanlon's voice.

"No beer. Maybe we should hit Picasso for some foie gras?"

"This is more intimate, don't you think?"

"I think you're still a cheap bastard." He pointed at Catherine with a finger covered in Cherry Garcia. "You know he used to make us put those little erasers on our pencils if we ran out of eraser before we ran out of lead."

She nearly started laughing before she caught herself. "He still does."

Brandon grimaced and sat at the table, popping the top on one of the Cokes and holding the open pizza box toward Catherine. "Give it a try. You know how they say that you appreciate stuff you earn more? Not true. Stolen stuff is always just a little bit better."

She hesitated for a moment and then took a slice, biting off an end and chewing energetically. "It *is* pretty good," she said through a full mouth.

"Christ," Scanlon said. "Just what I need. Two of you."

Brandon started in on the ice cream again. "So, did you ever figure it out, Richard?"

"Figure what out?" Catherine asked, reaching for a stolen Coke.

"What Brandon was up to when he was working for me. At the time, I couldn't put my finger on exactly what he was after, so we had to cover every base. You wouldn't believe the amount of money and man-hours we spent changing security procedures, locks, passwords, computer systems—all in case some of the people he worked with were still around."

"How much?" Brandon asked.

"Millions."

"Nice. I hope you looked like a compete fuckup."

"Oh, believe me, I did. Honestly, it's the reason I left and started this company. My credibility was never coming back."

They fell silent again and Catherine drummed impatiently on the table. "Okay, enough of this. Tell me. How were you going to rip off the casinos?"

"If I told you, I'd have to kill you," Brandon said, smiling broadly. "Besides, it'd be more interesting to see how Richard did."

Scanlon sat at the table but seemed reluctant to eat. "You weren't interested in the casinos at all."

"What do you mean?" Catherine said, motioning for Brandon to share the carton of ice cream in his hand.

"Have you ever considered where Las Vegas's cash goes?"

"Not really."

"Of course not. Why would you? But think about it now. The cash comes flooding in here every day. The casinos and local businesses take it in—literally tons of it. If they didn't get rid of it, it would just pile up in the streets."

Brandon quietly clapped his hands, genuinely impressed.

"Okay," Catherine said. "Sure."

"So how do you figure they do that?" Brandon interjected. "Get rid of it, I mean."

"I don't know. A transport plane? Maybe a motorcade of armored cars?"

Brandon grinned. "I used to go to this bar. There was a big bathroom on the first floor. You know, urinals, stalls. Whole thing was covered in graffiti. Upstairs, there was another bathroom. It was small and just looked like something that would be in your parents' house. After ten years, not a single word of graffiti."

She thought about that for a moment and then just shrugged.

"Don't you get it? Very few people in the world truly have the ability to think outside the box. You write graffiti in a public bathroom, but not in your mom's. The whole transport system is based on the theory that no one ever thinks outside that box."

"Except you," Scanlon interjected.

"Yeah. I wrote 'Fuck' really big on the wall of that bathroom right over a vase of fake flowers. Two weeks later, it was covered. Like you always said, Richard, it's all about leadership."

Catherine rolled her eyes and got up to look for a spoon.

"Years ago, when I worked for the FBI here," Scanlon started, "I helped set up a simple transfer based on the hide-in-plain-sight principle. If we'd created something more obvious and elaborate—the armored motorcade you mentioned—it would have attracted the wrong element." He thumbed toward Brandon. "And a plane doesn't solve your problem—you've still got to drive to it, load it, and then do the same thing on the other end."

"Exactly," Brandon said. "It's kind of an elegant setup, if you think about it. They keep it quiet and ninety-nine percent of the people in the world never give the flow of cash out of Vegas a moment's thought. The other one percent either aren't criminals or just assume there's some massively secure setup involving the army or something."

"So how *does* it get moved?"

Scanlon nodded toward Brandon. "Now let's see how *you* did."

"By regular old vans and sometimes semis, taking random routes to the Federal Reserve Bank in San Francisco, right?"

It was Scanlon's turn to clap.

"So the question I was trying to answer working for Richard was what the schedule was—I wanted to hit the semi, not the individual vans, obviously. And I needed to know the level of protection—air cover, number of guards, type of guards. That kind of stuff."

"Did you ever get that information?" Catherine asked.

"Not much of it. You can imagine that it's kind of hard to draw anyone into that conversation without being obvious. But I was piecing it together and meeting the people who could get me there." He turned toward Scanlon. "One thing I never figured out and it kind of haunts me: How much is in that semi?"

Scanlon didn't answer, a hint of uncertainty suddenly appearing in his eyes.

"Come on, Richard. It's a little late to get squeamish now."

"Yeah, I guess it is. Somewhere between a hundred and seventy-five and two hundred million."

Brandon let out a low whistle. "Oh, man. That's beautiful. Is your information still good?"

He nodded. "When I finally figured out what you

were after, I went to the security firm that oversees the transport and told them. They juggled a bunch of the procedures in case you'd figured any of them out."

"And were you one of the jugglers?"

"A paid consultant. I know everything."

"Irony," Brandon said, slowly shaking his head. "I love that."

"We've been through this four times already."

Scanlon was pacing back and forth across the room, his back aching from hours of sitting. He was tired enough to make it nearly impossible to think coherently, while Brandon seemed to be sucking energy directly from the air. The sad truth was that he was getting too old for all this. It was coming time for Brandon's generation to take responsibility for the world.

"Yeah, but I'm not completely clear on the—"

"You've got plenty to think about," Scanlon said. "We can deal with the minutiae tomorrow."

Catherine was sitting on the floor, dozing amid a collection of empty paper plates and wadded-up tinfoil.

"You just need a little caffeine," Brandon said, shaking the soda cans on the table, searching for one that hadn't been drained.

"What I need is to go home."

Catherine woke suddenly, tossing the hair out of her face. "Home?" she said groggily.

Brandon found something left in one of the cans, but instead of offering it to Scanlon, he drained it, stood, and wandered out of the room. He was deep enough in thought that he rammed the doorjamb with his shoulder and didn't seem to notice.

"I'm sorry I fell asleep," Catherine said, struggling to her feet. "But when he started into exactly how trailers are hooked to semis for the tenth time, it was like someone hit me over the head with a brick."

"It seems like overkill," Scanlon agreed. "But there's no point in second-guessing him on this kind of thing."

"You look horrible," she said, walking up and smoothing the shirt on his shoulders. "Are you sleeping?"

"Are you?"

She ignored the question and put a hand on his forehead. "You're not getting sick are you?"

"I'm fine," he said, gently taking her hand and putting a small piece of paper in it.

"What's this?"

He leaned in close to her ear. "An e-mail address and passwords. Memorize them and destroy the paper."

"What—"

"If you should ever run into serious problems and can't contact me, you'll need to get into that account."

He looked into her worried face and immediately felt a pang of guilt for being the cause of it. What choice did he have, though? There was no telling what Hamdi had planned for Brandon, and he didn't want to see her get caught between those two.

"It's okay," he said. "I can't imagine you'll ever need it. But you hope for the best and plan for the worst, right?"

Chapter Sixteen

Despite its being quite simple, Jamal Yusef read the e-mail a third time, closed it, and decrypted it again. The result was always the same.

Finally, knowing that the computer was draining the ancient car batteries providing power, he shut it down. The blood was pounding loudly in his ears, and when he tried to stand, his legs seemed incapable of supporting him.

Edwin Hamdi had been so smooth and logical during their courtship. He'd made perfect sense, gracefully countering every argument Yusef had put to him with talk of patriotism and the greater good. But none of this was theoretical anymore. Hamdi hadn't watched those people at the theater die. He hadn't seen them bleed, smelled them burning. With hands so slippery with blood, it was becoming increasingly difficult to hold on to that logic.

Yusef hesitated before opening the tent flap. He'd been barricaded inside since his return from Jerusalem—something that had likely not gone unnoticed by his men. What had they read into his self-imposed isolation?

When he finally stepped out into the blinding sun

his legs had steadied, but his hands still shook. They always did now.

Ramez was drilling the men, trying to get them into military formation and to march them in a straight line. Why, Yusef wasn't sure. Perhaps it appealed to the younger man's overdeveloped sense of order, though it generated nothing but frustration for everyone else involved. There was something about Arab culture that didn't mesh with military discipline. These were people ruled by passion.

Yusef grabbed a rifle leaning against a rock and fired it in the air, feeling a sickly burst of adrenaline as the recoil wrenched his arm. The men ducked involuntarily and then turned, looking both confused by his uncharacteristic outburst and relieved to be done with Ramez's endless drill.

It occurred to Yusef that he could kill them all right now. They were unarmed, lined up only twenty feet away. His clip was still nearly full. Eleven fanatical terrorists—men who would devote their lives to creating death and chaos—gone in a matter of seconds. And when he then put the gun to his own head, twelve.

But what good would it do? There were hundreds of other cells just like this one. And when the male relatives of these men got news of their martyrdom, they would join the cause. The mythical Hydra was alive and well in the Middle East.

"We have our money!" Yusef shouted.

He was immediately drowned out by the shouts of his men as they rushed forward, hugging him, kissing his cheeks, clasping his hands. After a few seconds, he managed to pull away, stepping back to examine the unbridled joy and religious ecstasy in their eyes. All except Muhammad. There was something else in those eyes. Jealousy. The thirst for power. And, of course, hate. But for whom exactly?

"God willing, we will soon have nuclear weapons and the enemies of Islam will tremble. America will fall to its knees and beg us for mercy! God be praised!"

Another cheer erupted, but he raised his hand, silencing it. "Secrecy is the most critical thing now. The Americans and the Jews have ears everywhere. We must maintain complete silence until our plan has been carried out."

The men all nodded eagerly, though Yusef knew it was more from excitement than agreement. Silence, like military formations, took discipline that terrorists, almost by definition, lacked. In fact, he was counting on that particular failing to cause the news to leak to compatriots, families, and sympathizers across the globe. It wouldn't be specific enough to cause them any serious problems—just another shout in the never-ending chorus of hate monitored by the CIA and Mossad. As usual, the source wouldn't be investigated until the attack had already occurred. And that investigation would lead right where it was supposed to—to an isolated band of Islamic fanatics.

"Our prayers have been answered," he said, turning his back on his men and starting toward his tent again.

Contacting the Ukrainians was never quick or simple. If he was going to stay on Hamdi's schedule, he'd have to start the process now.

Chapter Seventeen

There was only one potential escape route that Brandon could see: back through the stone and steel lobby, past the unusually vigilant guard, beneath five surveillance cameras, and through the thick glass doors that led to the street where Daniel was parked. Less than ideal.

Catherine moved aside and he stepped into the empty elevator, turning to watch her slip through the closing doors and press the button for the fifteenth floor. The camera above them looked on silently.

"Nice building. Lived here long?"

She didn't answer, instead stepping aside again as the doors glided open.

"Ladies first," he said.

Clearly she wasn't anxious to give him even the slightest opportunity to get away again. "No. After you."

The hall was sparsely decorated and overly wide— a configuration obviously intended to send a message that the people there were wealthy enough to waste expensive square footage with reckless abandon. No doubt the paperboy was suitably impressed.

"This is us," Catherine said, missing the lock with

her key a few times because she was unwilling to take her slightly bloodshot eyes completely off him. He reached out and steadied her hand, sliding the key in and pushing through the door.

There was a keypad on the wall—set too high for her to obscure with her body and she stood there impatiently until he took the hint and wandered deeper into the expansive condo. It was kind of a replay of the lobby, but with the addition of a few carefully placed pieces of leather furniture and a wall tapestry or two. Basically, a professionally decorated stopover for someone who liked to lose a few bucks in Vegas a couple of times a year.

He walked by an industrial kitchen that no one seemed to have ever cooked in and passed through a set of sliding glass doors onto a generous balcony. Despite the hour, it was still over ninety degrees, and he immediately started to sweat as he leaned over the railing and looked around.

There were balconies above, below, and on both sides, but none were close enough to get to without specialized equipment. He could go with the time-tested method of tying sheets together, but that tended to work better when the motivation was a late night rendezvous with your high school sweetheart and the worst-case scenario was falling ten feet onto your lawn. If he was going, he wasn't going via the balcony route.

But what if it had been possible? What if he just happened to have two hundred feet of rope in his pocket? Richard Scanlon was many things, but he wasn't a crook. Not in the classic sense, anyway. To take this kind of risk, he must be pretty certain of his information.

"Long way down," he said as Catherine stepped out onto the balcony.

"All doors and windows are alarmed and there are motion detectors in the living areas. The halls and elevator all have cameras," she said.

"So, I'm back in prison, huh."

"Don't say that. Look, I'm sorry about what we've done to you, but what choice did we have?"

He shrugged.

"You don't get off that easy. It wasn't a rhetorical question. I want to know. What choice do you think we had? Twelve nuclear weapons, Brandon. *Twelve.*"

"Fine. I understand why you did what you did. If you're asking for absolution, though, you're not going to get it. You don't get off that easy, either."

"This is where we're going to be staying for a while," she said, changing the subject. "There are two bedrooms. I gave you the master. You'll find—"

"So you evaded my question yesterday."

"What question?"

"Why did you become a criminal?"

She squinted at him, obviously trying to get across that it wasn't exactly the time for a philosophical conversation, but in his mind it was the perfect time. Talking tired was a little like talking drunk as far as the tendency for little bits of truth to slip out unbidden. And even more importantly, now he had a baseline he could use to interpret her. She'd been tough to figure out when he thought she was just an extremely gifted crook. But now it was clear. All that seething sincerity and discomfort were genuine.

"The opposite of you, I guess. My father, not my mother. He worked for Richard at the FBI before he died. I was only ten at the time. Richard lived right down the street and he did a lot for me and my mom. I suppose it sounds a little clichéd but he really was—is—like a father to me. He helped me get into college and, after that, helped me get a job at the NSA."

"So that's the reason you're a spy? To follow in your dad's footsteps?"

"I'm not a spy, I was an analyst at the NSA. This is my first field work."

"Really? I would have never known."

"Don't make fun, please."

Brandon couldn't help smiling. "Let me guess. Scanlon figured that some former Green Beret following me around would put me off, and you were the only smart, beautiful woman he had access to."

She seemed a little embarrassed by his statement, but he wasn't sure if it was the backhanded compliment or the realization that "temptress" was at least a part of her job description. Probably best to move on a bit.

"So then Scanlon starts his own company and hires you away from the NSA . . ."

She nodded. "A few years ago."

"To do what? What exactly is American Security Holdings?"

She didn't answer.

"Come on. Richard said that you'd tell me the story."

Not finding the answers she was looking for in the carpet of lights below, she finally just shrugged. "Part of the reason we got bogged down in Iraq was because the intelligence community was too politicized. It really wasn't their fault—it was just the way the system worked. If you wanted to do well and move up, you spun the facts to agree with what the president wanted to hear. Hardly anyone ever got fired for getting it wrong—only for telling him hard truths that didn't mesh with his worldview. With all the problems this caused and all the publicity it got, everyone expected things to get fixed, but honestly it got worse."

"Huge egos create their own truth," Brandon said.

"Tell me about it. Anyway, the Senate Intelligence Committee had a rare good idea. They approved a prototype program that would create a different kind of defense contractor—one that dealt solely in intelligence. ASHI was the first, and it did so well that there are now something like ten other companies doing similar work."

"What am I paying taxes for if you're doing the CIA's job?"

"You've never paid taxes," she reminded him.

"I was speaking figuratively."

"We don't do their job for them, we duplicate it. For instance, if we'd existed before the Iraq war, we'd have been sent all the raw data pointing to Iraq's WMD program, and we'd have done our own analysis and then distributed it to all the agencies that could use it. It's essentially a check and balance. We're not part of the political system." She pointed to the city below them. "We're not even in Washington. And we can't be fired for saying inconvenient things."

"But if you were being a pain in the ass, wouldn't the government just cut off your funding?"

"At the end of our contract, and the contracts of our competitors, our reports are examined by a nonpartisan group and the decision of whether or not to renew is based on an objective measure of the accuracy of our analysis. Well, as objective as anything can be that has to do with the government."

Brandon leaned against the railing, thinking about what she'd said. "So the CIA looked at these Ukrainians and decided it was a hoax or whatever. You guys said it was a real threat. The politicians sided with the CIA, so you decided to go it on your own."

"Basically. It was never our goal to run an illegal operation, and most of the organization doesn't know anything about it. But we felt like we couldn't just turn our backs on this."

"And now I can't either."

She seemed to be concentrating on not looking at him.

"He really likes you, Brandon. I can tell. I think he even admires you in a way. You might not believe me, but I'll bet Richard was genuinely hurt when he found out you were there just to use him. To betray him. Did you ever wonder if what happened to you wasn't as much that as his not wanting you to succeed in what you were planning?"

Brandon felt his stomach tighten. He was about to grab her by the arm and force her to look at him, to listen to him tell her about what it was like to be framed and watch your youth drain away in a prison cell. About the fact that if he was caught now, his life would be completely over. About how he didn't give a shit about Richard Scanlon's feelings. What about *his* feelings?

But he didn't.

"You're playing a pretty dangerous game here, Catherine."

"Don't you think we know that?"

"I wonder. I get the impression you think this is going to be a lot easier than it is."

"Even if we were to figure out a way to get our hands on Vegas's money—a very big if—the FBI and the cops are going to go nuts. There are only about eight guys and one woman in the world who would even think about attempting something like this. With my history, I'm going to be the odds-on favorite. No big deal for me at this point. I'm a convicted felon who beat up a guard and escaped from prison."

"Brandon, we—"

"Let me finish. This *is* a big deal for you. There are a lot of little circumstantial lines that can be drawn to Scanlon on this thing, and there aren't a lot of degrees of separation between you two. I imagine his plan is to hand the nukes over to the CIA and say, 'Yeah, I stole a little money, but if you guys had been doing your job I wouldn't have had to.' But you can't imagine how many things can go wrong between now and then. Are you sure this is your fight? Would your dad really want you involved in this?"

"Would yours?"

Brandon couldn't help laughing. "Yeah, I guess he would. Let me tell you how disappointed he is to have me for a son. Drives him nuts. He tried so hard to raise an upstanding citizen, but I guess I just couldn't fight my mom's genes."

Catherine didn't speak for a long time. Finally she turned toward him.

"There's a woman?"

"Huh?"

"You said there were eight men and one woman who would try something like this."

Brandon grinned. "Yeah. There's a woman."

"Do you know her?" Catherine sounded a little overly disinterested and Brandon's smile broadened. It was weird to be around a woman who just didn't have much lying in her.

"Yeah, I know her."

"What's she like?"

"Nothing like you."

Catherine's face fell a bit.

"Believe me, I mean that as a compliment. She's in her early fifties and looks like the evil warden from one of those low-budget women's prison movies. And she'll steal from anyone. Seriously, she'd hijack a food shipment to an orphanage if the money was good enough. Complete bitch."

That seemed to cheer her up a bit, but he didn't

allow himself to consciously speculate as to why. Too dangerous.

Suddenly she pushed herself off the railing and turned toward the door. "I'm going to bed. I assume you could figure out a way to beat our security if you really tried. Are you going to be here when I get up?"

He thought about it for a moment. "I'm not really sure."

Brandon adjusted himself into a slightly more comfortable position on the bed and tossed an expensive-looking vase in the air, making a precarious one-hand catch to keep it from shattering on the wood floor. He was dead tired, but knew there was no way he would be able to sleep. There was just too much swirling around in his head right now—most of it completely pointless.

Despite his best efforts, what Catherine said about Richard had managed to get some traction in his mind. There was no denying that they'd formed a pretty strong relationship during the time they'd worked together. Scanlon had never married and didn't have children, creating a deep-seated loneliness that Brandon had exploited every way he could. Not that he really did that sort of thing on purpose. It was more of a reflex. A highly evolved survival instinct.

But did that really absolve him? The truth was that Richard had been nothing but great to him until he found out he was being set up. Brandon had convinced himself over the past few years that it was just business, that it hadn't been Scanlon's money or even his company that would have gotten hit.

But he had stolen from Richard. Not some insured bauble, either. He'd stolen his credibility and the respect he'd earned from a life devoted to nothing but career. What did Richard have that was more important or irreplaceable?

Brandon had spent a lot of time sitting in his cell imagining elaborate ends to Richard Scanlon: Shark attacks. Quicksand. Falling safes. But that was all just bullshit. Neither of them had played by the rules and in situations like that, the better man tended to win. It was just that, until then, Brandon had always been the better man.

And then there was Catherine. Smart, beautiful, not a sociopathic kleptomaniac, and not sitting on the other side of a wall of shatterproof glass. What was she about? Maybe . . .

He shook his head violently, clearing her from his mind. Safer not to go there.

Finally, there was the job itself. While perhaps the facts of his life suggested to most people that he was kind of a scumbag, he wasn't so bad that he could just shrug off the thought of a million people disintegrating into a mushroom cloud. What if he managed to make a successful run for it and set up house in Central America? Would he one day walk out of his little grass bungalow to find out that Chicago was gone? That everyone—every single living thing—was dead? What would it be like to live the rest of his life wondering if he could have stopped it?

The most pathetic thing in all this, though—even worse than allowing himself to fall for the carefully proffered illusion of Catherine—was that he wanted to steal that money. He didn't even care if he got to keep any of it. He just wanted to pull it off. Oh, and then disappear into thin air before Scanlon could put a bullet in him. How sweet would that be?

Chapter Eighteen

"Cocktail?" Brandon said, reaching into the backseat and pulling a beer from the cooler.

"Shouldn't you be concentrating?"

He pulled the tab on the can, holding it to his ear to hear the hiss of carbonation. "I *am* concentrating. Pork rind?"

She crinkled her face in disgust.

"You're one of those health nuts, aren't you? I knew it."

"I am not a hea—," she started and then caught herself. "Seriously . . . Shouldn't we be looking for something?"

"Probably."

Catherine sighed quietly and squinted through the windshield at the strip of asphalt bisecting the empty Nevada desert. The speedometer read seventy but it felt to her like they weren't moving at all. The road was dead straight until it finally disappeared into a horizon of broken rock, dead plants, and burned-out mountains. According to the digital readout in the rearview mirror, the outside temperature was a pleasant hundred and two degrees.

"Slow down!"

Catherine jammed a foot on the brake and Brandon steadied himself with one hand while using the other to retrieve a digital camera from the glove box. He rolled down the window and snapped a shot of the Highway 95 sign.

"What was that?" Catherine said, accelerating hard enough to slam him back into his seat. "Was it important?"

"Souvenir," he answered, examining the photo in the screen on the back of the camera.

"I wouldn't think a guy in your line of work would be the photo album type," she said, staring into the side mirror. Nothing but empty road and heat distortion. For some reason, though, that just made her more nervous. Instead of accepting the obvious—that no one was out there—it made her paranoid that the people tracking them were more sophisticated than that. High-altitude surveillance planes? Satellites? Maybe they had access to those new—

"Can I give you some advice, Cath?"

"Huh?"

"Advice. Can I give you some?"

"Yeah. I guess."

"You really need to try to relax a little. This is going to be kind of a long process and if you wind yourself this tight now you're gonna explode before we even do anything illegal."

"I'm chauffeuring a fugitive around with open alcohol containers in the car," she reminded him.

It was amazing how trivial that sounded now. Obviously, the slope was a lot slipperier than she'd planned on. A month ago, she'd been the type of person who went back into a store to return excess change.

Brandon shook his head. "No, you're not. You picked up a hitchhiker you thought was going to die of thirst in the desert. And all you had to drink in the car was this cooler full of beer that you were taking to a picnic for your coworkers at the Ronald McDonald House."

He might be a psychopath but he was right. At this rate, could a stroke be far off? She sucked in a deep breath and let it out slowly, leaning her seat back a few clicks.

"Feeling better?"

"Not really, no. So? What do you think?"

"About what?"

When she turned to glare at him, he countered with a smile so relaxed and penetrating that it would have acted as a sedative on anyone unprepared.

"You know damn well what I'm asking."

She hadn't slept much the night before, instead rereading the information she had on Brandon and thinking about what he'd told her about his mother— assuming any of it was true. Maybe you really couldn't fight genetics. If someone programmed a computer to predict the personality and profession of a person born of Brandon's preternaturally charismatic mother and analytical father, it wasn't that far-fetched to think it would churn out a description of the man sitting next to her.

She'd read an article once on the evolution of

psychopaths—how any population of people could be expected to have leeches attached to the society they created. Remorseless people completely devoid of morality, who produced nothing and lived entirely by using others. It was hard to reconcile that description with her feelings about Brandon, though. Not surprising, she supposed. According to the article, most psychopaths had evolved to be incredibly charming and attractive. For obvious reasons, the ugly, obnoxious ones hadn't been all that successful.

"The heist," she said, realizing that she was being tested. He wanted to see if she could say it out loud. "Tell me about our chances of stealing this money."

"You want the truth?"

Her smirk at hearing the word "truth" come out of his mouth wasn't as heartfelt as it should have been. She found herself having to constantly remind herself that everything he said was probably a lie. Or was it? Christ . . .

"Yeah. I want your honest opinion."

"Okay. Even with Richard whispering his secrets in my ear, this is going to be dead hard. Impossible might be a better word."

"What do you mean 'impossible'?" she said a little too loudly for the confines of the car. "I thought—"

"You were relaxing, remember? Look, they're all impossible when you first start thinking about them. But there's always something. Some security flaw. Some angle they didn't think of. Unfortunately, as much of an unimaginative asshole as he is, Richard doesn't miss a lot."

"So you think you—we—will be able to do it?"

"If I had a gun to my head and a year to plan, maybe. Probably. But all I've got is the gun to my head."

"You talk in circles a lot, don't you?"

"Undiagnosed attention deficit disorder. The truth is, if I'd known then what I know now, I'd have walked away from this deal. Too many unknowns and uncontrollables. Even at two hundred million, the risk-return sucks."

"But the return isn't just money anymore, Brandon. It's millions of lives."

"Yeah."

She went back to staring out the windshield and he went back to sipping his beer until they began closing in on a slightly wider than normal area in the gravel shoulder.

"Stop up there, Cath."

"Why?"

He jumped from the car before it had completely stopped and walked along the shoulder, rolling his cold beer against his forehead. Catherine set the brake and ran after him.

"Is this it?"

"Is this what?"

"*It!* Where it's going to happen?"

He stopped and faced her, examining the white cotton sundress she'd chosen that morning mostly because she figured it made her look less likely to commit a major felony than the rest of her wardrobe. The moment the scrutiny began to make her feel uncomfortable, he started walking again.

"Nah, this isn't it. It's just nice out here. Prison's funny. Everything's so closed in. So crowded. At first you hate it, then you get used to it, then you get to kind of rely on it. This—," he motioned to the silent emptiness around them, "it's like the ocean."

He tossed his empty can on the ground and sat on a low boulder.

"But it seems good," Catherine said. "We've only passed five cars in the last hour—I counted. I'll bet there isn't anyone within thirty miles of us right now."

"It's probably less perfect than you think," Brandon said.

"What, you'd rather be in Manhattan? We could hijack the truck right here and no one would even know."

"Stealing money is easy, Cath. Keeping it long enough to spend it is hard."

"But we know everything! Richard's given you this thing on a silver platter."

He sighed quietly. "There are a thousand details. And if you miss just one of them, you're done. I mean, if every piece of information we have is dead-on and I can actually figure out a workable plan, our chances of getting busted are still about seventy percent." He motioned around them again. "Enjoy the open space while you can."

"You can stop trying to scare me. I've made my decision."

He nodded thoughtfully and began appraising her with even more intensity than before. This time he either didn't notice her growing discomfort or he chose to ignore it.

"Are you *sure* you want to be involved in this, Catherine? I mean, I have no real choice, and as much as I hate to admit it, I got into this line of work because I love it. What about you, though? You're a million miles from where you started."

"I don't have any more choice than you."

"Sure you do. These Ukrainians aren't really your responsibility. Besides, what if you do manage to stop them? What's to keep the next group of Eastern Eurotrash freaks from doing the same thing? Are you potentially giving up your whole life to just postpone the inevitable?"

Of course, she'd asked herself the same questions a hundred times. Almost verbatim, in fact. And she always came up with the same answer. "What if everyone took that attitude, Brandon? Then where would we be?"

He poked at his empty beer can with his foot. "Funny how things can escalate, isn't it? One day you're sitting in some office at the NSA programming a computer to pick out Arab-sounding names, and the next, you're hijacking trucks full of cash."

"Yeah. Funny."

A low hum began to encroach on the silence, and they both turned toward the sound. The glimmer of a chrome grill became visible, followed quickly by the unmistakable outline of a semi moving toward them through the haze. They watched it close on them, listening to the shifting of gears as it began to slow. A moment later, the passenger-side window slid down.

"You kids okay?"

"Fine," Brandon said. "Just enjoying the view, you know?"

"Whatever you say," the driver responded, obviously not sure why anyone would want to be outside the safety of their air-conditioned car in the middle of the Nevada desert. "You wouldn't want to break down out here."

"Can't argue with you there," Brandon said while Catherine held her breath and pretended to look out at the landscape, positioning herself so the driver couldn't see her face. She tried to will him to drive on, but then Brandon spoke again. He sounded like he didn't have a care in the world.

"You travel this road a lot?"

"All the time."

"Doesn't get much traffic, huh?"

There was a grinding of gears and the truck finally started moving away. "Like being on the moon, son."

Catherine realized she was still holding her breath and let it out in a noisy rush. When she turned back toward Brandon, he was sitting cross-legged on the boulder watching the semi through unfocused eyes.

What was he thinking about? How to steal the money? How to escape?

When he had been working his way into Scanlon's good graces, had it been a calculated effort? Or had Brandon genuinely liked the man and separated that from what he was really there for? Scanlon, even after being substantially harmed by Brandon, was the first to admit he wasn't evil—that he'd never really injured anyone in a material way. Who the hell was Brandon Vale?

"Can I ask you a question?"

For a moment she wasn't sure if he'd heard her, but then he seemed to come out of his trance. "Go ahead."

"How much of you is real and how much is a lie?"

It had come out sounding more like an accusation than a question, but he didn't look angry or insulted.

"If I knew that, I wouldn't be as convincing, would I?"

Chapter Nineteen

"What the hell's going on?"

Paul Lowe, the director of the CIA, and Edwin Hamdi both rose from their seats when President Morris walked in and slammed the door behind him. Lowe, a little more slowly—a mannerism designed to make clear his long personal friendship with the president.

Morris, though, was a much more complex man than his old friend gave him credit for. He tended to encourage what Hamdi saw as Lowe's arrogant flights of fancy, but was generally good at separating them from fact. The president's preference on most difficult issues was to listen to diametrically opposed sides and then make his own decision based on the effectiveness of the respective arguments. It was a reasonable approach, Hamdi supposed, but one that gave Lowe a dangerous amount of power. The man's knowledge of the history and politics of the region was admittedly encyclopedic, but because he viewed those facts through a filter of American, Israeli, and Christian patriotism, many of his conclusions were utterly wrong.

"Can't we get two goddamn months of peace and

quiet?" Morris said. "Is that too much to ask? What happened, Paul?"

"We have a video, if you want to see it."

"Turn it on."

"It was taken by one of the attendees," Lowe said, standing and aiming a remote. The screen came to life, showing the steps of a New York City synagogue crowded with well-dressed people clapping as a bride and groom descended.

He paused the video and pointed to the corner of the screen where a yellow cab was coming up the moderately congested street. "One-way, two-lane road. The cab is on the right side, away from the wedding."

He began clicking forward frame by frame, keeping his finger trained on the cab as it swerved into the left lane, taking advantage of a small gap that had formed between two vehicles. A few frames later, it had hopped up on the sidewalk and was plowing through the crowd, bouncing wildly up the steps until a stone pillar finally stopped it.

Hamdi concentrated for a moment on the frozen image of a young man pinned between the cab and the pillar, then scanned the rest of the screen, examining the broken and bleeding bodies strewn out on the ground. The bride herself had disappeared—the only evidence of her existence being a wisp of white train wrapped around a tire. Hamdi winced in a facsimile of horror and sadness that he didn't feel.

He had spent a great deal of time in the Jews' country. His first childhood memories were of how his father—an eminently reasonable businessman—was treated as a second-class citizen. How he had been forced to scrape and kowtow to get work that was well beneath a man of his abilities. Later, as a college professor, Hamdi had studied the Jews' fanaticism and racism. And finally, as a politician, he had witnessed their brutality.

It never ceased to amaze him how the world had been so fooled by the Jews. Why had this one group been persecuted so long and so energetically by the rest of the world? Because they brought it on themselves.

Not that Hamdi had any real passion for the destruction of the Jewish race—it was hardly practical and would create a great deal of unnecessary human suffering. But it was time for the Jews to be recognized for what they were—a small, relatively unimportant group of people who were putting the entire world in danger. It was a situation that, with Richard Scanlon's unwitting help, he intended to put an end to.

Lowe turned off the television and settled back into his chair. The president didn't speak for almost a minute. Finally, "Who was it?"

"The driver's name was Daftar Abaza. He's originally from Syria, but he's been living in the United States for almost three years. Spotless work history, no criminal record. We have very little on him at this point—nothing suggesting he has any terrorist ties. Obviously, we're digging deeper."

"So we have no idea who was behind this?"

Lowe paused to calculate the most advantageous spin. "We believe that if this was premeditated, he would have been in the correct lane. With the traffic, he risked not being able to move left. We think it was . . . an impulse."

"An impulse? Jesus . . . Did he survive?"

"He's alive, but in a coma. There seems to be some brain damage."

Morris folded his hands across his stomach and fixed his stare on the back wall for a few moments. "So no known terrorist backing. Essentially, this guy is just a nut who doesn't like Jews. It was a hate crime more than a terrorist act. So, that's good. Right?"

"Yes, sir," Lowe said. "There's no suggestion of any kind of coordinated effort."

Hamdi sighed audibly. Another example of Paul Lowe coming to precisely the wrong conclusion based on all the facts.

"You disagree?" Morris said, turning toward him.

"That it was an impulsive act? No. That this is good news? Yes. This incident is lighting up the extremist Web sites, sir—for the exact reason that it had no organized backing. The spin is that a devout Muslim doesn't need leaders, or even an organization to fight. This man, with no preparation and no weapons, killed or wounded a fairly large number of Jews. That is the message the terrorists are working to get out there. While we spend billion of dollars and thousands of American lives fighting wars against countries we think are terrorist sponsors, individuals and small groups can destroy us. The truck at the Mall of

America was a fertilizer bomb full of nails. No matter how much we want to believe that it would take a massive organization and the support of Iran to succeed in an attack that devastating, it's simply not true. This is just the logical next step in a terrorist network that is becoming increasingly decentralized."

The president drummed his fingers on his stomach, and Hamdi glanced over at Lowe, who wasn't bothering to hide his animosity toward his half-breed detractor.

"I'm already under heavy criticism for not retaliating for the mall attack. And now I'm going to have every Jewish person in the country screaming for blood."

"Of course," Hamdi said. "All these people understand is retaliation."

"Here we go . . . ," Lowe said.

Hamdi ignored him. "Who would we retaliate against? This man's family? An eye for an eye? Besides, the Israelis are continuing to mass their military on the border of Gaza. They're more than capable of extracting their own pound of flesh."

"And Egypt is doing the same," Lowe said. "We're still waiting for moves from Syria and Jordan."

"Goddamn Arabs," the president said, in an uncharacteristically obvious attempt to bait Hamdi. "They don't care enough about the Palestinians to take them in, but they're willing to set the entire region on fire for them. I'll never understand these people."

"Mr. President . . . ," Hamdi started, but Morris ignored him.

"Look, I've told Israel in no uncertain terms that they need to stay out of Gaza. But they know how powerful the Jewish lobby is here, and they sure as hell know how the average American voter feels about Arab terrorists. I don't think they're taking my threats seriously. And frankly, there's no reason they should."

"Sir," Lowe said, "the Israelis are an important bulwark in the Middle East. I think even Dr. Hamdi would agree with that."

"It's all moot," Hamdi said. "We've put ourselves in a position that we have no choice but to do whatever is necessary to protect Israel. They have a nuclear arsenal that they wouldn't hesitate to use if their country was in danger. We have no way of stopping them from using that option, so we have to make sure they're never put in a situation that they would be forced to consider it."

Morris turned toward Lowe. "Do you agree? Would they use nukes?"

"Sir, I think—"

"Yes or no question, Paul."

"Then yes. Their main concern is their own security, and they aren't going to walk away from it for us."

"And yet we walk away from our security every day for them," Hamdi interrupted.

"Come on," Lowe said. "The Israelis may not be perfect, but they're the most reasonable friends we have in that region. Are they unfair and heavy-handed with the Palestinians? Sure. But wasn't it you, Edwin, who once said that there are no victims in the world—

only the poorly armed? Bet you didn't know I read your book, huh? The Israelis are just giving back a little of what they've been getting for years. The Arabs run around expecting everyone to bow down to them because God loves them best and then they don't have the juice to back up their big mouths. And thank God. I mean, if an Arab country ever had military power— I mean real power—can you imagine what they'd do with it? They'd kill every infidel they could get their hands on, then they'd start going after each other. In fifty years, there'd be about a hundred people left on the planet and they'd all be skulking around trying to stab each other in the back because their Koran was printed in a different font than their neighbor's Koran—"

"Goddamn country the size of New Jersey," the president said, silencing his two advisors before one of their infamous shouting matches started. "And nobody can agree on anything except that I'm damned if I do and damned if I don't. I'm looking for solutions here, not academic arguments that dead-end in the fact that the situation is hopeless. Edwin?"

"Are we talking about the synagogue attack or Israel in general?"

"Both."

"I guess the answer is the same. There really isn't anything you can do. The cab driver is already in a coma and seems to have no connections to anyone we can reasonably punish. And Gaza? Well, Gaza has turned into just the disaster the Israelis had hoped. They'll use the chaos as an excuse to take it back and to stop any talk about further moves from the West Bank. What they'll do with the millions of Arabs who live in Gaza, I'm not sure. My guess would be that they'll foment terrorism against the U.S. so that we'll support whatever measures they want to take. I have to assume that their long-term goal is to kill or drive the Arabs out of the Occupied Territories so that they can settle them."

"A typically cheerful analysis. Same question, Paul."

"You know I don't agree with Edwin's conspiracy theories. Israel may not be perfect, but they're a strong ally in a part of the world where we don't have a lot of friends. And you have to understand that there are factions within Israel that aren't under the control of the government. A lot of times it's them, not the prime minister or the Knesset, that cause the problems. They can help us, they have helped us, and we should support them for that reason. As for the cab driver . . . We know he was from Syria."

"What's that supposed to mea—," Hamdi started, but the president held up a hand.

"What kind of targets do we have there?"

"Sir . . . ," Hamdi cautioned.

"We've firmed up our intelligence on a few training camps along the border," Lowe said.

"But it's still incredibly soft," Hamdi said. "Please, sir—"

"You have something better, Edwin?"

"Restraint—"

"Restraint? That's all I hear from you anymore! We

get hit and you tell me to just sit on my hands and explain to the American people why Homeland Security and the military that they pay billions for are completely useless in the face of a bunch of illiterate Arab fanatics. Syria is a problem for us and you know it. There are terrorist training camps all over that border, and the Syrian government isn't doing a damn thing about it."

Hamdi jerked forward in his chair, but then forced himself to take a breath before speaking. "Paul likes to point out that the Israeli government isn't complicit in many of the problems there, and I'd like to make the same argument about Syria. We expect them to know exactly who is and is not in their country and to completely control their border. But as the wealthiest nation in the world we can't control our own border with Mexico. And, frankly, our problems are no more a priority for them than their problems are a priority for us."

The president folded his arms across his chest and cocked his head a bit as he examined Hamdi. "You're always saying that we get in trouble by reacting without fully understanding what we're doing. Well, let me tell you what I'm about to do. I'm going to give an order to bomb a bunch of people who had nothing to do with the attack this morning and who may have nothing at all to do with terrorism. In the process, I'm going to give Islamic fundamentalists fodder to recruit another thousand terrorists. And you know what that's going to get me? Credibility with the American people so that they'll allow me to continue your program of conciliation."

Chapter Twenty

The room was typically spartan—not so much as an inspirational poster about teamwork to break up the white, windowless walls. The long, rectangular table was straight out of government surplus, and so were the six men sitting around it. They all looked up at Brandon from behind steaming cups of coffee, expressions registering everything from intense curiosity to intense distaste.

At Catherine's request, most of them had made some effort to soften their images, but it took more than a pair of worn jeans and slightly shaggy hair to disguise that they were all either former military or from some even scarier branch of the government. Even more obvious was that none of them had signed on with Scanlon to take orders from an escaped convict.

Brandon drained the lukewarm remnants of his own coffee and stood, still waiting for the caffeine to kick in. He'd spent the last week driving desert highways, visiting gas stations and airfields, touring the San Francisco Federal Reserve Bank, and plinking away on that invention of inventions, the Internet. It would have been nice to postpone this meeting until after he'd been able to get a decent night's sleep, but time was working hard against them.

He pointed to the man closest to him. "How many pull-ups can you do?"

No hesitation. "With which hand?"

Of course.

As much as he hated to admit it, you just didn't get this class of manpower working with the average American criminal. If this had been one of his typical strategy meetings, at least one person wouldn't have shown, one would be high, two would be fifty pounds overweight, and the rest would be suffering from near-terminal hangovers.

The question at hand, of course, was which of these disciplined and well-trained patriots was charged with putting a bullet in the back of his head when all this was over? Or was Scanlon on the up-and-up? Honestly, he was a trustworthy guy in a weird eighteenth-century kind of way, but Brandon wasn't one to bet his life on concepts as outdated as chivalry or honor. And then there were the millions of people who might just die if he screwed this up. Pressure anyone?

"Is everyone in the right meeting?" he said. "This is Stealing Two Hundred Million from Vegas. Parents of Problem Teenagers is down the hall."

Not so much as a tremor of a smile from anyone. "Start them out with a joke," his public-speaking professor had always said. Thank God he'd dropped out.

Catherine gently prodded his leg from her seat next

to him, prompting him to continue. He cleared his throat.

"Okay. My name's Brandon and I'll be your guide today. Let's start with an overview. Basically, we have money getting picked up at various locations in Vegas, then transported to the Federal Reserve Bank in San Francisco. A simple concept, made complicated by various truck configurations—sometimes a bunch of panel vans going out at different times, sometimes a single semi. Also, we have to deal with multiple routes and uncertain timing. The whole thing is super lo-fi. No armor, no motorcades, no machine guns."

Brandon glanced at Richard Scanlon, who was sitting with the back of his chair leaned against the wall. "The whole thing's pretty clever, actually. It's not that hard to hit an armored car that goes out at the same time every day. They're obvious on the road, and there are all kinds of ways to get into them. When I was planning this before, the randomness and lack of concrete information was crushing. Obviously, I wanted to hit the semi and not the multiple vans, but when was it going out? Which route was it taking? Where was it stopping on the road? The list goes on and on. As much as I hate to admit it, Richard made this money incredibly irritating to steal. Too many uncontrollable factors. Too many potential surprises."

Catherine slid a new cup of coffee in front of him and he took a grateful sip, motioning to the men around the table. "Crime is probably a little like war. Surprises are *always* a bad thing."

That got a few nods. They weren't exactly eating out of his hand, but at least they seemed to be listening.

"Now that Richard's feeding me information, it takes the main protection factor out of the equation. We should have only about a hundred insurmountable problems instead of the usual thousand." He pointed to Catherine. "Could you . . ."

She tapped a few commands into her laptop and a projector mounted to the ceiling shone the image of a map on the screen behind him.

"According to Richard, the next time a semi goes out is a little over a week from today—so we're really up against it time-wise. It'll travel the route I've highlighted in yellow to San Francisco. Anybody been on that road?"

The Pull-up King raised a hand. "I have. It's mostly dead straight and gets hardly any traffic. Couldn't be better."

"Honestly, it has its drawbacks," Brandon said. "Remember, it's not so much *getting* the money, it's *keeping* the money that's hard. I mean, you've got a couple of tons of cash in a big, obvious truck on a road that's really hard to get off of and has almost no traffic to get lost in."

He pointed to Catherine again. She changed the slide to one showing a plain white semi and two equally nondescript cars. "Here's what we've got. Two unmarked Ford Tauruses with one man in each. They're private guards—nothing superimpressive, but better than your typical yahoos. I think both of them are former state cops. We'll have some more detailed info on their backgrounds before we go." He turned his attention to Scanlon. "Either of these guys new? Or have they been on the job awhile?"

"Both veterans."

"That's good. They'll be comfortable. The last thing we need is some rookie paying attention to everything."

The man who had been introduced to him as Daniel the week before raised a hand. "No police or federal coverage?"

"None," Scanlon interjected. "Cops and feds don't protect property. And even if they did, I wouldn't have gotten them involved. It would just be more people with knowledge of this thing."

"Okay," Brandon said. "Moving along. The driver is unarmed. An actual truck driver and the same one every time. He's never been told specifically what he's carrying but since he's picking it up from the casinos and going to the Fed, we can assume he's guessed. And finally . . ."

Catherine anticipated him and changed the slide. This one showed a small Bell helicopter.

"There's air coverage. The copter keeps an eye on the semi and the traffic, but doesn't constantly hover overhead and draw attention. Remember, these guys are putting most of their eggs in the stealth basket. Can anyone here fly a copter?"

They all raised their hands.

"Why do I even ask?"

All hands sank again except for the Pull-up Czar's.

"Yeah?"

"We could take out the copter with a fifty-caliber rifle. You can buy—"

Brandon held a hand out, cutting him off. "You bring up an important point. There will be no fifty-caliber rifles. No rocket launchers. And absolutely no grenades. In fact, no one is going to get hurt at all. Anybody can steal money by killing people. We're going to see if we can take a higher road."

Daniel raised his hand. "What about satellites? Will there be anything overhead when we're doing this thing?"

Actually, it wasn't a bad question.

"It's possible," Scanlon answered. "But there's no way anyone would be able to get their hands on the information in time to interfere with us."

"More of a worry is the random element of vehicle traffic," Brandon said. "But it's fairly light. Also, the men in the chase cars are armed. Again, nothing fancy—just handguns." He looked around to see if everyone was tracking on the information. So far so good.

"Moving on to electronics. The semi has a GPS tracker—a commercially available model used by pretty much all trucking companies. Roughly the same unit has been installed in the chase vehicles. Another five GPS transmitters will be hidden in random bags of money in the trailer. All of these are being tracked real time by the security firm's head office."

That elicited some frowns and fidgeting on the part of his audience.

"The good news is that the company running this

operation is still using essentially the same technology they started with when they originally set
the thing up. You've got to love private industry—
they hate spending money to upgrade systems that
still work. So what they're getting is location coor-
dinates, direction, and speed. Also, they're getting
data from the engine management system—they're
notified of things like hard braking, horsepower, gas
mileage, and whatnot. That system also allows them
to shut down the engine with the flip of a switch.
Obviously, that means the truck and cars can't
deviate from course or make any unscheduled stops,
and they have to stay relatively close to each other.
But we have more latitude than if they were using
cutting-edge technology that read out three dots on
some Doctor Evil ten-foot screen. And last, but not
least, all three drivers check in with code words
every hour. Richard assures me he can get those
code words . . ."

Brandon picked up his mug and looked into the
eyes of every man sitting at the table. The lights were
definitely all on, but some were dimmer than others.
Time to find out what he had to work with.

"Okay. So now we're seeing the complexities. The
problem with the lonely road is that there's no way
off the damn thing. The cops can close in from both
directions, zoned in on the GPSes if there's any sign
of trouble. So? What do you think? Any ideas?"

Silence.

"Seriously. Anything? Anything at all?"

One of the men at the back spoke up. "We could

dig a cave in the desert, hijack the truck and cars, and drive in there. It would kill the GPS signal."

Brandon nodded noncommittally. "But how do we get the money out of there? The cops would descend on our last known position and since there's virtually nowhere for us to go, they'd eventually figure out to look for something underground. Plus, they'd be checking every vehicle coming off that road. And then there's the fact that digging caves is kind of time-consuming."

More silence.

Daniel put up a hesitant hand. "It seems like our problem is the tracking station. Why not take it out?"

Brandon kept his expression passive, unwilling to show that he was impressed. "I actually looked into that years ago when I first started thinking about this thing and it turned out to be too hard. They have two redundant sites—one in Vegas and one in Chicago—plus an open line to the police and heavy security in the buildings that are both smack-dab in the middle of town. Also, it takes a long time to make that drive—you'd have to hold the people for something like twenty hours without anyone finding out. Anyway, even if we could come up with something that would work, we'd need three times the manpower you see around you, and Scanlon tells me this is all we're going to get."

Daniel nodded, chewing his lower lip. "Well, the copter's gonna have to stop for fuel. I don't know anything about trucks, but I assume it will have to stop, too. Can we get them there? Or would it be too public?"

"Interesting you should mention that. It's one of the few things working in our favor. The truck has to drop money at the Fed when the Fed's open. That means it has to leave Vegas around nine P.M. and drive through the night. Combine that with the fact that it'll be driving through the middle of nowhere and that should keep our audience to a minimum. So let's assume we get control of all the vehicles. The monitoring station still knows exactly where we are. If we deviate, slow down, or do anything else unusual, they're going to shut down the engine and call the cops."

Daniel spoke up again. "What about offloading the truck while it's still moving?"

This guy was not only abnormally sneaky, he actually seemed to be getting into the spirit of things.

"Okay, but what about the GPSes hidden in some of the bags?"

"You'd have to scan each bag for a GPS transmission. If they're clean, toss them on the side of the road and have someone come through and pick them up . . ."

Brandon motioned for the guy to continue.

"What if you rebag them in orange so they look like garbage? You know, like those Adopt A Highway deals? Then we drive along in a garbage truck . . ."

Brandon blinked a few times. Where had this guy been all his life? He was a fucking prodigy.

"Consider me impressed, Daniel. Believe it or not, I tried almost exactly what you're suggesting. I rented some trucks and used an abandoned piece of highway in Utah to do a dry run. Getting the money off the semi was kind of a pain in the ass, particularly when you had to scan every bag for a GPS monitor. And picking it up was a nightmare—essentially, crawling along in multiple garbage trucks, loading them. Also, we had a hell of a time finding bags that didn't burst when they hit the ground. Caused a real mess trying to get that right. But even with all those problems, I liked it. Simple and straightforward. Until . . ." He pointed to Scanlon and everyone turned.

"It's how I would have stolen it, too," he said. "The signal from the GPSes in the money bags runs into a PC with a simple program that constantly compares their proximity to one another. It allows for a bit of cargo shifting, but nothing more. Moving any one GPS relative to the others would set off an alarm."

Daniel looked genuinely disappointed.

"Then how?" one of the men asked.

"Yeah," Scanlon said. "How?"

Chapter Twenty-One

Jamal Yusef was certain he was being led in circles.

The cavern, deep beneath the Carpathian Mountains, was almost cathedral-like—stalagmite pillars rose into an endless, suffocating blackness, and the ground was strewn with broken boulders the size of houses. Five minutes earlier, though, he'd been slithering on his belly, scraping his head on the jagged stone above and trying to control a vague panic that was almost certainly justified.

The most prevalent impression, though, was cold. Not like the Syrian desert at night and not like those winter nights in New York where the wind whipped between the buildings like a freight train. There was something malevolent about this cold. The stillness of it. The way it penetrated so quickly and deeply. Like a virus.

The man ahead of him was better prepared. He wore a down-filled jumpsuit with a thick hood edged in grimy fur. An equally filthy Kalashnikov hung over his shoulder.

He pointed right and Yusef looked down, squinting into the intermittent shadows. He hadn't been given a flashlight and was completely reliant on the one held by his guide. Unfortunately, it wasn't quite powerful enough and left about half the cave's deadly obstacles a bit ambiguous. Would a stumble to the right lead to a twisted ankle or a free fall through the blackness that would leave him impaled on a rock formation below?

He wasn't particularly anxious to find out. He moved as far left as he could, using his already numb hands to steady himself against a wet wall of stone.

The courting process had been a long one: more like two predators circling a carcass than a business negotiation. The Ukrainians were understandably cautious, and so was he.

Organized crime had identified terrorism as a growth industry but had yet to learn to deal with the fanatics involved. Religious ecstasy, while a good motivator, didn't necessarily create predictable business relationships. And so, while Yusef had proven his credibility as a terrorist, his reliability was still subject to substantial skepticism.

The tight corridor they'd entered twisted and climbed violently for another few minutes and then abruptly widened again. As they continued forward, Yusef could see the flash of preternaturally white faces hidden in small alcoves to both sides—armed men watching through dead-looking eyes.

The man leading him turned off his flashlight in favor of the glow of industrial lights set up on rusting stands every twenty feet or so, and then veered left into a small gap in the rock. A few moments later, the corridor dead-ended into a well-lit chamber dominated by a large, regal desk. It was covered in gouges and water stains, but in its day it would have been worthy of a czar.

The man motioned for him to stay and then disappeared, leaving Yusef with only the hum of a distant generator to keep him company. He used the time to try to calm himself, to stay in character. A fundamentalist terrorist wouldn't be uncertain. Or afraid. Or . . .

"Mr. Yusef!"

The voice seemed to come from everywhere as it bounced off the stone walls. He spun just in time to see two men emerge from the darkness.

"I've looked forward to meeting you in person," the man in front said with a moderate accent. He was wearing a crisp military uniform with the sleeves rolled over muscular forearms that seemed impervious to the cold.

"I'm Grigori."

"I, too, have been looking forward to this moment," Yusef said, shaking the man's hand. Grigori was the man he'd been corresponding with by e-mail for so long. He never really thought he'd meet the man face-to-face. Or perhaps he had just hoped he wouldn't.

The other man didn't speak or approach, instead moving into a shallow alcove and watching through bulging eyes that burned with something that wasn't quite clear. Insanity? Fury? The garish scar across his mouth identified him as Grigori's brother. Edwin Hamdi had provided physical descriptions of the two men as well as some basic background, though its reliability was questionable.

They were thought to be Ukrainian Jews. One brother had joined the military as a young man, while the other had become an enforcer for a local gang. Then, about ten years ago, and under murky circumstances, they had joined forces in a number of criminal ventures that had reportedly been quite profitable. How they had ended up here, though, and how they had come to possess nuclear weapons was unknown.

Yusef removed the backpack that had generated so much interest earlier and held it out. "A gift, Grigori. Whether we are able to come to an agreement on this transaction or not, I hope you will think of me again should you ever come across something interesting."

Grigori looked at the cash straining the sides of the pack and then tossed it to his brother with a few words in Ukrainian.

"A thoughtful gesture," he said, taking Yusef by the arm and leading him back out the way they had come. He could hear Grigori's brother—Pyotr according to Hamdi's intelligence—walking a few feet behind, and he glanced back, tensing when he saw the flash of a knife in the man's hands.

Pyotr made no move to close the distance between them, though, and Yusef was eventually forced to turn and focus on where he was going.

The chamber they finally came to was virtually identical to the hundreds he'd passed since he arrived, with one exception: It had a door. Or more precisely, a web of bars haphazardly welded together and attached to heavy hinges set into the stone. On either side was an armed guard, each of whom snapped to the loose facsimile of attention favored by military men who had abandoned their oaths in favor of self-interest.

Grigori used the key around his neck to unlock the gate and stepped aside.

Yusef hesitated for a moment, but knew he'd come too far to turn back now. Another glance at the knife-wielding Pyotr confirmed that he was well past the point of no return. Years past.

As soon as he stepped inside, the sound and smell of a generator kicking on surrounded him, and the level of illumination rose to the point that he had to shield his eyes with his hand.

Most of the wooden crates were still sealed, but one in the center had been opened, and Yusef could see metal peeking through what looked like hay. He reached out to touch it and immediately recoiled at the almost painful cold of the metal. Or perhaps that wasn't the reason at all.

Grigori was watching from his position at the gate and Yusef forced himself to retrieve the small tool kit he was carrying from his pocket. "May I?"

"Of course."

"You're satisfied, then?" Grigori said, slamming the gate closed again and carefully locking it.

Yusef barely managed to keep his voice from shaking. All twelve warheads were there and all twelve were fully operational. God help them.

"I'm satisfied."

They began walking again, this time side by side,

with Grigori's arm locked through his, as though they had been friends since childhood.

"Of course you are. And I, too, am much happier with meeting you. I find myself a good judge of men and I sense you are a man I can trust. But I must say that we have much interest in our product—from groups like yours as well as from governments."

"I'm sure you do."

"And these other bidders must be considered."

Yusef motioned behind him at Pyotr, who was still playing with the knife and staring at him with what Yusef had decided was inexplicable hatred. The backpack full of cash hadn't softened him at all.

"But have any of those other bidders provided you with half a million U.S. dollars? Or any gesture of good faith at all?"

"No," Grigori admitted.

"I'm not surprised. Even cells directly linked to Osama bin Laden have been scattered and cut off from their funding. As for selling to governments— this is very dangerous for you. The Americans are focusing almost entirely on the state sponsorship of terrorism. Countries like Iran and Syria are being watched very closely. While smaller groups—groups like mine—are going unnoticed."

Grigori nodded. "Much of what you say is true."

"And the risk of you trying to sell these weapons to multiple buyers is even greater. Twelve different buyers means twelve different chances for exposure. And what if one of the people—"

Pyotr began scraping his knife against the rock wall

as they walked, and Yusef's train of thought was briefly lost in the static of it.

"What if one of the people you sell to is captured? It would make the sale of the remaining warheads a very difficult matter."

"I assume you have an offer that will relieve me of all of these risks?" Grigori said, not bothering to hide his skepticism.

"I'm prepared to pay you one hundred and fifty million U.S. dollars for all the warheads."

To his credit, Grigori didn't react at all to the offer. He just continued walking through the cave, smiling politely.

"When?" he said finally.

"Obviously, there would be a number of details to be discussed, but ideally, I would like to have the transaction completed within two weeks."

Grigori's expression changed slightly at that. "Then you have the money?"

"I do."

"If this is true, then I see few details left to decide. You will remain here as my guest and we will discuss the price further. When we come to agree, we will send wire instructions. And when the money is confirmed to be in my account, you may take the items away."

Yusef shook his head and Grigori's face transformed into a slightly bored frown.

In these types of transactions, there was always a catch, and he was waiting for Yusef to get around to it. Undoubtedly he expected a rather complicated qualification of Yusef's statement that he had the money. The definition of "had" could be surprisingly murky.

"And how is this unacceptable to you, my friend?"

"The money is in cash."

Grigori stopped short, keeping his arm tightly linked with Yusef's.

"I'm sorry for my English. I am not sure I understood."

"Cash. The money is in currency."

Grigori thought about that for a moment. "This would be . . . It would weigh—"

"Well over a ton," Yusef said. "And it's bulky. It will take a good-sized truck to transport it."

"This is a great deal of cash."

"I understand the complications it poses for you, but we have acquired the cash and cannot launder it in the time frame you want to work within. That makes a wire transfer impossible."

Grigori started again, pulling Yusef along with him. "It would be most inconvenient. It would be quite expensive to handle so much currency."

Yusef nodded. "How expensive?"

"Twenty-five million."

"Am I correct in understanding that you're saying one hundred and seventy-five million in cash for all twelve warheads?"

Grigori thought about it for a moment and then nodded.

It was impossible to know if Pyotr understood their conversation, but suddenly the sound of the knife scraping rock gave way to hysterical shouting. Yusef spun and Grigori leapt in front of his brother, who was jabbing his knife in Yusef's direction while continuing his furious diatribe in Ukrainian.

Grigori spoke in a calm, even tone, but it seemed to just make Pyotr angrier. They continued like that for almost a minute, but when Pyotr took a step forward, the scene quickly changed. Grigori grabbed his brother by the front of his jacket and pulled him close, ignoring the knife and speaking with his lips less than an inch from the man's face. Finally, he shoved him back and pointed to the dark corridor behind them. A moment later, Pyotr was fading into it.

"I must apologize," Grigori said, once again linking his arm through Yusef's. "We are Jews and my brother keeps that religion like a neglected pet. Do you understand this?"

Yusef nodded.

"I myself am an atheist," Grigori continued. "Are you shocked? I'm curious: What offends a man like you more? A Jew or an atheist?"

There was no answer that could possibly benefit his position, so Yusef remained silent.

"Of course, you are right. It is best to keep business separate from our personal feelings. My brother hasn't learned this simple lesson. He is concerned that you might use our weapons to attack his people in Israel, though he's killed many, many Jews himself. More than you, I should think."

He stared directly at the side of Yusef's face from

a distance that felt much too close. Could he see the American in him? Could anyone anymore? The truth was that he really was a terrorist now. By virtually any definition.

Interestingly, Pyotr's psychotic ravings were exactly on target. The warheads—every one of them—would be detonated in Israel. In a month, that country and the Occupied Territories would simply cease to exist.

Yusef became aware of the fact that he was shaking but wasn't sure if it could be attributed to the cold. He believed in what he was doing—that it had to be done. But it was impossible not to be tormented by doubt there in the quiet darkness.

For the most part, America's relationship with the Middle East was moving in the right direction. Instead of being consumed with how to make war on the Arab people, Americans were starting to think about how to make peace with them. Oil prices were on an inevitable rise thanks to constricting supplies and China's increasing thirst—a situation that would eventually force the U.S. to break its desperate addiction to Middle Eastern petroleum and help ease the problems that addiction had caused.

And that left Israel. There was no way to eradicate the hatred and bigotry woven into the fabric of the Middle East since the very beginning of recorded history. Yusef had seen for himself that the future held nothing but escalation and the increasing involvement by the rest of the world in a situation that only God could resolve. And God had wisely elected to keep his distance.

After years of living in the Middle East—speaking with its people, watching its television, smelling its blood—he knew that the only solution left was to remove the problem. The homeland of the Jews and the Palestinians would be sacrificed for the greater good. And these warheads would be the tools of that sacrifice.

Chapter Twenty-two

The engine's roar echoing off the concrete floor and metal walls was almost enough to drown out REM's latest record. Brandon pulled his iPod from its Gucci case and adjusted the volume, bobbing his head to the beat.

The warehouse was enormous and virtually empty except for the eighteen-wheeler weaving dangerously through the widely spaced support columns. He counted the seconds it took to get from one end of the building to the other and calculated that Catherine was now topping forty miles per hour.

"Bet this was expensive."

Brandon spun and found Richard Scanlon motioning around the massive warehouse.

"Huh?" Brandon said, pulling one of the earphones out.

"I said, I'll bet this was expensive."

Brandon thumbed toward the semi. "Couldn't really do it in a ministorage, you know?"

That prompted a deep scowl from Scanlon. And he hadn't even seen the bill from the iTunes store yet.

"How's everyone doing?" he said, watching two men dangling from either end of a single rope slung across the top of the truck. As the truck weaved, the man on one side would swing helplessly away from the trailer, while the other was slammed into it.

"Okay, I suppose. We got Catherine a private tutor from a local trucking school and she's getting straight A's so far. But I have my suspicions that she's sleeping with the instructor."

That earned him another frown.

"Anyway, at the rate she's improving, she'll be fine by the time she has to do it for real." He pointed toward one of the men hanging from the truck, struggling to hold on to something that looked like an enormous roll of wallpaper that he had partially applied to the side of the trailer.

"The real stickers are still being made, but we managed to get some blanks to practice with. Unfortunately, they weigh a lot more than we thought."

The truck swerved and the man wrapped his arms and legs around the roll as he swung out into the air. His momentum pulled off a couple of feet of sticker, but when he was inevitably slammed back into the trailer, he was able to smooth it back down and apply a few more feet before he swung away again.

"At that rate, it's going to take an hour to get that sticker all the way across the trailer," Scanlon said.

Brandon nodded. "Just holding those rolls while you're hanging is really difficult—let alone getting them stuck on. And God himself couldn't get them straight."

"So what are you saying? That it can't be done?"

"Not by normal human beings. But as much as I hate to admit it, these guys aren't normal humans. They may be a little brain-dead, but if you point them in a direction, they don't let anything get in their way."

"They're not brain-dead," Scanlon said. "Not by a long shot. They just don't think in the same way you do. People like you and me spend all our time second-guessing orders. They get the job done."

"You can tell me that all day long, but I still think they're hopeless. Except Daniel. Now that's a guy you could steal some shit with."

"So what I'm hearing is that everything's under control?"

"My end is fine. You just make sure you come through with yours," Brandon said, walking over to a concrete pillar and opening a glass case containing a fire hose.

"What are you doing?" Scanlon asked.

"I'm curious about how well those things will stick if they're wet."

The force of the hose almost knocked him backward, but he managed to stabilize himself and use the stream to blast the man hanging from the side of the truck as it passed by. To his credit, he found a way to maneuver so his back took the brunt of the jet, swearing loudly enough that it was audible over the roar of the motor and the hiss of the hose. Catherine didn't even slow down. She just turned on the truck's wipers.

"Is that really necessary?" Scanlon said. His tone suggested that he already knew the answer to his question but disapproved of the pleasure Brandon was deriving from dousing his new colleagues.

"The long-term weather forecast looks good, Richard, but you can never trust a weatherman. If everything goes right, we'll be doing this on a straight, dry road. Everything never goes right, though, you know?"

Brandon pointed to a steel box with three buttons on it. "Push the blue one, would you?"

Scanlon did and they were engulfed in darkness for a few seconds before Catherine found the truck's headlights. Maybe it was just his imagination, but Brandon would have sworn that she actually sped up a bit. That was the spirit.

"How are you doing with all this?" Scanlon said as he watched the two men struggle to complete their tasks in a darker, wetter reality.

"All of what?"

"You know what I'm talking about: Being broken out of jail, being backed into a corner on this job. Being responsible for millions of lives. It's a larger arena than you're used to working in."

Brandon pulled the remaining earphone from his ear and hung it over his shoulder. "You know I just want to do my patriotic duty, boss."

Scanlon let out a quick rush of air that was impossible to read. It may have been a laugh. It may have been a death sentence.

The bottom line, Brandon knew, was that he needed to get the hell out of Dodge after this thing was over. If Scanlon was on the up-and-up, then he'd just shrug and forget about it. If not, a head start wouldn't be a bad idea.

The exact logistics of his escape, though, were starting to look a little complicated. His old accomplices were undoubtedly being watched by Scanlon's people, and if not, certainly by the cops. He had no money of his own to speak of. No passports or IDs anywhere close. And if his face wasn't already adorning every post office in the country, it soon would be. If he was particularly lucky, he might get a spot on *America's Most Wanted*. A career in television. Just what he needed.

The ironic thing was that it would all be incredibly easy if he just sabotaged the heist. But how could he with this much at stake? So now he had to figure out a way to pull the damn thing off but then disappear before he became more useful as a liner for a shallow grave than a thief.

"It's turning into a disaster, Brandon."

He glanced over at Scanlon, who was no longer watching the show, but staring off into the darkness at the edge of the headlights.

"What is?"

"The world. This country. You should be pissed off about what my generation is leaving you."

"Should I? The way they tell it, everything's going great."

Scanlon's smile seemed a little sad. A little tired. "Only believe about ten percent of what the government tells you."

"What are you talking about, man? You *are* the

government." He pointed down at Scanlon's feet. "Look at you. You're wearing wingtips, for God's sake."

The truck sped by again and Brandon opened the hose up for a few seconds, dousing the man hanging from the other side.

"I worked so hard for so many years to just try to keep things at a simmer," Scanlon said. "And now everything's exploded. The government decided to go out of its way to make the rest of the world fear and hate us and then told me to protect the American people from that world. The problem is, it's impossible."

"Is that why you quit the Bureau?"

He nodded.

"But it's gotten better since then, right? I mean, all you ever hear is how much money they're spending on homeland security."

"Just because you spend money doesn't mean you get anything for it."

Brandon shrugged. "I honestly don't think much about the government. If they ever start a draft, I'd dodge it. I don't really pay taxes. And the chances of me getting shot by some security guard is a hell of a lot higher than me getting blown up by some Arab guy."

"So you'd describe your political philosophy as apathy."

"Nope. Enlightened self-interest and practical self-reliance. What am I supposed to do? Sit around and wait for the government to show up with a handout? I'd be waiting a long time."

Scanlon shook his head slowly. "It wasn't always this way. But now it seems like it gets worse every year. The government's become completely effort-based. They tell you that they're working to put ten thousand cops on the street, and when they do it, everyone cheers. But that isn't a goal. The goal is reducing crime. Funny how no one ever mentions that." He folded his arms in front of him, still staring into the darkness. "Think about it. Billions of dollars and millions of man-hours have been spent on border security since 9/11. Do you know what's been accomplished? Nothing. How do I know? Because the country is still full of illegal immigrants and cocaine. If we can't stop that, how can we stop a terrorist from strolling across our border with a nuclear weapon?"

"You know what you guys just can't seem to understand, Richard? It's all about motivation. If drug dealers get a bunch of coke over the border, they get a new Ferrari. If a Mexican gets a job in Texas, he feeds his family. If a Muslim terrorist sets off a bomb in Washington, he gets fifty virgins in the afterlife. But if some government employee catches one of those guys or doesn't catch one of those guys, he gets the same paycheck. It's a losing battle."

"People work jobs for more than just a paycheck, Brandon."

"Yeah, I know—power and notoriety, right? Come on, Richard. How many people do you know in the government who aren't in it mostly for themselves? I mean, when a senator can't sleep, is it because he's thinking about what's best for America or about how he's gonna get re-elected?"

Scanlon didn't answer, instead silently watching the truck speed back and forth through the warehouse.

"But not you," Brandon continued. "You're a true believer. Here to save the day."

Scanlon seemed unwilling to look away from the darkness. "No. I'm getting old. And I couldn't do any of this even if I was thirty again. *You've* returned to save the day. It's up to you now."

The truck sped by again, but Brandon didn't turn on the hose. "Are you dancing around a point here, Richard? Because if you are, I have no idea what it is."

"I want you to be a fundamental part of this organization, Brandon. Not just a one-time contractor. We're a little off the map here, and you're used to working in that territory."

Brandon had no idea how to respond to that and didn't for a few moments. "What about my vineyard in South Africa?"

"It's there if you want it."

The truck pulled to a stop about twenty-five yards away, and Daniel came jogging out of the darkness toward them.

"How'd it go?" Brandon said, relieved to have an excuse to escape from his conversation with Scanlon before it got any crazier. He was starting to think the old man was losing it.

"Chuck is having some problems getting the thing on straight. He just doesn't seem to have an eye for it. You should let him do the copter and put me—"

Brandon shook his head. "You're in the copter Daniel. Buy the guy a level or something."

Catherine jumped from the cab as the two dripping men lowered themselves to the ground and began peeling the stickers from the side of the truck in preparation for round five. Or was it six?

"The stickers work fine when they're wet, but the swinging's a problem," Daniel continued. "It'd help if we could get a line under the truck to attach both guys together. That way they wouldn't come away from the trailer on corners. Hard, though. You can't just toss the rope underneath. It might get caught in the wheels, which would definitely ruin your day."

"It should be straight and dry where we're doing this, Daniel. But you never know."

"Train for the worst and hope for the best."

"I couldn't have said it better myself."

"Nice shooting," Catherine said, wringing out the sleeve of her shirt.

"You look good out there, Cath. How's it feeling?"

"No problems. I'm still getting the hang of it, but in a few days I'll be solid."

"Hey, one more thing, Brandon," Daniel said. "The wind is really catching the stickers—and there's gonna be even more wind out there in the open desert. I've been thinking, can we get little crescents cut into them? Like banners have? It might reduce the drag."

Brandon grinned and glanced over at Scanlon. "See? That's why I love this guy. Great idea. I'm on it. Lunch?"

Daniel looked back at his men. "I'd like to do one

more run with the weaving first. Probably not a great idea to do it with them full of raw fish eggs and champagne, you know?"

"Suit yourself," Brandon said, turning the warehouse lights back on and swinging an arm around Catherine's damp shoulder. "You'll have a snack with me, though, right? You're looking a little peaked."

"Am I?"

"Wasting away to nothing."

"You always know just the right thing to say, don't you?"

It was only an old card table, but the silk tablecloth and artistically arranged dishes gave it an air of elegance. Brandon had found an ice sculptor who'd do a giant dollar sign and a missile for a reasonable price, but decided at the last moment that it might be over the top.

"You've gotta try this stuff, Richard," he said pointing to a can covered in Cyrillic writing floating in ice water. "It's beluga."

Scanlon's jaw tightened and he glared at Catherine. "Did you authorize this?"

She pretended not to hear, concentrating instead on filling a plastic plate with peeled shrimp.

"How much did it cost?"

"If you have to ask, you can't afford to eat it," Brandon said, sprinkling some chopped egg on a cracker. Scanlon stood with his feet planted for a few seconds, but then just picked up a plate.

"What's the story with those," he asked, pointing

to a table stacked with plastic devices that looked like a cross between air fresheners and hot air popcorn poppers.

"Signal jammers—work on cells and satellite transmissions. Got 'em off the Net. Wait . . ." Brandon dug around in his pocket and held out a plastic box the size of a pack of cigarettes. "I got this little portable one free with my order. If you're ever in a movie or something and someone starts talking on their cell, turn it on and they're done. Illegal, but supersatisfying."

"Hey, Brandon?" Catherine cut in. "Didn't we get sour cream?"

Scanlon tried glaring at her again, but she saw it coming and averted her eyes.

"Oh, here it is. Never mind."

Chapter Twenty-three

Despite the thick down parka Jamal Yusef was wearing, he was forced to pace back and forth across the small chamber in order to stay warm. He stopped and held his hands up to the lightbulb hanging overhead, but it was too distant to provide any heat. Instead, it just swung gently from its cord, causing the stone walls to sway in time.

Yusef glanced down at the cot that was the only furniture in the poorly disguised prison cell, but then just pressed his back against the wall and stared into the black gap he'd entered through hours before. There were no bars like the ones protecting the warheads. Grigori had led him there through a mind-boggling maze of passageways that Yusef would have no chance of finding his way back through. Any attempt at escape would almost certainly end with his corpse at the bottom of a ravine or floating in an icy subterranean lake.

Not that he really had anything to escape from. The deal was done and Grigori was satisfied with the cash delivery plan they'd negotiated. Yusef would leave tomorrow to coordinate the details with Hamdi. Then it would just be a matter of Grigori living up to his end of the agreement—something that seemed fairly certain at this point. A single, quick, megamillion-dollar sale was ideal for him. Every day he held those nukes, every time he contacted another potential buyer, he took an enormous risk. No, Grigori would be happy to see them go, to pay his men, and to disappear forever.

So why did Yusef want to run to the blackness beyond that gap and just keep going?

A few hours ago it would have been an impossible question to answer, but now, here in the cold silence, it was completely clear: He'd wanted the warheads to be fake. Or better yet, not to exist at all. He'd wanted this to be another one of the countless hoaxes that flowed from Eastern Europe every day.

He believed in Edwin Hamdi and knew from his own long, depressing experience that the destruction of Israel was the world's best chance of exchanging the existing balance of terror for an admittedly delicate balance of peace. In the long run, he believed that millions would be saved—making the limited casualties caused by his actions irrelevant.

The problem was that yesterday those limited casualties had been nothing but an abstract concept. Now they were real. And with every moment that passed, his imagination gave them just a little more flesh and bone, families and personalities.

When the perfect blackness he was staring into began to show hints of gray, Yusef took a hesitant step forward. A light. Someone was coming.

It occurred to him that he hadn't eaten in almost twenty hours. Perhaps Grigori realized this and was bringing him something? Best not to starve your best customer.

When instead Pyotr appeared, Yusef managed not to step back again—less out of courage than the knowledge that there was nowhere to go.

The smears of dirt that had been so evident before were gone from the man's face, making the scar across his mouth glow white in the shifting light. His black hair was slicked back now, and he'd changed into a slightly less tattered jacket. Perhaps his religious convictions had faded a bit in light of the amount of money Yusef was offering.

That hope was quickly dashed when Pyotr began screaming again. The spit billowed from his mouth along with a stream of unintelligible words, though he was only jabbing the air with his finger and not the blade he'd had earlier.

Yusef stood completely motionless and silent, as though faced with a rabid dog. If he just didn't react, it seemed likely that Pyotr would quickly tire of shouting at a man who couldn't understand him.

Instead, his voice rose, and he began inching forward, motioning wildly with both hands. Yusef looked around for something he could use to defend himself, but there was nothing. The loose rocks that were strewn all over this godforsaken cavern didn't exist in here—probably cleared out for the very reason that they could be used as weapons.

With his strategy clearly not working, Yusef began moving sideways, trying to keep as much distance as possible between him and the slowly advancing man.

"Calm down," he said smoothly. "This is just business. Business you'll profit greatly from."

Pyotr circled right, dragging his fist against the wall next to him, leaving a shiny streak of blood as the sharp rock cut his skin.

It occurred to Yusef that he wasn't really frightened. Not in the generally accepted definition of the word. His years surrounded by constant violence, cruelty, and fanaticism, had numbed him. Even in a place where life is cheap, it seemed that your own would be an exception. But it wasn't.

"What?" he heard himself shout. "What do you want from me? If you—"

"Pyotr!"

Grigori's voice. It was impossible to tell how close he was in the ambiguous acoustics of the cave.

"Pyotr!"

They both fell silent and stopped circling. Pyotr's eyes widened to the point that they were nearly perfectly round and, perhaps inevitably, the knife came out.

What the Ukrainian lacked in training, he more than made up for in experience. He came charging straight forward, anticipating his opponent's move to the right and cutting it off.

The time between the moment Yusef realized that he had nowhere else to go and the moment the blade began entering his chest seemed impossibly long. He thought about the people who had died in that Israeli theater, about the look of joy in Muhammad's eyes. About the warheads.

Oddly there was no pain, only a weakness that caused him to sink to his knees and then tip onto his back. He felt his head hit the edge of the cot and then he was on the ground, staring up at that single bulb swinging hypnotically above.

"Pyotr!" he heard again, this time louder but in a way more distant. A moment later Grigori's face appeared above him. He heard the ripping of fabric as his jacket was torn open and then more shouting in Ukrainian.

Yusef struggled to keep his eyes from closing but found himself blinking more and more slowly. At least he wasn't cold anymore.

Finally, the darkness came—more complete even than the darkness filling the cave. And with it, the realization that he was no longer part of this. It was finally over.

Chapter Twenty-four

Brandon Vale had never been much of a sleeper.

It wasn't that he didn't aspire to descend into dreamless unconsciousness every night, or to wake up in the morning with a cleared mind and rejuvenated body. It was just that there was always so much to think about. His past, how this job or that job could have been done better, what would happened if brain-eating zombies took over the world. And now, two days out from the Vegas heist, his mind was relentlessly turning over every misstep in the sixteen-hour training days he and his team had been enduring. Not to mention obsessing about nuclear warheads, Ukrainian psychos, and Catherine Juarez. He reached for his iPod and scrolled through the screens until he found the song he was looking for: "It's the End of the World as We Know It (And I Feel Fine)." If you looked hard enough there was a sound track for every possible situation.

He kicked the blanket off and settled back into staring up at the dark ceiling. When the song was over, he scrolled through some more, finally finding one that was perhaps even more appropriate. "Alone Again Or."

The door to the room opened a few inches and he propped himself up on his elbow, squinting into the sliver of light. "Catherine?"

He didn't recognize the two men who entered, and neither of them said anything. One quietly closed the door and stood in front of it while the other dug clothes from drawers with a precision that suggested he'd been through them before.

Brandon swung his feet to the floor, catching a pair of jeans and a shirt as they were thrown at him. Before he put them on, though, he made a final adjustment to the iPod. The Dead Kennedys seemed to be the band that best captured this particular moment: "Forward to Death."

Sadly, it wasn't the first time Brandon had been shoved in the trunk of a car. Not even the second or third. At least it wasn't one of those subcompacts. Or one with the spare tire right in the middle. Those things could put a kink in your back that wouldn't loosen up for days. Of course, rigor mortis would do the same thing.

He put a hand out and braced himself as the car accelerated around a turn and then closed his eyes in the darkness, wondering what had happened. Had Scanlon decided that he had enough information to pull this thing off on his own? If so, he was in for an unpleasant surprise.

Now *there* was a moral dilemma. Right before they shot him, should he yell "Wait! Before you kill me, let me write down the stuff I didn't tell you!" After all, a nuclear holocaust wasn't exactly the legacy he wanted to leave behind.

No, Scanlon was way too smart and not quite arrogant enough to make such an obvious mistake. Besides, if he had been planning this the whole time, what was all that stuff about wanting Brandon to join the team permanently? What possible benefit was there to be gained by making that offer if it wasn't real?

And what about Catherine? He couldn't quite read her. What he did know, though, was that she was very interested in protecting her mentor. Did she see Brandon as a threat? If she thought it was in Scanlon's best interests, would she go behind her mentor's back? No way.

And so he was left with the only remaining option: That he hadn't met all the players in this thing. And at this point, he didn't think he wanted to.

Edwin Hamdi had received two e-mails regarding the Ukrainian warheads. The first was the one he had been waiting so long for: a properly encrypted and authenticated message saying that the warheads were real, operable, and that a deal had been agreed upon. The second had come a day later from Yusef's account, but clearly not written by him.

In slightly tortured spelling, it told the story of Yusef's accidental death from a rock fall and suggested that it might still be possible to complete the agreed-upon transaction in the event that the hurdles created by his unfortunate death could be overcome.

Having no other contact information, Grigori had sent the e-mail to Yusef's account where it had then been read by Ramez, his second in command. It was he who had forwarded the e-mail to Hamdi's account, along with a passionate note stating his willingness to die if necessary to complete the transaction. It was, after all, the will of God.

Hamdi held a printout of the email that he had unwisely made, running slightly shaking fingers over the black letters one more time before sliding it into a shredder.

Yusef had always been the weakness of the plan—his uniqueness, his irreplaceability. Virtually everyone else involved was expendable.

Ironically, perhaps, Ramez was in some ways an acceptable, if unwitting, substitute. Based on the information Yusef had provided, his young protégé was an educated, reliable man dedicated to the cause of peaceful Arab self-rule and not just senseless bloodshed. The problem was the Ukrainians. It had taken them a great deal of time to become comfortable with Yusef—a man who had spent years carefully building his credibility. It seemed unlikely that this Grigori would be interested in beginning that courtship process all over again. Not when they could sell to other buyers.

Of course, that simply could not be allowed to happen. Hamdi had purposely hidden the existence of the warheads from the American government and, therefore, was solely responsible for the government's inaction. If these weapons were sold and used in an attack on the United States, it would be his fault.

He put his elbows on the desk in front of him and let his head sink into his hands. This plan had been so long in its development—perhaps since he was a child, watching the newly christened Israelis march arrogantly through the land of his ancestors, taking what and who they wanted.

The sound of an opening door drifted in from the outer office, followed by a quiet knock. The only light in the room was provided by a small desk lamp, and Hamdi adjusted it so that it shone directly outward.

"Come."

The door swung open and Brandon Vale came through, prompted by a shove from one of the men behind him. He was wearing only a pair of jeans and a T-shirt with the slogan RUNS WITH SCISSORS.

"Have a seat, Brandon."

He didn't immediately obey, instead standing there trying to put detail to the figure behind the light. After a few seconds, he gave up and dropped into the chair in front of Hamdi's desk.

Despite the uncertainty of his situation and the hair still matted from bed, he appeared much more intelligent in person than in his photos. It was hard to quantify exactly—something in the subtle shifting of his features as he took in what was around him. It was enough to cause Hamdi himself to look around at the dim, empty office, to make sure there was nothing Brandon could use to identify it later. If indeed there was a later for him.

"I take it you wanted to see me?" Brandon said

finally. He didn't sound or look afraid, but the overall effect wasn't bravado or even genuine courage—more an acceptance of the fact that there were things he could control and others he could not. A very sensible philosophy.

"Richard Scanlon isn't in charge of this operation. I am."

Brandon nodded.

"I've seen to the closing of all your accounts—I even had that little safe-deposit box in Chicago emptied. I assume you're smart enough to know what you're dealing with here?"

Brandon crossed his legs, bouncing a bare foot casually in the air as he spoke. "The fact that Scanlon didn't come up with this all by himself? That someone is backing him? Sure. Why not?"

Hamdi waited to see if he would say more. He didn't.

"Richard has a great deal of confidence in you. He seems to actually believe you'll succeed in this theft."

"And you don't?"

Hamdi didn't answer the question, because he honestly wasn't sure of the answer. "Let's just say that I've been anxious to meet you. A man with so much power—"

For the first time, a hint of doubt crossed Brandon's face. "Power?"

"Of course. The lives of millions of people are in your hands."

Doubt turned to irritation. "You guys have really *got* to quit saying that."

"My apologies. May I ask you a personal question, Brandon?"

"Seems like you can do anything you want."

"An astute observation. Tell me, how do you feel about the position you find yourself in? Does a person like you even care?"

"It's a little late for an interview, isn't it? Seems like I already got the job."

Hamdi's smile would have been imperceptible, even if Brandon could see his face through the light. Scanlon was right. In his way, he was an impressive little bastard.

"I swear I don't know what's wrong with you people," Brandon continued. "Of *course* I care. Notice that no one's ever been hurt in a job I've done? Can you say that? I bet I have more of a respect for life than you."

Hamdi leaned back and watched the bouncing of Brandon's foot become manic.

It was hard to believe that the planet's future—or lack thereof—was going to rest on the narrow shoulders of a thirty-three-year-old thief.

Chapter Twenty-five

Daniel leaned back carefully, listening to the creaking wood for any sign of collapse. The building behind him, a massive structure with a gracefully arching roof and enormous holes that had once held windows, was in the final stages of its existence. He'd entered earlier through one of the many openings in its walls to explore, but the combination of darkness and debris made walking too dangerous. So now he was sitting in the dirt, back pressed against peeling boards, gazing out at the moonlit landscape.

Not that there was much to see. A flat plain extending to a distant mountain range that had swallowed the stars. It reminded him of an even more primitive airfield in Pakistan he'd visited years ago. What a cluster-fuck that had been—one of those missions that had the look of disaster even from the warmth and safety of an aircraft carrier. A lot of people had died that day. But not as many as would die if he screwed this up.

He looked at the glowing hands of his watch for what must have been the thousandth time and for the thousandth time felt a brief surge of adrenaline—something he'd thought he was long past.

Not so surprising, really. This wasn't exactly a typical operation for him. No government absolution, no high-tech military backing him up, no authoritative voice vibrating his earpiece. It was so much more complicated than that. Now he was taking orders from a nutty little crook no older than he was. And worse, he was unable to completely douse the spark of pride he felt at having been chosen by that crook for the only completely autonomous part of this mission.

Daniel pushed himself to his feet and started toward the dark runway in front of him. In truth, Brandon wasn't all that bad. Get him in shape and teach him to shoot, and he wouldn't be the worst guy to have watching your back in combat. Hell, with him on board, they'd have not only found Osama bin Laden, but made a killing selling all his stuff as souvenirs.

A distant star started moving a little too steadily, catching Daniel's eye and prompting him to pick up his pace a bit. This particular airfield was possibly the only thing in the operation that was almost completely free of drawbacks. It was about ten miles from the middle of nowhere, surrounded by nothing, and manned by no one. As Brandon had continually pointed out, though, that didn't necessarily mean it wasn't going to blow up in their faces. No complacency. Ever. In some ways, Brandon was very much an iPod-listening, Birkenstock-wearing, slightly mumbly version of Daniel's old team leader.

The light drew nearer and Daniel leaned his shoulder against an old shack about thirty yards from the fuel pump that would be the helicopter's destination. He was wearing a pair of black jeans, a black T-shirt, and black cowboy boots that made him virtually invisible if he stayed still.

He resisted the urge to raise a hand to protect his face against the sudden hurricane of dust, instead just closing his eyes and ignoring the million little needle pricks against his cheeks.

The chopper blades wound down and he slowly opened his eyes, letting them adjust to the glare of the helicopter's lights and watching the pilot jump. He seemed relaxed, confident. Not entirely unexpected since he'd made this run no fewer than a hundred times over the years with no problems.

Daniel waited until the man finished fueling before he started forward, screwing a silencer into the end of his pistol. Of course, it was just for show. A dead pilot wasn't going to get him very far.

"Nice rig," he said. "I used to fly one just like it."

The man dropped the hose and jumped back, staring as Daniel separated from the darkness.

"Who are—," he started, but then fell silent when the end of the silencer touched his forehead.

"Okay, so I was a little low when I guessed three hundred pounds."

Brandon adjusted his grip a bit, sliding his hands deeper into the unconscious woman's soft, damp armpits. The man holding her feet—Carl something—continued teetering backward obediently, but looked like he was ready to kill someone.

The wooden sidewalk they were staggering across

ran along the front of a Shell station built to look like an elaborate Old West stage stop, and it was a little too uneven to be practical. Things got a bit easier when they stepped onto the gravel parking lot and headed for a car parked away from the well-lit pumps. Brandon had originally chosen a nondescript economy car for the job, but based on the size of the station's night cashier, he'd had to go with an old Lincoln Continental instead. It wasn't just theater-seat and coffin manufacturers that had to adapt to the widening of America.

After a couple of precarious swings, they got the cashier into the foam-lined trunk. Carl reached up to close it, but Brandon stopped him, arranging the woman into what seemed like a more comfortable position and wiping away the spit running down the side of her mouth. Not exactly a featherbed, but no harm would be done beyond a drug hangover and a stiff neck.

"Couldn't we have left her?" Carl asked, rubbing one of his wrists. "They'd just figure she had a stroke or something. Bitch must weigh half a ton."

"What if she got an on-the-ball emergency room doctor who figured out she'd been drugged and brought her out of it while we're still on the road?" Brandon said, carefully closing the trunk.

Carl grimaced—a surprisingly menacing expression—and climbed into the driver's seat while Brandon ducked his head through the passenger-side window. "Park out on the highway and let me know if anyone comes up the road."

"I know. You already told me a hundred fucking times."

Carl, never one to hide his irritation with taking orders from an ex-con, stepped on the gas and forced Brandon to jump back in order to avoid getting hit.

"Screw you, too," he yelled when he was sure Carl was out of earshot.

He turned back toward the gas station, sliding his hands under his shirt to protect them from the cold night air. The gas station was perched on top of a mountain, about twenty yards west of a two-lane rural highway. The thin air couldn't hold the heat of the day, but neither could it seem to hold the bright fluorescent lights illuminating the pumps. They carved a circle a couple hundred feet wide and then faded into the shadows of the surrounding pine trees.

The phone in his pocket began to vibrate and he reached for it, taking a deep breath before picking up. When he heard the unmistakable noise of chopper blades, he let the breath out loudly.

"You're not going to believe this," Daniel shouted. "But it went perfectly! We're coming up behind the convoy now. ETA about two minutes to them and about another hour to your position."

"You're the man, Daniel. Call me if there are any problems."

"You got it. I'm out."

"Yeah!" Brandon shouted, raising his hand and turning toward two men walking a well-groomed poodle in the grass off to the side of the station. "We got the copter!"

Not only did they seem ambivalent about the news, they refused to even look at him.

His fault he supposed. They were the guys he was using to take control of the two chase cars protecting the semi. The problem was that both of them would scare their own mothers. They had faces, physiques, and body language that pretty much screamed former CIA assassin. And in order to counteract their "I'll twist your head off like a bottle cap" aura, he'd had to resort to desperate measures.

The answer to the question "How do you make two overly muscular guys with buzz cuts nonthreatening?" had come to him in a dream. Gay couple.

And not just any gay couple. To soften these guys, he'd had to go flamboyant—leaving them wearing a fair amount of pink and more than a little fringe. Sure, he could have gone the less humiliating hippy or handicapped routes, but what was the fun in that?

"One hour," he shouted, turning toward Catherine. "Everybody got that? One hour!"

She was sitting on the curb in front of the little general store eating what he estimated to be her fourth ice cream cone. When she'd taken the first one, she'd actually left money for it on the counter. Of course, he'd pocketed it.

"What do you think?" he said, walking up to her. "So far, so good, huh?"

"We haven't done anything yet," she pointed out. "This is the easy part. Isn't that what you told us a hundred times?"

He smiled and sat down next to her. "The reality

of being an outlaw's a little more nerve-wracking than the fantasy isn't it?"

She nodded miserably. "All I can think about is what will happen if we get caught. You know I haven't spoken to my family at all since this started? I have this elaborate scenario built up in my head where my mom's crying into one of those phones you talk over in prison—you know, the ones where you're separated by glass?"

"Yeah, I'm familiar with them."

She scrunched up her face in an apologetic wince. "It's not so much the possibility of going to prison as the fact that I can't exactly go on TV and tell everyone that those nukes are out there. Everyone would just think I'm a regular crook—" She winced again. "I just keep putting my foot in it tonight, don't I?"

"No worries. I understand what you're saying. If you want a piece of advice, it helps to try to live in the moment. If you think about right now and not a few days in the future, this is a hell of a rush."

"I guess. Not exactly the rush I was expecting, though."

"What were you expecting?"

"The thrill you get from, I don't know . . . sky diving."

"And what did you get?"

"The slow, crushing stress of waiting to find out if your biopsy's malignant."

He laughed out loud. "You paint such a pretty picture. You're right, though. You have to have a screw loose to do this for a living. And you have to be a complete lunatic to enjoy it. Which is probably a good thing. The world doesn't need too many of me."

"I don't know," she said. "There are a lot worse out there."

He pretended not to have noticed the compliment or the tone with which it was delivered. "Well, cheer up. I guarantee you there are no cops lurking in the woods and you can believe me when I tell you that I have no scruples at all about divulging top-secret information. I will personally tell your mother and the rest of the world what stand-up people we are if it comes to that. But who knows? It might not. It's only two A.M. and we've already got the copter and the cashier. Life is good."

"Thanks. I feel so much better," she slurred through a mouth full of ice cream.

"Oh, come on. You do a little, don't you?"

She smiled almost imperceptibly. "Okay. Maybe a little."

Brandon leaned over and grabbed the Coke sitting next to her, tossing it ten feet into an open garbage can.

"Hey! I was drinking that!"

"Not too many bathrooms once we get going," he said, starting around the side of the building. "And you've had enough caffeine."

It took a few moments for Brandon's eyes to adjust to the building's shadow and pick out the two men hidden in it.

"You two hear that?"

"Yeah. One hour. We're ready."

"Where'd you get that stuff?" he said, pointing to their clothing. They were both dressed entirely in black, with strategically padded pants and plastic body armor covering their arms, knees, and torsos.

"The motorcycle stuff you got us was sturdy as hell, but it was a little heavy," one of them responded. "Daniel found this. It's for mountain biking."

"Is it going to be enough?"

"We hope so, sir."

Brandon shrugged. "Me, too. So, one hour. And stop calling me sir."

"Are you absolutely sure I can't help you find anything?" Brandon asked.

There were a lot of drawbacks to his plan, but the inability to control stupid shit was practically a theme. And a perfect example of that theme was the jackass who was now wandering around the tiny store examining every item of snack food as though it were a precious gem. There hadn't been so much as a rabbit hopping across the highway in the last forty minutes and then this pinhead rolls up in his bright yellow Hummer.

"You should check out the Smart Food. That stuff kicks ass," Brandon said hopefully.

The man gave him a brief smirk and then went back to reading the ingredients on a box of Ho Hos.

Brandon glanced out the glass door and saw his gay couple watching. If this dumbass didn't make a decision soon, his morning was going to take a significant turn for the worse.

"Cheetos?" Brandon suggested, stealing a quick glance at his watch as the man started toward the counter carrying a bag of chips. He was one of those flashy young rich guys who seemed to have no time for anyone but themselves, which was a good thing, since Brandon was completely undisguised. The bitter truth was that everyone and his brother was going to know he pulled this job. Not only were there basically flashing neon signs pointing to him at every turn, but all those bastards needed to nail you these days was a little flake of skin or a hair. A quick match with a similar cast off from his prison bunk would add yet another conviction to what was becoming an overly long list of convictions.

"Ten minutes!" Brandon shouted, stepping through the glass doors and watching the taillights of the Hummer turn onto the highway and disappear.

Catherine was already sitting in the decoy truck hidden a few hundred yards up the road, and his gay couple was still walking their now somewhat tired poodle. Brandon was about to check his watch again when he caught the sound of a distant helicopter. Carl's voice crackled to life in his ear a moment later.

"I got the chopper and what looks like three sets of headlights. They're approximately five minutes from your position."

"Did everybody get that?" Brandon said, using the throat mike hidden beneath his turtleneck. "Five minutes."

They all responded and he started back to his cash

register, feeling the giddy light-headedness he always did when a job was about to go down. This time, though, there was a less familiar glimmer of dread beneath it.

They came around the corner in a perfect line, the unmarked white Peterbilt pulling a similarly unmarked white trailer, flanked by two nondescript Ford Tauruses.

They eased into the station and all three drivers got out. Brandon watched from behind a snack cake display as the guards looked around the station and, not registering a threat, went for the pumps. The truck didn't need refueling and the driver headed for the bathrooms. When he reappeared, he lit a cigarette and stood just outside the door.

The poodle began to bark right on cue, and its new owners cooed convincingly as they shepherded it toward the pumps. Still no recognition of threat from the guards. More like vague amusement.

Brandon started across the small store, opening the door, and stepping outside. At the sound of the little bell screwed to the frame, the quiet gas station erupted.

Pistols appeared from the pastel waistbands of the formerly innocuous gay couple's pants and the two body-armor-clad men hiding alongside the building burst out holding submachine guns.

"Anybody who moves is dead!" one of the men said. Brandon wasn't sure who, but the delivery was perfect. He almost threw his own hands up.

The team fanned out in a maneuver that could only be described as elegant, with one pistol-wielding and one machine-gun-wielding man covering each guard from an angle that wouldn't allow a stray bullet to hit anything that could blow them all up. Neither of the chase-car drivers—both formidable-looking men— had any chance to react at all. Surprise and fear crossed their faces for a moment, replaced quickly by anger and resolve as they slowly raised their hands.

The truck driver nearly sucked in his cigarette, freezing for a good three count before turning to run and finding himself staring down the barrel of Brandon's unloaded pistol.

"Relax, man. Keep smoking," Brandon said, locking the door without taking his eyes off the driver. Based on their information, he wasn't going to present any real problems. He wasn't a former cop or anything and not even much of a tough guy as truck drivers went. Plus, he'd been married for twenty-four years and had two girls in college. That kind of a lifestyle had a way of making a man sensible.

"Are you guys fucking crazy?" someone shouted over little Pierre's barking. "Do you have any idea how much security there is on this truck? There is no way you can get away with this. But you might still be able to run . . ."

Brandon grabbed the driver by the shoulder and pushed him in the direction of his two companions, who were now lined up against the pumps.

"Gentlemen, if I could have your attention, please," Brandon said, leaving the driver under the watchful eye of one of his armored colleagues and jumping up on the hood of a Taurus. "Obviously, we want what's in this truck. Now, I understand that some of you have police backgrounds and are good at what you do, but we've spent years planning and training for this and we're professionals, too. There's no reason for anyone to get hurt. Plan A doesn't include any violence at all. But most of our backup plans end up with all of you dead. In fact, I think it's fair to say that none of the men aiming guns at you can even remember how many people they've killed in their lifetimes."

His speech was having the desired effect. He definitely had everyone's attention, and the two guards seemed to be losing whatever confidence their work history might have provided them. On the negative side, the driver looked terrified. Brandon was going more for hopelessly intimidated. Intimidated people did exactly what they were told. Terrified people did stupid, pointless stuff.

"Look," Brandon continued. "This truck is not full of medication for your mom. Or an anthrax virus terrorists could get their hands on. It's just money. And not even *your* money. If it disappears, the whole thing's just gonna end up as a pissing contest between the government, the casinos, and a bunch of insurance agents. Nothing worth dying for. So if we all stay cool, in twenty-four hours you'll be sitting in a police station telling your story and we'll be sitting on some unextraditable beach sipping drinks out of coconut shells. Does everyone understand?"

They just stared.

"That wasn't a rhetorical question. Does everyone understand?"

Heads started bobbing and then a few mumbled yeses. Lucid, but not very enthusiastic. Brandon glanced at his watch. These stops were carefully monitored by the security company running this operation. They recognized that it was then the shipment was most vulnerable and timed the stops to the second.

"Okay, then. Let's saddle up."

The pumps were removed from the cars' tanks and the drivers were herded into their respective vehicles, with one swishy killer in each passenger seat. The two men in body armor climbed into the cab of the truck, dragging a black duffle behind them. The driver started to follow, but Brandon grabbed him by the back of the shirt, shaking his head and pointing to a set of headlights coming up the road.

The decoy truck, which he'd found on eBay, was an almost exact duplicate of the one containing the money: A ten-year-old white Peterbilt with a mattress behind the seats and an old-school bolt-on wind fairing on top.

It glided to a stop and Catherine jumped out, jogging over to him and giving the driver a quick appraisal. "Everything okay?"

"Perfect," Brandon said a bit hesitantly.

"Then why do you sound so worried?"

"Because it means all our bad luck is going to come at once."

She managed an eye roll that actually had some humor in it and then jerked forward and kissed him on the cheek. He was surprised enough to actually stumble backward.

"Good luck," she said, disappearing into the cab of the real truck and slamming the door behind her. Brandon stood there for a moment rubbing his cheek, then started pulling the driver toward the decoy.

Chapter Twenty-six

Brandon watched the truck Catherine was driving ease into the left lane and he leaned forward to see better. Instead of staring at the cash-stuffed trailer, though, he watched the dark windows, trying to get a glimpse of what was behind them.

"Did you see that kiss?"

The driver tensed, wringing a drop of sweat from his hand that slid down the steering wheel.

"My relationships with women have been screwed up my whole life, you know? Started with my mother, I think. Then I went into this kind of work and that made it even worse. I mean what kind of woman would put up with me running all over the country at a moment's notice and waiting for the cops to kick in our door? I'll tell you: Not good ones. Not ones like her . . ."

The driver's eyes were locked straight ahead and his face was frozen and pale enough to be almost corpselike. Brandon pulled the pack of cigarettes from the man's shirt, lit one, and held it out. "Seriously, man. You need to relax. Weren't you listening to what I said earlier? The only way you can get hurt is if you do it to yourself. And why would you, right?"

The man's nod had a panicked earnestness that made Brandon wonder if he was actually listening or if he was just in the mode of agreeing with everything. He accepted the cigarette, though, and it seemed to help a bit.

"Okay, Rob . . . It is Rob right? Rob Taylor?"

The particular tilt of this nod suggested that he was now aware Brandon knew where his daughters went to school. Definitely not a step in the right direction.

"Okay, Rob. Here's the deal. There's been no change. You're just going to drive this truck exactly like you would the real one." He showed the man a list of code words Scanlon had provided. "You're gonna check in on nice regular intervals just like you always do. The last thing you want is to get stuck in crossfire between us and a bunch of SWAT guys, right?"

No answer.

"Right?"

"Right."

Brandon reached beneath the seat and retrieved a belt made of surplus military webbing and parts from cell phones and walkie-talkies. The buckle had been replaced by a small padlock.

"Put this on under your shirt."

"What is it?"

"Just put it on, please."

A glance at the gun in Brandon's waistband brought Taylor around and he did as he was told, skillfully maneuvering the truck as he slid the belt around his waist. Brandon tightened it and clicked the lock shut, then flipped a switch that caused a red light to come on.

"We can hear everything you do and say over that thing," Brandon said. "It's essentially a speakerphone with an open line."

All true. It turned out that one of Scanlon's guys was a wizard with electronics.

He reached over and pulled up the man's shirttail. "See that wire? The thick black one? It's not actually a wire at all. It's plastic explosive. Not much. Just enough to cut you in half."

Now that was a lie. It was really a piece of stereo cable he'd picked up at Radio Shack.

"Oh, my God! Oh, Jesus!"

"Now listen to me, Rob. Concentrate now. If for some reason, you were to shut off the connection between us, then I can reroute the power to the explosive and . . ." He let his voice trail off, feeling increasingly guilty. He'd not only never hurt anyone in his history of criminal acts, he'd never threatened anybody. But there just hadn't been time to come up with something more elegant.

"I got a family. I—"

"Good," Brandon said. " 'Cause the last thing I want to do is blow you up. People getting cut in half by explosives tend to attract a lot of attention. And people in my profession hate attracting attention. We hate it more than anything."

He pulled a modified walkie-talkie from his pocket and spoke into it, confirming that his voice was clearly audible over the speakers installed on the belt.

"Okay, sounds good. You know, they say communication is the cornerstone of a good relationship."

"They do?"

"I think so, but like I said, I haven't had a lot of luck with relationships."

"I wonder why?"

Brandon grinned. "You know, if you think about it, this could be the best thing that ever happened to you. When it's all done, you can sue your boss for mental duress and probably collect workman's comp for the rest of your life."

Chapter Twenty-seven

As much as Daniel tried to fight the feeling—and he was fighting it hard—this was fun. Sure, the special ops missions he'd been involved in provided a hell of a rush and were satisfying on some deep patriotic level, but fun? Never. Too much blood and suffering.

Maybe Brandon wasn't as nuts as everyone thought he was. Which was crazier: getting rich stealing money from the air-conditioned homes of people who didn't need it or making twenty grand a year crawling around some godforsaken desert shooting people who'd never done anything to you? Not such a tough call when you thought about it in those terms.

The helicopter drifted down as it passed over a low, sunburned ridge, coming close enough for him to see the jagged rocks glowing in the dim morning light. The convoy was about a mile in the distance—two identical cars and two identical semis—moving steadily away from the reddening horizon. The rest of the road was completely empty—a shiny black ribbon going on forever in both directions. There was a stark beauty to it that made him feel good, like they might just pull this thing off. But then, he'd once had the same feeling in Iraq and that day had turned into a disaster.

A dull beeping started over his headphones and he glanced at the pilot, who was tapping the instrument panel with his knuckle.

"What?" Daniel said over the thumping rotors.

"Engine light," the pilot said.

"Bullshit!"

The man pointed to the gauge and Daniel leaned over, putting a hand on the grip of his pistol in case this was some kind of half-assed trick.

The light was actually on. Pulsing red and continuing to sound. So if it was a trick, it was a little more than half-assed. He'd put almost thirty hours in this particular model over the previous week and wasn't aware of any way to fake that warning unless it was a system put in place specifically in anticipation of a hijack. If that was the case, though, Scanlon hadn't known anything about it.

He glanced into the aging face of the pilot and saw a convincing mix of worry and outright fear—but he'd had that since Daniel first stuck a gun in his face.

"What's the problem?"

"I don't know." Another few taps on the gauge. "But we're going to have to set down."

"No!" Daniel shouted, as though he could keep them aloft by sheer force of will. He felt a trickle of sweat roll down his back as he looked out over the barren landscape. What now? Brandon had given him this job because he could think on his feet, but at this moment his mind was a blank.

"You said you could fly this thing," the pilot said, starting to sound a little panicked. "If that's true, then you know if we stay up here, we could lose the engine."

Daniel started to slide the gun from his waistband, but then stopped. It was easy to fall back on threats, but what good was that going to do now? He leaned forward in his seat and looked out at the convoy continuing blissfully up the road. What would Brandon do?

"Fix it," Daniel said.

"Fix it? I can't fix it! It's the fucking engine!"

"No way. It's a trick," Daniel said, keeping his voice completely calm. "You faked it."

"Are you kidding? How could I? There's a—"

"Shut the fuck up!" Daniel shouted and then immediately softened. What was it Brandon had told him? No one wanted to die for other people's heavily insured money.

"If this is some system you guys set up, you better fucking well turn it off. Because if we go down, I've got to cover my tracks. And that means I leave you in that seat with a big dent in your skull."

The pilot hesitated for a moment, then started to descend.

"Vegas control, this is helicopter 008 Echo. I have an engine light on and am landing immediately. Estimated position eighty miles west of Bridgeport."

"008 Echo, are you declaring an emergency?" came the response.

Daniel shook his head.

"008 Echo. Not at this time, tower. Will advise if I need assistance."

About a hundred feet above the deck the pilot increased power and slowed their descent, aiming for a relatively flat patch of ground just ahead. He was completely absorbed by what he was doing, with no thought at all to what would happen once they landed—a sure sign of someone who thought he might not survive long enough to be killed.

"Dumb fucking luck," Daniel muttered and then reached for the stick. He shoved it forward, dipping the helicopter's nose violently and listening to the pilot shout panicked obscenities as he fought to regain control.

The impact was a little more dramatic than Daniel had planned for. Just because you knew how to fly a helicopter didn't necessarily mean you knew how to crash one. His harness stopped him from going through the buckling glass in front of him, but he felt at least one rib—probably two—break as it came tight. The sound of the blades digging into the ground and the bending of metal penetrated his headphones for a moment and then was gone, disappearing into a silent darkness. Instinctively, his hand went for his gun and he managed to get a weak grip on it but couldn't do much more. He wasn't sure how long he spent in that semiconscious state, but when his vision finally cleared enough to look left, he found an empty seat.

Two clumsy kicks got the door open, but he was stopped by the harness when he tried to get out. A few seconds of fumbling and he was on the ground, tripping over rocks and pieces of what was left of the helicopter.

The pilot looked like he'd come through the crash significantly better off. He was running into the dawn, heading for the highway that was probably a little less than a mile away. Worse, he seemed to be holding a pretty good pace.

Daniel started after him at a slow jog, his head continuing to clear as the pain in his side intensified.

After the first minute of his pathetic effort at a chase, he was starting to think it was hopeless. He was slowly losing ground, leaving little doubt that the pilot would make the road. At minute two, though, the gap seemed to have stabilized. Minute three shrank it a bit.

Daniel knew he wasn't moving fast—his balance was still barely sufficient to negotiate the uneven terrain, and it was impossible for him to take anything but shallow breaths. What he was, though, was steady. It suddenly occurred to him that for an average person, even one much younger than the pilot, a mile-long run through the desert was a nearly impossible task.

It took a lot longer than it should have, but Daniel managed to close to within twenty-five yards of the man, who was now looking back over his shoulder every few seconds and nearly falling every time. He was obviously pushing himself too hard and his breathing was clearly audible as he started up a steep bench that climbed about a hundred and fifty yards before flattening out into the roadbed.

Daniel slowed slightly, matching the man's pace as they started up the grade, concentrating on keeping his stride even and relaxed. His vision was a hundred percent now, and his balance probably seventy percent. Overall strength was lower, probably fifty percent. And there was blood in his mouth. A lot of it.

By the time the pilot was a third of the way up the hill, he was expending more energy just thrashing around than moving forward. Daniel fought the urge to speed up, gauging that he'd overtake the man about twenty feet from the top of the hill and wanting to be as rested as possible when he did.

The pilot managed a final burst of speed when he saw he was about to be caught, but it wasn't enough. Daniel fell forward and batted the man's foot with an open hand, tripping him and leaving him on the ground gulping desperately for air. He didn't seem to have the strength to get up, so he tried to keep going by crawling through the loose rocks and dirt. Daniel rose and covered the distance between them at a walk, finally falling on the man and working an arm around his neck to cut off the air he so desperately needed. There were a few moments of increased thrashing and then the pilot passed out.

Daniel rolled off him and lay against the slope, searching for just the right rock. He finally found a properly jagged one and hit the unconscious man in the forehead a few times hard enough to raise a good bruise and cause a few shallow cuts that looked much worse than they were. Then he fished a syringe from his pocket and jabbed it into the pilot's thigh, depressing the plunger with one hand while he dialed his cell with the other. A moment later Brandon's strangely comforting voice was vibrating his ear.

"Yo."

"Hey. Got some bad news."

"Shit. What?"

"We, uh, crashed."

"Tell me this is a bad connection and you didn't say crashed."

"I said crashed."

"Goddammit! What happened? Are you okay?"

Daniel struggled to his feet and lifted the pilot over his shoulder, ignoring the sensation of his broken ribs slicing his insides. "I'm fine. A warning light went on and we had to set down. I made sure we went down hard."

"Shit! Do you think it was a trick? Something they set up in case they got hijacked?"

"I doubt it," Daniel said, choosing his footing in the loose soil carefully. "I told the pilot that if we went down I'd have to bash his head in and make it look like an accident to cover my ass."

The brief silence over the phone wasn't entirely unexpected. "Oh, man. You didn't—"

"Relax. He's fine. I gave him the tranquilizer and banged him up a little. It'll look like he got knocked out in the crash. The point is, I think he believed me. I don't think he wanted to die, you know?"

"Shit!" Brandon shouted again. "You're sure you're okay, though, right?"

"I've had worse," Daniel said, though he wasn't certain it was true.

"Okay. You've gotta make sure there aren't any tracks around the copter—that everything looks natural. You probably don't have much time before someone shows up."

"I'm on it."

"Then can you maybe hole up under a rock a little ways away? We can send someone for you tonight."

Daniel braced himself against a boulder and hopped off a two-foot drop, grimacing as the pilot's weight came down on his shoulder. He was pretty sure he had some internal bleeding. The question was whether or not Brandon needed to know that. There wasn't a whole lot he could do without jeopardizing the operation and he didn't need to be worrying about a wounded man on the field. "Yeah. No problem. Early tonight would be better, though, huh?"

Chapter Twenty-eight

"Goddammit!" Brandon shouted, kicking the dash-board repeatedly until he realized he was terrifying the already sweat-drenched driver.

He stopped attacking the dash and instead tapped out a manic, but less threatening rhythm on his knees. Stupid helicopter. Now he had to deal with the possibility that this was some signal Scanlon didn't know about.

"No!" he said out loud, causing the driver to flinch noticeably. "It happened, right? Nothing can be done. Nothing."

Normally, something like this would have caused him to immediately fold up his tent and send everyone home. Not really an option under the circumstances. In fact, he hadn't even bothered to think about a way to abort safely. If they were driving into a SWAT team, then they were driving into a SWAT team. At least this time he'd go down with a little style.

He shook his head violently. "Focus, dumb-ass!"

The sun was still low on the horizon, causing distended shadows to grow from the rocks and shrubs lining the road. Beyond that, it was impossibly bright. Generally, he wasn't all that shot in the ass with working under a spotlight, but timing and logistics had dictated that this thing go down in broad daylight. The upside, though, had been that they'd be able to do the heavy lifting on a straight, flat section of asphalt.

He stared out the windshield at the steep, twisting road in front of them for a few seconds and then rolled down the window to look back at the truck containing Catherine and his money.

"Son of a bitch," he muttered, pulling his head back in and putting a hand on the driver's damp shoulder. "It's not you, Rob. I'm just in a little bit of a bad mood."

"Okay."

Brandon's earpiece crackled to life with the voice of one of his men. He wasn't sure which.

"We've been notified that the helicopter had to make an emergency landing." The tone was that artificial calm all soldiers seemed to aspire to. There was nothing more unreliable than a man who didn't have the sense to know when to start panicking.

"They're sending a replacement copter."

"ETA?" Brandon said into his throat mike.

"A little less than an hour."

"Everybody get that?"

He counted the responses.

"How're you guys feeling about this road?"

There was a short pause before one of the armored men riding with Catherine answered.

"Is there any choice?"

"No."

"Then I guess we're feeling good about it."

"Shit," Brandon muttered, pulling out a heavily annotated map and confirming what he already knew: There wasn't a straight section of road for thirty miles—putting a bit of a damper on his plan to have Taylor pull up alongside the lead car and let him jump into the sunroof. The way his luck was going, they'd end up in a head-on. It looked like the steep, arcing hill just ahead was as good as it was going to get.

"What's the slowest you'd ever go up that next hill?" he said, pointing.

The driver swallowed hard. "I don't know. I . . . I can't make more than thirty fully loaded. I'm not lying to you, there's just—"

"So if you cut it to, say, twenty for a few seconds, it wouldn't be weird."

"No. There could be a slower vehicle on the road. Or a bad headwind."

"Okay. That's what you're going to do. And I'm gonna jump out. We ne—"

"Jump out? You can't jump out! What if your phone gets broke? What if the signal cuts off? What happens to me! I've got this bomb—"

"Dude! Relax, okay? Just relax. Do I look stupid to you? There are backup transmitters. Remember— if anything happens to you, I don't get my money. And I want my money. Right? That's the whole point."

The driver fell silent and nodded, dislodging a drop of sweat from his nose.

"I know it's hard, but you should try to enjoy this," Brandon said, opening his door and stepping out onto the running board. "You'll probably end up making a million bucks going on the talk show circuit. Think about it: You'll be rich and famous and I'll just be rich. You got the better end of the deal."

The seat belt he was gripping slipped and he swung out over the asphalt, barely managing to get hold of the windowsill in time to keep from falling. A moment later, a gust slammed into the door, pinning him between it and the frame. When the wind finally relented, he threw himself back into the cab.

"Okay, that was scary. Let's try plan B."

This time he kept the door closed and crawled through the window, feet first. At least he had something solid to hold, though finding the running board with his toe turned out to be more exciting than he'd expected. It took too long and too much adrenaline, but eventually he found himself standing in a relatively secure position outside the truck.

"Brandon!" he heard Catherine say over the radio. "What the hell are you doing?"

"I'm getting out!"

He had to shout over the rush of the wind and grinding of gears as the truck began to slow. "Okay, guys! Back off as far as you can and open your rear window."

"Roger."

"Rob!" he yelled through the open window. "Take it down to twenty."

"I'm at twenty."

Brandon looked beneath him at the road rushing by at what seemed more like a hundred.

"You sure?"

"I can read a speedometer!"

"Okay, okay. No need to freak out."

No more time for procrastination. He took a deep breath and let go, twisting to face forward and trying to hit the ground running, hoping that he might be able to stay on his feet. Instead, he pitched forward, slamming shoulder-first into the asphalt and rolling uncontrollably through the gravel at the edge of the road. When he finally came to a stop, he just lay there trying to assess the damage. He hadn't ended up under the wheels of the semi, which was good. But he felt like he'd been beaten with a bat.

He pushed himself to his feet and started a limping jog up the hill, craning his sore neck to see the white Taurus bearing down on him. By the time the car came alongside, he'd actually managed to increase his speed to a point that the burning in his chest was almost as sharp as the pain in his shoulder.

He reached out with his left hand and got hold of the sill of the open back window, but immediately began to stumble, his fingers slowly slipping.

"Slow down! I can't—"

An arm suddenly appeared from the passenger-side window and slammed painfully up between his legs, lifting him to the point that he could get his head in the window. He grabbed the edge of one of the seats as the pressure between his legs was replaced by a hand under his chin and another on the back of his head, pulling hard enough that he thought his neck would break.

"Goddammit!" he whined as he slumped into the

back seat, feet still sticking out the window. "You didn't have to do that!"

Unsure what part of him hurt the worst, he curled into the fetal position and took turns holding his groin and rubbing his neck.

The man in the passenger seat looked back at him, a deeply satisfied expression crossing his foundation-smoothed face. "Quit bitching and get your ass up. This is your fucking plan."

"Hey, screw you, too." He wiped a trickle of blood from his lip, wincing at the dagger-like pain in his shoulder. Scanlon's gorilla was right, though. No time to feel sorry for himself.

Brandon struggled into a sitting position and retrieved an elaborate video camera from the floor-board.

"Look out," he said, purposely kneeing the man who had pulled him inside as he stood up through the open sunroof. It was still early, but the wind blasting him was already getting hot. He squinted at the two semis in front of them and reached down to pat the driver on the shoulder. "Okay! You're clear. Pull up between Catherine's truck and the decoy."

Brandon jockeyed the camera into a more comfort-able position as the car accelerated. Catherine gave him a quizzical look and mouthed "Are you all right?" as they passed.

"Okay. Is everybody set?" he said into his throat mike.

Affirmatives from everyone.

"Okay, then. Let's go." He wedged his legs a little

tighter against the seats below, stabilizing himself as they wound along the road's sharp corners and steep rises. "You've got about forty minutes until the replacement copter comes overhead."

A moment later, a man in black body armor and helmet came through the truck's open passenger window, grabbing hold of the wind fairing and using it to pull himself gracefully on top of the cab. By the time the second man had completed the same well-practiced maneuver, his partner was already using a battery-powered drill to remove the bolts from the fairing. Brandon watched the whole thing through the movie camera propped on his uninjured shoulder.

Their inability to control public access to the highway had demanded a little creativity. While the traffic was incredibly light—particularly at dawn—it wasn't nonexistent. And that made it likely that someone was going to drive by and see his men applying enormous stickers to the side of a moving truck. Not exactly something you ran into every day and possibly worthy of a quick call to the police.

The answer had come to him while he was surfing channels on Catherine's TV. He'd landed on a game show where contestants risked their lives in all kinds of ill-conceived stunts for some meager prize or other. On that particular night, they had to ride a bike across a foot-wide plank suspended between two high-rises after eating live worms from a bucket of mud. Anyone who'd do that, he figured, wouldn't think twice about rappelling off the side of a moving vehicle.

Brandon zoomed in on the second man, unidentifiable in his helmet, as he pushed the fairing bracket out of the way and replaced the bolts with eyehooks that he then clipped himself and his partner into. Both men were also connected by climbing harnesses to the ends of a single rope, most of which was contained in a black bag between them.

"Come on, guys," Brandon said into his throat mike. "Let's pick it up. We've got to do this two minutes faster than your record, and these turns are gonna kill you."

Of course, he was just talking to relieve his own nervousness. The men on that truck had done this over a hundred times in training and were undoubtedly moving no faster or slower than they could.

The fairing came free and they threw it as far as they could off the side of the road, then climbed down between the cab and trailer.

"Thirty minutes," Brandon said as they played out the rope between them and then flipped it up onto the trailer.

"Careful, guys . . ."

They evened out the rope so that they each had the same amount, unclipped their safety lines and jumped out at precisely the same time. Brandon tensed as they swung away from the trailer and then slammed into its metal sides. When they were satisfied that they were stable, they began sliding the two massive sticker rolls from custom-made sheaths on their backs.

"Car! We've got a car coming!" the man in the passenger seat below him yelled.

"Everybody stay cool," Brandon said, making a bit more of a show of handling the camera. "This isn't a problem."

The two men hanging from the sides of the truck acted as though they hadn't even heard the warning—just like they were supposed to. One of them had already positioned the start of his decal and the other was struggling a bit as the truck came around a corner, causing him to arc out in the air.

"Hold it steady, Cath," Brandon said.

"You want to drive?" came the reply.

Of course there was nothing she could do. The road wasn't straight.

"Not for two hundred million dollars. You're doing great."

He could hear the car approaching in the oncoming lane and he kept his eye glued to the camera's viewfinder while concentrating on his peripheral vision. The minivan slowed and moved as far as possible onto the dirt shoulder, its driver pointing at the men dangling from the truck as his two children pressed their faces to the glass in back. Everyone was smiling and talking a mile a minute. Perfect. . . .

Once the car was out of sight, Brandon lowered the camera and glanced at his watch. "You've got less than fifteen minutes!"

"That's not helping!" one of them replied.

"Sorry."

They were swinging all over the place, despite Catherine's best efforts to take the apexes out of the curves. As one was pressed into the trailer, working furiously, the other hung helplessly in the air waiting for his turn.

But it was working. They continued to make progress and the decals actually looked fairly straight from Brandon's angle.

"Sorry, guys, but I've got to say it. Five minutes. The replacement helicopter is gonna come overhead in five minutes."

He used the camera's zoom to scan the sky. Nothing yet, but he could feel the sweat starting to turn cold as it ran down his back. He had a sixth sense for these things. Time was running out.

They were only a few feet from the back of the trailer, increasing their pace as the rolls got lighter. Just a few more minutes. That's all they needed.

"Oh-oh," he said as a tiny dot appeared in the direction of Vegas. "I see it! Finish up!"

The road in front of them swept right, bordering a deep, rocky valley. The oncoming lane looked clear, but it kept coming in and out of view, making it impossible to be sure.

"Pull back," Brandon shouted at the driver below him. "Move into the left lane and bring me up next to the cab!"

"What the hell are you talking about?" he said. "I can't see around these corn—"

A gun appeared in the hands of the man in the passenger seat and a moment later they were coming alongside the cab of Catherine's truck.

Brandon dropped the camera into the backseat and leaned out, grabbing the sill and trying to ignore the searing pain in his shoulder. The moment he had a grip, the car accelerated again, causing his legs to slide out of the sunroof and leaving him dangling from the truck's door, kicking for the running board. Catherine grabbed him by the back of his shirt with one hand and steered with the other.

When he'd found his footing he glanced right and saw his man pull out a knife and cut the rope he was suspended from. They were probably going in excess of thirty miles an hour and both men hit the road hard, rolling and skidding wildly along it. When they finally came to a stop, one jumped up immediately and began gathering the rope, while the other staggered toward the edge of the road, falling a few times before his partner caught up and wrapped an arm around his torso.

"A little help?" Brandon said, jumping up and trying to pull himself through the window. This had always been part of the plan and they had gotten fairly good at working together to get him inside the cab. Unfortunately, his injured shoulder wasn't doing much for his athleticism, and the curves were straining Catherine's ability to drive with her knees.

"Brandon! You're blocking me. I can't see!"

He stopped about halfway through the window and checked the road ahead. "A little more to the left. Good. Hold it there." He pushed forward, jabbing her with knees and elbows, while she tried to maintain control.

"Where's the copter?" he said, pulling his legs the rest of the way inside and dragging them across her on his way to the passenger seat.

She looked in the side-view mirror, adjusting it upward to view the sky. "A ways back still."

Brandon dialed Carl's number and pressed the phone to his ear.

"Yeah."

"Our men are down. Mile marker one ninety-two. The copter's a couple of miles behind us."

"I'm on it."

He stuffed the phone back in his pocket and leaned forward, looking at the vehicles in front of him. The decoy truck was continuing smoothly through the curves about a hundred yards in front of them, bracketed by the two chase cars. Their truck—the one with the money—now had a trailer proclaiming Budweiser to be Crisp, Clean, and Refreshing. That, combined with the missing wind fairing and Catherine's feminine arm hanging partway out the window, would make it completely unrecognizable. As long as they stayed close enough to the decoy truck and the chase cars to keep the GPSes happy, no one would be the wiser.

The sound of rotors became audible, and Brandon ducked down, watching the helicopter pass overhead and then retreat to a more discreet distance.

"Jesus," he said, flopping sideways in his seat.

"You almost gave me a stroke when you jumped out of that truck!" Catherine said. "Are you okay?"

"I'll live."

She let out a long breath and looked over at him. "I can't believe it worked. It did work, didn't it? They aren't just playing with us."

He shrugged painfully. "My instincts say we're okay. But I guess we'll know for sure soon enough."

She downshifted as the hill steepened.

"So, you were worried about me, huh?"

"No," she said, pulling a handkerchief from her pocket and holding it out to him. "You're bleeding."

He took it and dabbed at his forehead. "You're sure you weren't just a little worried?"

"Maybe a little."

He smiled. "Anything on the police scanners?"

"Dead quiet."

"Nice. Look, when we get to a place you can pass, I want you to pull ahead of those guys."

"Aren't we going to follow them?"

He shook his head. "With the copter up there, we don't want to give the impression we're tailing. We know where we're going, so we'll stay just ahead. It'll make it seem like their fault that we're so close."

She depressed the accelerator and they began closing the distance to the vehicles in front of them. He nudged her leg with his foot. "Pretty cool, huh?"

Chapter Twenty-nine

It was only a little after nine in the morning and Richard Scanlon's office had already turned claustrophobic. He strode out into the hallway and started down it, nodding silently to the people he passed and trying to find something to occupy his mind. He finally ended up in the empty break room pouring a cup of coffee that he didn't want.

Scanlon wasn't accustomed to feeling helpless, but there was no other way to describe his present situation. Not only was he not in charge of the drama playing out in the desert a few hundred miles away, he wasn't even involved. There had been no practical way to monitor communications and, frankly, there had been no point. The sad truth was that he would only be in the way. This was Brandon's show.

It was a critical lesson that was easy to learn, but almost impossible to adhere to: You pick good people and let them do their job.

He tried to fill his mind with the image of driving those warheads to Langley and ramming them down the throat of that jackass Paul Lowe.

Of course, that wasn't really the plan. They'd

actually be left on an uninhabited island for retrieval by the navy. But the end result would be the same. They would be kept from the maniacs trying to get them and the American government would finally be forced to let go of their obsession with state sponsorship and concentrate on the much more immediate threat posed by the weapons that were already out there.

"Richard?"

He turned and saw his secretary peeking around the doorway.

"There's a Steve Ahrens from the FBI here to see you. He doesn't have an appointment."

Scanlon stopped stirring his coffee and stared blankly at her. He'd known that eventually the FBI would be showing up on his doorstep, but not this soon. There was no way they could have tracked him down this quickly. No, that wasn't true. If the hijacking had gone wrong and his people had been caught, Brandon would gleefully give him up before the police even got the cuffs on him.

"Richard? Are you all right? Do you want me to tell him you're busy and have him come back?"

Scanlon blinked a few times and then just shook his head. "No. Have him wait in my office."

"Steve? I'm Richard Scanlon."

The man standing in the middle of the office was too young for Scanlon to have known from his own days at the FBI, but he'd heard the name. By all reports, a top-notch agent.

"Nice to meet you," Ahrens said, offering his hand. "I've heard a lot about you, sir."

Scanlon looked around his otherwise empty office. It seemed that they were alone. A good sign?

"Have I caught you at a bad time?" Ahrens said. "I know I should have called ahead."

"There are no good times, these days," Scanlon said, concentrating on keeping his voice calm and his posture relaxed. He sat in one of the chairs in front of his desk and offered the other to Ahrens.

"I take it you're aware that Brandon Vale broke out of prison recently," the young agent said.

"Your office called me. Thanks for the heads-up."

Ahrens nodded and held out a five-by-seven photograph. "We have an informant who thinks he's seen Vale in Las Vegas."

Scanlon examined the photo and then handed it back, making sure he didn't reveal the relief he felt. The Bureau wasn't on to him. Not yet.

"That could be my aunt, Steve."

"Yeah, it's not a great shot. Apparently it's from one of those camera phones, taken at the Rio. The informant knew him, though. Not well, but he'd met him before. Insists it's Vale. I figure the chance at about fifty-fifty."

Scanlon nodded slowly. "So what's your thinking?"

"Well, he had outside help on the jail break. There's no question of that. Honestly, though, the escape itself was a little strange."

"How so?"

"It wasn't a carefully planned, elaborate scheme like the other things we suspect him of. Left a lot to chance. Haven't figured that out yet."

Ahrens fell silent and Scanlon knew he had no choice but to throw in his two cents. It would seem odd if he didn't.

"I agree. He's a planner. There's more there."

"Yeah. I'll get it. I just need some time. Anyway, back when he was working for you, it seems pretty obvious that he was casing the place. But he never talked. Did you ever figure out what he was after?"

"Not for certain. It's Vegas—there's a lot of money around. Casinos, transfers, wires. He was like a kid in a candy store, I would imagine."

Vague, but essentially true. He'd planned carefully for a conversation with the FBI, though not this one precisely.

"Could he still be after one of those things? Maybe there were other people working with him? Maybe they finished the groundwork and now that they're ready to pull the job, they need Vale back?"

Scanlon shrugged. "Or maybe he just wanted out of prison and paid someone."

"Yeah, that's the obvious answer, but honestly he didn't have that much time left. And why come back here? That suggests something to me."

"It's interesting conspiracy theory. And possible, I suppose. Though I have to tell you that we went back and changed every security procedure I'd been involved with. Cost millions."

Ahrens leaned back in his chair, a pained expression

spreading slowly across his face. "Then maybe he's after you for helping to put him away."

"After me? You mean out to do me physical harm? Oh, I doubt it."

"So you're not worried he might just walk up and shoot you?"

"Nah. Not his style. I like your first theory better. Do you have any idea how embarrassing it was for me when we discovered who he was? If he wanted to get me, he'd come here and pull whatever job he'd been planning—make me look like even more of an asshole than he already has."

Ahrens nodded thoughtfully. "I wonder. Prison can change a man, you know?"

Scanlon tried to keep his expression passive. Just what he needed—the goddamn FBI crawling all over him in the interest of protecting him from Brandon Vale.

"Trust me, Steve. I know this guy. He'd figure you're watching and stay as far away from me as he can."

"Yeah," Ahrens said, standing and extending his hand. "You're probably right. Thanks for your time. And if you wake up at night with any brilliant ideas, give me a call. I could use a few."

Chapter Thirty

"Where are they?" Catherine said for what must have been the fiftieth time.

It was ten thirty in the morning and the unforecasted fog Brandon had been hoping for was nowhere to be found.

He squinted through the windshield glare at the stop-and-go traffic, spotting one of the chase cars about fifty yards ahead. A quick check of his side mirror revealed neither the decoy truck nor the other chase car.

"Relax, Cath. We're in San Francisco traffic. The people monitoring the GPSes are going to give us a boatload of slack. There's no way to stay together in this crap and they sure as hell don't expect anyone to steal their money now. Even if you figured out a way to offload the truck under the noses of a thousand commuters, the cops would be able to catch you on a skateboard.

"Maybe we should slow down," she said, staring into her mirror and coasting up too fast on the Porsche in front of them.

"Cath!"

She slammed on the brakes and he lurched forward, grabbing the dash.

"I'm sorry. I—"

"Jesus Christ!" he said, cutting her off. "What's your job? To get us to the Fed without crashing, right? Let me worry about where everyone is."

She tried to look away, but he could still see her distraught expression.

"Hey, I'm sorry, Cath. But all it takes is one little fender bender and everything goes up in smoke."

"I know," she said finally. "You're right. I shouldn't be thinking. I should just drive."

"Come on. Don't be that way. You should always be thinking. I'm just asking you to focus on what you're doing right now. You've driven this route, what, five times before? And all in worse traffic than this. Everything's gonna be fine."

"There's so much . . . It's hard."

"I know."

He watched her carefully, making sure she was paying attention to the road. "What are you thinking about?"

"Everything. Terrorists. Nuclear bombs. You. Me. Us. The guy driving the other truck. World War III . . ."

He smiled and shook his head. "Is that all?"

"The police. I've been thinking about them, too. Oh, and that helicopter . . ."

"Look, I know exactly what you're going through. I have the same problem. But how many of those things can you do anything about from behind the wheel of this truck?"

"None, I guess."

"You guess?"

"Okay. None."

He glanced in the side mirror again and saw the decoy truck appear around the corner. "There it is. Don't look! Watch where you're going. But trust me it's there."

She seemed to relax a little, but her knuckles were still white around the wheel.

Brandon rolled down the window and hung partway out of it. The helicopter wasn't visible, but he knew it wasn't far. With the buildings rising all around them, it would have to be virtually overhead to be visible. At this point, though, air cover was more a formality than anything else. When Scanlon had created the transfer protocols, he'd assumed that delivery was a foregone conclusion by this point. Shame, shame.

Brandon heard the crackle of static in his earpiece and pressed a finger against it to hear more clearly.

"This is car one. We've reached the Federal Reserve Bank and are beginning to circle the block per procedure."

Brandon rolled his eyes and imitated the deep, businesslike voice on the radio. "We're beginning to circle the block per procedure."

"Now who's not focusing?" Catherine said, clearly nearing the end of her rope on this thing. Any further attempts to lighten her mood might prove dangerous, so he just moved a hand to his throat mike. "Copy that."

She downshifted and checked her mirrors, easing the truck right around a sharp corner. "Here we go."

The Federal Reserve Bank of San Francisco was a predictably imposing building that looked like it could survive a direct hit by one of the nuclear bombs Richard Scanlon was so anxious to get his hands on. Across the back of the building, though, was a surprisingly run-of-the-mill delivery area—simple bays where various types of vehicles dropped off cash, checks to be cleared, and all the other things that made America great. Security wasn't as impressive as most people would have imagined—just an easily climbable chain-link fence and a couple of guards.

Brandon slid the walkie-talkie from his pocket and pressed the button on its side while Catherine continued to creep forward through the traffic.

"Rob, can you hear me?"

He'd been checking in every hour with the truck driver, trying to make sure he was as calm as a man who thought he had an explosive locked to him could be.

"I can hear you."

"Hey, it's almost over. Before you know it you'll be sitting around with Oprah telling her your story. Okay. Here's the deal. You're going to do everything exactly like you normally do. We couldn't get the combination for the lock on the back of the real truck, though, so we jammed the one we put on your truck. If they ask you about it, just say you don't know what's wrong with it. No explanation—you just want to get out of there and go home, right?"

"Yeah."

"Okay, then. I'll be listening in through the phone

on your belt. I've also got people inside the Fed, so any hand signals or written notes are going to be a really bad idea for you."

All lies, of course. He had no one inside, and hadn't been able to figure out if the Fed monitored radio and cell signals in the dock. Most likely, they didn't, but he couldn't take that chance.

"I understand."

"Rob. Is this your money?"

"No."

"Is anyone going to be hurt by me stealing it?"

"No."

"Okay, then. When you come back out, you're going to follow the chase cars. They're going to take you somewhere to get that plastique off you and they're going to get you some pizza and hold on to you until we can offload the real truck and get out of town. Probably twenty-four hours or so. I don't want you to worry about it. We haven't hurt anyone in this thing and there's a reason for that. If I get caught, I don't want to get nailed for murder and spend the rest of my life inside, right?"

"Right." Even over the marginal connection, he sounded skeptical.

"Good luck, Rob." One last look at the walkie-talkie and he switched it off. It was out of his hands now.

Catherine stepped on the clutch and began revving the engine in a way that made it sound like the truck was about to stall. They were about a hundred yards from the gate leading to the Fed docks—close enough for him to make out two uniformed guards standing on the other side of the fence.

"Okay, slow it down," he said.

Catherine rode the clutch to a full stop and then used it to jerk the truck briefly forward a few times. It didn't take long for the horns to start and then for the traffic behind them to begin death-defying maneuvers to get around.

"I see it!" Catherine said. "Coming up behind us."

Brandon adjusted his side mirror slightly and watched the decoy truck slowly close on them. Catherine shut off the ignition for a moment, turned on the flashers, then started it up again, revving the engine wildly and lurching toward an empty bus stop a few feet from the dock gate.

"Watch your timing," Brandon cautioned.

"What do you think I'm doing?"

"Sorry. Keep your eyes on the road and I'll watch the decoy. It's thirty yards back."

She continued jerking forward as the traffic flowed around them, grinding gears and feathering the accelerator artistically.

"Twenty yards."

When they got to the bus stop, she pulled into it and stalled the motor. After a few futile-sounding attempts to get it started again, Brandon jumped out and crawled beneath the cab, pretending to search for the cause of their engine problems.

He wiggled along the asphalt, watching the wheels of the decoy truck as it rolled by and stopped in front of the Fed entrance. A moment later, the gate began to open and the truck pulled through.

"Car two passing by the Fed," he heard in his

earpiece. "The truck has entered and we're starting around the block."

Brandon's heart was pounding a mile a minute—just like it always did. Not at the possibility of being caught, which had never scared him for some reason, but at the thought that this thing might actually work.

"The truck's backed into the bay and stopped," Catherine said over his earpiece.

"This is car one. We've called in and confirmed delivery."

"Car two. We've called in delivery."

"Jesus," Brandon whispered to himself, scooting into a position where he could see through the bottom of the Fed's fence. The decoy truck was just visible sticking out of the center bay. He assumed that the driver was out of the cab unhooking the trailer but without an open line to him, that was only an educated guess. Just as likely, he was telling his story to Fed security and calling the cops. No sense in worrying about that now.

While this plan left more things to providence than he normally would have tolerated, it wasn't the worst thing he'd ever come up with. The idea was simple: If it was impossible to steal the money on the open road, you had no choice but to steal it at the Fed.

The GPS system used by the security company for monitoring the convoy wasn't sensitive enough to know the difference between sitting in the Fed's delivery dock and sitting twenty yards away in the bus stop, so their slightly outdated technology was telling them—and the chase cars were confirming—that the money had been delivered. The only thing going on that was even slightly out of the ordinary was the Budweiser truck broken down just outside the gate.

"This is car one. The helicopter has confirmed delivery."

"Yes!" Brandon said, a little too loudly. Only one more hurdle. Assuming the driver hadn't ratted them out, the Fed guys would be noticing that the lock on the trailer was jammed. When they got it off and found the truck full of the expected bags, they'd call in the final delivery confirmation.

He was surprised when he saw the trailerless decoy truck begin to roll out of the bay after only another minute. He'd figured on it taking a while to cut the lock off, but they must have had problems with it before and been prepared.

He dragged himself from beneath the truck, wincing at the excruciating ache coming from his injured shoulder. Catherine fired up the motor—stalling it a few times before bringing it to a sickly purr.

He jumped in, keeping his eyes on the cab of the decoy truck as it disappeared around a corner.

"Oh, my God . . ." Catherine said in a low voice that was hard to hear over the engine.

"What?"

"You did it. You actually did it."

He smiled broadly. "Was there ever any doubt?"

"Yeah. There really was. Now can we get the hell out of here?"

He shook his head. "With all the confirmations in,

the security company will be shutting down its tracking operation pretty fast—they've been at it nonstop for over fifteen hours after all. But let's give 'em a few minutes to make dead sure no one's still watching."

She worked the accelerator to make the truck seem as though it was still warming up and Brandon rubbed his hands together vigorously, smile ever widening.

"You're in a good mood," Catherine observed.

"Are you kidding? If I was a football player, I just won the Super Bowl. If there was a Nobel Prize for larceny, I'd be composing my speech right now. In fact, I'd be right at the part where I thank all my lackeys."

She didn't turn toward him, but her teeth flashed briefly in the sunlight. "I'm curious. Does this feel better than normal?"

"What do you mean?"

"You know, because you didn't do it for yourself. That you put yourself at risk for other people."

"I don't know. Are you going to let me roll naked in the money?"

"Maybe if we have time—"

"Before you shoot me?"

Her smile disappeared so suddenly, he wondered if it was ever there. "You still think I'd do that?"

Brandon turned in his seat and examined the side of her face. "You know, I really don't anymore. I actually think you'll be surprised when they do it. But then you'll just put it out of your mind and keep marching on like the good soldier you are."

"I—"

"Time to go," he said, cutting her off.

She glared at him for a moment and then shoved the truck into gear, easing back out into traffic. "You're a hell of a clever guy, Brandon. But you're paranoid."

He nodded slowly. "You have no idea."

The way he let the sentence hang seemed to worry her. "Is that supposed to mean something?"

"I hope you believe me when I tell you that I wish it didn't have to be this way."

"You're starting to scare me, Brandon."

The concept he'd presented to her and Scanlon was that the security firm would just turn off the GPS monitors upon delivery confirmation and go home. After that there would be no record generated and so the truck would essentially be lost in space. They'd just drive to the warehouse he'd rented, turn on the signal jammers and unload the money at their leisure.

Of course, it wasn't really that simple.

"Remember what I told you about details, Catherine? It's all about the details."

"Oh, no," she said quietly. "Brandon, tell me you didn't screw us on this thing."

He shrugged. "Well, you do have a little problem."

She turned left along the route they'd laid out and found traffic light enough to allow her to speed up a bit. When she spoke again, her voice had gained in volume. "What problem?"

"Think about it, Cath. How long before the Fed guys realize that trailer is full of nickels, ones, and newspaper?"

"We figured about two hours."

He nodded. "And how long for us to unload?"

"About five hours to scan all the bags for GPS transmitters and load them into vans."

"So there are three hours that they know they've been ripped off and we're still digging around in the truck. What will they do with that overlap?"

"They'll try to track the GPS signals in the money bags. But we've set up the jammers in the warehouse so there's no way they can get a signal."

"And?"

"And what?"

He shook his head in disappointment. "I'm going to tell you the secret of planning great crimes, Cath. Are you listening?"

She watched him out of the corner of her eye, but her expression was unreadable.

"One word: perspective."

"Perspective," she repeated.

"Exactly. You come up with your plan and then put yourself in the shoes of everyone involved. An amateur will always run through things from the perspective of the criminal—themselves. In your case, everything you see through the window of this truck. I, on the other hand, will run through the job a hundred times—from your point of view, from the point of view of the cops, from the point of view of some guy walking by our broken-down truck on his way to Starbucks—"

"What the hell are you trying to say, Brandon? That you screwed me on this? That you sabotaged the job?" Her voice was nearly a shout now, despite the open windows and their proximity to about a thousand ears. "You don't care anything about those warheads or the people they could kill. You—"

He reached over and clamped a hand over her mouth. "So why don't you take a shot at answering my question again. When the security company people figure out they've been had and turn their monitors back on, they won't get a signal. What then?"

"What do you mean what then, you son of a bitch?" she said when he pulled his hand away.

"I mean, if you were them, what would you assume?"

"That the signal was being jammed."

"Right. Thank you. And by then they'll probably have figured out that the Budweiser truck broken down next to the Fed had something to do with all this. What will they do with that information?"

Catherine was silent for a moment, turning the question over in her mind. "They'll calculate how far we could have gotten in the time we've been missing, then they'll call the phone companies, the trucking companies, and anyone else who uses satellite transmissions to find out where they're having signal problems."

"I knew you had it in you," Brandon said.

"How long have you known this?"

"I don't know. A few years?"

Her eyes narrowed dangerously. "Fine. What now?"

He shrugged. "The Bay Area is a signal transmission disaster—what with all these mountains and valleys and buildings. All you need is a quiet natural dead spot to unload."

"And I suppose you know just the place."

"Coincidentally, I do."

"What do you want?"

"I want to survive."

"Paranoid," she repeated, bringing the truck to a stop at a red light.

"Look, my job is done—terrorists and warheads inhabit your world, not mine." He opened the door and slid out onto the street. "Keep heading toward the warehouse. In a little while, when I'm confident I'm not being followed, I'll give you a call and tell you how to get to a dead spot where you'll have all the time you need."

She refused to look at him, instead staring straight ahead through the windshield. It wasn't really how he wanted to say good-bye, but there wasn't much of a choice at this point.

"It's been nice knowing you, Catherine. Good luck."

Chapter Thirty-one

Steve Ahrens stood just inside the yellow police tape surrounding one of the bays at the back of the Federal Reserve building. If he had his way, he'd have shut down the whole block, but the bank was just too important. The flow of trucks, vans, and armored cars continued unabated, weaving through the investigators and lab techs inhabiting the fenced parking area.

Not that it really mattered. There were no answers here. He glanced up at the top of the building and the deep blue sky beyond. Nice afternoon, though.

The representative from the Fed was standing next to an empty semitrailer having a heated conversation with the assistant special agent in charge of the San Francisco FBI office, though they were too far away for Ahrens to hear what they were saying.

He tried to match their grave, angry expressions, but after only a few seconds broke into a smile again. In truth, this was one of the best days of his career. The terrorism and white-collar crime that the FBI was so focused on these days, sucked—a nasty combination of futile, depressing, and dull. But this was a whole different ball game. It would be entirely accurate to say that there was nothing in the world he would rather do than spend the next few weeks figuring out how Brandon Vale had pulled this off. God bless him.

Ahrens shoved his hands in his pockets and strolled toward the trailer, stopping when he was close enough to hear the two men's conversation, but not so close as to be noticed.

". . . so when you couldn't get the lock off the back, that didn't raise any alarms?"

"Not really. It wasn't the first time we've had to cut it off. You know, those things get old, they rust, they malfunction. It happens."

The FBI man sighed quietly, taking on a vaguely depressed expression that Ahrens just couldn't understand. Maybe it was that the ASAC was so much older. Whatever it was, though, he seemed inexplicably blind to how incredibly lucky he was that someone had chosen his jurisdiction to walk away with the better part of two hundred million dollars. It was like winning the cop lottery.

"And it took you another four hours to figure out the money was gone?"

"Three and a half," the Fed representative shot back. "The bags we offloaded first had a lot of change and ones, which isn't all that unusual. When we noticed we were a quarter of the way through the truck and the denominations hadn't gotten any larger, we started to get suspicious. That's when we dug to the back and found the bags full of newspaper. At that point we called the security company and you."

Ahrens glanced toward the back of the bay and spotted the security company's rep talking urgently into his cell phone. A moment later, he hung up and started in their direction.

"Special Agent Dolan?"

"What?" the FBI ASAC snapped.

"The helicopter pilot's still unconscious, but now they're thinking he's been drugged. The chase cars, the truck, and the drivers have all fallen off the face of the earth."

"And the GPSes?"

"We stopped monitoring them when the Fed called in a safe delivery. No way to retrieve the data now— it doesn't record anywhere."

"But they were working until then."

"Five by five according to our people. They've turned everything back on now."

"And?"

"Nothing. No signal at all."

Ahrens crossed his arms and leaned back against the trailer, watching an agent a few years younger than him jog up.

"Have you gotten anything on signal jamming?" Dolan asked him.

"We've talked to everyone we can think of and no one is aware of any strange dead spots."

"So no one's actively jamming the GPS signals."

"That's our read, sir."

"Then they've set up in a natural dead spot. How many within a couple of hours of here?"

"Hundreds," the young agent replied. "They also

could have lined a building with signal absorbent material. We're checking with all the manufacturers about recent purchases."

Another long sigh. "And the Budweiser truck?"

"We've talked with every distributor and trucking company we can find. As far as we can tell, that truck doesn't exist."

Ahrens wandered back out of the bay, ducking under the tape and scrolling through the address book on his phone. When he found the number he was looking for, he hit dial.

"American Security Holdings."

"Richard Scanlon, please. This is Steve Ahrens."

"He's out of the office. Let me see if I can connect you to his cell."

The phone went silent for a few moments before being picked up again.

"Steve. What can I do for you?"

"Guess where I am."

"Where?"

"Standing in the loading dock at the San Francisco Federal Reserve Bank."

Silence.

"Are you there still there, Richard?"

"I'm still here. But I'm not sure I want to be."

Ahrens grinned. "When you and I were talking this morning that brilliant little bastard probably already had the money hijacked."

"The money transfer from Vegas."

"Yup."

Ahrens had to pull the phone away from his ear to

bring the stream of obscenities that followed to a listenable volume.

"We set that goddamn thing up so it would be impossible to get to! And then we rearranged all the procedures after he went to jail. Shit, I was just talking to some of the guys who have the security contract on that. They had the thing down to a science."

"Apparently not enough of a science," Ahrens responded.

"How sure are you that it was Vale?"

"No evidence at all at this point, but come on. Who else?"

"How?"

"I'm not entirely sure yet, but I've got a few ideas."

"Shit. Look, I've got to run, but call me when you put the details together. And if in the meantime you catch that son of a bitch, do me a favor and shoot him in the ass."

Chapter Thirty-two

"Nice shoes."

Brandon glanced down at his feet and fought back a grimace. They weren't shoes. They were work boots. Honest-to-god work boots. He'd found a secondhand clothing store that let him trade his expensive new threads for a basic jean sweatshirt ensemble and a few measly dollars.

"Thanks."

The man sitting on the other side of the tiny room had a thick, tangled beard and an insane glint in his eye that made him look like an unhinged member of the ZZ Top fan club. Combined with his ragged and malodorous clothes, he'd pretty much nailed the shopping-cart-pushing homeless-man thing. Brandon was going for more of a "hardworking guy down on his luck" look.

"Nice pants."

Brandon nodded noncommittally. "Thanks."

They both jumped up when a plump woman in her late twenties poked her head in. "I'm ready for you now, Brandon."

He walked hesitantly into the small, cluttered office and stood facing the desk. "I'm Jennifer Ralston," she said, sticking her hand out. "I hear you wanted to talk to me."

She had an unnervingly steady gaze and a handshake that hovered somewhere between empowering and overpowering.

"Brandon Ellis," he said. "But I guess you knew that already."

Ralston, by all reports a tireless advocate for those who wanted to better themselves, ran the homeless shelter Brandon had slept in the night before. And though he really had no interest at all in bettering himself, he was willing to fake it occasionally.

"So what can I do for you, Brandon?"

"I need a job and I heard you might be able to help me find one."

Her expression wasn't suspicious exactly, but it was clearly designed to impart that she'd heard every hard-luck story ever devised. "I see . . . Tell me, what brings you to us, Brandon?"

It occurred to him how much fun it would be to just tell her the truth. He was willing to bet that she hadn't heard anything like *his* story before.

"I suppose the same thing that brings a lot of people here. I moved from the Midwest with barely enough money to make the trip, had some bad luck . . ." He let his voice trail off for a moment. "And here I am."

"Do you have a drug problem? Please excuse my bluntness, but I've found speaking directly is the best way to communicate. Understand that I'm not being judgmental. We have all kinds of programs to help you."

This really sucked. Couldn't Catherine have had the

simple decency to leave her cash-stuffed purse open on the kitchen table instead of demanding a fistful of receipts every time he spent a quarter? Now he was out on the street with no money, no IDs, and no bank accounts. At least none he wanted to risk trying to get to.

"No drug problem," he said, not meeting her eye. "Can't even afford to drink anymore."

She drummed her fingers on a stack of notebooks, silently appraising him.

No question, she was a tough nut. At one time or another, she'd probably been faced with half the con men, sociopaths, and grabby losers on the planet. But he wasn't asking for much—just a way to make enough money to get him across the border.

"I do have some contacts, Brandon. But I also have a lot to lose by calling them on your behalf. I've used my credibility with them to get a lot of people jobs—to help a lot of people. And every time I send them someone who . . . who isn't up to it, I lose a little bit of my ability to help people in the future."

He nodded. "I totally understand, Ms. Ralston. But I'm really smart . . ."

That was true.

"And I'm super hard working . . ."

A bit of an embellishment.

"I've just had some bad luck lately . . ."

The understatement of the year.

He hit her with his most earnest and subservient smile, but found it difficult to keep it plastered to his face. It was horrifying enough to have to get a job, but to have to beg for one? That was just cruel.

Chapter Thirty-three

"Tree. Out. Yes?"

Brandon wiped the sweat from his face, forgetting to take off his glove first and leaving his eyes full of dirt.

"Goddammit!" he shouted, blinking through the tears as the tiny Mexican man looked on impatiently.

"Brandon! Tree! Yes?"

"Hey, don't mind me. I'm just going blind here," Brandon replied. The Mexican just shook his head in general disapproval.

They were standing on the expansive lawn of some semi-rich guy who apparently hadn't been watering his plants. The trees in front of the house had dropped all their leaves and the shrubs were turning an alarming shade of black.

Why was this his problem? Because that evil witch Jennifer Ralston had gotten him a job on a land-scaping crew. Now he hadn't been expecting a job selling lingerie to supermodels, but he had been hoping for something air-conditioned. A cushy banking gig. Or a security guard. Yeah. That would have been sweet.

"Tree," the man said for the third time, jabbing a

finger at it and then a thumb toward the truck in the driveway.

"Lunch," Brandon countered.

"Cómo?"

"Lunch! Uh . . . *Almuerzo. Si? Almuerzo.*"

The man glanced at his watch, a bit confused. *"Son las diez."*

"Bullshit."

He held his wrist up as proof. Nine fifty-eight A.M. How was that possible? That meant he had . . . six more hours of this.

Another quick jab in the general direction of the tree and the man was off, leaving Brandon to sag against his shovel. His injured shoulder was killing him, though he knew that it was more psychological than physical—his subconscious protesting this waking nightmare.

There had been nothing about the heist in the local paper. The cops had apparently decided to keep things quiet. That wouldn't last long, though. Pretty soon, his picture was going to be on every television in America and the million problems he already had would double. At least.

If he were more of an optimist, he'd just lie low until the nuke story broke and then reappear just in time for the parade in his honor. A vague smile spread across his face as he pictured himself sitting on a flower-covered float, perfecting that insincere wave that beauty contestants did so well. Brandon the Savior. Brandon the Hero.

It wasn't going to happen that way, though. If there

was one thing the government didn't like, it was to be embarrassed. They'd sweep the whole thing under the rug, placating Scanlon and his crew with this promise or that and then sending a hit squad after the little thief who had made it all possible.

It was getting hard to keep track of his ever-expanding fan club: Scanlon's guys, that creepy asshole who'd snatched him from Catherine's place, the cops, the FBI. And who knew? If things went right, maybe the Ukrainians and a bunch of Arab terrorists would join up, too.

On the bright side, though, he'd just stolen a quarter of a billion dollars. No one could take that away from him. Figuratively speaking, anyway.

He stuck the shovel in the ground and slammed a foot into it, ignoring the woman staring at him through a bay window about thirty feet away. She'd been there on and off all morning, obviously worried that the men crawling all over her yard were going to steal her blind the moment she turned her back. Not that it was a bad idea, but it would be a little obvious if he tried to wander off with a big screen TV shoved down his pants.

A few more semienergetic kicks to the shovel got him nowhere. Roots. Or rocks. He sagged on the handle again. Nothing was ever simple.

"When I told them you'd get a job, they all said I was crazy."

He pretended he didn't hear and went back to digging.

"Brandon?"

"Very clever. My hat's off to you. Now go back and tell them you didn't find me."

"It's a little late for that," Catherine said.

He finally turned to face her. She was standing there in a pink skirt and white blouse, arms crossed in front of her chest and eyes downcast. At that moment, there wasn't anywhere in the world she wouldn't have seemed out of place.

"Maybe it's not you or Richard, but somebody out there wants me dead. You'd be stupid to risk me getting caught and telling my story."

She shrugged. "We have lousy criminal minds. Isn't that what you keep telling us?"

Brandon waved a hand around at the other men on the crew. "Which is why you decided to come here and kill me in front of a bunch of witnesses?"

"Stop it, Brandon. You know I wouldn't ever hurt you."

"Then what are you doing, Catherine? Wait. Let me guess. You're here to give me my cut. That's mighty big of you."

She didn't answer, instead just holding out a hand. He stared at it for a few seconds before dropping his gloves and taking it. They walked down the driveway and out the gates in silence, ignoring the stares of his new colleagues.

He climbed into the back of the limo first, seeing Scanlon there and then glancing up front and noticing that Carl was behind the wheel. How convenient. Someone who had made his hatred clear from the beginning.

"Where's Daniel?" Brandon said, settling into the deep leather seat as Catherine slammed the door behind them.

The silence that ensued started to make Brandon sweat. Were they going to kill him right there, parked in the middle of affluent American suburbia? They were. Of course, they were. That's why Carl was there. Daniel hadn't wanted to be the one who pulled the trigger.

"I don't know exactly how to say this," Scanlon said as the limo accelerated away from the curb.

Brandon's mouth suddenly went completely dry.

"Daniel . . . Daniel didn't make it."

Brandon blinked a few times, the complex details of the heist flooding back into his mind and temporarily drowning his fears.

"You've got to be kidding! He got caught? I thought he was a Green Beret or something! Shit! Listen to me. We've got to—"

Catherine put a hand on his arm and he fell silent.

"What Richard means is that Daniel . . . died."

"What? What do you mean, *died?*"

"Apparently, he had internal injuries from the helicopter crash," Scanlon said with a calm that came off as completely artificial. "We couldn't get him on his cell or his radio and I had to send Carl out there in broad daylight to find him. He was lying under a boulder unconscious. He died on the way to the hospital."

"But . . . He can't have . . . People don't die doing stuff like this. They don't . . ."

Catherine slid an arm around his shoulders and he leaned forward, propping himself on his knees. It was getting hard to breath. It had been his plan—his fault that Daniel was in that helicopter.

"He had to know he was hurt," Brandon managed to get out. "Why didn't he say something? I'd have come back for him. I wouldn't have left him out there to . . ." He could bring himself to say the word.

"He knew that, Brandon. It's why he kept it to himself. He knew he couldn't risk jeapordizing the operation—"

"The operation? *The operation?* Are you—"

"Listen to me," Scanlon said. "This isn't your fault. You planned and executed this thing perfectly. No one else could have done what you did. But you can't control everything. You just have to put it behind you and move on."

It occurred to Brandon that he'd never really known anyone who died. Sure, deep down he knew his mother had, but it was more like she'd just gone away. Suddenly, he felt like he was going to throw up.

Scanlon leaned forward and opened a small refrigerator, pouring three whiskeys. He held one out to Brandon. "Take it."

He did, and watched Scanlon hold up his own glass. "To Daniel. To his courage. And to you, Brandon. You did it. You actually did it."

Scanlon and Catherine drank, but Brandon just slumped back into the seat. "Yeah. I did it."

Everyone in the car fell silent, and Brandon watched the liquid in his glass slosh back and forth as Carl maneuvered the limo through the congested city streets.

"Why are you here?" he said finally. "Not just to tell me about Daniel."

"No," Scanlon replied.

Brandon eyed the door handle but managed to resist testing it. "What do you want?"

Scanlon ignored the question. "Taking off like that was stupid, Brandon. It could have ended with you getting caught. Or worse."

"Seemed like a good idea at the time."

"We can't have you running around trying to scrape together enough money to jump the border. You know that."

"So you're going to kill me."

"Brandon, you've got to get over this idea that we're going to kill you," Catherine said. "If you want to walk away from us—and we both understand if you do— then we need to go back to the original plan. A new identity, a new face, a property in South Africa, and enough money to keep you out of trouble for the rest of your life."

"Is that a joke?"

"It was our agreement wasn't it?" Scanlon said.

Brandon didn't respond immediately, trying instead to figure their angle. He came up blank. "I don't get it."

"It couldn't be more simple. We can't afford for you to be found, and if we leave you here, you will be. The FBI knows it was you, Brandon—I don't have to tell you that. We have to keep you out of their reach."

"Bullshit," he said and turned to Catherine. "Come on. Give it to me straight. What's the catch?"

She shrugged. "There is no catch. We have a plastic surgeon in Argentina that's going to do the work and you'll stay there until you've recuperated enough to get pictures for new IDs. Then we'll show you how to access the ten million we've deposited for you and fly you to your house in South Africa. That's it. You'll never see us again."

"Nothing's ever that simple."

Scanlon took a sip from his glass and swished the fluid around in his mouth for a moment. "Well, there is one thing I wanted to talk to you about."

Brandon nodded knowingly. "Here we go."

"We have a little problem . . ."

"I don't know if I'd call it little," Catherine interjected.

"The thing is, we have another job that we need help with. It's ironic, but it seems that you're the only person we have who's qualified."

"You've got to be kidding me. Seriously—You're joking, right?"

"No. It's not a joke," Scanlon said.

"I just left one of your guys to die out in the desert. I find it hard to believe I'm the best you can do."

He was surprised when Carl spoke. "Daniel wasn't your fault, Brandon. You did what you had to do and he did what he had to do. Sometimes that's all there is."

The distaste that had been so evident before was completely gone now.

Scanlon nodded in agreement. "Look, all I'm asking is that you hear me out. If you don't want the job, you'll be on a plane to Argentina this afternoon."

"I don't need to hear you out. I don't want the job."

Scanlon ignored him and pulled the whiskey bottle from the refrigerator again. "Can I freshen those up?" Both Brandon and Catherine shook their heads. He poured himself another healthy shot.

"So what you're telling me is that you didn't enjoy one minute of stealing that money? Or maybe that you don't think it was a worthy cause?"

"It was okay."

"And what about South Africa? I've seen your place there. It's a beautiful old Cape Dutch house surrounded by fifty acres of vines."

"Almost sixty," Catherine corrected.

"Well, there you have it. Almost sixty acres. And all the money you could ever spend. I imagine that's your idea of paradise, isn't it? Time to putter?" He thumbed in the general direction of where they'd picked him up. "Do a little gardening, sip wine by the pool. There is a pool isn't there?"

Catherine nodded. "One of those negative edge designs overlooking a little valley."

"A valley," Scanlon said. "I really envy you. It sounds so . . . peaceful."

Brandon stared out the tinted window, watching the traffic go by. Scanlon's delivery wasn't exactly subtle, but the point was depressingly valid. If all this was true, what would he do with the rest of his life?

Fish leaves out of his pool? Stomp grapes? He tried to picture himself walking along a golf course in a pair of plaid pants and a matching cap.

It wouldn't hurt to just listen, right? If Danny had been willing to die for this thing, the least he could do is sit there and listen.

Chapter Thirty-four

"I have to say I wasn't sure that we'd ever get to this point," Scanlon said, leading Edwin Hamdi through the empty building toward his office. "But the plane's in the air."

"And Vale? How is he?"

"He's scared to death of Eastern European criminals."

"And does that concern you?"

Scanlon shook his head. "Any sane person in his position would be afraid. He just doesn't bother to hide it. This is a lot to pile on him, Edwin. We both know that."

"After the death of my man in the Middle East, there wasn't a choice."

Scanlon let out a humorless laugh, flipping on the light to his office and starting toward the small bar in the back corner. "I don't doubt that. I know how you feel about Brandon. Must be killing you to have it all come down to him."

Hamdi accepted a drink with a polite nod. He'd never been much of a drinker. While the powerful Islamic faith of his father had never taken hold of him, it was hard to completely discard so much cultural heritage. Today, though, was different. For perhaps the first time in his life, he would welcome oblivion.

"I have to admit that in many ways you were right about him, Richard. He does have unique qualities that have proven quite useful." Hamdi took an uncharacteristically long pull from the glass in his hand, but resisted the urge to immediately take another. "I don't think I've ever thanked you, Richard. I want to now. For all your hard work and for everything you've put at risk. This operation wouldn't have succeeded without you."

His tone had an unintended finality to it, but Scanlon didn't seem to notice. He was too caught up in the idea that he would soon be turning over a planeload of nuclear weapons to the U.S. Navy.

And while that wasn't going to happen, the end result of their actions would be effective beyond Scanlon's wildest imaginings. The warheads would be transported to Israel, placed in strategic positions by Yusef's men, and after a short time, detonated. Not only would the constantly escalating tensions caused by Israel's existence come to a long overdue end, but the United States would finally be forced to give the problem of loose nukes the attention it demanded.

The problem with America's desperate addiction to Middle Eastern crude and the irrational decisions that addiction caused would remain, of course. But in Hamdi's estimation, the situation was self-correcting. With China's thirst growing and world production peaking, the coming years would see price increases that would force the U.S. to restructure its energy strategy. The Middle East would become a political backwater with little more significance than sub-Saharan Africa.

"I'm glad you're starting to see Brandon's value," Scanlon said, as Hamdi finished his drink and went to the bar to make another one.

"I think it would be a bit hypocritical for me to deny it at this point."

Scanlon was in many ways a brilliant man, but also a fundamentally emotional one—tied to ideas of right and wrong that the modern world had turned into dangerous conceits.

"When all this is over we'll see that he gets a pardon," Scanlon said. "Or maybe something a little quieter. Going forward, I hope we can work it out that he can continue to play some role in the organization. He's got a lot of talent."

"Yes, he does," Hamdi said, his voice barely audible. "We'll see if we can work something out."

He just wasn't good at this. Scanlon had to be sacrificed—one man's life was meaningless when compared with an opportunity for peace in a world moving toward the brink. It was one of those rare times, though, that Hamdi wanted to turn away from the logic of that conclusion. He not only admired the man, but liked him. The idea that he had to die while the incompetent and corrupt men who had made all this necessary were allowed to live was a cruel joke.

But an inescapable one.

In a few hours, the honorable and patriotic Richard Scanlon would be silenced—along with Catherine,

Vale, and the rest of his men. His legacy would be a strange one. There was little hope that the FBI would overlook his involvement in the Las Vegas theft, but Hamdi had done—and would do—everything possible to make sure that Scanlon's name would never be tied to Israel and the warheads. He deserved that much at least.

Hamdi looked down at his glass, watching the ice flash in the lights overhead. Soon his real role in all this would start. He would take on the task of directing the world's actions toward a post–Israel Middle East, working to replace the horror and panic he was about to unleash with peace and sanity. Perhaps one day the dispassionate hindsight of historians would recognize that neutering the Jews had been the first step in creating a permanent peace in the world.

Chapter Thirty-five

Every time Brandon slumped against the curving wall behind him, he was immediately jerked fully awake by the powerful vibration of the plane's props. He finally crawled to the middle of the floor and wove himself into a well-anchored cargo net, trying to think happy thoughts. None came to mind.

He'd always had a mild distaste for flying, though it wasn't so intense that it couldn't be mitigated by a wide first-class seat, some decent wine, and the fawning attention of a cute flight attendant.

This particular flight didn't have an attendant, though. Or wine. It didn't even have seats. Just a gloomy fuselage filled with wooden crates and thin, frigid air.

He pitched to the left when the plane hit an air pocket, feeling his stomach bob helplessly on a sudden wave of adrenaline. From where he was lying, he could see Catherine in the cockpit, one eye on the black windscreen and the other on their creepy pilot.

Oddly, she seemed more relaxed than he'd ever seen her. It appeared that courting death a million miles from home was less frightening to her than courting arrest on the warm and familiar roads of the

American West. Unfortunately, he was a bit more realistic when it came to risk assessment. At this point the best he could hope for—beyond surviving, of course—was to get through this thing without crying in front of her.

He'd never even gotten to see it. Two hundred million dollars in glorious, gleaming cash. The greatest—and most likely last—achievement of his life.

These were sad times for thieves—an age in which virtually everything of value was contained in computers and fiber optics. You couldn't run your fingers through a wire transfer. You couldn't smell numbers on a computer screen. No matter how many zeros there were.

Standing unsteadily, Brandon left the relative safety of the cargo net and lurched toward the closest crate. He ran his hands along the rough, unmarked wood and then tried to pry his fingers beneath the well-secured lid. Just a quick peek. What could it hurt?

"Step away from the money," he heard over his earphones.

Behind him, Catherine was leaning out of the cockpit, staring at him with mock severity. She finally broke into what might have been a mildly psychotic smile. She seemed almost happy to be there.

"We're getting ready to land, Brandon, and it's going to be rough. Hold on, okay?"

He did as he was told, threading himself through the cargo net again and thinking about South Africa. Golf probably wasn't so bad. People were always doing it.

The nose of the plane dipped suddenly, causing the already dim lights in the fuselage to sputter and finally go out. Brandon gripped the net tighter.

The story Scanlon had told him was less a briefing than a vague outline. The bottom line was that the last guy they'd sent to meet with the Ukrainians had suffered an "accident." Details, beyond the fact that it had been of the fatal kind, were hazy at best.

And so the organization found itself with a job opening for someone with very specific qualifications. The Ukrainians—a cautious and clinically insane lot— were not going to accept one of Scanlon's fair-haired boys as anything but what they were: American spies. As a career criminal well known in the circles the Ukrainians traveled, though, Brandon was another matter. Suddenly, everyone was happy again. Except him. And, of course, the guy who had the accident.

As promised, the plane hit hard, driving the side of his head into the floor and causing him to slide uncontrollably toward the cockpit until the cargo net went taut. He closed his eyes as the plane bounced wildly down what he suspected wasn't really a runway, opening them only when they had come to a full stop.

"Up and at 'em," Catherine said, grabbing him by the front of his down parka. She pulled him to his feet and dusted him off. "You okay, Brandon? You look kind of pale."

He nodded, but didn't say anything. The closer death came, the more chipper she seemed to get. It was, he hoped, a trait explainable by the fact that she was actually some kind of supersecret agent able to kill a man in a thousand different ways without wrinkling her skirt. More likely it was just blissful ignorance.

He'd once known a guy who got sideways with the Ukrainians. They'd killed him and his whole family—his daughter's poodle alone had thirteen separate stab wounds. Brutal, but not unheard of. What set this particular incident apart was that they had pulled his fish out of their tank and carefully stomped on each and every one.

"Let's go," she said, jumping nimbly through the door behind their pilot. Brandon followed reluctantly, sitting on the threshold and sliding delicately to the ground.

"Where are we?"

He could see only general outlines illuminated by a sliver of a moon. Otherwise there was just darkness and silence.

"Ukraine," the pilot replied.

Brandon was about to tell him just how fucking helpful that piece of information was, but then thought better of it. Their pilot was an evil-looking bastard that neither he nor Catherine had ever seen before. His skin was a dark brown and he had a thick accent that wasn't Arab but something close. Brandon guessed he was a Serb, but wasn't sure since he'd never met one.

"Did anyone bring a hibachi?"

"Shhhh!" Catherine hissed, putting a hand on his arm and freezing in a mannerism that reminded him of a hunting dog locking onto a duck. A few seconds later, he heard it, too. The distant hum of a motor. No, motors—plural.

They stood their ground, listening to the sound grow louder, until something burst from a stand of trees a few hundred yards away. Then another and another. Brandon began backing toward the plane, but wasn't fast enough to avoid being surrounded.

None of the All Terrain Vehicles had their lights on, but his eyes had adjusted to the point that he could make out a few details. Each driver was wearing a thick jumpsuit, a helmet, and elaborate night vision goggles. The overall impression was of something out of *Star Wars*.

The engines wound down to a low rumble, prompting Catherine to take a step forward. "Do any of you speak English?"

No response, other than for one of the men to jump off his vehicle and rush to them. He ignored Catherine and the pilot, bringing his thick goggles to within a few inches of Brandon's face. Whether or not he was satisfied wasn't entirely clear when he spun Brandon around and began frisking him. That seemed to be the signal, and the other two men jumped off their ATVs in order to carry out a similar search of Catherine and their pilot.

When they'd finished, the man standing behind Brandon pointed to the ATVs. Catherine started toward one of them, but Brandon blocked her with his arm.

"Money's in the plane, dude. Where's our stuff?"

The man pointed toward the ATVs again.

"Hey, fuck you. We came through on our side of the deal and we're not going anywhere." He kept his voice even, oozing practiced calm all over the place. "So why don't you and the rest of the Darth Vader squad here run off and get our warheads? Then we can just get the fuck out of each other's lives."

This time the response was a bit less ambiguous: The man pulled a .45 from his holster, cocked it, and pressed it against Brandon's forehead.

The trip took what seemed like hours, but since Brandon hadn't thought to bring a watch with illuminated hands he wasn't sure. His injured shoulder ached from holding on as they pounded their way along what seemed like impassable fields of rocks and roots. When they finally slowed and the engines died, Brandon had completely lost his bearings. Undoubtedly, exactly what was intended.

The three men who had brought them there walked over to a large dead bush and pulled it back while their pilot leaned against a tree and looked on. For some reason, he reminded Brandon of those pictures of Old West villains propped against a wall in their coffins. God, he missed Daniel.

"Is this normal?" Catherine whispered in his ear.

"You mean, is this the way it went down the last time I bought a bunch of atomic bombs from the Ukrainian mob?"

She rubbed her sides through her down parka. He couldn't really see her face in what little moonlight could fight its way through the trees and instead watched the icy vapor of her breath as she spoke.

"Yeah. That's exactly what I mean."

"I'd say they're probably going to torture us to death and then take the money." He nodded toward the pilot. "Where'd Scanlon dig him up?"

"Don't know. None of our guys were qualified to fly that plane. You should have seen that landing from where I was sitting. I thought we were dead."

"We probably are."

"Not exactly a ray of sunshine today, are you? What were you lecturing me about in the truck? Something about not worrying about things you can't control?"

Brandon pretended not to hear, squinting into the darkness as one of the men disappeared into the ground.

"The entrance to the cave," Catherine said.

They moved closer and Brandon peered at the small hole the man had slipped into. It was probably only two feet in diameter and more black than anything he'd ever seen.

"No fucking way."

The Ukranian standing next to him said something indecipherable and jabbed a finger toward the hole.

"I said forget it."

This time when the man aimed the gun, Brandon just stared defiantly into it. "What are you doing?" Catherine said, gripping his arm. "Come on, this guy isn't screwing around."

"I've got a little bit of a problem with confined spaces."

She let out a choked-off laugh. "Are you kidding? You're a thief. You make your *living* crawling through things."

"Windows. Once in a while heating vents. Not holes in the ground."

"Relax, Brandon. Okay? I'll go first. How will that be? You just follow. Can you do that? Follow me?"

It was at least another two hours before they stopped again. Led by a man with a single, dim flashlight, they'd climbed down ropes, waded through ice-clogged streams and squeezed through passageways so tight Brandon had been certain he'd get hopelessly stuck and die there in the cold, still darkness. But he'd managed all of it with only one panic attack—freezing when the back of his jacket hung up on the jagged roof he was slithering beneath. Catherine heard him hyperventilating and somehow managed to turn around and get him unstuck, offering words of encouragement with her face close enough that he could feel the heat from it.

Now they were walking through a natural amphitheater that seemed to swallow their guide's light. An improvement, but even if he couldn't see it, Brandon could still feel the millions of tons of stone and dirt between him and the sky.

"What now?" Catherine said, when the man leading them stopped. Her voice seemed to come from nowhere and everywhere at once.

Brandon didn't answer, shoving his hands into his pockets and trying to absorb himself in the pain as they thawed out. It was time for him to get his shit back together. If he could think, they might get out of this. Probably not, but maybe. If he couldn't, they were almost definitely screwed. Catherine seemed totally in control, but this wasn't her world. It was a criminal transaction and that was his thing.

"Brindoon!"

They all spun in different directions at the butchering of his name, unable to tell where it was coming from. A moment later, a light appeared, rocking back and forth as the man holding it rushed toward them.

His face seemed to float inside the fur-trimmed hood he wore, pale to the point of being ghostlike and dominated by a deep scar that twisted his mouth into something between a deranged smile and the baring of teeth. There was no gun on his hip, but instead a long knife in a badly stained sheath. Stained with what, Brandon didn't want to know. God, he hated the Ukrainians.

"Brindoon!" the man said again, pushing past Catherine and their pilot to grab Brandon by the shoulders and kiss him firmly on both cheeks.

"Cash! Yes! Of course! California!"

Brandon smiled uneasily, looking into the man's glistening eyes and not liking what he saw there. This guy wasn't a little nutty, he was the-voices-told-me-to-do-it crazy.

"Cash," Brandon said. "Yes, we have cash."

"I must apologize for my brother. His English is quite poor, even when he's not overexcited."

Brandon looked past the man still holding him by the shoulders and spotted a taller, thinner man in a carefully preserved military uniform.

"He's been an admirer of yours for quite some time," he continued. "It seems that you stole from a brokerage company in Ohio some years ago. Pyotr heard about it and used your idea on a bank in Moscow. It worked very well and he made a great sum of money."

"Uh, yeah," Brandon mumbled. "That was a good job. I came out of that all right, too."

"Good job! Yes! California!"

"Huh?"

"He means San Francisco. The American news programs have been very much telling the story of the Federal Reserve."

"Really? That story broke? Are they mentioning me by name?"

"Oh, yes. Very much so. The details of the theft haven't been made public, though, and my brother is most anxious to hear them."

With that, Pyotr slung an arm around Brandon's shoulders and led him into the darkness.

Chapter Thirty-six

After two drinks with Edwin Hamdi and three more since he arrived home, it was time to admit that they weren't helping. Or maybe it was the television that was the problem.

Richard Scanlon muted the volume and watched the correspondent speak silently from Damascus. It had been inevitable, of course. After the Mall of America explosion, and the recent incident at that New York synagogue, someone was going to get bombed. And Syria was an easy target. Next time he saw Hamdi, he'd have to ask if they'd had any hard intelligence or if they'd just attacked whatever was at hand. No, on second thought, he didn't want to know.

Scanlon turned off the television and wandered into the kitchen of the modest suburban home he'd never gotten around to moving out of. A quick search of the refrigerator netted a bowl of leftover pasta, some pie, and a salad that had wilted almost to the point of no return. He got as far as setting it all out on the counter before he realized he wasn't hungry.

By now Catherine and Brandon had landed in Ukraine and, as expected, were completely incommunicado. He wished he'd been able to send them off with someone he knew, but none of his men were qualified to fly a cargo plane, particularly under the difficult nighttime conditions the mission demanded. The pilot was Hamdi's contribution, and he'd given his word that the man was top-notch. For some reason, though, that didn't make Scanlon feel any better.

It was still hard to make himself believe that any of this was going to work. Through all the planning, the problems, and the desperate solutions, the idea of success had never seemed like much more than a well-formed dream. But now it was almost within reach.

At first, Scanlon thought the knocking was his imagination, but when the doorbell rang, he gave his watch a curious glance and started down the hallway. The sad truth was that no one really ever came to his door—particularly after ten o'clock.

He pulled open the door without looking out first, preoccupation overpowering caution, and found Steve Ahrens smiling uncomfortably on the porch.

"I thought the FBI was a strictly nine-to-five outfit these days," Scanlon said.

"You know what they say: Neither rain nor sleet nor dark of night."

"That's the post office."

"The truth is that I was in the neighborhood and I saw your light."

An obvious lie. Scanlon knew he should tell the man to come by the office in the morning when he was fully sober and better prepared, but the idea of some company—even dangerous company—was fairly attractive at this point. Anything to take his mind off not knowing whether Brandon and Catherine had made it to the meeting, whether they had the warheads, whether they were dead . . .

"Well, in that case, I guess you should come in. Can I get you a drink?"

"No, thanks, I'm driving."

"I've been watching it all play out on TV."

"The heist? It was bound to leak. Too big and too many people involved."

"The press seems to have already pinned it on Brandon Vale."

"Yeah, that didn't come from us, though. Some reporter who used to be a Vegas cop broke that and everybody jumped on it like a pack of wild dogs."

"What they aren't saying is *how* he did it." Scanlon motioned toward the sofa and took a slightly elevated position in a chair.

"No, we've managed to at least keep that part quiet. It looks like he hijacked the truck, the chase cars, and the helicopter when they were refueling and brought in a duplicate truck."

"But the GPSes . . ."

"You're going to love this," Ahrens said with a hint of admiration audible in his voice. "He had all four vehicles drive really close together and then used guys on ropes to put Budweiser stickers on the truck with the money. Then he parked that truck right next to the Fed while the fake one went in and dropped off a trailer full of basically nothing. Then, when everyone called in a safe delivery and turned off the tracking equipment, he just drove away."

Scanlon remained silent for a few seconds, acting as though he was working through the scenario. "I told them to upgrade their GPSes to read out on a map. To give them more precise locations. They didn't think it was worth the expense."

"Honestly, it probably wouldn't have mattered. With the Fed, the chase cars and the copter all calling in delivery, a little deviation in the reading probably would have been written off as an electronic glitch."

"Sure you don't want a drink?" Scanlon asked.

He shook his head. "The whole thing is kind of fascinating, don't you think? Vale escapes—with help—and disappears. Then this."

"Well, if you're asking if I think the press is right and there's a connection, I'd have to say yes," Scanlon said.

"Yeah, I don't think there's any question at this point. It's amazing that he was able to pull it off with you and the security company changing so many of the procedures after he went to prison."

He was clearly leading to something, but was mindful of Scanlon's political position and the fact that he regularly played golf with the head of the Vegas FBI office.

"Oh," Ahrens continued, a little too casually. "I almost forgot. Bill Crane says hello. He says he bumped into you a few months back and that you guys kind of rekindled your relationship."

There had been no way to get the information

Brandon needed other than to "bump into" the guy in charge of securing the shipment. Scanlon had been as subtle as he could, but it had still left him hopelessly exposed.

The bottom line was that if this operation went south and he didn't get the nukes, he was going to take a fall. And while he wasn't happy about that, what choice had there been? To turn his back on his country?

"He mentioned that you and he had talked about the transfer recently. It's a shame that when you were going over the details you didn't restructure it again. Then maybe Vale couldn't have pulled it off."

Ahrens ended with a polite smile, but the accusation was clear in his eyes.

"So you think I did it?" Scanlon said, leaning back in his chair and crossing his arms in front of him. "That I fed Brandon the information he needed?"

The expression of horror that spread across the young agent's face was clearly intended to look affected. "Hey, I never said—"

"I'm not sure you've fully thought this through, Steve. I'm already rich, and all I do is work." He motioned around the threadbare house. "What would I do with the money? New curtains?"

"You know, it's interesting. The timing of those friendships you rekindled kind of coincided with the government walking away from a two hundred million dollar contract with your company. Funny how that's about how much got stolen."

Scanlon didn't bother to hide his surprise. "I'm

impressed. The funding of companies like mine isn't exactly in the public record."

Ahrens shrugged. "I hear things."

"Well, I'm not sure how much you know about my company, but if you dig deep enough, you'll see that we're in a fairly strong position financially and that the government is happy with the job we're doing. The funding snag hit everyone after the Mall of America explosion. It isn't going to last. And even if it does and my company goes belly up, I've got enough personal wealth that . . . Well, let's just say I wouldn't starve."

Ahrens chewed his lower lip for a moment. "Yeah, I've looked into all that, and what can I say? You're right. You aren't on the hook for any of the company's debt and you have a personal net worth in the ten-million-dollar range."

"So what's my motive, Steve? Boredom?"

Another noncommittal shrug. "Your old coworkers at the casino say that when Brandon Vale worked for you, you two were pretty close."

"Have you ever met Brandon?"

"No."

"As much as I hate to admit it, he's a pretty likable guy. Smart, too. If he wasn't so set on being a crook, he probably would have ended up being my boss."

"I'll tell you, Richard, everywhere I look on this thing, I find something that fascinates me more than the last thing. I did some reading on that diamond heist you helped send Vale away for. Sloppy. Nothing like the precision operations he'd been suspected of pulling before. Not so much his MO."

"No?"

"You've never been married, have you, Richard?"

A smile spread slowly across Scanlon's face. "So I'm gay now? Brandon and I had a lover's quarrel, and I framed him for the diamond heist? Then, just recently, I realize that I can't live without him and I break him out of prison. And to make amends, I help him steal two hundred million dollars."

"Sounds pretty stupid when you say it out loud, but it feels like the right general direction. On a long, twisting road, though."

"Well, I admire outside-the-box thinking, Steve. I really do. But you may be a little far outside the box with that one. Keep after it, though. See where it takes you."

"Oh, I imagine I won't have a chance."

"Why not?"

"I'm guessing you'll be onto my boss by the time my feet hit your lawn. And by midmorning tomorrow I'll be sitting in a basement somewhere working on car theft statistics."

The funny thing was that this kid and Brandon had a lot in common. Ahrens had come here essentially to stare him down in his own house—to say, "I may not be able to do anything about it right now, but don't think you're smarter than me." That took balls.

"Do you like being an FBI agent, Steve?"

"Sure. Sometimes it's a little boring and bureaucratic, but then something like this pops up."

Scanlon stood and offered his hand, indicating that

the interrogation was over. "Well, if you ever get too bored, come and talk to me."

"Are you offering me a job, Richard?"

Scanlon laughed. "It's not a bribe—the job wouldn't be all that good. It's just damn near impossible to find talented people these days. You can't imagine the lengths I have to go to."

Ahrens gripped his hand firmly, holding it a little longer than he had to. "Oh, you'd be surprised at what I can imagine."

Chapter Thirty-seven

Brandon had his arm linked through Pyotr's and, surprisingly, was having to fight the urge to tighten his grip. Normally, it wasn't his policy to cling so energetically to murderous sociopaths, but this cave was slowly sucking the life out of him. The longer he stayed in it, the smaller, deeper, and colder it seemed to get. One false step and he was sure he'd find himself hopelessly lost, with nothing to do but stare into the darkness while the walls closed in and hunger slowly killed him.

He shook his head violently and tried to refocus on the here and now—the unintelligible babble flowing from his guide, the not-all-that-comforting ring of light emanating from his flashlight.

"Catherine?" Brandon said. "Are we going to see Catherine?"

"Yes, of course." Pyotr's tone was less than authoritative.

"Did you fly here on a polka-dot spaceship?"

"Yes, yes."

Brandon fell silent again, stooping to get through a low passage running with water.

He'd been too preoccupied with the constricting

passageways to even notice when he and Catherine were separated and for some reason he felt deeply guilty about that. One moment they'd all been together—Pyotr, him, Catherine, their pilot, Grigori— and the next, he'd glanced back and seen only darkness.

Where was she? What were they doing with her? There were grimy military guys everywhere in this godforsaken place. It was worse than prison, and he remembered what the guys in prison were like. It didn't take much more than a quick flash of Kathy Bates on television to drive them into a sexual frenzy.

"It will work, yes? Good plan. Good plan."

Brandon glanced over at Pyotr and nodded. "Good plan."

They'd spent the last few hours going over artistic, but undetailed diagrams of a museum somewhere outside of St. Petersburg. It was apparently Pyotr's intention to relieve it of some of its more valuable treasures and he'd developed a complex scheme that seemed to be based almost entirely on old episodes of *Mission Impossible*.

After an elaborate and mostly pantomimed presentation, he'd asked Brandon's opinion, putting him in a rather delicate position. The truth—that it was perhaps the stupidest thing he'd ever seen—probably wouldn't make him any friends. On the other hand, saying it was perfect didn't seem credible.

The fact that he was still alive suggested that he'd lucked into the right balance of gushing enthusiasm and constructive criticism.

They took a hard left and Brandon thought he could see a dim glow encroaching on Pyotr's flashlight. It grew in intensity and a few moments later, he was squeezing through a narrow slot into a chamber lit by a single bulb and furnished only with an old cot. Their pilot had taken up a position on the cot, and Catherine was sitting on the ground, leaning against the back wall. She jumped to her feet and took a few quick steps toward him, but then stopped herself. "What's going on, Brandon?"

He'd wondered if they were going to ever see each other again and, if they did, whether there would be suspicion in her voice at his extended absence. There wasn't.

"I have no idea. Are you all right?"

"Cold."

Pyotr waved to them, smiling widely. Or maybe that was just his scar mutating in the bad light. "Come!"

Catherine moved up next to Brandon and tried to slip a hand in his, but he shook his head. Their pilot—whose name he still didn't know—stayed a few feet behind.

"It's been hours," Catherine whispered. "Where have you bee—" She fell silent and sniffed the air. "Have you been drinking?"

"Just a few," he said quietly. "I didn't want to be rude."

She smirked, but still no hint of suspicion.

"What do you think's happening?"

He shrugged numb shoulders. "They've been unloading the plane—counting the money and making sure it isn't counterfeit. By now they have a pretty good idea that we've come through on our end."

"So now they're going to give us the warheads?"

He didn't answer.

"Brandon?"

"I don't know."

They came out into another cathedral of a chamber, this one echoing with splashing water and the hum of generators. Pyotr swept a hand dramatically toward two wooden wagons, each hitched to a team of four horses. Brandon squinted past the spotlight aimed at them and examined the hay overflowing the edges of the carts.

"Uh, okay. What?"

Pyotr seemed a bit deflated at his reaction.

"What my brother is trying to tell you is that we've confirmed your payment and your merchandise is there."

Brandon and Catherine both spun in time to watch Grigori separate himself from the shadows. He had a crowbar in his hand, which he held out. "I assume you'd like to examine one?"

Catherine accepted the crowbar and then proceeded hesitantly toward the wagons. Brandon was about to follow, but stopped when Grigori spoke again.

"I'm surprised to see you here."

"Me?" Brandon said. "What do you mean?"

"Terrorists? Nuclear weapons? You've had a most impressive career, but it's been one of less . . . What is the word I am searching for? Dangerous. Less dangerous crimes."

Brandon heard the crunching of Pyotr's boots as he took up a position a few feet behind. His second interview in as many weeks, and another serious penalty for blowing it.

"You know that diamond heist I went in for?" Brandon said, forcing the image of Pyotr's knife from his mind.

Grigori nodded.

"Well, I didn't do it. Fucking government framed me, and they were going to make damn sure I never saw the light of day again. These guys offered to get me out and set me up with a new identity and enough cash to live on for the rest of my life. Sounded like a good deal to me."

"Did it?"

"Hey, I don't owe anybody anything."

Grigori pointed toward Catherine, who had the top off a crate and was digging hay out of it. "And your companion? She has a similar story?"

Brandon had anticipated questions about her and decided that she was one of those subjects that demanded a completely over the top lie to be credible.

"Catherine's a freak. She'd kill you, me, and half her family for fifty bucks. I don't know if she was born that way or if something happened to—"

"And yet you work with her."

"It makes her . . . predictable. And I like predictable."

Another few seconds of silence passed before Grigori spoke again. "It's a very valuable and very rare quality in the profession we have chosen."

Brandon felt a hand clamp down on his injured shoulder and winced, but it was clear that the grip was a friendly one. He'd passed.

Pyotr led him toward the carts where Catherine was leaning into one of the crates, screwdriver in hand. When they got to within a few feet, she looked down at him with an impressively dead expression. "They're what they told us they were."

It occurred to Brandon what a strange image it was. The end of the world in the back of an old hay cart. He extended a hand toward Pyotr. "Pleasure doing business with you, my man. Now let's load 'em up and we'll be on our way. The faster we can get in the air, the better it is for everyone."

Pyotr looked a bit perplexed. He slapped one of the horses on its swayback, creating a cloud of dust that hung in the bright lights. "Good. Strong."

Brandon blinked a few times and shrugged. To him, they looked like they should be wearing hats and giving kids rides at a state fair, but then what did he know about horses?

"Yeah, they're nice. Now, where's the truck? Let's load 'em up."

Pyotr's confusion deepened and he used a stalagmite for support as he put all his energy into trying to understand.

"No truck, Brindoon. Horses. Yes?"

Chapter Thirty-eight

The doorbell sounded a second time and Richard Scanlon squinted at his alarm clock. Three A.M.

He rolled onto his back and threw off the sheets, letting out a long, frustrated breath. Steve Ahrens had taken up a rather obvious position in front of his house, sitting in classic stakeout mode along the curb across the street. And while Scanlon didn't begrudge him his shot at intimidation, it was three in the goddamn morning. Time to clarify the ground rules a bit.

He swung his legs off the bed and stood, grabbing the pants and shirt draped across the back of a chair. By the time he'd dressed and made it to the stairs, his irritation had faded a bit. When he'd been a young agent, he'd have done the same thing—woken the old guy up and hit him with a zinger question while he was still groggy. He was a smart kid and that was smart police work.

When his feet hit the tile of the entry, he was already mentally rehearsing answers to worst-case-scenario questions. Ahrens would undoubtedly not disappoint.

"Mr. Scanlon?"

He spun in the direction of the voice fast enough

that he nearly lost his balance, saving himself from falling only by sticking a hand against the closed front door.

"I'm sorry," the man said, stepping forward and allowing himself to be illuminated by the glow of the streetlights outside the window. "I didn't mean to startle you."

He had a short, military haircut complemented by a respectable, but hardly elegant suit and tie. Certainly not your typical burglar.

"Who the fuck are you and what are you doing in my house?"

In his peripheral vision, Scanlon saw a similarly dressed man appear in the hallway leading to the kitchen.

"Mr. Hamdi sent us. He needs to see you."

"Jesus Christ," Scanlon said in a harsh whisper. "Do you realize that there's a goddamn FBI agent watching the house? He—"

"Yes, sir. We're aware of that."

Scanlon fell silent as the man pulled the front door open. His colleague moved up from behind.

"I need to get a pair of shoes and—"

"There's no time, sir. I'm going to have to ask you to come with us now."

To emphasize the point, they each took an arm and ushered him through the door.

"What the hell's going on?" he asked, but immediately regretted it. They wouldn't know. Had something gone wrong with the warheads? Had something happened to Catherine and Brandon?

The grass was wet beneath his feet as they moved toward a black SUV parked by the curb. Across the street, he could see that Ahrens's car was still there. A streetlight reflected off the windshield, its glare lessening as they continued relentlessly forward.

One of the men broke into a jog and opened the back door of the SUV, though Scanlon wasn't really paying attention. He continued to concentrate on the car across the street, watching the shadow behind the wheel begin to take shape—turning from a vaguely organic form to a man slumped motionless against the steering wheel.

"No," he said as he was shoved into the back seat. The door slammed behind him and he twisted around as they pulled away, unable to take his eyes off Steve Ahrens's body.

Chapter Thirty-nine

"I can't believe they stole our plane!" Catherine shouted, more giddy than angry. Her expression was impossible to see in the dim light, shadowed by the enormous fur-trimmed hood of her jacket. Brandon could make out the dull white of her smile, though.

"You just can't trust some people," he said, too quietly to be heard over the roar of the engines.

After being sent off by Pyotr with a slap on the back and a hand-drawn map, they'd spent seven hours coaxing those stupid horses over what amounted to miles of muddy goat path. They'd assumed that they were headed back to their plane, but when they finally arrived at the spot marked X, they found a cargo plane that looked like it had seen service in World War II.

As disconcerting as the patched bullet holes in the side were, the wires and singed insulation hanging from the inside of the fuselage were worse. And then there was the cockpit, where their pilot was sitting on a folding chair, using a penlight to see the instruments. He'd gotten the thing in the air, though, something Brandon would have bet good money against. The question now was whether they'd be able to stay there.

"Come on, Brandon, this is a good day!" she said drumming her hands wildly on a poorly secured crate full of hay and thermonuclear weapons.

"I'd appreciate it if you'd stop doing that."

"What? This?"

She pounded out another rhythm, this time loud enough to be heard over the drone and rattle created by the slow disintegration of the plane.

"Look what you've done, Brandon! You're a hero! Are you just going to sit there looking glum? Is it the money? You wanted the money?"

"No. It's not the money."

"Wait! Don't tell me! You still think we're going to kill you. That I'm going to throw you out the door of the plane."

"I—"

"Come on! We're going to land this plane on a little uninhabited island in the middle of the ocean, Richard is going to call the cavalry, and next thing you know we're going to be sipping champagne on an aircraft carrier. We have saved the day!"

"Yeah, right," Brandon said. "Until the government classifies all this because they don't want to be embarrassed and it kills me to keep me quiet. They'll probably give the credit to a couple of cops and they'll say, 'Oh, we thought he had a gun.'"

She came around the crate and sat next to him. "Richard's a big fan of yours, Brandon. I know you don't believe that, but he is. He was really impressed with what you did in Vegas, but the fact that you agreed to do this . . . Trust me. You don't have anything to worry about. If someone comes after you, it's going to be over his dead body."

Brandon pulled his knees up and wrapped his arms around them. "Then it wouldn't be a problem for you to drop me off in Bhutan with some cash?"

She didn't answer, instead just leaning forward and kissing him. Not on the cheek, either. Full on the mouth.

When she pulled away he just stared at her, frozen. "What . . . What was that for?" He sounded a little panicked, even to himself, and cursed himself for not coming up with something more suave.

She kissed him again, this time longer and harder. Once he got over his surprise, he kissed back, running a hand gently down her back, ninety percent because he'd wanted to ever since they'd met and ten percent to confirm she didn't have a knife she was going to whip out the second his guard was down. He felt bad about being so suspicious—she'd say paranoid—but with everything that was happening, it was hard to give in completely to trust.

The sound of the motors deepened, and he felt a tingle in his stomach that didn't have anything to do with Catherine. They both pulled back and looked at each other, then at the now closed cockpit door.

"Why are we going down?" Brandon said. "Are we there already?"

She shook her head. "It's probably just weather or something. Relax. It's over. We did it."

He shrugged and lay back on the floor, pulling her down on top of him. She propped her elbows on either side of his head, bringing her face to within a few inches of his. "I have to admit, I had my doubts."

"About what?"

"You. When Richard told me we were going to break you out of jail, I thought he'd lost his mind. And when he told me I was the one that was going to be responsible for you . . ."

"Yeah?"

"I was so nervous when we met. And then when you jumped out of the car in Las Vegas . . ."

"Sorry about that. I know it made you and . . ." His voice trailed off. It was still so hard to say the name.

"It's forgotten. And I think Daniel would say the same thing."

The angle of the plane's descent steepened and Catherine had to throw a hand out to keep from collapsing on top of him. They both looked at the cockpit door again and Brandon began chewing his lower lip nervously.

"I know you think I'm nuts, Catherine. But does this feel right to you? We've been going down for a long time."

"Like I said, it's probably just weather or something." She pushed herself to her knees and then stood awkwardly. "I'll check."

He wasn't really surprised when the cockpit door turned out to be locked. More like vaguely disappointed.

He propped himself against one of the crates, watching Catherine pound on the door with her fist.

Wouldn't you know it was the only solid thing in the entire goddamn plane?

Strangely, he still felt pretty good about everything. Not ecstatic or anything, but it could have been worse. He believed that Catherine sincerely didn't know what was going on. It would have really hurt if she was the one who betrayed him. And Scanlon? He wasn't completely sure, but he had decided to give his old boss the benefit of the doubt and lay the blame for what was going to happen to him at the feet of that creepy bastard who'd had him dragged out of bed in Vegas.

Catherine threw herself against the door, but it was going to take a lot more than the soft shoulder of a hundred-and-twenty-pound woman to get it open. Finally, she turned and shouted, "What's going on? Why won't he let me in?"

Brandon shrugged.

"The crates!" she said, steadying herself against a sudden bout of turbulence. "We can slide them into the door."

She teetered over to one and grabbed the edge, but he didn't move.

"What's wrong with you?" she yelled. "Help me!"

"Can you fly it?"

"What?"

"The plane? Can you fly it? Because if not, smashing an atomic bomb through the door isn't going to get us very far."

She couldn't move the crate by herself so she staggered back to the cockpit door and pounded on it some more. "Open the door! Can you hear me? Open the door!"

"Catherine! Sit down! You're going to get hurt. We're landing and there isn't anything you can do about it."

She looked around the windowless fuselage and gave the door one last frustrated kick before sitting down next to him and grabbing hold of a strap securing one of the crates. She stared straight ahead for a few seconds, then looked over at him. "You know something, Brandon. What is it?"

"Don't worry. You're going to be fine. They're just dropping me off somewhere so there aren't a lot of awkward questions."

"Awkward questions about what?"

"If I'm there when your aircraft carrier shows up to get the nukes, a bunch of people are going to see me and recognize me from the news reports about the Fed job. Better for me to go away before that. It makes things simpler."

Her expression of defiance was clear even in the bad light. "No way. Not for me."

"I know. But in the end, you won't say anything."

Defiance turned to anger.

"Of course, I'm going to say something! I—"

"Oh, come on, Catherine. Scanlon will hit you with a bunch of words like 'unfortunate' and 'unavoidable' and tell you how millions of lives were at stake. Then he'll hum 'The Star-Spangled Banner' and you'll never give me another thought."

He realized how unnecessarily harsh his words

sounded, but he was having a hard time controlling the anger building inside him. He hadn't wanted to die in that cave, but if he had, at least he would have gone down trying to save millions of lives. Now he was dying for nothing more than to keep a few powerful men from being mildly inconvenienced.

"Hey, fuck you, Brandon! You think—"

The wheels touched down hard enough to cause them both to slide helplessly across the floor and into the cockpit door. Brandon wrapped his arms around her as the plane bounced wildly along what felt like a field of boulders, trying to force the crates behind them from his mind. If one broke free, they were going to have a whole new set of problems.

The plane pitched left suddenly, driving Brandon's head into a fire extinguisher hard enough to fill the air with the dull ring of metal. He was barely aware of the plane coming to a stop and Catherine's weight disappearing from him. He blinked hard when a bright light washed over him, but couldn't focus or regain enough equilibrium to sit up.

There was shouting—a woman's voice, then a man's, then Catherine landed on top of him again. By that time, his vision had cleared enough to see the pilot opening the door in the side of the plane and he squinted out at what looked like an endless blue sky hanging over an equally endless plain.

Catherine stood again, this time grabbing him by the front of his jacket and pulling him to his feet. With an arm slung around her shoulders, he was able to remain upright, but beyond that he couldn't do much

more than watch the pilot as he disappeared through
the door and was replaced by two Arab-looking men
pointing rifles.

Chapter Forty

The office was small and barely furnished: a metal desk of a vaguely seventies design, a couple of chairs, and badly painted walls devoid of artwork. If there had been a set of windows behind the desk, it would have reminded Scanlon of a private investigator's office from an old black-and-white movie.

He tested the handcuffs holding him in his chair, only to find that they were just as secure as they had been five minutes ago. He'd considered shouting for help, but at this time of night there would be no one to hear. Besides, the two men who had brought him there were undoubtedly standing just on the other side of the office's only door.

And so he would wait. For what? Hamdi. And death. There was little doubt of that after they'd killed Steve Ahrens. He'd never keep quiet about that. Not if he was still alive.

The real question was why.

He could only assume that the warheads were fakes or the Ukrainians had stolen the money and kept them. Those had always been risks, but Hamdi had no direct exposure to them. Obviously, he didn't trust Scanlon to keep his mouth shut and was going to shut it for him—severing the only link to him. Very thorough.

The door behind him opened and Scanlon twisted around to watch Hamdi enter.

"Hello, Richard."

"Edwin."

"I'm sorry we have to meet under these conditions."

"Why are we? I understood the risk I was taking. I would have kept your name out of it."

Hamdi closed the door and took a seat behind the desk. His expression was a mix of sadness and resolve, though Scanlon noted that the resolve was etched a bit deeper.

"What happened to Catherine and Brandon?"

"By now, I imagine both are dead."

Despite knowing that would be the answer, the words spoken aloud hit him hard. He took a deep breath and let it out slowly, trying to fight off images of Catherine as a young girl. Of her graduation. Of moving her into her first house. Of the death he'd sent her to.

"I'm sorry, Richard. She was a wonderful young woman. And I'd actually come to admire Brandon."

"What happened?" he said, cutting Hamdi off. "It was all a hoax? Or do the Ukrainians still have them?"

"Neither. We have the weapons. The transaction went perfectly. If anything, the substitution of Brandon probably was a positive development."

Scanlon straightened in the chair, his handcuffs

ringing loudly in the small room. "Then what the fuck's going on, Edwin?"

Hamdi frowned and averted his eyes toward the desk in front of him. "One of the most difficult decisions I've ever made was whether to let you die thinking everything had gone to your plan or to tell you the truth. In the end, keeping you in ignorance seemed . . . disrespectful."

Scanlon leaned forward as far as he was able. He'd never fully trusted Hamdi, but that was more the result of his nature than any real reason to believe that Hamdi's motivations weren't the same as his own. "Then I guess you have the floor, don't you, Edwin?"

Hamdi didn't respond immediately, obviously considering his words carefully. "I never intended to turn the warheads over to the authorities, Richard. Right now, they're being hidden in various strategic positions around Israel and the Occupied Territories. They've been modified with timers, and in three weeks they'll detonate. I'm sorry I couldn't tell you—the truth is that your help in the planning and execution of this would have been very welcome. But, of course, it's not something you would have agreed to involve yourself in."

Scanlon opened his mouth to speak, but no sound came out. His mind began replaying his long relationship with Hamdi, but he could find nothing that reconciled what he was hearing with the man he'd come to know. Sure, he had no love for the Israelis, but he'd always framed that distaste with logical political arguments and offered equally practical assessments of

Arab failings. Had it all been a lie? A cover? After an entire life in law enforcement, was Scanlon so easily duped?

"You're . . . You're telling me that you're just another fucking religious fanatic? Another psychotic anti-Semite? You—"

Hamdi held a hand out, silencing him. "Please, Richard. Of course not. At best I'm a pragmatic agnostic. And in many ways I admire the Jews. They wanted Palestine and they did what was necessary to get it. That kind of determination is what it takes to succeed in the Middle East. What was it you yourself said about the Iraq war? That in order to win, we needed to stop apologizing and go out and kill a hundred thousand civilians, then make it clear that we would kill another hundred thousand if necessary. That when we suspected someone of insurgency, we should kill him, his family, and everyone in his village. But you also recognized that Americans simply don't have that kind of resolve."

"That's not exactly what I said, though, is it, Edwin?" Scanlon said through clenched teeth. "I said we don't *want* to have the resolve. We aren't butchers, and we aren't willing to become butchers."

"And so we embark on a war in which the primary strategy for victory is hoping that the Arabs welcome their Christian invaders with open arms?" Hamdi shook his head disapprovingly.

"So you're telling me the Israelis did exactly what they had to in order to hold that land, and for that you're going to unleash a nuclear holocaust on them?

Think for a minute, Edwin. That doesn't sound insane to you?"

"Don't act as though you don't understand what I'm trying to accomplish, Richard. We both know that in a time of proliferating WMDs, the existence of Israel has become an impossibility. Whether that fact is the fault of the Arabs or the Jews is irrelevant. America and the Jews have become a single entity to the Muslims—another fact you're fully aware of. So far, we've avoided a major attack on the U.S. mainland, but how much longer? How much longer will we allow a few million Jews to hold the safety and prosperity of the entire world hostage? Hard decisions have to be made. The needs of the many must supersede the needs of the few."

"They've pulled out of Gaza, Edwin. They—"

"Yes, they pulled out. And then they did everything possible to see that the Palestinians failed—from keeping security provisions in place that would stifle their economy to sending people to fan the flames of hatred between the different Palestinian factions. The Jews are every bit as bigoted and fanatical as the Muslims—make no mistake of that. They would kill every man, woman, and child in the world to hold the land that they believe God gave them. But again, I'm telling you what you already know."

"Jesus Christ, Edwin! Listen to yourself! Israel has started down the path of peace. They're tearing their country apart trying to find a way to live with the Arabs."

"To no effect, I'm afraid."

"You're going to kill millions of people! You'll be the greatest mass murderer in history. What the fuck gives you the right—"

"In fact, an al-Qaeda splinter group will be the greatest mass murderers in history. My role will be to direct America's policies in a way that creates a lasting peace. In fact, I hope to minimize casualties as much as possible. The Israeli government will be warned, and I've allowed time for evacuation. Obviously, it will be challenging logistically, but certainly possible with the help of the international community."

"You expect a whole country to just pack up and leave? That's your plan?"

He shrugged. "Of course, many people will choose to stay for whatever reason, and they'll be killed. But that is their decision, not mine. And as a practical matter, they will be the most fanatical and, therefore, the most . . . expendable."

"Didn't Hitler say something like that when he got started?"

"Oh, come now, Richard. Hitler used millions of peaceful Jews as a tool to rally his people into a vicious war. Do you really think that's a good analogy? I'm simply relocating millions of Jews who are threatening the entire planet's stability."

"Relocating? Jesus, Edwin. To where?"

"I imagine that most will be absorbed back into the countries they came from."

Hamdi's outward appearance suggested little but resolute calm. He had obviously convinced himself that he was the impartial architect of the only possible solution. But Scanlon knew that was bullshit. No one was impartial.

"And why were there so many Jews in other countries, Edwin? Because they had been driven out by the persecution of the Arabs. What's next for you? Are you going to nuke the Midwest and give it back to the Indians?"

Hamdi smiled humorlessly. "The Jews will be reabsorbed by the Western world, and the Palestinians, with a bit of coaxing, will be absorbed by the Arab world. And with that, a problem that we both know was going to end in disaster will simply cease to exist. The West Wall, the Al-Aqsa Mosque, and everything else will be gone. The land that gave rise to the disastrous myth of God will be a wasteland of irradiated sand. And because this was done by a Muslim terrorist organization, the Arabs will see it as a victory despite the hardship it will pile on them. They always do. As for the Jews, they will no longer have a Holy Land to kill for, and they'll busy themselves building new enclaves from which to practice their particular brand of racism."

"So your solution to disputes between people is to destroy the thing they're arguing about? That's a great plan, Edwin. Think how many neat little solutions you could come up with if you just had a hundred more warheads? You could get started right away on Tibet. And what about Kashmir? Of course, there wouldn't be much of the world left after you were done."

"Perhaps not," Hamdi said seriously. "Or maybe

people would learn to create equitable solutions to those disputes in the face of the alternative."

"Amazing how well behaved people can be when you have a gun pressed against their temple."

"Don't be so melodramatic, Richard. It doesn't suit you. You act as though I made this decision yesterday based on an article in the newspaper. I've personally worked to broker peace between the Jews and the Palestinians. I've studied and written on the subject for most of my life. I've tried to direct America's policies—"

"And it's working! You've completely changed the administration's stance toward the issue. You're—"

"Too little, too late, Richard. I fought tirelessly for years and have managed to change a few insignificant policies, but not the attitudes that created them. What is the likelihood that the next administration will continue pushing in a direction that's at odds with what most Americans believe?"

"If they see that—"

"No. The problem with Americans is that they always want to force the fantasy of who they are on everyone else. They say that we can succeed in the Middle East by appealing to the moderates—a strategy that doesn't even work in U.S. elections. We believe we are the only truly moral country, despite incredible murder and crime rates, the fact that we produce virtually all of the world's pornography, and consume most of its narcotics. We say that al-Qaeda are horrible terrorists because they killed thirty-five hundred people on September eleventh, but consider ourselves peace-loving when we kill and torture tens of thousands in Iraq. We demand democracy and then are surprised when, just like in America, religious fundamentalists are elected. The stage is set for endless fighting, Richard. You know this."

"So kill them all and let God sort them out? That's your solution?"

"The time for compromise and half solutions is over, Richard. The stakes are too high."

Scanlon pulled hard on his cuffs, nearly toppling the chair and feeling the bones in his wrists strained almost to the point of breaking. How could he have been so stupid? How could he have allowed this to happen? He wrenched his hands forward again, this time feeling the skin beneath the metal shackles split. Finally, he went still, his head hanging and warm blood dripping from his fingertips.

"Eventually, the oil will run out," Hamdi said. "And the Middle East will collapse back in on itself. The question is what will happen in the meantime? This is a giant step in the direction of controlling the region without killing millions of Arabs and turning America into a security-obsessed totalitarian state."

Scanlon heard a desk drawer open and looked up to watch Hamdi pull a gun from it.

"It won't surprise you to know that I've never killed anyone," he said. "I was going to have one of my men do it but again it seemed like an insult. I have a great deal of respect for you, Richard. In fact, I consider you a friend."

Scanlon stared at the black silencer extending from

the gun's barrel but didn't bother pulling against the handcuffs again. There was no point. It was over. He'd killed Catherine, Brandon, and now how many others? A million? Two?

Had it all been arrogance? Had he gotten involved in this to prove that he was smarter than the men he'd left behind in the government? Had he been blinded by that?

"You'll understand if I don't take a lot of comfort from your friendship, Edwin."

Chapter Forty-one

"Shit."

Brandon continued to lean on Catherine for support, though the effects of the blow to his head had dissipated enough that he could stand on his own. They both stood completely still, focusing first on the armed men screaming at them in Arabic, then on the warheads.

Brandon didn't speak the language, but the meaning was fairly clear. He raised his hands and shuffled along behind Catherine, who was being dragged toward the door by her hair.

The sun was hot overhead, and Brandon shaded his eyes as he jumped down to the sandy strip that passed for a runway. There appeared to be twelve men total, not including their pilot, who was quietly speaking to a guy who had the air of being in charge. Everyone was wearing desert fatigues and most were armed either with a shoulder-slung rifle or a holstered pistol. To their left were twelve parked vehicles—everything from little economy cars to Mercedes to army trucks. Other than that, nothing. Blinding sun, sand, and sky.

Brandon shook his head in disbelief. He'd actually

been overly optimistic in his prediction that he'd be dropped off, shot, and buried in an unmarked grave. Who would have guessed?

Catherine was about ten feet away, struggling against a dusty-looking man with one hand tangled in her hair and the other wrapped around a rifle. He was laughing, holding her head at waist level and jerking back and forth as she tried uselessly to free herself. The man guarding Brandon was more cautious, standing back a bit and aiming his rifle directly at Brandon's head.

"Let go!" Catherine shouted, and gave one last jerk backward. The man did as she asked, with timing calculated to send her toppling into a group of broken rocks.

"You okay?" Brandon said, prompting the man next to him to push the barrel of his rifle a little closer.

"What the hell is going on?" she said, slamming a hand down on the ground and raising a small cloud of dust. "Where are we?"

"Not on some tropical island waiting for the navy," Brandon said.

"You don't sound very surprised. Did you have something to do—"

"Come on, Catherine. Get real. Somebody screwed us. This would be an example of why you don't get involved in shit that doesn't concern you."

The man hovering over her shouted an unintelligible order and seemed a bit perplexed when she ignored him.

"So what are you trying to say, Brandon? That

Richard's sold us out to—," she pointed at the man hovering over her. "To him? No way."

"And yet here we are," Brandon said. "Take it from me. Loyalties can get a little murky when numbers get into the nine digits."

"Bullshit!"

She was an odd sight sitting there in the rocks with her hair in her face and still wearing the heavy parka she'd had on in the plane. He was still wearing his, too, and he could feel the sweat starting to run down his sides.

"This isn't going to happen," she shouted. "There's no way I'm going to allow this to happen!"

Brandon let out a long breath, but otherwise remained motionless in deference to the man aiming a gun at him. He didn't want this, either. He didn't want to die. He didn't want to watch her die—or worse. And he sure as hell didn't want to see these psychos drive off with twelve nuclear weapons in the back of their cars. But what could he do? The truth was that he was completely out of his depth. How stupid had he been to agree to do this? What had he been thinking?

The man guarding Catherine was yelling again, apparently wanting his new toy to stand. Incredibly, she continued to completely ignore him.

"What do we do, Brandon?"

He looked along the barrel of the rifle aimed at him and into the eyes of the man at the other end. Like the man hovering over Catherine, he was registering their conversation, but clearly he didn't understand any of it. And their compatriots were all busy unloading the plane under the watchful eye of that scumbag, double-crossing pilot.

Brandon had to raise his voice to be heard over the man still shouting at Catherine. "I'm not Danny. I don't know what to do."

"I assume you agree that we're going to be dead in an hour."

"I guess."

"Then if I were to do something stupid, you wouldn't have a problem with that."

He didn't answer immediately. He was a person who needed time to think, to plan. To consider every contingency. Now she was asking him to make life-or-death decisions without so much as a coin toss. "I don't know," he said finally. "Are we talking just dumb, or really moronic?"

The man standing over Catherine was screaming now, obviously losing a fair amount of face by being defied by an unarmed woman. She looked up at him, took a deep breath, and screamed back. "Would you shut the fuck up? I can't hear myself think!"

That was the last straw. The man switched his rifle to his left hand and grabbed hold of Catherine's arm. She offered some token resistance but in the end let him get a good grip and start pulling.

Brandon was the only one who seemed to notice that she wasn't letting go of the softball-sized rock her hand was resting on. She allowed herself to be yanked upward, adding to the momentum of the rock that was already moving in a smooth arc toward the man's head. Oddly, he didn't even flinch. Thousands of years of women cowering at the feet of his ancestors had left him unable to process even the possibility of this attack.

Brandon's relationship with women had been a little less one-sided, and he shifted his attention to the gun aimed at him.

The crack of stone against skull prompted the man in front of him to hesitantly adjust his aim toward Catherine.

Brandon charged, ducking low and driving upward with his legs, trying to lift him off the ground and dump him on his back.

It turned out not to be as easy as the jocks at his high school had made it look. While the man's feet did briefly leave the ground, when they came back down they were still under him. The blow to Brandon's back felt like it came from the butt of the rifle, and though it mostly just glanced off, it was enough to send him sprawling facedown in the dirt. Every muscle in his body seized when he heard the brief burst of automatic gunfire, and then he went completely slack. So this was where it was going to end. Bleeding to death in the middle of—

"Brandon! Get up!" Another short burst of fire. Then another.

He turned his face out of the sand and opened his eyes only to find himself staring at the bleeding body of the man who had been guarding him.

"For God's sake, Brandon! Get up!" Catherine shouted again. She sounded farther away this time.

It took another few seconds for him to realize that he hadn't been shot. He was alive. In fact, other than a little sand in his mouth, he felt fine.

A sharp burst of adrenaline dissipated the lingering effects of his brief death and he wrestled the rifle from the dead man's hands. Instead of standing, though, he rolled into a position that allowed him to aim the gun in the direction of the plane.

Amazingly there was another man down near the landing gear and three more scrambling for cover. Catherine was moving sideways at an oddly casual pace, inching toward the line of parked cars while peering intently through her rifle's sights. She seemed to have figured out how to switch it to semiautomatic and was delivering extremely accurate fire in the direction of anyone who exposed even a few inches of skin.

Brandon used the faint glimmer of hope he felt to force himself to his feet and start a stumbling sprint toward the vehicles Catherine was so methodically closing in on.

By the time he crossed behind her, she had adjusted her aim from the open door of the plane to a stack of rifles leaning against the landing gear—the existence of which explained why no one was shooting back. Yet.

The first vehicle he came to was an old canvas-covered army truck and he dove through the missing passenger-side door, sliding behind the seat and finding the keys dangling from the ignition. It started on the first try and he ground it into gear, popping the clutch and flooring the accelerator.

A spray of sand and dust shot from beneath the tires as he twisted the wheel to the right, spinning 180 degrees and skidding to a stop in front of Catherine. She switched the gun to full automatic and emptied her clip into the rifles beneath the plane before jumping in.

"Go!"

He did as he was told, releasing the clutch and sending the truck fishtailing toward the open desert.

The sound of shots started a few moments later, and Brandon pressed harder on the accelerator, finally easing up when he started to worry that he was going to push it through the rusting floorboard.

"Jesus Christ!" he shouted. "You killed those guys! I knew it! I knew it the whole time."

She leaned her head out of the missing door and looked behind them. "What are you talking about? You knew what?"

"You're some kind of government superspy!"

When he glanced over at her and saw her expression, he felt some of his hard-won hope slip away. "You're not?"

She shook her head. "We got lucky. They underestimated me because I'm a woman and they tossed their rifles to unload the plane."

"But you were hitting what you aimed at!"

"My dad was into hunting and he didn't have a son—"

"Oh, great! That's just fucking great," Brandon said, skidding around a large boulder and nearly putting the truck on two wheels. "So if we get attacked by a deer, I have nothing to worry about."

"Hey! Who just got you out of that?"

"Are you kidding? Who got me into it?"

She didn't seem to have a response for that, so she leaned out the door again. After less than a second she pulled herself in and slammed her back into the seat.

"What?"

"They're coming up behind us. Fast."

"How many?"

"Just the Mercedes."

"Do you think the others are going to try to head us off?"

She shook her head. "I doubt it. They've got a couple hundred million dollars worth of nuclear warheads sitting in a plane. They're going to concentrate on that. Can you go any faster?"

"I'm floored."

She grabbed the rifle he'd taken, checked the magazine, then sat there with it in her lap for a moment, thinking.

"Bear right," she said, pointing to a tilted ridge where the sand had blown away to reveal fissured, sun-baked earth, strewn with boulders.

"We could get stuck!"

"Not before a Mercedes does."

"How close are they?" Brandon asked. There were no side mirrors and the back of the truck's cab was a solid patchwork of wood and metal.

She peered out again, but as soon as her head cleared the edge of the door, a burst of automatic gunfire sounded. Brandon took a hand off the wheel and jerked her back inside, causing the truck to swerve violently.

"Brandon! What did you tell me in San Francisco? Drive the truck!"

"But they were shooting!"

"You let me worry about that! Two hundred yards."

"They're about to get a lot closer."

He braked, but not so much that all four wheels didn't come off the ground when they left the sand. The cracks in the hardened mud grew wider and the rocks larger as they continued forward, forcing him to slow even more.

It was at that moment the shooting started in earnest. Not the drone of automatic fire, but the much more frightening sound of careful, individual shots and the ring of metal as they hit the truck.

Brandon veered left, trying to keep the back of the vehicle to the men shooting at them. There was a loud crack of splintering wood behind him and a neat bullet hole suddenly appeared in the windshield.

"Shit!" he yelled, as he was forced to slow the truck even more in order to maneuver through a group of rocks big enough to do fatal damage to the underside of the vehicle. He glanced at the speedometer. Fifteen miles an hour. No. Kilometers an hour. What was that? Eight?

Catherine ducked her head outside and then immediately pulled it back. "They're either stuck or stopped."

"They're not hitting us anymore," Brandon said

hopefully. The terrifying sound of bullets striking metal and wood no longer followed each shot.

"They're going for the tires."

"Of course," Brandon mumbled, downshifting and refusing to look again at the speedometer.

"You're gonna have to go faster, Brandon. They can catch us on foot at this speed."

"Hey! You think you can do better?"

She looked through the windshield at what he had to work with and let out a long breath between her teeth.

"Do *not* wreck this truck or get it bogged down," she ordered. "Better to go too slow than too fast, understand? When you get out of range or you find some cover, wait for me."

"What do you mean, wait—"

She swung her feet out the door and jumped to the ground, clutching the rifle in her hands.

"Catherine! What are you doing? Get back in the truck!"

But she was already in a crouched sprint, heading for a jumble of boulders about twenty yards away. Brandon took his foot off the accelerator when a puff of dust exploded only a few feet from her. She dropped to the ground and slithered the last few yards on her stomach, pushing the rifle in front of her. When she had her back pressed safely against a boulder she waved him on.

"Catherine! Come back! You're going to get yourself killed!"

She ignored him, spreading her parka on the rocks

beneath her and peeking out through a narrow gap between two boulders. He kept creeping forward as she sighted carefully along her rifle and squeezed off a round. The Mercedes was close enough that the sound of shattering glass was clearly audible.

He shifted down again and stepped on the accelerator, the breath catching in his chest when he did. She was right—their only hope was for him to keep going. But watching her disappear from his peripheral vision turned out to be harder than anything he'd ever done.

Chapter Forty-two

The rear wheels lost traction and the truck began an uncontrolled slide back down the hill before hitting a more solid section and jerking forward again. The slope was a treacherous mixture of rocks, crevices, and sand bogs, forcing Brandon to clear his mind of everything that didn't relate to gaining a few more feet of ground. Right now, there wasn't anything he could do about Catherine, or the gunmen behind him, or his role in Armageddon—other than to try to keep the truck moving.

The front wheels finally cleared the top of the hill, launching briefly into the air and then slamming down on the small plateau. He heard the underside of the truck grinding against something and he slammed his foot to the floor, feeling the vehicle finally level out and accelerate over the gloriously open terrain. After about two hundred yards, he skidded to a stop, jumped out, and ran back through a blinding cloud of dust. The closer he got to the edge of the plateau, the lower he crouched, finally dropping to his knees and crawling the last few feet.

The valley below looked completely dead—an endless expanse of brown and tan bordered by mountains so far away that they might have actually been a distant storm. The plane and the men swarming it were nowhere to be seen, lost in the gentle roll of the terrain.

Catherine, though, was easy to pick out. She was lying on her stomach about a half mile away, her rifle barrel resting between two boulders. The Mercedes was still there, too, and from his elevated vantage point, Brandon could see two men huddled behind it.

One of them suddenly popped up and there was a puff of smoke from the end of his rifle, followed quickly by the ring of the shot. Catherine didn't react at all. She just lay there, motionless. Waiting.

But for what?

He scanned the horizon again, looking for the telltale plume of dust that would signal the approach of reinforcements. Nothing. And with a little luck, it would remain that way. With almost two hundred million dollars' worth of nuclear warheads to worry about, the escape of a couple of captives wouldn't be much more than an irritation. Whoever was running that particular horror show was undoubtedly saying the same thing Brandon would have: Get the stuff loaded, split up, and get the hell out of Dodge.

The same man popped up again, but this time Catherine got a shot off and he jerked back, disappearing from view.

"Nice!" Brandon said aloud, thinking he'd been hit

A moment later, though, he reappeared, pressing his back against the car and looking depressingly healthy. It must have been close, though, because after what looked like a heated discussion, both men crawled through the open passenger-side door. A moment later, they were speeding away, hunched down in their seats to keep clear of the rear window.

"Yes!" he shouted, and then looked back nervously. Nothing. Just the old truck and a million miles of sand.

When Catherine finally appeared at the edge of the plateau, Brandon already had the truck running. She jumped in and he took off, driving in the exact opposite direction the Mercedes had gone for want of a better plan.

She'd left her parka in the rocks and was now down to a pair of cargo pants and a sweat-stained turtleneck with the sleeves pushed up as far as they would go. Her breathing was too heavy to allow her to speak, but she did manage to check her rifle's clip before laying it down on the floorboard.

Brandon wanted to say something, but wasn't sure what you said to a woman who had thrown herself out into the middle of the desert and traded shots with a bunch of Arab terrorists so you could drive away.

"Thanks," turned out to be the best thing he could come up with.

She leaned forward until her head almost touched her knees and massaged the stitch in her side. When she sat upright again, her breathing was a little more under control. "You're welcome."

She pulled off her turtleneck, leaving her in just a jog bra, and wiped her face with it. "Watch the road."

"There is no road," he said, turning fully back toward the windshield and trying to hold the truck steady. "Any thoughts on where we are?"

"No."

"Aren't you supposed to be an expert?"

"On what? It's a desert, Brandon."

He dared a quick sideways glance. She didn't look scared at all. And the men she'd just killed didn't seem to be registering, either. Mostly, she just looked pissed—like at any minute she was going to twist his head off. Better to just shut up and give her some space.

For the next fifteen minutes, she just stared out the open door, oblivious to the suffocating heat, the dust blowing in her face, the sun beating down on her bare skin.

In that time, Brandon confirmed that the fuel tank was full ten times, made certain that no one was following them twenty times, and looked around the empty cab of the truck at least fifty times. At half an hour, he felt like he was drowning in the silence between them.

The front of the truck suddenly slammed down, bouncing wildly and almost causing him to lose control. Catherine threw a hand out to steady herself and he leaned through the missing door, examining the vague outline of a dirt road stretching into the distance. He jammed his foot against the brake and twisted the steering wheel, spinning the truck 180 degrees.

"If those guys in the Mercedes come looking for us, it'll probably be on that road," he said. "But we don't have any food or water and we have no idea where we are. We can't just drive around the desert until we run out of gas."

She sat there motionless for a few moments, the life starting to slowly come back into her face.

"What the hell happened, Catherine?"

She shook her head. "It had to be the pilot. He must have cut a deal with a terrorist group."

Brandon frowned and flopped back in his seat.

"What?" she said.

"Come on, Cath. Why the hell would Scanlon even tell that pilot what our cargo was? And even if he did, why wouldn't the pilot just have taken the money? These aren't easy items to fence. You don't just post them on eBay or flash them to people walking by on the street."

"I know that you and Richard have your differences, but there's no way you believe that he just handed twelve nuclear warheads to a bunch of terrorists."

Of course, they had no proof those guys were terrorists, but they sure as hell fit the profile. And while he didn't completely trust Scanlon, it was hard to imagine him selling out Catherine and his country.

"Richard isn't the only one running this thing," Catherine said hesitantly. "There's someone else."

"Yeah? Who?"

He still didn't know if Catherine had been involved in his being dragged out of her condo that night, and until now he hadn't wanted to know. But if there was any time to discard whatever illusions he was nursing, this was probably it.

"Who, Catherine?"

"I don't know," she said, refusing to look at him.

"This is no time to—"

"I'm telling the truth! The only thing I know is that some of the information we've gotten and some of the resources we've had access to . . ." Her voice faded for a moment. "Richard's well connected, but he's not *that* well connected."

"So someone in the government."

She nodded.

"But you have no idea who. Richard never said a word about who was standing behind him on this."

She looked a little uncertain.

"Jesus Christ, Catherine. Spit it out!"

"He never said anything directly, okay? But he told me that if I ever had a problem and I couldn't get in touch with him . . ."

"Yeah?"

"He gave me an e-mail address and a password— made me memorize them."

Brandon let out a long breath. It wasn't exactly a presidential pardon and a SEAL team, but at least it was something. "Okay. Then we need to find a computer."

She laughed bitterly. "We're not even sure what continent we're on."

"Then we're just going to have to find out."

"And how do you propose to do that?"

He pointed and she followed his finger, squinting through the windshield at a distant figure riding what looked like a camel.

Chapter Forty-three

After a lifetime of seeing the worst in people, Brandon was finally getting to enjoy a glimpse of the other side. Camel Guy—he hadn't entirely caught the man's real name—had been ridiculously helpful. After some rather obvious gawking at the fit of Catherine's sweaty turtleneck— who could blame him—and a few communication difficulties, he had gotten across that they were in Jordan. When directions to the country's capital degenerated into a frustrating pantomime, he had them follow him to his village, where he borrowed a car and led them through thirty miles of back roads to what passed for a highway. At the end of all that, he'd refused money, handed them some home-cooked food, and sped off back to his village.

Their overdue good fortune had continued when a German couple had given them the heavily anno-tated tourist guidebook that Catherine was now immersed in. It would have almost been enough to make Brandon think there was hope for humanity if he hadn't been personally involved in dooming a large portion of it.

He looked around at the little outdoor café, futilely searching for something familiar. There were no comforting smells, no intelligible sounds, no Western faces. Just a television endlessly repeating footage of Syrian children blown apart by American bombs and the curious stares of the people around them.

He was having a hard time getting his balance. At least when he'd been on the run in Vegas there had been familiar tools to work with—places he knew he could run to, a language he spoke, a system he understood and could subvert. Here he just felt helplessness.

"Finding anything, Cath?"

She froze for a moment, gripping her copy of the *Lonely Planet Jordan* like it was the cure for cancer.

"We're going to have to call Richard."

He let out a long, slow breath. "Then he'll know we're in Amman."

"He'd have guessed that already."

"Why not go to the American embassy and tell our story? You've got credibility."

She shook her head. "We have no idea who in the government is involved in this and how much power they have. It's the first place they'd expect us to run."

Of course, she was right. But their remaining options would barely fill a postcard.

"What about getting out of the country?"

"How? We don't even have passports?"

"No," Brandon said. "But we've got almost two grand in U.S. dollars between us. I could make some calls and maybe get the name of someone here who can help us."

"You mean a criminal."

"I wouldn't be too snobby, if I was you."

"So you're suggesting we just run."

"Well . . . Yeah."

"What about the warheads?"

He leaned across the table and lowered his voice. "What about them? I mean, I'm not any happier about this than you are, but what can we do? We're in the middle of fucking Jordan, and if it wasn't bad enough that the friends of those guys you shot are probably looking for us, we've got some government psycho sniffing around, too. I say we get the hell out of here, and when we've found some place safe, we call the cavalry. I'm not being entirely selfish here. If we get killed, then the game's over."

"Well that *is* generous of you, isn't it?" she said angrily, then immediately fell silent. "I'm . . . I'm sorry, Brandon. I'm really tired. And really scared."

"It's okay." He nodded toward her book again. "Did you find a place we can get on the Internet?"

She didn't respond, instead just staring over his right shoulder.

"What," he whispered, adrenaline surging through him. "Is it one of the guys from the plane?"

She just pointed.

He turned slowly, but instead of finding a group of Arab men wielding those big curved swords he was certain people in this part of the world favored, he came face-to-face with himself.

"You've got to be kidding me . . ."

The photo on the television was his mug shot—a typically dreary picture of him with bed-head and a serious five-o'clock shadow. He looked around, but no one seemed to be paying attention. And even if they had been, he doubted anyone would be expecting to find the man on television sipping coffee in Jordan.

The Internet café was more high tech than Brandon expected. Of course, it was in a building old enough for Jesus to have worked on it, but the connection was reasonably fast and the computers didn't seem to be in danger of catching fire.

They settled into a station near the back, as far away as they could get from a young couple arguing in French. Catherine punched up a Web mail account and typed in her password. She moved her hand to the enter button and let it hover there.

"What?" Brandon said.

"Richard said to look at this account if I couldn't get in touch with him. We haven't tried."

Brandon responded by slapping her hand out of the way and pushing the enter key himself. The screen went blank for a moment and then a simple in-box appeared with one unread e-mail. Honestly, he'd expected some techy video of Scanlon to come up like on the old spy shows, but it was just text. It wasn't even all that long.

> *Catherine:*
> *I know that if you're reading this, something's gone very wrong. Despite that, if you haven't done everything you can to contact me, I'd urge you to*

*stop reading and do so immediately. You know that I
will do everything in my power to help you.*

She tapped the screen above the sentence about
contacting Scanlon and shot Brandon an irritated
glance.

*If you have tried to contact me and I haven't
responded, I'm probably beyond being able to help
you. So all I can do is tell you as much as I know
about what's happening.*

*As I know you suspected, I was never the sole
driving force behind this—I have a strong ally in
Washington. His name is Edwin Hamdi.*

"Shit," she said quietly.

"What?" Brandon said. "Who's Edwin Hamdi?"

"The national security advisor."

"Is that a big deal?"

"You don't follow politics much, do you?"

"Not really."

"The president probably has Hamdi's home
number on his speed dial."

"Great. That's just great."

*It's likely that there are other people high up in
the various intelligence agencies involved as well, but
I've been insulated from them by Hamdi and so I
can't give you their names.*

*I don't know what's happened to you, Catherine,
but it's possible that Hamdi can help. On the other*

hand, he could also hurt you. I've never entirely trusted him, but my suspicions were never very well founded. It's possible that he might want to use the retrieval of those weapons to propel himself politically. I don't know.

If Brandon is still alive and still with you, he should give Hamdi a very wide berth no matter what you decide. Without me to stop him, I imagine he'll have Brandon killed if he has the opportunity.

You, on the other hand, need to calculate the risks and benefits of keeping Brandon with you. I believe he can be trusted and, as you already know, he can be quite resourceful.

I've left five million dollars in an account in Argentina with both your names on it. I was extremely careful, but I can't guarantee that Hamdi doesn't know about it.

I'm sorry I got you involved in this, Catherine. I hope you understand that I felt I had no choice. You're the only person I've ever completely trusted, and I think the only person I've ever really loved.

Richard

At the bottom was the information for the bank account Scanlon had mentioned. Catherine scrolled down looking for more, but there wasn't anything.

After one more read, she finally deleted the e-mail and then went to work on the browser's history, clearing every trace of them ever having been there. By the time she was finished, a tear was beginning to work its way down her cheek.

Chapter Forty-four

"Turn right at the next cross street," Ramez said, looking out at the poverty-stricken Tel Aviv neighborhood. The crumbling concrete dwellings that lined the narrow street were quiet during this part of the day, with most of their Arab inhabitants gone to work cleaning Jewish toilets. Manicuring Jewish lawns. Groveling for the privilege of living on land that had been theirs for so many centuries.

Despite the fact that Muhammad's knees were jammed up beneath the steering wheel and his head was scraping the roof, he was maneuvering the car smoothly, ever vigilant of the speed limit and traffic laws.

Ramez concentrated on his side mirrors, looking for police and military but seeing only the still, empty street.

"Here. It is here," he said, pointing to a house distinguishable from all the others only by the wooden bay door in its façade. Muhammad eased to a stop in the middle of the street and Ramez stepped out.

The key he had been given worked with surprising ease in the old lock, and the door slid up on a well-oiled track. He had to fight to stay calm as he directed

Muhammad inside. A few more seconds and it would be done. God be praised, just a few more seconds.

When he finally pulled the door closed, everything went dark. He listened to his breathing for a few moments, the tension he'd felt since Yusef's death beginning to release him. He'd been shocked and deeply saddened by his friend's courageous death and had been proud to take on the responsibility for this mission. But he hadn't been completely prepared for what it would feel like to be solely responsible for carrying out God's will.

Muhammad turned on the car's headlights and Ramez examined the cluttered space around them. They weren't in the middle of the city—not even close. But proximity didn't matter to what they had in their car. The destruction would spread from this point like the hand of God. In an instant, everything that men had spent so many centuries building would be gone.

He squinted into the bright light coming through a crack in the door and imagined the neighborhood later in the day when it would be transformed by children returning from school and parents from work. How many would die? How many would disintegrate in the unimaginable heat and force that the Americans had created so many years ago to exterminate the Japanese?

They would meet God as martyrs. Unwitting warriors in the final battle against the Jews. The battle that would carve out the cancer that had infected their ancestors' land for so long.

"Our time is now," Muhammad said, unfolding himself from the car.

But not really a car anymore. It had been transformed. It was God's will made tangible.

"We can't risk leaving here," he continued. "We can't."

"You understand the plan," Ramez said, watching the much larger man come toward him. "You understand what is expected of us."

Muhammad put a key in the trunk and pulled it open, moving old blankets and other carefully arranged debris that hid the warhead. His eyes burned in the reflected light.

"Once we leave, there is no certainty, Ramez. The warhead could be found. It could malfunction. But we're here now. We have the power to be certain. We have the power to do God's will. You know how to do it. To reset the timer so that—"

"Yes," Ramez said. "I know how to do it."

It was hard to discern what was more destructive to Islam. The Jews? Or was it Muslim men with minds so paralyzed by hate that they would fight endlessly for an undefined future that could never exist. Men like those in Iraq who wanted so badly for the Americans to leave but then created such violence and instability it ensured they would stay. Or Yasser Arafat, a man who had existed not to serve God and his people, but only to feed his own thirst for power.

If this conflict continued on the same path, the end of the Muslim people was certain. They had to come together as a unified front against America and the

Jews. They had to strive for real strength and to recognize acts like the destruction of the World Trade Center as the meaningless tantrums they were. Cohesiveness, discipline, and a common goal. With those things and their oil reserves, they would have the power to force the rest of the world to its knees.

Muhammad continued to stare down at the promise of death and glory contained in the car's trunk as Ramez reached for a two-by-four leaning against the wall. "You're right," he said, using both hands to raise the board above his head. "It is your time."

Chapter Forty-five

"Edwin Hamdi is not some kind of terrorist mole," Catherine said, pacing as manically as the tiny hotel room would allow. "He's a former college professor who's worked for several administrations and has direct access to the president. He's been checked out in every way possible—particularly because of his Arab background. Can you imagine the scrutiny?"

Brandon fell onto the bed and propped his head on a pillow. Catherine had stopped in front of a cracked window, backlit by the desert sun. They'd bought clothes more appropriate for the climate and culture, so she created a rather formless silhouette that was still strangely beautiful.

"Who are you trying to convince here, Cath? If you think Hamdi's so trustworthy, then let's give him a call. Tell him what happened."

She wrapped her arms around herself, then let them fall to her sides again. "We could . . ." Her voice faded for a moment. "We need to find a phone. We need to try to get Richard."

Everyone had limits, and as near as he could tell, she'd reached hers. The chain of command she'd relied on, the moral certainty she'd become so accustomed to, were all gone now, and she was grasping at just about anything.

"You know that's not a good idea, Cath."

"You still think he did this? You think he betrayed us?"

"No. I don't. I think this Hamdi guy has his own thing going on and . . ."

"And what?"

"And I think Richard's dead. Anything we do to try to contact him is only going to hurt us."

The silence that ensued was long enough to suggest that she knew what he was saying was true.

"I still have friends at the NSA. What if we call them? Tell them what's happened?"

"That would be an interesting conversation," Brandon said. "Hi. I just bought a bunch of nuclear warheads and gave them to some crazy-looking Arab guys so they could load them into cars and drive away."

"Do you have a better idea?" she nearly shouted. "Or do you think we should just sit here?"

"Hell no, I don't think we should just sit here. I think we should get the fuck out of here. Look, Jordan's no different than anywhere else—money talks. When we had two grand between us, getting out of here was gonna be a trick. With the five million Richard left us, not only can I get us out of here, I can get us out of here with cocktails and air-conditioning."

"To do what?"

He propped himself up on his elbows. "I say we

go to South America. If Hamdi is involved in what just happened, he's going to do everything he can to make sure we can't hurt him. And that means we have to get as far off the map as we can."

"Nothing you can say is going to make me believe that Edwin Hamdi is a terrorist."

He fell back on the bed again, a loud rush of air flowing from his lungs. "Kind of a subjective label isn't it, Cath? If the British had won, George Washington would be a terrorist. Maybe it's more complicated than you're thinking. What if he just doesn't feel like the American government is taking the terrorist threat seriously enough? Maybe he's gonna have one of those guys set off a bomb in a not-so-populated part of the U.S. and then lead the team that finds the rest of them? I don't know much about politics, but I'll bet at that point the American people would let him fight the war on terrorism any way he felt like. Or maybe he wants to use them on one of our enemies—North Korea or Iran or something—so America won't be blamed. There are all kinds of things that could be happening here. But none of them have anything to do with us."

She looked vaguely panicked as her eyes darted around the room. "How sure are you that you can get us out of here?"

He fought the relieved smile that was in danger of spreading across his face. "I'm a little out of my element here, so it might take some time. But I'm sure."

"And that's what you want to do."

Hell yes, it was what he wanted to do! The image of an anonymous little hut in Paraguay was so beautiful right now it nearly made him want to cry. And if he ever got there, he was going to pay someone to repeatedly hit him in the head with a brick until he forgot all about Richard Scanlon, Jordan, warheads, and just about everything else from his recent past.

That's what he wanted to say. What he should say. What he would say if he wasn't completely nuts.

"It's your call, Cath. I'll do everything I can to help you, no matter what you decide."

She leaned back against the wall while he tried to will her to give him the go-ahead to get them the hell out of there.

"We could still send my friends at NSA an e-mail about this."

"Absolutely," Brandon said hopefully. "We could send it right away."

"But then what?" she said. "What if there are people at the NSA who are involved? What if they think it's a hoax? We're just going to hit send and walk away?"

"What else can we do, Cath? Drive around asking if anyone's seen something that looks like a nuclear warhead lying around? I understand what you're saying, but sometimes you've just got to pull back and regroup. When we're safely out of here, we'll be in a hell of a lot better position to follow up on this thing than we are now."

She fell silent again, this time for more than a

minute. Finally, "Okay. We e-mail my friends and then we run."

Brandon resisted the urge to jump up off the bed and kiss her, instead just nodding gravely.

Being about six inches too tall, their truck had resisted every effort at hiding it in an underground parking garage. In the end, they'd been forced to leave it in the back of a small, razor-wire-encircled lot guarded by a single middle-aged man in grubby traditional dress. Fortunately, the general temperament of parking lot attendants seemed to cross cultural lines, and he could barely even be bothered to look at them as they passed by.

Brandon ducked his head in the driver's side and Catherine did the same on the passenger side, beginning a thorough search of the cab. It was the only piece of evidence they had, and Catherine wanted to see if they could find anything helpful before she sent her e-mails.

"Christ," Brandon mumbled.

"What? Did you find something?"

He pulled an empty soda bottle from beneath the seat, holding it up so she could read the label: Mecca Cola.

"Nothing quenches my thirst after a hard day of killing infidels like—"

"This is serious!" she said in a loud whisper. "You—"

"I know. I'm sorry," he said, leaving her to search an empty glove box while he walked around back.

The bed of the truck was covered with green canvas in a configuration that conjured thoughts of wagons from the Old West. Instead of a wooden gate, though, there was a heavy flap held closed by rope.

He glanced behind him for what must have been the hundredth time since they'd left the hotel and saw that the sun had sunk almost to the tops of the roofs across the street. Above, the sky was still an almost malevolent blue, promising nothing but dry, punishing heat for the next century. He hadn't been in Jordan long, but he was starting to get an idea of why these people were so pissed.

The rope came free with a little effort and Brandon threw the flap back. It took a moment for his eyes to adjust to the shadow inside, and when they did, he froze.

After a few seconds he heard Catherine's muffled voice from the cab. "Brandon? Is there anything there?"

When he didn't answer, she came around the back of the truck and stood next to him.

"Oh, my God."

"Okay," Catherine said, trying to steady her voice. "We can't panic. We just need to stay calm and think this through."

They'd retreated across the street and were standing in front of a crumbling stone house with laundry hanging from the windows.

"Didn't you see them putting it in there?"

"Like I had time to look over all the cars before I decided which one to steal?"

"Don't get mad," she said. "I'm not saying it's your fault. It just happened, okay?"

The truck was clearly visible from where they were standing, parked innocently along the back wall of the lot. It seemed strangely natural there, as though it had been stalled in that space for years. Nothing at all would suggest that it contained a weapon capable of flattening Amman and everything around it.

"That's it," she said. "We have to go to the embassy."

"No. No way."

"Brandon—"

"Hamdi's going to be watching for that. I know you don't think he's a terrorist, but are you sure? Because if you're not—"

"I don't know if you've been paying attention," she said, in something between a shout and a whisper. "But there's a—"

He clamped a hand over her mouth. "We stick to our plan. With one slight modification. Tomorrow morning we're going to buy a couple of shovels and we're going out to the desert and bury that thing. Then, when we're confident your NSA buddies are on the up-and-up, we'll tell them where it is. This works for us, Cath. Think about it. When they lay their eyes on that thing, our story's gospel."

Chapter Forty-six

A dull glow had started on the other side of the shutters, but it wasn't strong enough to overcome the darkness in the room. In fact, the more Catherine stared into it, the darker everything seemed to become.

She was lying on her side in the lumpy bed with Brandon right behind, his arm thrown across her. She moved slowly so as not to wake him, gently gripping his hand and pressing it against her bare stomach.

Their role as a married couple had left them with a single bed in an un-air-conditioned room so hot that she'd had to strip down to her bra and panties in order to sleep. Or at least that's what she'd convinced herself of last night. The obvious truth was that it had been a rather desperate and poorly conceived come-on—a ploy to help her forget. If only for a little while.

Of course, Brandon saw her advances for what they were and gracefully deflected every not-so-subtle hint, feigning complete ignorance with an ever-deepening glint of worry in his eyes.

The problem, though, wasn't so much that he seemed to think that she was slowly going crazy, it was that she wasn't sure if he was wrong. She hadn't slept at all, despite the temperature dropping at least forty degrees overnight. Instead, she'd just lay there, her mind repeatedly failing to process all that had happened. Every time she tried to calmly think through their situation, she found herself drowning in the enormity of what she'd done.

Because of her, there were eleven nuclear warheads out there. What if they were smuggled into the United States? Even if her friends at the NSA took her warning seriously, how many could they hope to intercept? Five? Six? That left most of America's largest cities gone and tens of millions of people dead or dying horribly. It left the world order in shambles and perhaps millions more starving. It left the Middle East open to a retaliation that was impossible to even imagine.

She felt the waves coming over her head again and she squeezed Brandon's hand tighter, closing her eyes and just trying to keep breathing. He was the only person she had left, but he didn't belong there with her. She had no right to let this destroy him, too.

He wanted her to run with him, but what then? He'd been so smooth in trying to convince her how critical her survival was, but it was a lie. Once she told the NSA what she knew, she would have no purpose other than to inhabit a richly deserved prison cell and to watch the deaths of the millions of people she had doomed.

A few angry shouts filtered through the shutters along with the strengthening light, and Catherine finally closed her eyes. She saw the warheads, and Richard, and Brandon. She saw fire and endless deserts.

The shouting outside grew in volume and she tried to shut it out. Only when it was replaced with something that sounded like a speech did she open her eyes again. The voice was unamplified, but had a rhythm and pitch that identified the message as political.

Brandon stirred, pulling her tighter against him and mumbling, "Shut up, man," into the back of her neck.

The voice became a shout and then fell silent after coming to an important sounding conclusion. A moment later cheers forceful enough to rattle the windows erupted.

Brandon bolted into a sitting position, blinking groggily. "What the hell is tha—"

The sound of gunfire brought him fully awake, and he shoved her onto the floor, landing on top of her with his feet still tangled in the sheets. The cheering was deafening now, but there were no more shots as Brandon dragged her to the wall.

"They couldn't be . . . ," he started. "No. No way. They couldn't be out there for us, could they?"

Catherine shook her head violently, trying to clear it. Had they left a trail? Had they missed something? She just didn't know.

Brandon must have seen her helpless expression because he gathered up the sheet twisted around his feet and wrapped it around her. "It's okay. We're going to be all right."

When he tried to stand, she held his arm. This was insane. She had to pull herself together. This wasn't his responsibility.

"Come on, Cath. I have to—"

"No! I'll do it."

"You're not—"

She leaned forward and kissed him, his momentary surprise allowing her to stand and move into a position where she could see through the gap between the shutters.

The street was crammed full of men to the point that they seemed to be a single entity, ebbing and flowing, shouting as though from a single, massive throat.

Almost directly across from their hotel was a man standing on the hood of a car, straining to be heard. Another burst of machine gun fire erupted, and Catherine resisted Brandon's effort to pull her back to the floor. The shots weren't aimed at them. In fact, they weren't aimed at anything. It was just the Arab equivalent of a standing ovation.

The hotel manager flashed his slightly plastic smile as they descended the stairs, raising his voice to be heard over the roar of the crowd outside. "Good morning."

His English seemed perfect, but was really just the result of some narrowly targeted practice. "Good afternoon" and "Good evening" had an equally upper-crust British feel, but beyond that his communication skills were unreliable at best.

Brandon pointed to the closed door at the end of the lobby. "What's happening out there, Hussein?"

The man's eyes widened for a moment, indicating

surprise at the question and not just his normal comprehension problems. "You no hear?"

"Hear what?"

"Israel," he said and then made a motion that resembled a baseball umpire designating a runner safe.

Catherine had positioned herself behind Brandon, having learned that despite playing the respectable married woman, Hussein found dealing with her directly rather distasteful.

"I, uh, don't understand," Brandon said, prompted by a jab in his lower back.

Hussein squinted for a moment and then came up with "Israel, bomb. Atomic." Then an exploding noise.

"What?" Catherine shouted, coming out from behind Brandon to face the hotel owner for the first time since they'd arrived.

"Cath—I've got thi—"

"What did you say?"

She hadn't thought that she had any adrenaline left after feeling nothing when the shooting had started outside their window. Now it was coursing through her again. "Tell me what you said?"

When Hussein just stood there staring, she went for the door.

"No! Danger!" he said, running to block her path.

"Get out of my way!"

"Catherine . . . ," Brandon cautioned.

"Did you hear him? We've got to go, Brandon. Now! He can't keep us here."

Brandon grabbed her by the arm and pulled her out of earshot of their host.

"I heard what he said, Cath, but I'm not sure what he meant. Are you? And what are you going to do about it? Look, I haven't said anything up till now, but you're not thinking straight. We need to wait until things cool down out there and—"

"Then don't come with me."

"Cath—"

"I'm serious, Brandon. Look, I can't tell you how much I appreciate everything you've done. But you should stay here and concentrate on getting yourself out of the country. If I can come, I will. But this isn't your fight."

Brandon went through the door first, with Catherine right behind. She had a death grip on one of his hands and the other was clamped around the cloth belt at his waist.

While Hussein had no real affinity for either of them, he did recognize their value as conduits for American dollars. His hope that his favorite paying customers would live to spend a few more nights had prompted the donation of some of his and his wife's old clothes.

The overall effect of Brandon's disguise was mediocre at best, but most of the people on the street were too occupied to pay much attention. She, on the other hand, was almost completely enshrouded, with only a narrow strip around her eyes that made the crowd they were pushing through even more frightening and claustrophobic. She had a purpose again, though, and she used that to shut out everything but getting through the cheering, jostling men around them.

"Are you sure you want to do this?" she shouted in his ear. He didn't answer.

She'd tried to get him to stay behind, but it was just an act. She would have never made it by herself and, even more selfishly, she wanted him with her. Once again, Brandon Vale was trapped in a situation he had nothing to do with. And once again, he'd proved that he was much more than most people would give him credit for.

The sun had finally cleared the rooftops and the air was so humid with sweat that the shop windows were beginning to fog. The crowd moved back suddenly, pinning them to a wooden fence as the speaker continued to speak from the hood of his car. Catherine wrapped her arms around Brandon's waist and just held on.

She wasn't sure how long they were stuck there, but eventually the mob shifted and they started forward again, slipping through a quickly narrowing gap between men whose barely controlled religious ecstasy had them leaping up into the air with such force that they nearly fell every time they landed.

A few lucky dodges and a fair amount of shoving left them standing in front of the gated door to the Internet café they'd been in the day before. Brandon pulled Catherine in front of him and grabbed the bars on either side of her, partially insulating her from the chaos of the crowd. "Is there anyone in there?"

She pressed her face against the bars, then slipped a hand through and pounded on the glass door. A moment later, the owner of the café appeared at the back to wave them off. He was about to turn away when Catherine pulled the cloth from her face and hair. The man inside froze for a moment and then rushed forward while Brandon turned to confirm that they weren't attracting any undue attention.

The gate clicked open and they both slipped through. The café's owner immediately slammed the bars shut again and locked them in place with a panicky twist of his key ring. When he finally faced them, he jabbed a finger violently in the air. "This is insanity! Why are you here? Have you not heard what has happened?"

"I'm sorry," Catherine said in a voice meant to be soothing, but sabotaged by an undercurrent of panic. "Is your connection still working? We need to get on a computer."

He glanced over his shoulder at the crowd now pressing against the increasingly flimsy-looking gate. "Take one of the computers at the back. The *far* back."

The headline on CNN.com was bad, but not as bad as the ever-escalating images Catherine's mind had conjured on her way there: "Israel Threatened by Nuclear Terror."

She skimmed the article, paraphrasing for Brandon while he watched the crowd outside.

"They put one of the warheads in front of a government building in Jerusalem and then called the police and the press. They said they had eleven more—"

"Ten," Brandon corrected.

"They say all of them have been set with three-week timers and that they're hidden all over Israel and the Occupied Territories . . ."

She fell silent, her initial relief that no one had been hurt disintegrating. There were millions of people in Israel. Thousands of years of human history . . .

"Catherine?" Brandon said. "Come on, stay with me. Why would anyone do something like this?"

She took a deep breath and let it out slowly.

"Cath?"

"There's some Islamic rhetoric about the Jews being a blight on Arab land and an affront to God, and identifying the terrorists as a group no one has ever heard of. Their warning included the serial numbers on the warheads. The Russians are stalling but . . ." She fell silent.

"What?"

"It says that the American government has confirmed that the numbers are valid."

"So? We knew that."

"The quote is from Edwin Hamdi."

"Hamdi," Brandon repeated quietly. "But why would he be involved in something like this? Aren't we friends with the Israelis?"

She leaned back in her chair, the computer screen going slowly out of focus. "Think about it, Brandon. Both the Jews and the Palestinians think God gave them Israel and neither is ever going to budge. The problem gets worse every year, and every year we get dragged farther into it."

"So you're saying he just decided to get rid of the problem?"

"I don't know. It seems crazy, but there's sort of a twisted logic to it. Give the warheads to a bunch of Muslim fanatics and tell them to destroy Israel . . ."

"But the Arabs *want* that land! It's all tied up with their religion and history. They'd be cutting their nose off to spite their face."

She nodded. "You just summed up the Arab people, Brandon. And terrorists are even worse. They don't care about accomplishing anything meaningful for their people—they just like to make grand, pointless statements."

"Then why the warning? Wouldn't it be a bigger statement to just set them off and kill everyone?"

"Hamdi," she said. "I've never met him, but he doesn't have the reputation of being a maniac. He wouldn't want to kill millions of innocent people. He's giving them a choice—a chance to move on."

Brandon opened his mouth to protest again, but for some reason didn't. "So what do we do?"

She thought about that for a long time, and the more she did, the more her mind cleared. She had almost no chance of stopping this, but now at least she had enough information to try.

"You're going to get out of the country and disappear, Brandon. You're going to run somewhere you'll be safe."

"You mean *we*. *We're* going to get out of here and go somewhere safe."

"No."

"Catheri—"

"I can't walk away from this, Brandon. I can't."

Chapter Forty-seven

The mix of fear, anticipation, guilt, pride, and so many other emotions was virtually impossible to fully hide, and Edwin Hamdi cast his eyes down whenever he could. There was something hypnotic in the swirling grain of the desk in front of him, something that helped him maintain the carefully constructed aura of calm he had wrapped himself in.

Of course, the operation had not gone entirely to plan—they never did. Catherine and Brandon were still on the run, probably somewhere in Jordan. Worse, they had one of the warheads, making it necessary to revert to a contingency placement strategy that, while suboptimal, would still leave Israel and the Occupied Territories completely uninhabitable.

In the end, Hamdi was certain that their escape would prove to be little more than an annoyance. They had been powerless to stop the deployment of the warheads, which were all now in place with timers counting down. And there was no reason to believe that Catherine had any knowledge of his involvement.

It was unstoppable now. Inevitable. In three weeks the world would be a very different place. A place where the Jews were scattered and marginalized. A place that he would have the opportunity to mold.

"So this is real," President Morris said. His back was turned and he was standing in front of the large window that looked out over Washington.

"There is no way to be completely certain," Hamdi responded. "But all evidence suggests that it is."

"And you believe that they will make good on their threat."

"I do."

The president finally sat, pointing to the only other man in the room. "What's the CIA's position?"

Paul Lowe folded his arms in front of his chest in a mannerism he displayed only when he was in the uncomfortable position of agreeing with Hamdi. "If they've really got the nukes, they're going to do everything they can to make sure they're detonated. Unless someone stops them, Israel is going to take a hit—"

"A hit? Jesus Christ, Paul! We're talking about their complete destruction! We're talking about an environmental disaster that could affect the entire region. Hell, the entire *world*. How are we going to stop this?"

"I don't think there's anything we can do," Hamdi said. "We're talking about a terrorist cell that we have absolutely no information on. None of our informants have ever even heard of them—"

"They're out there somewhere, Edwin. And that means they can goddamn well be found."

"Yes, sir. They're out there. But spread out and underground. And what if we did manage to find one of them before the detonation? It's unlikely he would have any information beyond where he'd hidden the warhead he was directly responsible for. As for finding the ringleader . . . Well, our history with Osama bin Laden is instructive regarding the chances of that happening."

Morris's face had continued to redden throughout the conversation and he seemed on the verge of one of his infamous outbursts, but instead, he just turned his attention to Lowe. "How the hell did we miss this, Paul?"

"Prior to your administration, building an intelligence network to track loose nukes in the former Soviet Union wasn't a top priority. We've been making progress, but it takes time to put that kind of infrastructure in place. At this point, we believe that the warheads were purchased from a Ukrainian organized-crime group, but we have very little information on that group or exactly how they got hold of the weapons—"

"Time," Morris interrupted. "The one thing we never have." He took a deep breath and let it out slowly. "I talked to the Israeli prime minister this morning. So far, they've managed to control the panic and they're organizing evacuations of their major cities, as well as creating task forces to search for the warheads. Jordan and Egypt have agreed to accept the Palestinians and, for the time being, give them refugee status. They aren't being as generous with Israel's Jews."

"I've spoken to my contacts there," Hamdi said. "And from what they tell me, they'd be willing to allow the Jews to move through their countries and leave from their ports. However, they will only accept them unarmed and in civilian vehicles."

"So we need to get probably ten million people over the border in the next three weeks and they want to frisk every goddamn one of them?"

"I believe the searches will be perfunctory, sir, but nonnegotiable. Neither country is anxious to have millions of armed, displaced Jews inside their border. During the cold war, I think we would have taken a similar position if the entire population of the Soviet Union needed to pass through the U.S."

Lowe actually nodded at that "They want guarantees from both the U.N. and us that the Israeli Jews will be immediately removed and that we will side with the Arabs should there be any clashes."

"I think this is reasonable," Hamdi said. "Even generous, based on their history. The Arabs are also concerned about the current mobilization of Israeli forces and the possibility that they could be used as an invasion force."

"The Jordanians, Egyptians, and Syrians are putting everything they've got into strengthening their border positions," Lowe added. "And they're requesting U.N. support. The fact that the Israelis haven't ruled out retaliation is making things worse."

"Yes," Hamdi agreed, becoming increasingly mesmerized by the chaos he had created. "Lashing out blindly would be incredibly counterproductive for the Israelis at this point. Every Arab nation, as well as the Palestinian government, has condemned this act."

"They've pointed out problems with radioactivity, and the destruction of Al-Aqsa, and the Palestinian homeland," the president corrected. "That's hardly what I'd call a condemnation."

"Hatred of the Jews is very potent in that part of the world. No government can come out too strongly against this act until they see how popular it is with the common man—particularly in light of the fact that they are allowing the Israelis to cross their territories."

"And by all indications, it's pretty popular," Lowe said. "We're seeing massive celebrations breaking out all over the Middle East."

The president fell silent for a few moments. "I can't help thinking what could have happened if they'd gotten those nukes into the U.S. Our ten largest cities . . . gone."

"Yes, sir," Hamdi said. "We should use this as an opportunity to strengthen the policies of peace you've been pursuing as well as our commitment to controlling the loose-nuke problems. If Israel, with its minimal borders and history of police state tactics, can't keep this from happening, we can't expect to, either."

Morris stared at him for a moment and then started slowly clapping. "We're looking at the complete destruction of a country and the deaths of God knows how many people and you're still calculating the angles."

Hamdi kept his expression completely impassive. "This is a horrible tragedy, sir. But if these people are destined to die or be displaced, we should do everything we can to see that some good comes from it. One of the most dangerous and contentious situations in history is going to simply cease to exist in three weeks and we need to be prepared to exploit that reality—for the good of everyone."

"How?"

"I understand that we're already mobilizing virtually all our resources to help with the evacuation. That's the right action. But we have to go out of our way to try to be evenhanded—to put as much effort into the problem of Arab evacuation as we do Jewish evacuation. We need to be focused on making it appear as though we value an Arab life just as much as a Jewish life."

The president leaned over his desk, a brief flash of anger crossing his face. "We *do* value an Arab life as much as a Jewish life."

Hamdi cursed himself silently. The power of being at the center of this particular moment in history was making him incautious. "I misspoke, sir. My apologies."

Chapter Forty-eight

"This isn't a plan, Catherine. This is no plan. We need to think this through. Come up with something—"

Brandon grabbed hold of the truck's dashboard as the front wheels dropped into a rut and jumped back out, causing a cloud of dust to billow through the missing doors and into his eyes and mouth.

"It's the *only* plan," Catherine shouted over the whine of the struggling engine. "And you know it. We don't have any idea who to trust in the American government and we sure as hell can't trust the Arabs. But we know for sure the Israelis don't want their country destroyed."

"That's not exactly the same thing as trusting them, though, is it?"

She glanced over at him. "I told you not to come, Brandon. This isn't your fight, and even if it was, there's nothing you can do. You should take Richard's money and run. You earned it."

"Damn right, I earned it!" he yelled, more for his own benefit than Catherine's. "Damn right . . ."

He settled back in the seat and squinted through the windshield at the bizarre scene outside. It wasn't the devastated barrenness of the desert that was so fascinating—he was actually starting to get used to feeling like he was on Mars. It was the narrow line of cars and pedestrians extending into the horizon. He watched a young woman and her two children walking behind a tiny car stuffed with possessions. Then a pickup overflowing with a family that seemed to encompass four generations—each hiding from the sun beneath a dusty umbrella. And on and on.

Catherine swerved right to avoid a donkey with what looked like an antique writing desk strapped to its back and nearly got bogged down next to a soldier tracking the procession of refugees from a sandbag-protected machine-gun emplacement. Another hundred yards took them past a group of U.N. soldiers trying keep everyone moving peacefully forward. They gave the truck a quick glance as it bounced by, but didn't seem particularly interested. They had more important things to worry about than two people speeding toward a country that was now well beyond security concerns.

"There's got to be a better way, Cath. If we just stop and thi—"

"We've been driving for hours, Brandon. What have you come up with?"

She was right. He'd thought about it from every angle and come up blank. Now he couldn't help feeling like anything that happened to her was his fault. He was supposed to be good at this.

"I'm sorry," she said, unwisely taking a hand off the wheel and squeezing his leg. "I know that if you had a couple of months you'd probably figure out how to break into the prime minister's house and drop this thing in his living room. But we don't have a couple of months."

It seemed as though she hadn't so much as blinked since they'd left Amman. She was completely consumed by the idea of either putting all this right or dying in the attempt. The problem was, she didn't seem all that concerned with which.

"But like you said," she continued, "it's not much of a plan. And that means that there's nothing you can do to help—"

"Are you trying to get rid of me?"

The truck hit another series of ruts and she had to put her hand back on the wheel.

"You can get away, Brandon. You can live out the rest of your life. I don't want to be responsible for something happening to you. Can you understand that? It would be . . . It would be too much. To know that you . . ." Her voice faded.

"I'm just as responsible as you are for this. If I hadn't gone to Ukraine, the warheads would still be in that cave. Maybe I can't live with that, either."

He wondered if that was true. Or if he really was just there for her. Not that it mattered. Most likely, they'd be dead in an hour with nothing at all to show for it. Just a pointless heroic gesture that would quickly be swallowed by a mushroom cloud. And while that wasn't really his MO, what was the alternative? Get out of the truck and walk back to Amman with endless scenarios of her death running through his head? Watch the destruction of an entire country from the comfort of his South African mansion, knowing that there had been a chance that he could have stopped it if he'd just had the courage to try?

"There it is," she said, releasing the accelerator and letting the truck drift to a stop.

The checkpoint was nothing more than a narrow opening in a tangle of razor wire that went out about fifty yards on either side, ending in sand drifts deep enough to bog down any vehicle short of a tank. There were two machine-gun positions dug in on either side, but the guns were pointed away from them and toward a similarly armed Israeli checkpoint about a hundred yards farther down the road.

Catherine pushed the scarf she was wearing off her head, revealing her long, dark hair. "So there's nothing I can say to convince you to turn around and get out of here?"

"That you're going with me."

She shook her head. "I can't, Brandon. You know that."

"Yeah. Then I guess I'm staying."

He wasn't really surprised when she let out a long breath and sagged a bit in her seat. She didn't want to face this alone any more than he would have.

"Any ideas?" she asked, peeling off the rest of the hotel manager's wife's clothes. A group of men walking by slowed a bit, only to be disappointed by the cargo pants and billowy white shirt she had on underneath.

"Not really," Brandon said, studying the checkpoint. He pointed to an open section in the razor wire where an entire family was lying face down in the dirt while a group of well-armed Jordanian soldiers searched their Lexus. The next car was only about a foot behind, as was the next car, and the next. "We're not getting through that way. And we can't swing wide—it'd give too many people too much time to shoot us. Besides, we'd just get stuck in the sand."

"So straight through the razor wire," she said, tying her hair in a knot behind her head.

"I guess so. Go slow at first, though. We're in a military truck, and with the position of the sun, those guards are going to have a hard time seeing through the windshield. Don't give them any reason to get fired up—I mean, at this point, what harm can anyone do to Israel?"

She nodded and started forward, leveling out her speed at a nonthreatening ten miles an hour as they closed in on the checkpoint.

"Figure out what path you're going to take and concentrate on that, Cath. Remember it, because you're probably going to have to do some of it blind. I'll worry about the guards. Wait for my signal."

They continued forward, getting surprisingly little attention at first. When they made it to within a hundred yards, though, one of the guards pulled his head out of the Lexus and turned to watch their approach.

"It's too many people," Catherine said. "Too many guns. We're not going to make it." There was nothing in her tone that suggested she wanted to turn around. It was more of a resigned observation.

"Just keep it steady," Brandon said, sticking a badly

shaking hand out of the truck and holding it over the roof in greeting. The guard didn't wave back, but he didn't reach for the rifle slung over his shoulder, either. At fifty yards, the other guards abandoned the Lexus and began ambling in their direction.

"You're sure that bullets can't set off that warhead."

Catherine shrugged. "I'm pretty sure."

"Well, then I guess you might as well floor it."

The acceleration was more violent than he'd expected and he grabbed the edge of his seat as she swerved right, aiming for a section of razor wire as far from the guards and machine gun emplacements as she could get.

The quickest of the guards already had a bead on them and Brandon watched for the muzzle flash, praying his half-assed theory was right.

Nothing.

Two more men managed to get their rifles off their shoulders and aimed, but they didn't fire either.

The razor wire ripping apart on their hood sounded a bit like shattering glass and Brandon leaned toward the middle of the truck to avoid getting cut.

"Why aren't they shooting?" Catherine shouted, as they came into range of the Jordanian machine gunners.

"They think we're Arab terrorists!" Brandon yelled back, grabbing the wheel and aiming them at a similar line of razor wire on the Israeli side. "Get down!"

The sound of gunfire started and a moment later the windshield exploded, filling the air with shards of glass. Brandon crammed himself as far as he could beneath the dash, trying to hold the wheel steady with one hand and to pull Catherine down with the other. She hung up for a moment and by the time she managed to work her way to the floorboard, she was bleeding badly from a series of gashes across her forehead.

"Keep going!" he shouted. "Hold on! We've got—"

The front of the truck suddenly dipped and he was slammed forward as the back wheels came off the ground.

It all seemed to happen in slow motion, just like everyone said: the truck beginning to tip, his sweaty hands sliding from the wheel, the increasing momentum as he fell backward. Despite the realization that he was going to end up on the ground with the truck on top of him, he managed to remain surprisingly calm. Mostly he felt regret. Not sharp. Just kind of nagging.

When the truck finally hit, though, he wasn't under it. The cab skidded along on its side and he could feel the sand building up behind him, pushing him toward Catherine. It was then he noticed her hand gripping the front of his shirt and realized that it had kept him inside.

The increasingly familiar sound of bullets hitting metal grew loud enough to drown everything else out. It seemed inevitable that the gas tank would be hit, enveloping them in a ball of fire. Or maybe a bullet would penetrate the vehicle and make its way through Catherine and then into him . . .

But the old truck held. Whatever weapons the

Israelis were using couldn't penetrate the heavy steel it had been constructed from. Eventually, someone realized that, and everything went silent.

"Americans!" Brandon shouted, though not as loudly as he'd hoped. His second try was better. "We're Americans! Don't shoot! We're Americans!"

He used his sleeve to wipe the blood from Catherine's forehead as she tried to blink it from her eyes. "Told you it would work."

Chapter Forty-nine

"Kind of dicks, aren't they?" Brandon said, motioning with his head toward the angry-looking soldier sitting across from them.

"Brandon, don't make things worse than they already are, okay?"

He and Catherine were sitting next to each other in the back of an Israeli army truck, speeding along in what most people would agree was the wrong direction. He stretched his legs out and rested them on a wooden crate, prompting the kid guarding them to start shouting and shaking his rifle. Brandon's Hebrew was pretty much nonexistent, but the meaning was still clear. Don't use the thermonuclear weapon as an ottoman.

"Shut it," Brandon said, adjusting himself into a more comfortable position and trying to get the blood flowing into his shackled hands. The soldier aimed his rifle, and Brandon gave him a bored frown. He'd never expected to survive their border crossing. Or his prison escape. Or the Ukrainians. Hell if he was going to be intimidated by a high school kid with a bad afro.

He let his head loll to the left and looked at the similarly restrained Catherine. "So how are we doing?"

"Maybe not quite as well as I'd hoped. I figured the Jordanian guards wouldn't speak any English, but for some reason it never occurred to me that none of the Jewish soldiers would, either."

The Israelis were understandably upset that someone had just tried to crash through their barricades with a nuclear weapon in the back of their truck. There had been a lot of shouting, sign language, and brandishing of weapons, but it quickly became clear that this was a situation that demanded a bit more nuanced communication.

"Can't plan for everything," Brandon said.

"Go ahead and say it. You would have." She forced a hopeful expression that was barely visible through the dried blood on her face. "But, hey, we're not dead."

In truth, he'd been fishing for a little reassurance, but it looked like "we're not dead" was the best she was going to do.

"So, what now?" he said, not sure he really wanted to know.

"When we get where we're going, they'll separate us. Interrogate us."

"Great." He leaned his head back against the canvas behind him. "That's just great."

"I told you not to come. I told you—"

"It's not your fault," he said, turning toward her and trying unsuccessfully to get her to look at him.

"Just tell the truth. Okay, Brandon? Tell them everything they want to know."

"Everything?"

She nodded, still not meeting his eye. "Don't try to be clever. I know you're good at it, but these people . . . They'll see through it."

The implication was clear. Tell the truth and maybe they won't turn the electrodes taped to his balls up to eleven. Why were they trying to save the world again?

"Are you looking for something?"

Brandon ducked out from under the table and sat upright in his chair. "The electrodes."

"Electrodes?" A broad smile spread across the man's face—an open, easy, friendly smile. A smile that said he'd just returned from coaching the local Little League team and was about to start his volunteer shift at the old folk's home. It wasn't real, of course, but as a professional, Brandon could appreciate the effort that must have gone into developing it. The truth, just visible behind it, was that this guy was about an inch from pulling out a knife and starting in on Brandon's fingers.

Beyond that subtle vibe, though, everything was quite pleasant. They were sitting in something that felt more like a conference room than an interrogation room and Brandon had a cup of really good coffee steaming away in front of him.

"I think you've been watching too many movies," the man said in slightly accented English, squinting at the screen of his laptop. Finally, he pushed the computer aside and raised his reading glasses to the top of his head. "That's quite a story, Brandon."

"Yeah. I guess it is."

It had all happened exactly like Catherine said. They'd been separated the moment they arrived in his empty, spooky, little town, and an hour later the man sitting in front of him had arrived to politely listen to Brandon's stream-of-consciousness recounting of his past few weeks.

"Where's Catherine? Is she okay?"

The man nodded, but seemed preoccupied with the difficult task of finding holes in Brandon's story. He'd been on the Internet through the entire interrogation, verifying what he was being told. The bottom line was that there just weren't many paths that could take Brandon from an American jail cell to delivering a nuke across the Israeli border.

"So they're still liking me for the Fed heist, huh?" Brandon said, trying to break the silence before it broke him.

The man ignored the question. "You still want to stand by your statement that you've never met Edwin Hamdi?"

"Like I said, I think I did—when he had me pulled out of the condo—"

"It seems a bit incredible that he would involve you to this level with no prior issues."

"Issues? What do you mean, issues?"

"For instance, maybe you don't like Jews? Or perhaps you are a supporter of the Palestinians?"

Brandon took a slow sip of his coffee, being careful not to burn his mouth. "I want to be completely clear on this: If you put a gun to my head—and I'm not suggesting you should—I couldn't find Israel on a map."

"Brandon!" Catherine threw her arms around his neck as the door was bolted behind him. "Are you okay? I thought I was never going to see you again!"

"Wasn't so bad," he said, losing himself in her warmth for a few seconds before pulling back to look at her face. It was clean and he could see black stitches peeking out from the edge of a bandage on her forehead. "How was yours?"

"Okay, I guess," she said, taking him by the hand and pulling him over to a sofa pushed up against the wall. Once again, the room wasn't what he'd been expecting. More college apartment than gulag.

"They'll be cross-referencing our stories now, trying to figure out if we're lying. But I think they believed me. What about you?"

He shrugged, still looking around nervously. "They didn't want to believe me, but why would I lie? Their whole country's going to be gone in three weeks."

She agreed. "It's a little late for tricks."

"Okay. So they'll think about it for a couple hours and figure out we're telling them the truth. What then?"

"They'll try to find—"

"I mean what about us?"

"Oh."

He waited, but she remained silent.

"That's it? Oh?"

"How would I know? I don't—"

"Yes, you do."

She stood and walked across the room, getting as far away from him as she could before turning and pressing her back against the wall. "I told you not to come with me, Brandon. I told you to run."

"I think we've established that."

She stared at the blank wall above his head. "If they can't find the bombs with the information we've given them, then they'll probably just leave us here to die in the blast."

"And if they do find them?"

"Then . . . . Then they'll probably just kill us to keep the whole thing quiet. I imagine they'll let the U.S. government know what happened and hold it over their heads. The Israelis have never been very happy with the Morris administration's conciliatory stance toward the Arabs."

Brandon nodded slowly, feeling a wave of sadness that actually obscured the fear of the past few hours. He'd almost gotten to the point that he could imagine a real life for himself. A life where he came up with a way to get his rush from something more productive than stealing. A life that maybe included Catherine. Of course, he'd always known it was nothing but a dream, but at least it had been a vivid one. Almost vivid enough to think about it becoming real one day.

Chapter Fifty

Edwin Hamdi sat quietly in the backseat of his car, staring past his two bodyguards into the darkness beyond the windshield. It was after ten p.m. and the traffic was almost nonexistent as they pulled off the exit leading to the quiet neighborhood he'd lived in since his move to Washington.

He turned in his seat and watched the trees lining the road as they were briefly lit and then swallowed up again. There was a certain serenity to be derived from the familiarity and stillness, though he knew it was nothing more than an illusion. The chaos he'd created was out there—building and destroying, killing and saving. Reshaping the world.

The evacuation of Israel was going as well as could be expected. After endless promises and reassurances—as well as a number of outright bribes—the Jews were finally crossing into Jordan and Egypt. Combined with the massive airlift effort as well as the involvement of thousands of ships from all over the world, it appeared that the Jews would once again be saved. Deserving or not.

Sadly, but not surprisingly, the Palestinians were not faring as well. While they were on track to achieve a more or less full evacuation, the question of what would happen afterward was still unanswered. In many ways, they were a people unwanted by the world. The West wasn't anxious to absorb an uneducated mass that it considered largely radical and violent, and the Arabs weren't particularly interested, either. While the Jews were moving toward new and eventually permanent homes, the Palestinians were flooding haphazard refugee camps.

Of course, there were also those who refused to leave. Some estimates put the number at a quarter of a million—primarily fanatical Jews who would not let the land they thought they so richly deserved be pried from their fingers.

The sound of crunching glass and subsequent deceleration interrupted Hamdi's train of thought and he put a hand out to brace himself. "Did we hit som—"

He fell silent when he saw two small holes in the windshield, one in front of each of his men. A moment later, a dark figure with a rifle appeared in the street, running hard toward the car.

"Drive!" Hamdi shouted throwing himself forward and wedging himself between the front seats. The man on the passenger side was completely still, his head resting against the side window, while the driver was slumped forward against the steering wheel.

"Drive!" he yelled again, though he knew both men were dead.

The car drifted to a stop and Hamdi jammed a hand against the driver's knee, trying to get his foot to depress the accelerator. Instead, the lifeless body just tipped to the right.

The sound of crunching glass was louder this time, and came from behind.

Hamdi jammed himself beneath the steering wheel and reached the gas pedal just as a powerful hand closed around his ankle. The car leaped forward and he was jerked violently back, slamming his head against the edge of the wheel.

"Help!" he shouted weakly. "I'm Edwin Ha—"

The pressure around his ankle disappeared and was immediately replaced by an arm around his neck. He reached behind him and tried to claw the eyes of the man who was holding him. At the same time, he heard the driver's side door open and his bodyguard's body being dragged from the car.

The blind rage that suddenly boiled up inside him provided enough strength to twist around and partially face his attacker, who was still hanging partway out the broken back window. He swung a fist at the man's head and bit down on his forearm, filling his mouth with the metallic taste of blood.

Instead of releasing him, though, the man just increased the pressure on his neck. After a few moments, Hamdi's strength abandoned him and he was shoved to the floorboard as the car began a smooth U-turn. The arm around his neck disappeared and he gasped for breath, too consumed with getting air into his lungs to notice the handcuffs closing around his wrists.

As his mind cleared, panic began to take hold. He

pulled painfully against his shackles and tried to rise to his knees but was held in place by a knee in his back. It was becoming hard to breath again, but this time it was his own fear robbing him of oxygen. He forced himself to stop struggling and to concentrate only on his breathing. He had to regain control. To stay calm.

"Where are you taking me?" he finally managed to get out.

"Somewhere we can talk."

Hamdi had always prided himself on being a strong-willed man, someone able to do what was necessary when others wouldn't. In truth, though, that conceit had never really been tested. It would be now.

"Do you know who we are?" the man said.

Hamdi didn't answer immediately, instead letting the warmth and vibration of the floorboard seep into him. "The Jews."

Chapter Fifty-one

The gaps between the boards that made up the door were almost a half-inch wide but there was nothing but darkness beyond. Brandon's hand hovered over the ancient knob for a moment before he tried to twist it. Locked. Or more likely just stuck.

"I can't get it open, Colonel."

Colonel Iyov Silva, the man who had so pleasantly interrogated him weeks before, strode across the living room they had just torn apart, accelerating to almost a run before slamming a foot into the door. The crunch of splintering wood filled the tiny house, but it held. Silva lined up again and delivered another kick, this time pulling part of the jamb away from the wall and sending the door cartwheeling down a flight of stairs.

"Colonel," Brandon started, "it's over. There's no more time."

The man ignored him, stepping cautiously onto the stairs and feeling along the wall for a switch. When lights came on, he let out a long breath.

"Catherine! Another dirt floor!"

The clanging of metal sounded somewhere in the house and Silva descended into the cellar to start the now familiar process of digging through old furniture and dusty boxes.

"Did you find something?" Catherine said as she ran into the living room holding three long metal spikes.

Brandon didn't answer, instead concentrating on the glassy sheen of her eyes. As near as he could tell, she'd completely lost it. Completely.

They'd spent the last three weeks crawling through the abandoned buildings of this cluttered Israeli city, futilely searching every closet, basement, and attic. His hands were cracked and bleeding from manhandling furniture and jimmying doors and his back was killing him from the wooden floor he'd been using as a bed. Not that he'd really slept since they'd arrived—instead, he just lay there, waiting for someone to decide that they'd outlived their usefulness and kill them both.

He grabbed Catherine's arm as she tried to get by and held her there for a moment. "Cath. Jesus. It's today. Do you understand me? I've been keeping track of time. The bombs go off today."

When she looked up at him, all that was visible was the blank desperation that had replaced hope in her. He let go and she ran down the stairs after Silva, asking the same doomed question she had a thousand times before: "Did you find something?"

In her mind, she was solely responsible for all of it—the destruction of Israel, the deaths of countless people, the greatest ecological disaster in history. The superlatives just went on and on.

Maybe he should be thankful. They hadn't been tortured or summarily executed like he'd expected.

Instead, they'd ended up here, working on one of the countless task forces charged with finding the warheads before they detonated.

"Shit!" he yelled, slamming a hand against the wall and dislodging some of the hundred-year-old paint. "Shit! Shit! Shit!"

He wanted to take the steps three at a time, but the dim light and rotted wood demanded a less dramatic entrance. When he finally hit the dirt floor, his eyes hadn't completely adjusted, but he could still make out Catherine using her spike to penetrate the earth in a careful grid pattern designed to uncover something the shape of a warhead. Silva was doing the same, though more slowly. Every time he was forced to move one of the old pieces of junk that littered the basement, he stared at it like it was a family heirloom.

"What the hell's going on, Colonel?"

Silva looked up from an old photo album resting on an ironing board. "What?"

Brandon held up his left hand, displaying an empty wrist. "You took my watch, but I'm not stupid. I can count. Today's the day they said the warheads would detonate. It's too late. We're not going to find them."

"There's still time," Silva responded. "Still a chance."

"How much time?"

He didn't answer.

"When are they going to go off, Colonel?"

"How would I know that?"

"Because you've found some of them. Not this one, but you've found some of them."

"I don't know what—"

"You've found some?" Catherine said. She stopped what she was doing and looked at Silva with an expression so pleading that Brandon found it hard not to turn away.

"Come on, Colonel. Tell her."

Silva seemed to soften for the first time in the weeks they'd been together. He glanced at his own watch and then nodded slowly. "Yes, Catherine. We've found others. In fact, we've found all of them—except this one."

Her face animated slightly and she sagged against the spike in her hand. Brandon walked over and wrapped an arm around her shoulders. She was completely exhausted. Honestly, he had no idea what was keeping her going, but whatever it was, some of it seemed to have just drained from her.

"The bombs were all set to detonate at the same time, right? When?"

"Soon."

"Then get us the hell out of here. We're not going to find it."

"How can you be so certain?" Silva said. "If you have any information you neglected to provide me, now is the time."

"Jesus Christ," Brandon said angrily. "Have I ever done anything that would lead you to believe I'd give my life to blow up a bunch of dirt I'd never set foot on until a few weeks ago? And what the —"

Silva held up a hand and Brandon fell silent.

"You're a very exhausting man, Brandon. Has anyon
ever told you that?"

"You don't believe we know anything, do you?"

He shook his head.

"Then let's get the fuck out of here! We've don
what we can, Colonel. You've evacuated, you'v
searched, and you've found all the bombs but one
You've saved your country . . ."

Silva pulled a single cigarette from his pocket an
lit it. "We captured Edwin Hamdi shortly after yo
told us about him. Our best interrogators were sent—
men I've worked with for years. It didn't take long fc
information on the location of the warheads to begi
to flow. At first it was worthless, but as the questionin
went on, it improved."

He took a long drag on the cigarette and then looke
at it in a way that worried Brandon.

"Given time, anyone can be broken down," h
continued. "Even the strongest and most clever c
men. But we didn't have time. We had no choice bu
to begin the questioning . . . forcefully. The drawbac
to that approach, of course, is the toll it takes on th
subject. By now he is exhausted, confused. Even if h
wanted to tell us where the remaining warhead is, it
possible he would no longer be able to."

Brandon didn't respond immediately, trying to shru
off the matter-of-fact description of the brutal tortur
he and Catherine had doomed Edwin Hamdi to.

"Then it's time for us to go, Colonel."

Another drag on his cigarette. "Yes, it's time to go.

★   ★   ★

When they stepped outside, the sun was directly over-head, eradicating shadows and giving everything the look of an overexposed photograph.

The city appeared to be completely dead, but Brandon knew it wasn't. After sunset, it was speckled with intermittent lights. Mostly old people, a soldier had told him. People who preferred to die in their homes than to try to embark on a new life in their final years.

At its height, there had been at least five hundred men assisting in the search—smashing in doors with sledgehammers, tracking progress on laptops, eyeing him and Catherine with a mix of curiosity and suspicion. A few days ago, though, the city had been deluged with a procession of trucks, helicopters, and busses—all of which were quickly crammed with soldiers and sent on their way. As far as Brandon could tell, there were only about a dozen of the original search crew remaining. Maybe less than that now.

"The next address is just across the street," Catherine said, pulling a pen from her pocket and marking the paper in her hand. She started forward, but Silva gripped her shoulder. "Perhaps we should take a short break and enjoy this beautiful day?"

Men began to appear in doorways, moving slowly toward the middle of the empty street, shaking hands and talking softly amongst themselves. Brandon watched as some wandered away and others huddled together. Silva just stared up into the empty sky.

"You're not leaving," Brandon said. "Jesus . . . you're not leaving."

"No," Silva said.

"Why," Brandon said. "Why would you stay here."

Silva shrugged. "I suppose we all have our ow reasons. Some because they cannot walk away fro the land of their God. Others—"

"Are you crazy?" Brandon shouted. Everyone the street turned to look at him. "Are you all craz A nuclear bomb is going to go off here! You're goir to die! Do you understand? Die!" He moved awa from Silva and spoke directly to a knot of me standing near the sidewalk. "What's the point? To heroes? People won't remember. To pray? It wor work. If God wants you dead, let him come dow here and kill you. Don't do it to yourself!"

Honestly, he wasn't even sure any of his audien spoke English. There wasn't any reaction at all to h words.

"No!"

At the sound of Catherine's shout, he spun arour and saw her backing away. "You can't die here! Yo can't make Brandon stay. This is my fault. You dor have to die because of me."

Colonel Silva, the man who a few weeks ago ha been so willing to torture and kill them, walked up her and put a hand on her back. "It's not your fau Catherine. You're not to blame. And I'm sorry yo and Brandon are here. I didn't agree with that dec sion. It—"

The hum of an engine stopped him in midsenten and everyone turned toward the sound, watching sand-colored panel van skid around the corner ar ear down on them. Brandon took a few hopeful steps ›ward it. Had they found the nuke? Had they hanged their minds and decided to evacuate him and ‹atherine?

The van skidded to a stop about twenty yards away, nveloping them in a thick cloud of dust. Brandon rabbed Catherine by the arm and followed the men 1oving toward the vehicle. This might be their only hance.

The driver jumped out and ran around to throw pen the vehicle's rear doors. He ducked inside for a 1oment and when he reappeared, he was dragging ʻhat looked like a dead body behind him.

The smell hit Brandon almost immediately—but ot the stench of death. It was the stink of old sweat nd blood. He covered his nose and continued to edge ›rward as the driver released the collar of what had nce been an expensive suit and let the limp man fall › the ground.

Catherine mumbled something and he looked over t her. "What?"

"Hamdi," she said quietly. "It's Hamdi."

By the time a rough circle had formed around the rostrate man, he was showing signs of life. They all ʻatched as he struggled to his knees despite the zip e securing his hands behind his back.

He seemed rather small, with a dark complexion nd eyes that still seemed intelligent despite their ›vollen and cracked sockets. His feet were bare and ‹randon could see that they were covered with black 1arks that looked like burns.

Catherine squeezed his arm, probably wonderir the same thing Brandon was: What had this man gor through over the past weeks?

How did people live like this, Brandon wondere for the thousandth time since he'd been broken o of prison. *Why* did they live like this? Killin, torturing, oppressing. Playing hopelessly complicate games that could only be lost. He'd occasionally fe some guilt about how he made a living, but n anymore. He'd done more harm in a month workir for the good guys than he could have in a thousar years of stealing and con games.

The driver of the truck started shouting at Hamo motioning toward the men encircling him, trying get him to look at them. Brandon didn't understar the language but could get the gist: "You've lost. The heroic men and others like them have stopped you

Hamdi raised his head slowly, ignoring the Israel and focusing only on Brandon and Catherine. H stare was almost violent, and Brandon wanted mo than anything to back away. But he couldn't.

Hamdi didn't move or even blink until the driv pulled out a pistol and aimed at his head. It seeme to take all the strength he had left, but he manage to spit on the man.

"*Stop!*" Catherine tried to jump forward, b Brandon held her. There was nothing she could do

Hamdi looked at them one last time and said som thing. It wasn't loud enough to hear but Brando could read the movement of his lips.

Congratulations.

The sound of the gun and Catherine's scream vibrated the air and Hamdi's head jerked forward, briefly ringed by a halo of blood.

For almost a minute, everyone just stood there, gazing down at the dead man in the street, absorbed in their own thoughts. Finally, one by one, they began to wander off.

Brandon wrapped an arm around Catherine's waist and managed to get her to come with him. But to where? He picked a street that no one else had chosen, and they just walked along it in silence. Waiting.

He was surprised when she spoke. He'd assumed he would never hear her voice again.

"You know I never wanted you to get hurt."

"Yeah. I know."

It was strange. Normally, he would have been consumed with trying to figure a way out of this. But there was none. And for some reason he felt almost at peace with that. In a few minutes, it would be over. In the blink of an eye, everything would turn to nothing.

Catherine slowed and finally stopped, pulling him toward her and kissing him. They were still locked together when he saw a dull flash through closed eyelids—like a camera going off at a distance. They both ignored it, shutting out everything except each other.

To Brandon, it was a moment that seemed to go on forever. Then he realized it really was going on forever. There was no sound of an explosion, no scalding wind, no screech of buildings as they were pulled from their foundations. Just the still warmth ᴏ the sun and of Catherine.

When he pulled away, she opened her eyes an they looked at each other for a moment.

"Are we dead?" she asked.

"I don't think so."

He took her by the hand and walked back dow the road to an open square where they could see ove the tightly packed buildings and into the surroundin desert.

It was impossible to judge distance accurately, bᴜ based on the scale he imagined, it had to be well ove a hundred miles away. The shape was just like on TⅤ A tiny line thrusting from the ground and spreadin out into the inevitable mushroom cloud.

He could hear the shouts of the men who had staye behind but wasn't immediately able to process wh⍺ had happened. Was there another bomb? No. Silⅴ said they'd found all but one . . .

"Hamdi held out," he mumbled to himself. "Th⍺ has to be it. Hamdi held out. He didn't give them th right location of the last bomb. It wasn't here! We— He fell silent.

Colonel Silva and his men were gathering at th other end of the square, staring out at the gracefull expanding cloud with almost the same intensity ⍺ Catherine.

Brandon pulled on her hand but she didn't movᴇ A second, harder pull was no more effective. H leaned in close to her ear, keeping Silva in his periph eral vision. "Time for us to go."

Chapter Fifty-two

"This is it," Brandon said, sinking to his knees and rubbing what was left of a metal fork on a rough patch in the floor. He'd been carefully grinding it for what felt like years now, fashioning a makeshift lock pick that a more technically minded crook could have turned out in a day.

He glanced back and saw Catherine staring blankly at the table she was sitting behind. It was a position that was becoming a little too familiar.

"I'm serious. This is the one. Guaranteed."

"We're on a ship," she said, not looking up. "Probably in the middle of the ocean."

Their escape from the town where, to hear it told, God saved them, hadn't worked out so well. He'd managed to get Catherine to break into a run—no mean feat these days—but had quickly discovered that there weren't a lot of transportation options. The city's fleeing population hadn't left so much as a skateboard behind.

Plan B had been to hide out and wait for everyone to start flooding back, then to lose themselves in the chaos until they could figure a way to slink out of the country. And that probably would have worked if it hadn't been for some screeching old lady jumping up and down pointing her finger at them. Who would have thought that the ultimate instrument of his destruction would be wearing a housecoat?

"What are we going to do if the door does open?" Catherine pressed. "Where do you think we're going to go?"

He stopped grinning. "Did you ever think that maybe I don't want to just sit here and wait for someone to put a bullet in the back of my head?"

She didn't respond and he immediately regretted snapping at her.

"I'm sorry, Cath. I didn't mean it like that. I just need something to occupy my mind, you know?"

Over the time they'd been imprisoned there, Catherine had sunk into a fatalistic melancholy that all the yelling in the world wasn't going to break her out of. Every day she seemed to figure out a new way to heap more blame on herself—a new way to make herself directly responsible for one third of the nuclear attacks that had ever occurred on earth.

The truth was that they didn't really know anything: Not where the nuke was detonated, not what kind of damage it had done, not how many casualties there had been. It didn't matter, though. She'd convinced herself that whatever was going to happen, she deserved worse.

He, on the other hand, was less resigned to their situation. And while she was probably right that there was nothing he could do about it, at least he could fan the flames of false hope enough to keep his sanity.

He finished grinding and crawled over to the door, taking a deep breath and sliding the homemade pick into the lock. He jockeyed it back and forth for a few seconds, closed his eyes, and gave it a twist. The click seemed impossibly loud in the small space. Terrifying and satisfying in roughly equal amounts.

"What was that?" Catherine said, jumping to her feet and starting to slowly back away.

He pushed the door with the tip of his index finger and it swung partway open to the sound of Catherine hitting the wall behind her.

It had been an interesting time. He wasn't certain how long they'd been there—no windows or clocks had been provided—but his best guess was a couple of weeks. They'd spent the endless hours telling their life stories with the honesty of the doomed, speculating about what the world's reaction to all this had been, and finally, making love. Though she seemed to do that with fatalistic resignation, too.

"Lock it back, Brandon."

"What? No way."

"But we're . . ." She fell silent.

The one thing they hadn't talked about was the future. It was just understood. The Israelis would keep them around for a while in case there were any more questions, but once the situation was under control, he and Catherine were going straight into the drink.

"Come on, Cath. They're gonna kill us anyway, right? Why not go look around?"

She just stood there, holding up the wall.

"Don't worry," he said. "We won't get away. You'll be dead in a week. I promise."

"What's that supposed to mean?"

He pushed the door the rest of the way open and stepped aside. "It means, ladies first."

The metal corridor was uniformly white and narrow enough that they couldn't walk side by side. He decided to let Catherine lead, but it left their progress a bit halting.

"The trick to hiding in plain sight is bored politeness," he said quietly.

"What?"

"I'm thinking we're on a navy ship and that most of the people on it probably don't know who we are or what we're doing here. There's nothing we can do about the fact that we look out of place, so it's all about attitude."

She stopped suddenly. "Brandon, we can't—"

He put a finger to his lips and then pointed up the corridor. After another moment's hesitation she started out again.

"Bored politeness," she said.

"That's all there is to it. Trust me. People are suspicious of anyone who's overly friendly or overly stand-offish. But no one thinks twice about someone who's vaguely good-mannered."

"Okay. Let's say that works. Where are we going?"

It was a good question. He'd actively ignored that particular subject, satisfied to immerse himself in the mechanics of getting through the door. The deck seemed like as good a goal as any. If they were docked and insanely lucky, maybe they could just stroll away. If not, maybe they could swim for it. Most likely not, but if they stayed below, there was no chance at all.

This was one of those rare times he wished he were the violent type—the kind of guy who would go down fighting, taking as many people with him as he could. He'd tell Catherine to run while he single-handedly took out a team of Israeli commandos. A death fit for a made-for-TV movie.

"It'd be nice to see the sky one last time," he said.

She stepped through a small doorway and turned right, slowing significantly when she saw a man in an Israeli navy uniform coming toward them.

Brandon stuck a hand in her back and subtly pushed her forward until they both had to stop and turn sideways to let the man by.

He looked a bit perplexed, but Catherine gave him a short nod with a disinterested smile, and he moved on.

"How was that?" she said when they were alone again.

"Beautiful," he whispered, putting a hand on her back again, but this time just to touch her. "I liked the hint of arrogance you brought to it. Works with the whole military thing."

She pointed to a set of metal stairs. "So when we get to the top, what are we going to do? Jump over the side? We're probably a thousand miles from shore."

"Not quite a thousand."

They both stopped dead at the lightly accented voice behind them.

"Too far to swim, though, I think."

When they finally turned, Brandon was surprised to see a pudgy, unarmed man with gray hair that seemed to be controlled by unseen static.

"Keep going, Cath."

She didn't move.

"Cath—"

"He's the prime minister," she whispered to him.

"The prime minister of what?"

"Of Israel," the man said. "The prime minister of Israel."

"Seriously?"

He nodded and motioned toward the stairs. "Shall we?"

Brandon had to shade his eyes when they stepped outside. The sky was dead clear, reflecting off the ship's white paint and the ocean around them. The shore was there, but distant enough to be at the very edge of his vision.

"Come on," he said, slipping a hand in Catherine's and pulling her along behind their huffing guide.

The deck was full of sailors, all working at their tasks in complete silence. Other than a few respectful nods and enigmatic stares, the crew seemed satisfied to ignore the two Americans trudging along the deck.

The prime minister—whose name Brandon wracked his brain to recall—walked up to the rail circling the deck and leaned against it, looking out over the water. Brandon's eyes had adjusted to the bright sunlight and now the shoreline was a little clearer, though it still wasn't much more than a uniform brown streak that went from horizon to horizon.

They waited for the man to speak, but he just stood there, taking in the view long enough for Brandon to glance over at Catherine and raise his eyebrows. She just squeezed his sweaty hand.

"Look, uh, sir. We—"

"Ten of the eleven were deactivated," the prime minister said, cutting him off. "There is nothing left of Beersheba and the land around it will be uninhabitable for some time. We estimate over three thousand dead, though it's too soon to know for certain. The evacuation of millions of people in the span of a few weeks is a virtually impossible task, even if they're eager to leave. There was no time to consider those who were determined to stay behind."

Out of the corner of his eye Brandon saw Catherine sag against the railing and for a moment thought she was going to collapse. Despite the fact that the number of casualties was much less than she'd fantasized, there was one critical difference: Those three thousand people weren't bloodless guesses and tortured calculations. They were real.

He had no idea how to talk to a prime minister, but Catherine obviously wasn't in any condition to contribute, so he decided to lay his hand on the table. It might be the only chance he got.

"So, it looks like we saved your country, huh? Seems like we should get something in return."

"It does?"

"Sure. I mean, getting a nearly empty city blown up is still pretty bad, but it could have been a lot worse."

"Yes, but isn't it true that you also caused our problems? While I appreciate that you helped us find most of the warheads . . ." He motioned toward the shoreline. "My country has still been ripped apart."

"That wasn't our fault, sir. Those things were for sale and we were told to go get them off the market. It might not have worked out perfect—"

"Obviously not."

"But what if we hadn't done anything at all? They would have still been sold to terrorists and at least a few of them probably would have ended up in your country. There would have been no warning then. They'd have just gone off. In Jerusalem. Or Tel Aviv. Or both."

The prime minister, whose name Brandon still couldn't remember, actually smiled. "You're an extraordinarily convincing young man, Brandon. Have you ever considered politics? I feel almost compelled to thank you for delivering a planeload of nuclear warheads to terrorists bent on Israel's destruction."

Brandon wasn't exactly sure how to take that and he glanced back at Catherine for help. She didn't even seem to know he was there. She just stared into the glare coming off the water, trying to see the faces of those three thousand dead.

"Just for the sake of argument, Brandon, what do you think would be fair compensation?"

"I'm not trying to be greedy, sir. A couple of pass-ports and two plane tickets to South Africa would do it. We could even fly coach."

The man's smile grew wider for a moment, but then disappeared when he fixed his gaze on Catherine. "There's been a great deal of debate as to what to do with the two of you. It seemed very clean to send you to look for the final bomb and then to just lose you in the detonation. But when you survived, the situa-tion became more complicated. Of course, most of us still agree that weighing you down and throwing you off the ship would be in everyone's best interest."

"Not ours," Brandon said.

"No, I suppose not. But you have to understand that both my country and yours are very interested in keeping what has happened quiet."

"So you're going to kill us," Brandon said, subtly nudging Catherine in a futile attempt to get her to participate in the conversation that was going to deter-mine whether she lived or died.

"I don't know what to do with you, Brandon. I really don't."

Epilogue

"Do you think this is enough?"

Brandon waved a hand through the thick smoke enveloping him and peered at the large bowl in Catherine's hands. Who would have thought she would be a gardening prodigy? The lettuce leaves were a uniform, unblemished green, and the tomatoes were perfectly round and bloodred.

"Looks good to me. Oh, and when you come back out, could you bring some beer? The cooler's almost empty."

She had short blond hair now, a smaller, straighter nose, and slightly elongated eyes that went a long way toward relocating her Spanish heritage to somewhere in Asia. Combined with the smile that seemed to grow broader and more relaxed every day, sometimes even he didn't recognize her.

Their surgeries had been done in Argentina, where they'd lived in complete seclusion for a rather painful and tedious five months. Once they were fully healed and had their carefully prepared cover stories straight, the Israelis had provided them with passports and greased the skids for permanent residency in South Africa. He took back everything bad he'd ever said

bout those guys, despite their repeated refusal to pay
or him to get Brad Pitt's chin.

"Kind of a lot of smoke," Catherine said, coming
round the elaborate stainless steel grill he'd bought.
'Are you sure you know what you're doing?"

"Hey, who's in charge of the meat?" He flipped a
udu steak that was partially on fire and waved her
way.

A quick roll of the eyes and she started toward
he house, weaving through the people drinking and
alking on their lawn. He watched her until she
lisappeared, enjoying the sway of her skirt and the
lash of newly whitened teeth as she passed by their
guests.

Being cautious by nature, Catherine had been
gainst hosting a block party for their new neighbors.
t was understandable in light of the fact that they
vere wanted not only in connection with the Vegas
eist, but for questioning in the murder of an FBI
gent who'd been found parked outside Richard
Scanlon's house.

Strangely, the possibility of her eventual appear-
nce on America's ten most wanted list didn't seem
o weigh on her all that much. Or maybe it wasn't
hat strange. The deaths of all those people in Israel—
stimates had stabilized somewhere in the thirty-five
undred range—made everything else seem irrele-
ant. He'd done what he could to convince her it
vasn't her fault, but nothing worked. In Argentina,
he'd practically lived in front of the television, face
vrapped in bandages and teetering on the edge of

clinical depression. It had been so hard for him to ju
sit there and helplessly watch.

Finally, when they'd been relocated to Cape Town
he'd decided that if he couldn't convince her to forgiv
herself, then he was going to help her learn to liv
with it. He'd bought a couple of motorcycles an
talked her into heading out across Africa with him
When they returned two months later, she was startin
to come out of it. Flashes of real happiness were mor
and more frequent.

Of course, they still kept up on what wa
happening. Edwin Hamdi's disappearance had gotte
a lot of press at first, including speculation that it wa
somehow connected to the terrorists who had place
those nukes all over Israel. Now, though, it was almo
as if he never existed—even a Google search couldn
find current information on the investigation. Not s
surprising, he supposed.

As for Israel, it was back to what passed as norma
in that part of the world. People were returning i
droves, while Syria and Egypt's armies continued t
hover on the borders, trying to decide whether to tr
to take advantage of the chaos. The convention
wisdom, though, was that it was all for show. Israe
had made it subtly clear that after being the victim o
a nuclear attack by Arabs, they wouldn't hesitate t
return the favor.

Brandon flipped a few more steaks and shot a squi
gun at a particularly stubborn flare-up, wondering fo
the thousandth time if the world wouldn't have bee
better off if they'd just left Israel to its own devices

Catherine reappeared in the doorway of their new house, and started toward him with a tray full of neatly sliced vegetables.

"You forgot the beer."

She set the tray down on the edge of a table and came up behind him, wrapping her arms around his waist and leaning into his ear. "I met your new friend."

"New friend?"

"Dominic. He's not from the neighborhood, is he?"

"Uh, no. Just a guy I met."

"Seems nice."

"Yeah, he is."

"He tells me he works for a bank. A vice president, I guess."

"Yeah. I think that's right," he said, grabbing a stack of cheese slices and using them to top the burgers.

"A bank, Brandon?"

"So?"

She dug a knuckle painfully into his ribs.

"Oh, come on, Cath. Now who's being paranoid?"

"So this is just a coincidence? You're saying I owe you an apology?"

"Hell, yeah. A big apology."

Her grip loosened and she leaned her chin on his shoulder for a few moments. "Okay, then. I'm sorry."

"You should be," Brandon said, wiping his hands on a towel. "I'll tell you something, though. They do have atrocious security here . . ."